A BEGINNING AT THE END

Also by Mike Chen

Here and Now and Then

A BEGINNING AT THE END

MIKE CHEN

ISBN-13: 978-0-7783-0934-5

A Beginning at the End

For questions and comments about the quality of this book, please contact us at CustomerService@Harlequin.com.

BookClubbish.com

Printed in U.S.A.

For Mandy, the strongest person I know.

A BEGINNING AT THE END

PROLOGUE

People were too scared for music tonight. Not that MoJo cared.

Her handlers had broken the news about the low attendance nearly an hour ago with some explanation about how the recent flu epidemic and subsequent rioting and looting kept people at home. They'd served the news with high-end vodka, the good shit imported from Russia, conveniently hidden in a water bottle which she carried from the greenroom to the stage.

"The show must go on," her father proclaimed, like she was doing humanity a service by performing. She suspected his bravado actually stemmed from the fact that her sophomore album's second single had stalled at number thirteen—a far cry from the lead single's number-one debut or her four straight top-five hits off her first album. Either way, the audience, filled with beaming girls a few years younger than herself and their mothers, seemed to agree. Flu or no flu, some people still wanted their songs—or maybe they just wanted normalcy—so MoJo delivered, perfect note after perfect note, each in time to choreographed dance routines. She even gave her trademark smile.

The crowd screamed and sang along, waving their arms to the beat. Halfway through the second song, a peculiar vibe grabbed the audience. Usually, a handful of parents disappeared into their phones, especially as the flu scare had heightened over the past week. This time nearly every adult in the arena was looking at their phone. In the front row, MoJo saw lines of concern on each face.

Before the song even finished, some parents grabbed their children and left, pushing through the arena's floor seats and funneling to the exit door.

MoJo pushed on, just like she'd always promised her dad. She practically heard his voice over the backup music blasting in her in-ear monitors. *There is no sophomore slump. Smile!* Between the second and third songs, she gave her customary "Thank you!" and fake talk about how great it was to be wherever they were. New York City, this time, at Madison Square Garden. A girl of nineteen embarking on a tour bigger, more ambitious than she could have ever dreamed and taking the pop world by storm, and yet, she knew nothing real about New York City. She'd never left her hotel room without chaperones and handlers. Not under her dad's watch.

One long swig of vodka later, and a warmth rushed to her face, so much so that she wondered if it melted her face paint off. She looked off at the side stage, past the elaborate video set and cadre of backup dancers. But where was the gaffer? Why wasn't anyone at the sound board? The fourth song had a violin section, yet the contracted violinist wasn't in her spot.

Panic raced through MoJo's veins, mental checklists of her marks, all trailed by echoes from her dad's lectures about accountability. Her feet were planted exactly where they should be. Her poise, straight and high. Her last few notes, on key, and her words to the audience, cheerful. It couldn't have been something she'd done, could it?

No. Not her fault this time. *Someone else is facing Dad's wrath tonight,* she thought.

The next song's opening electronic beats kicked in. Eyes closed, head tilted back, and arms up, her voice pushed out the song's highest note, despite the fuzziness of the vodka making the vibrato a little harder to sustain. For a few seconds, nothing existed except the sound of her voice and the music behind it—no handlers, no tour, no audience, no record company, no father telling her the next way she'd earn the family fortune—and it almost made the whole thing worth it.

Her eyes opened, body coiled for the middle-eight's dance routine, but the brightness of the house lights threw her off the beat. The drummer and keyboard player stopped, though the prerecorded backing track continued for a few more seconds before leaving an echo chamber.

No applause. No eyes looked MoJo's way. Only random yelling and an undecipherable buzz saw of backstage clamor from her in-ear monitors. She stood, frozen, unable to tell if this was from laced vodka or if it was actually unfolding: people—adults and children, parents and daughters—scrambling to the exits, climbing over chairs and tripping on stairs, ushers pushing back at the masses before some turned and ran as well.

Someone grabbed her shoulder and jerked back hard. "We have to go," said the voice behind her.

"What's going on?" she asked, allowing the hands to push her toward the stage exit. Steven, her huge forty-something bodyguard, took her by the arm and helped her down the short staircase to the backstage area.

"The flu's spread," he said. "A government quarantine. There's some sort of lockdown on travel. The busing starts tonight. First come, first serve. I think everyone's trying to get home or get there. I can't reach your father. Cell phones are jammed up."

They worked their way through the concrete hallways and industrial lighting of the backstage area, people crossing in a mad scramble left and right. MoJo clutched on to her bottle of vodka, both hands to her chest as Steven ushered her onward. People collapsed in front of her, crying, tripping on their own anxieties, and Steven shoved her around them, apologizing all the way. Something draped over her shoulders, and it took her a moment to realize that he'd put a thick parka around her. She chuckled at the thought of her sparkly halter top and leather pants wrapped in a down parka that smelled like BO, but Steven kept pushing her forward, forward, forward until they hit a set of double doors.

The doors flew open, but rather than the arena's quiet loading area from a few hours ago, MoJo saw a thick wall of people: all ages and all colors in a current of movement, pushing back and forth. "I've got your dad on the line," Steven yelled over the din. "His car is that way. He wants to get to the airport *now*. Same thing's happening back home." His arm stretched out over her head. "That way! Go!"

They moved as a pair, Steven yelling "excuse me" over and over until the crowd became too dense to overcome. In front of her, a woman with wisps of gray woven into black hair trembled on her knees. Even with the racket around them, MoJo heard her cry. "This is the end. This is the end."

The end.

People had been making cracks about the End of the World since the flu changed from online rumors to this big thing that everyone talked about all the time. But she'd always figured the "end" meant a giant pit opening, Satan ushering everyone down a staircase to Hell. Not stuck outside Madison Square Garden.

"Hey," Steven yelled, arms spread out to clear a path through the traffic jam of bodies. "This way!"

MoJo looked at the sobbing woman in front of her, then at

Steven. Somewhere farther down the road, her father sat in a car and waited. She could feel his pull, an invisible tether that never let her get too far away.

"The end, the end," the sobbing woman repeated, pausing MoJo in her tracks. But where to go? Every direction just pointed at more chaos, people scrambling with a panic that had overtaken everyone in the loading dock, possibly the neighborhood, possibly all New York City, possibly even the world. And it wasn't just about a flu.

It was *everything.*

But…maybe that was good?

No more tours. No more studio sessions. No more threats about financial security, no more lawyer meetings, no more searches through her luggage. No more worrying about hitting every mark. In the studio. Onstage.

In *life.*

All of that was done.

The very thought caused MoJo to smirk.

If this was the end, then she was going out on her own terms.

"Steven!" she yelled. He turned and met her gaze.

She twisted the cap off the water-turned-vodka bottle, then took most of it down in one long gulp. She poured the remainder on her face paint, a star around her left eye, then wiped it off with her sleeve. The empty bottle flew through the air, probably hitting some poor bloke in the head.

"Tell my dad," she said, trying extra hard to pronounce the words with the clear British diction she was raised with, "to go fuck himself."

For an instant, she caught Steven's widemouthed look, a mix of fear and confusion and disappointment on his face, as though her words crushed his worldview more than the madness around them. But MoJo wouldn't let herself revel in her first, possibly only victory over her father; she ducked and turned quickly, parka pulled over her head, crushing the product-molded spikes in her hair.

Each step pushing forward, shoulders and arms bumping into her as her eyes locked on to the ground, one step at a time. Left, right, left, then right, all as fast as she could go, screams and car horns and smashing glass building in a wave of desperation around her.

Maybe it was the end. But even though her head was down, she walked with dignity for the first time in years, perhaps ever.

Six Years Later...

Excerpt from *The Post-MGS Resource Report* as Commissioned by Acting President Tanya Hersh:

Ultimately, the Commission came to the following conclusions:

- *Potential for water, energy, communication, and infrastructure distribution were nearly half of pre-outbreak levels.*
- *Offers of support from former tech-sector leaders can support infrastructure logistics with tools for automation and management.*
- *Farming should be migrated to local population centers.*
- *Widespread manufacturing will take at least a decade to restart but unopened goods of all kinds can be recovered, centralized, and distributed by federal convoys.*

With a roughly 70% reduction in the American population due to the MGS pandemic, these resources remain widely available, and harnessing them creates new jobs for an economic reset. The Commission believes that the largest risk to stability in government-supported Metropolitan Zones is so-called "Post-Apocalyptic Stress Disorder" (PASD) and the way it destabilizes families, the building block of society. It is the Commission's recommendation that all possible initiatives be focused on restoring the nuclear family unit, regardless of gender or sexual orientation, as well as the stability found in blood relations. Children, ultimately, are society's future.

State and local municipalities should be given discretion in managing these situations as needed to ensure federal resources maintain focus on larger-scale infrastructure as well as coordination with international governments for Project Preservation.

PART 1:
STRANGERS

CHAPTER ONE

Rob

President Hersh to address first fatality in new flu epidemic.

Rob Donelly sneezed as he considered the latest headline out of the Miami Metro. In surrounding cubicles, keyboards paused and conversations hesitated. It wasn't a giant interruption; work didn't grind to a halt, the San Francisco Metro's local area network didn't fall apart, and no one headed for the exits. But inside the office of PodStar Technologies, that single sneeze was a subtle bump in the road to the workday, and Rob heard the hum of a portable air sanitizer start up. If he stood up and looked around, he probably would see the purple glow from the device's germ-killing UV light.

People weren't going to like headlines about flu deaths. Was it providing facts or feeding paranoia? Rob opted for the former, hitting the Approve button despite his initial hesitation.

Protests explode outside CDC's Atlanta headquarters. Valid news but maybe too much? The directive in the months since the Greenwood Incident was to lay off anything that might induce fear or trigger symptoms of Post-Apocalyptic Stress Disorder. While PodStar maintained the region's spotty network, that also meant culling the news for public consumption due to limited public bandwidth—which meant Rob became the filter for the San Francisco Metro to the world.

Looter gang raids government trucks leaving distribution center. Violence involved with that one, so pass.

Father offers reward for missing pre–End of the World pop star MoJo. MoJo? That pop star that his wife, Elena, had loved before quarantine? Rob shuddered as one of her songs instantly got stuck in his head. Elena would have laughed at him for that—and the fact that their daughter, Sunny, *still* listened to MoJo, even without her mom.

Still, pop culture fluff felt desperately needed in 2025, so sure, post it.

Unrest grows as governments, Reclaimed Territory communes argue resources and access. Political, so nope.

Major League Baseball announces new season, twelve reactivated teams starting next spring. Hell, he'd bookmark that one for himself. If only Elena were around for the news that baseball would be back.

He clicked Approve, immediately posting those articles up for public consumption, then continued scrolling. Somehow, conspiracy-level rumormongering made it onto here as well—theories that rolling blackouts were a precursor to a new outbreak rather than shoddy infrastructure, or accusations that the regular Metro blood drives were really a secret international project to examine antibodies. Rob quickly swept those away and checked the source; apparently, the new flu outbreak in Florida brought out the paranoia in their local media.

No thanks.

His back pocket came to life with a sudden buzz. He hit the Silent button on his 2018-era smartphone, a relic of a different kind now that apps were essentially defunct, then moved back to the task at hand. The next headline seemed to sap his strength.

New survey shows stability, not love, highest priority in marriages.

One simple sentence. And yet, it struck Rob with the weight of death—not five billion deaths, but a single one. He blinked back his tears, the *feel* of Elena's limp hand an ever-present shadow over his own. Stability instead of love. Before everything, romantics would have scoffed. These days, stability seemed like a luxury, if both were impossible.

He clicked Approve without reading the article when the phone buzzed again. One look shook him out of his stupor.

The school.

A month ago, they'd called because Sunny "planned a trip out to Reclaimed to visit a recently departed classmate"; even without the general distrust of the Reclaimed communes, he'd gotten a lecture for not emphasizing the risks of going beyond Metro limits. And last week, it was when Sunny "went missing" by searching the different classrooms to get a Band-Aid for her scraped knee rather than simply asking for help. Both times, the day ultimately ended with Rob telling her to slow down and wait for the grown-ups, along with a hug and a heavy sigh.

What did she do now?

He clicked the green button to answer. "Mr. Donelly, this is Kavita Eswara."

"Oh. Right." Sunny's principal. "How are you?"

"Fine, Mr. Donelly. But we need you to come into the school. Sunny got into an altercation."

"'Altercation'?"

"Well, you could call it a fight. We need to talk."

"Wait," Rob said, rubbing his forehead, "my Sunny hit someone?"

"That's right. She's in the office right now, but she's a bit… wound up. Mr. Donelly, this is the third time I've called you this month. You need to come down."

"Wait—but, we always talk these things out. She's never *hit* anyone before."

"Has Sunny started counseling?"

The question lingered, taunting Rob with all the things he wanted to avoid. "Well, no. Not yet."

"I believe we agreed that would be sensible following her last outburst."

"I know, but I can't really afford it right now. We've only got single Residence License coverage. It's nowhere near as good as the married rates." *And counselors would poke around into things that aren't their business.*

"Mr. Donelly, we should discuss this further when you pick her up. Can you come now?"

"Is this about the students who moved out to the Reclaimed Territories? I explained—"

"No, Mr. Donelly, it's not about that. It's not about PASD," she said, using the colloquial pronunciation of *passed*.

"We suspect it's about her mother."

For a second, the only noise was the low murmurs and clacking keyboards of the office. "Her mother?"

"Any mention of her mother gets Sunny in hysterics. And any physical violence requires me to file an immediate Family Stability Board hearing by the school. They may follow up with a social normalcy audit. So, we should talk. Come to the principal's office. If you can bring a character witness, that would be helpful." The Family Stability Board. Metros were empowered at state and federal levels to protect the world's most important remaining resources: children. With growing neglect cases or worse, social normalcy audits marked the first step of intervention—a process that could end with kids rehomed in dorms.

But that was for the messed-up cases. Not like Rob and Sunny. There was no Greenwood-style murder-suicide and cult, just some pent-up angst and emotional outbursts. That couldn't be enough to actually take Sunny away.

Could it?

"Right. Okay, then." What could Sunny have said? He'd made her promise to never, ever talk about Elena to anyone. "I'll get there as soon as I can."

Rob and Elena had read plenty of parenting books when Sunny was born, but there was no manual on the psychological toll of global death and a continuous fear of any hint of another pandemic. The list of what-ifs swirled around, speeding up until one thought broke through and repeated.

What if someone told Sunny that Elena was actually dead?

Rob stood, keys jangling in hand, and they rattled as he marched through the cubicle farm toward the fourteenth-floor elevator. Each step felt heavier than the last, the weight of his dying wife's final words and his daughter's violent outburst propelling him forward. He hit the call button and stepped inside as soon as the doors slid open.

As the elevator descended to the parking levels, Rob tried searching on his phone for ways to pass a social normalcy audit. He vaguely heard the elevator ding, and he knew that someone else stepped in, but his focus remained on keeping Sunny out of the government's hands.

Then the lights died and the floor dropped out from beneath his feet.

CHAPTER TWO

Moira

"I think I want to cancel the wedding," Moira Gorman said to her wedding planner.

Krista Deal, an impeccable combination of professionalism laced with sass, was speechless, perhaps for the first time since Moira and Frank hired her. Her gray eyes went wide. Then she inhaled sharply. Then little creases of concern formed around her mouth, the dim freckles on her cheeks freezing. Krista's lack of response was disquieting, forcing Moira to look all around the small cafe—at the empty tables around them, at the baristas who brewed drinks and served pastries from behind silicone breathing masks, through the window at occasional passersby. Her eyes darted back to Krista, who still seemed lost in thought after a second, and averted her gaze, instead counting the floors up at the skyscraper across the street, all the way to the PodStar Technologies office where she worked.

The door opened behind Moira, bringing in a gust of wind.

Footsteps followed, then a woman's muffled voice. "Where are your masks?"

Krista's gaze broke, focus sharpening then trailing upward. Moira looked behind her to see an older woman, face hidden behind a disposable mask.

"It's hard to drink tea with a mask on. But we'll just be a few more minutes," Krista said, all proper enunciation and tone, like she dealt with this all the time. Which she probably did, bouncing from place to place to constantly meet people, pick up things, shake hands while she planned events. Most people limited their contact with other human beings these days, but Krista seemed to seek it out. In a different world, Moira would have loved to peer into her brain to see what made her tick. Maybe Krista loved people? Maybe she felt invincible? Maybe she just didn't care?

The older woman reached into her backpack and pulled out two more disposable masks, then tossed them between Moira and Krista before heading to the cafe's counter, an audible "You're putting us all at risk" under her breath.

Moira adjusted in her seat before pushing the short locks of black hair back behind her ear and looking back at Krista, who seemed grounded again. "So like I was saying, I think I want to cancel the wedding. It's for the best. It really is," Moira said. "I just… I like Frank. A lot. He's a wonderful guy, really. His family is great. I'm just not *in* love with him."

Moira expected words of sympathy. Of understanding. This was, after all, what Krista did. Surely it had to happen from time to time, especially in the era of PASD. And Krista did all types of events—she'd once called herself "the gopher for people afraid of going outside." Talking with the managers at the King Hotel, going to City Hall to get paperwork for newlywed tax credit applications, even driving around to various stores for the white running shoes for Moira's wedding outfit; the to-do list meant encountering so many different immune and respiratory systems that even the biggest contagion skeptic would do a double take.

Moira had asked her to do all those and more, and Krista always accepted without a flinch. Yet Krista's reaction here seemed like the worst news in the world next to another viral outbreak.

"Well," Moira finally said, "after I tell Frank, you can cancel the—"

"There's a cancellation penalty." Krista's tone was unusually tense, and the words came out in a tight, clipped fashion, mouth pursed over her dimpled chin.

"What?"

"A cancellation penalty," Krista repeated, though some of her normal cadence had returned. "It's in the contract. Either fifty percent of the retainer monthly until the originally scheduled date or a forty-percent lump sum of the balance."

"Oh. Well, of course. I mean, we wouldn't leave you in a lurch."

"But think about it." Now she was smooth, professional, almost soothing in her voice. "Plenty of couples get cold feet. We're five months out. It happens around this time. The paperwork, the selections, the logistics. It makes it real. So while I understand that you may be feeling this way, it's totally natural. You just don't want to do anything rash, that might be harder to undo."

"Maybe you misunderstood me," Moira said after several seconds. "I don't love Frank. I never have."

"Listen," Krista said. She pulled out her phone, a flip phone manufactured several years before the End of the World. It opened with a flick of her thumb, and Moira wondered why Krista would use such a device. Smartphones couldn't download apps or stream videos anymore with the world's shoddy infrastructure, but taking photos seemed important for her job. "I think it's— Oh. Oh, look."

"What's that?"

Krista held up her phone, the screen's blocky text only capturing a few words. "New headlines on the Metronet." Moira took it in her gloved hand, the headline *New survey shows stability, not love, highest priority in marriages* seemingly tailored by fate for the moment. The article loaded line by line until she could finally scroll down, skimming details about how PASD and Metro life and the general sense of unease that naturally arrived after surviving a pandemic that wiped out five billion people turned stability into the most desirable trait in a partner—not passion, not attraction, not job prospects.

Simply knowing that the other person would be there.

"Did you plant this?" Moira asked with a laugh.

"Nope. It just popped up on Metronet. I was going to pull up a text from an old client who also had cold feet." She smiled, a precise move of curled lips, soft eyes, and raised cheeks framed by neat blond hair, dimpled chin, and a relaxed posture. "What you're feeling is totally natural. Both from a wedding perspective and this," she pointed around them, "this world. Do me a favor?"

"What's that?"

"Just think about it. Don't make a decision one way or the other for a few days. Take a walk, sleep on it, whatever you need to think it through. And," she laughed, "*don't* talk to Frank about it. Deal?"

It'd been a year since Moira had met Frank at a speed-dating event, and four months since he'd surprised her with a ring after they ran a charity marathon together, one of the Metro's annual benefits for reconstruction funds. A few more days couldn't hurt.

"Sure," she said with a sigh.

Krista's knees banged into the table as she stood, and she shook her head with a laugh. "Oh, yeah. How could I forget? The retainer—in cash. Do you have it?"

"Oh, of course." Moira reached into her bag and handed over a small envelope. It disappeared into Krista's purse, and Moira watched as she quietly left the cafe, only offering a quick wave, her hair getting tossed by Bay Area wind. Krista disappeared into the lobby of the skyscraper, and though Moira probably should have also gone in and returned to PodStar on the fourteenth floor, she didn't.

Instead, she left the cafe, the autumn breeze chilling her ears, and walked. First past the block of still-boarded-up storefronts, then past the untouched newspaper stand with a yellowed pre-quarantine newspaper, then past the converted hotel that was now government housing for those who couldn't afford Residence Licenses, the only passersby a pair of citizen patrol volunteers in their familiar red vests. At the corner, she stood, loading up the Metronet to read that article again when another headline stole any thoughts of Frank, weddings, or life in San Francisco.

Father offers reward for missing pre–End of the World pop star MoJo.

Six years ago, she'd sprinted out of Madison Square Garden, away from life as a celebrity and away from the father who controlled her every move. Instead she ran to the people that would become her family in a cross-country caravan of sun-beaten cars, surviving on limited fuel and even less food.

They'd protected her then as a band of overland survivors. But they couldn't protect her now, not while she lived in the San Francisco Metro and they stayed in their Reclaimed commune.

Moira reread the headline three full times before the phone slipped out of her trembling fingers. She bent down to pick it up, though she was interrupted by the sound of screeching tires and clanging metal. When she looked up, steam came out of one car T-boned into another, and around them, stoplights and window signs had all gone dark.

CHAPTER THREE

Krista

Seconds of panic suffocated Krista as she pushed through the revolving door of the big corporate building, one of the few reopened skyscrapers in San Francisco dedicated to office space and businesses. One breath in, one breath out, and though she didn't have the space or attire to go through her usual nerve-soothing yoga routine, the breathing was enough.

After all, it had only taken her about a minute to get over the End of the World and step into her new life. So facing the loss of her business, her Residence License, and everything else she'd fought and clawed for since quarantine ended—hell, since she left her terrible mother and deadbeat uncle long before the MGS pandemic—she wasn't going quietly into the night.

She just needed a plan.

In an alcove of the lobby, by a water fountain with a sign stating *No longer in service*, Krista stepped aside and reached into her purse, feeling past a pair of knitting needles and her business card holder to get to Moira's envelope. Moira had been so *calm* minutes ago, no sense of urgency or panic or anything else that might bring a flush to her olive-toned cheeks, despite the loaded weapon of her words. Krista's fingers jammed through the bills, counting and recounting the total until her hunch proved true.

There wasn't enough. She knelt down, doing the math in her head, but the numbers weren't there. Of course this would happen. It's not like she was karmically due for a cash counting error in her favor or anything.

What remained unpaid was a Residence License bill, one with smarmy red ink stating it was due for renewal at City Hall by the end of next week. Fail to pay it and her whole life unraveled, the entire foundation of independence she'd built for herself since leaving for college. No Residence License, no home of her own, no vehicle of her own. She'd even have to give up her cat—and she was not bailing on Mick even though he was a crotchety old feline these days. They'd survived the outbreak and quarantine together, they could survive this.

Somehow.

That didn't even include the issue of Moira almost breaking her contract—but that would have to wait. Krista considered the small stack of reserves hidden in a small safe in her bedroom closet, the reboot-your-life money she always kept on hand in case she just needed to pick up and *go*.

She vowed never to touch her safety net. But maybe she'd need to, just to make it through this hump.

And almost on cue, Krista's phone buzzed.

Except this wasn't a client swooping in at the very end. Or Moira texting to say that she'd decided Krista was right, and that she really loved Frank after all and wanted to have an even *bigger* budget, along with a long list of corporate-event referrals.

Instead, it was an email. An email of emails, in fact. Krista watched as the bits and bytes traversed through the shaky data network and loaded line by line on her phone.

To: Krista Deal
From: San Francisco Email Archive Services
Subject: New Server Restored! See Past Emails From Kristen Francis Now!

Dear Krista Deal,

Email Archive Services is happy to announce the completion of our latest email server restoration. And with our new Pacific Metro server clusters, the past is now at your fingertips—no more waiting for the national server to connect. Just imagine, re-reading messages from Kristen Francis and other loved ones. Remember getting these?

June 2018: I'm sorry about last night
August 2018: Sober this time
January 2019: Trying again
March 2019: Rehab

We're currently working on restoring data from other pre–End of the World hardware and will have even more data available soon. Sign up now by calling 415-RECOVER.

Note: Your privacy is important to us. To stop receiving these notifications, reply to this email with the word "Unsubscribe" in the body of the message.

Kristen Francis, the type of mother who thought it was so clever to name her only child after herself—the type of mother that was worse than a worldwide pandemic. Clean? Sober? Alive? Krista checked the dates; of course she didn't remember these messages. They'd arrived during that window between her cutting off her mother and the start of the End of the World outbreak. Those messages meant nothing then, and they'd mean nothing now.

No thanks.

Krista hit REPLY immediately, then typed in the word UNSUBSCRIBE before sending it off.

Only forward. Never back. That's what she discovered years ago. Krista snapped back and loaded up the Metronet headlines, anything to get away from her mother. *President Hersh to address first fatality in new flu epidemic.* She clicked on the article, though immediately switched off when she saw the name Dr. Dean Francis mentioned regarding communicable diseases.

No thanks, part two. Krista kept Uncle Dean firmly out of her orbit.

Father offers reward for missing pre–End of the World pop star MoJo.

Reward?

It was probably nothing, but she clicked it anyway. At this point, she'd take anything.

Evan Hatfield, the father of pre–End of the World pop star MoJo, made headlines several weeks ago in the UK when he announced that he believed he found evidence that his daughter was alive. Yesterday, he made an even bigger splash on both sides of the Atlantic by claiming that not only was MoJo—real name Johanna Hatfield—alive, but living on the West Coast of the United States in a Metro area.

Krista skimmed the bulk of the article, which covered MoJo's final performance at Madison Square Garden and her discography, along with speculation that this was all a publicity stunt designed to go with Hatfield selling recently uncovered demo tracks and unpublished songs—a well-timed media event to offset the public's growing paranoia about recent flu reports out of south Florida. Krista was about to snap her phone shut when the last quote caught her eye.

"I'm happy to report that Reunion Services has offered to partner with me in my search to find my family. As it stands, whoever confirms the location of my daughter will receive a large payment. An unprec-

edented award with an unprecedented opportunity: this search is open to any and all Reunion Services agents, not just a single assignment. Of course, I ask that you respect her privacy in doing so. This is, after all, a family affair."

An unprecedented award? Krista was technically a Reunion Services agent—really, anyone with a Residence License could be one—and though she'd even completed a few contracts, the money hadn't been worth the hours of calling and sifting through records. Plus you had to actually *make* the connection, and the last gig kind of wrecked that for her. She'd seen some weird, even uncomfortable stuff dealing with families and supposed loved ones while planning events, but nothing even approached the Reunion Services contract where a man looked for his sister, only leaving out the tiny detail that they were estranged.

Reconnecting people without consent veered too close to her own blood ties, enough for her to disable text notifications of new available contracts.

Except when "an unprecedented award" was involved. And for a pop star? She was a public figure; MoJo had to know something like this was coming. The singer might even be in on it for some sort of career relaunch.

Plus, that kind of money would change everything. Maybe Krista could ride things out until everyone got over the current wave of paranoia and returned to the more fun kind of post-apocalyptic life, one that still went to PASD support groups and cried a lot, but also at least had weddings and work events. And if MoJo was supposedly in a California Metro?

Between her networking skills and MoJo's assumed location, Krista had a head start. She sent a text to the automated Reunion Services number to enable gig notifications. The first response showed that this MoJo business was indeed true. Including the reward.

Those anxieties? Krista told herself her favorite piece of advice.

Get over it.

Krista stared at her phone, an outdated model even by today's standards, but its battery lasted way longer than a smartphone—which meant a lot when Metros still urged residents to conserve power and the occasional blackout wasn't a surprise. A low-resolution photo of MoJo was trickling down pixel by pixel on her screen. She squinted at the final image, though there was no way to tell who the real person was between the photo's quality and the teen singer's wild spiky hair and star painted over her left eye. Add a good six years to the mix and there was no telling who MoJo was now.

But it was a start. Funny how technology and social media created millions of jobs a few years ago, and now one pandemic later, the *lack* of such a thing created this glorified bounty hunter service. Krista considered the possibilities when the door behind her opened, a man walking past her in a business suit and silicone breathing mask. Even behind the mask, under the suit, the man's demeanor screamed PASD.

PASD from…what? Mourning? Fear? Every symptom counselors and therapists used to make big bucks these days? People tiptoed through life now, and PASD was more like paused.

Paused.

Definitely a more appropriate term than PASD.

Krista smirked at her own cleverness.

They looked at each other for a second, and she stood, stomach in, chest out, and gave her shoulder-length blond hair a toss worthy of a shampoo commercial, then walked to the elevator, a little sashay thrown in for good measure.

Not that she wanted this guy's attention that way. It was more of a general statement—even at twenty-nine, men offered little more than a distraction, and she didn't have the patience for distractions of any type, particularly Y chromosomes. Her last extended fling felt more like completing a social and sexual checklist, and even the energy expended to avoid his calls was too much trouble.

But in a morning filled with rumors and unease, *someone* had to demonstrate that life still moved on. It might as well have been Krista. After all, she'd learned that lesson long before any mutant viruses ended the world.

Only forward. Never back.

And definitely never paused.

Krista marched straight to the elevator, chin held high, the opposite of the shell-shocked vibe that she'd carried when leaving Moira just a few minutes ago. The elevator dinged, opening to a tense-looking man staring straight at the ground. He stood a few inches taller than her, no mask on, brown hair, his eyes and facial structure and light tan complexion giving away that one of his parents was probably Asian.

Most importantly: wedding ring.

Case closed. Not a potential client. "Excuse me," she said to the man, extra level of professional saccharine in her tone.

He remained unmoved, and Krista let an instinctive eye roll go as she reached around him to hit the already lit Parking 4 button. The elevator door slid closed, which was the last thing that Krista saw before the things went black and the floor dropped out from beneath her.

Excerpt from *Mayor Sees Potential for National FSB Initiative, San Francisco Metro Times*:

San Francisco's Mayor Janovitz proclaimed the Family Stability Board initiative a massive success after a trial run of six months. "Over the last half year, we have reduced migration to Reclaimed Territory communes by 32% while getting more families and individuals into PASD therapy and support groups. In addition, we have intervened with 19 at-risk families, rehoming the children to FSB dorms while the parents receive psychiatric treatment," said Janovitz. "We're an inspiration to Metros all over. In fact, we've received several inquiries asking how other Metros can adopt this initiative, even unifying into a national standard."

However, the Mayor refused to address fallout from the recent Greenwood Incident, which has shaken both the local Metro residents and nearby Reclaimed communities. When pressed, his only comment was, "The loss of any life at this point is too much, but when five hundred people vanish without a trace, it's troubling." He refused to comment about whether Kay Greenwood and the Fourth Path cult were categorized as missing or presumed dead.

CHAPTER FOUR

Rob

Rob *needed* to get to Sunny's school.

Fortunately, the elevator stopped falling after a second, jolting to a halt. That was a start.

He—they, actually, as a woman had walked in while he was lost in thought—was surrounded by pitch-black and thick air, the only illumination coming from the green LED *1* above the door. Something overhead clicked and a *thud* echoed in the space, then the floor dropped again.

Not as bad this time, just a fraction of a second, enough for him to stumble and grab the handrail before emergency light kicked in, dim floor lighting causing his eyes to adjust to the sudden visual change.

And then it hit him.

He hadn't been in a room so cramped, so dimly lit since five years ago, that horrible day, that horrible moment in Quarantine CA14, a converted prison.

"Do you need some water?" a woman's voice had asked at

the time while he knelt in the storage closet turned infirmary, a room slightly bigger than this elevator, with one big difference.

The storage closet had a hospital bed for his unconscious wife.

Shadows had cast from one emergency light in the corner. It was starting to dim, meaning the crank on it would need a refresh in about ten minutes. "Thank you," he had replied before looking over. He recognized the woman from the quarantine community—she'd maybe been in Elena's book club—but couldn't connect her face with a name. Without Elena to pull him aside and whisper names, he was lost. Even after they'd been married for several years, her social graces never rubbed off on him.

He nodded at the woman, then turned back to Elena. The door shut without any further words.

Right when the latch clicked, all of Rob's hopes funneled into an audible gasp from his wife. For maybe ten or fifteen seconds, Elena had a surge of life. It radiated past her bruised skin and the layers of hospital tubing, animating her more than he had seen in hours. She turned to Rob, though her half-opened eyes seemed to look past him.

"Don't be so serious," she said in a rasp.

"I'm here," he said. "I'm here. Sunny's right outside. Everything will be fine. Look at you, you look badass like that." His brain spun, trying to say things to engage her, but her eyes glazed over, a failure to focus that clashed with the slightest of smiles that came to her mouth. "Things will be fine. You'll heal up, we'll get out of quarantine. I can finally show you the little cove off Point Lobos my parents used to take me to. I can't believe we still haven't gone. We'll take Sunny." He continued blubbering nonsense, a mixture of forward planning and apology and asking for forgiveness and spouting out how much he loved her, how they were going to make it, how Sunny couldn't *wait* to see her again.

A minute, maybe two passed as he continued, the whole time

Elena looking at him but staring elsewhere until finally she sunk back into the cot. "And be good to yourself," she whispered before letting out a final exhale.

He threw the door open, his jaw and temples aching from a continuous scream for help. Down the hall, Sunny's cries only amplified with every passing shout. At some point, the quarantine's head doctor and nurse pushed past him, medical terminology and beeping instruments filling his ears.

The whole memory became a muted blur, a never-ending list of questioning. If only he'd been a little faster the night before, a little stronger, that sort of thing. That morning, they would have sat in their bunk, making paper dolls or something joyfully frivolous with Sunny and the other quarantine children.

Rob may have shielded Sunny from the rioting mob hours prior, but he wasn't quick enough to protect Elena from their fury and chaos, or loud enough to flag down the necessary quarantine medical staff when he saw her on the concrete floor. Those facts created a bottomless chasm of guilt. Absolution never arrived, not a year later when quarantine ended, and not now, this instant some five years following the quarantine, here, in this elevator.

He wasn't sure how much time had passed, caught in the flood of emotions triggered by claustrophobic walls and bad lighting.

"Guess we're stuck," the woman said.

Rob finally looked up, struggling to pull himself back into the moment. But she was right. There they were, caught in an elevator with no power. He pulled out his phone and looked at the coverage icon, only to find a big black X in the corner.

No signal. No way to call a character witness for the hearing. And he was already going to be late. And beyond that, how was he going to *explain* everything?

"Come on," he said, jamming the buttons on the panel. He pressed the emergency phone icon, again and again.

Nothing.

"You know how much time has passed?" Rob asked the woman.

"Four, five minutes? The power outage a few weeks back only lasted like thirty."

"Yeah, but one lasted a few hours not that long ago. You get any phone signal in here?"

She pulled her phone out of her purse, then shook her head. "You have some place to be?"

"My daughter, I gotta—" Rob hesitated, catching himself before he revealed too much. "I have to pick her up from school."

"Ah. Well, we may be stuck here awhile." Something in the woman's demeanor shifted; Rob couldn't quite pinpoint it given the lighting, but it was a whole body change—even her tone seemed to dance a fine line between polite and calm, like a nurse talking someone through surgery. "I'm gonna knit."

The elevator's four metal walls gave off a tiny echo with every word. Rob leaned forward to make sure he'd heard her correctly. "Knit?"

"Good way to pass the time. I always carry some yarn and needles with me just in case. My cat winds up with all sorts of odd-shaped toys this way." She settled into the floor, knees awkwardly tucked under her pencil skirt and coat folded into a seat cushion. "My name's Krista, by the way. I'm an event planner."

"Rob. I work upstairs." He reached down to her on the floor, offering a hand to shake. "Let's find a way out of here."

A good hour passed. Rob's chipped fingernails offered evidence that the elevator door would not budge. Even in the dim view of emergency light, the ceiling held no access panel, just overhead bulbs and mirrored tiles.

They were stuck. And during that time, Rob's thoughts shifted from finding a way out to what would eventually happen once they *did* get out.

He'd have to talk. And he was terrible at talking.

He talked to his daughter, of course. He talked to professionals. But people? In a social setting with the purpose of enjoying each other's company? That was different. Those skills had atrophied years ago without Elena taking the lead. But he had to have these conversations, whether he was good at them or not. With the principal and possibly worse waiting at the school, he'd need as much practice acting so-called *socially normal* as possible.

Krista made for good practice, a blessing in disguise. He wouldn't necessarily call it charm but he'd managed to get a bit of reasonable conversation out of Krista. Nice superficial topics, things that would keep any social normalcy audit scorers happy. Krista was a wedding planner. Krista had a client on his floor, Moira the admin (She was engaged? Who knew?). Krista grew up in upstate New York, went to Hofstra University. In turn, he'd told her the same types of details. He grew up in San Francisco. He was quarantined at CA14.

He didn't mention Elena.

Simple facts, though the lack of light probably disguised that he'd had to force the words out.

Still, all things two friendly people would discuss. Social, stable, and very normal, which was a start, but an hour later and he hit the point where he had to go *there*. There was no recruiting anyone to go with him to the hearing, not with him already being late.

Krista rubbed her cheeks and let out a contagious yawn, one that Rob fought against repeating. "So," he said, strategically opening with small talk, "were you knitting a scarf for someone?"

"Nah. I only had a little bit of yarn in my purse, so it's just a rectangular *thing* to pass the time. It's twenty-twenty-five, you'd think we'd have, like, holographic yarn by now. You ever wonder what technology'd be if the End of the World never happened?"

"I suppose not. They have those cool vacuum robots in our building."

"Twenty-twenty-five sounded so *futuristic* when we were kids. But there are no flying cars. My cutting-edge car technology is a navigation system that doesn't even work. I mean, people have reverted to CDs. Old technology, touchy-feely movies, music with no edge. It's like we've paused as a society." In the dim light, she grinned to herself, like there was an in-joke that he'd missed.

"I wouldn't know. I'm more of a sports guy." The elevator gave a low creak as Rob adjusted his weight on his corner of the floor.

"The only good thing my family ever did for me was introduce me to punk rock. The real pre-pandemic kind, not the weak stuff you get after an apocalypse."

Rob smirked at the remark. She'd done that as the time wore on, going from professional politeness to adding in various bits of passive-aggressive snark. He couldn't tell if he found it witty or annoying. Either way, he had to move beyond the polite banter.

He was running against the clock here.

"Hey, look," Rob said, biting into his lip. "This is going to sound weird."

"We're stuck in an elevator in a world where people wear gas masks as fashion statements. So weird is relative. Let's get over it."

"Right. Good point. Well, what I mean is, I…" Rob sucked in a breath of stale elevator air. "I have to meet with my daughter's principal. Something, um, happened. And I'm probably gonna get grilled. So if it's not too weird, I have to practice what I'm going to say. Especially since I'm gonna be late."

Krista's knitting needles stopped clinking. "As in, you're gonna practice a speech?"

"Kind of. Sort of. Actually, I'm not totally sure."

Her tone softened and got quiet, in a controlled and focused way that made part of Rob wonder if she was loaded with empathy or if it was a professional trick. "Are you all right?"

"Yeah," he said with a laugh. "No. Not really. I'm easy to read, huh? Sunny's had some behavior…issues lately. And because of that, they have to file a Family Stability Board report. Best case, it's this hearing that I'm late for. Worst case…" His voice trailed off. His eyes shut, squeezing tight enough to tense his cheeks. "It makes no sense. I'm just trying to protect her from this world and now *this*. They want to know if we're 'socially normal'? Come on."

"Well, you wanted to practice. So are you? 'Socially normal'?"

"Sort of? Not really?" Rob rubbed his face with a low groan. "I take her to soccer. We keep to ourselves. Seems safer these days. I mean, the damn Greenwood incident made it all worse. One bad apple, you know?"

"I actually haven't read too much about Greenwood."

"Well, it's scared everyone. Everyone's on the verge of snapping and they're worried about whether we have barbecues or visit support groups. I don't think that explains why Sunny hit someone."

"Oh. Well, good job raising a little ass kicker."

Rob didn't smile.

"I'm joking," she said. "Kids fight. It's what they do. And they lived through the End of the World. Kids are tougher than most people these days."

"She's only seven."

"See, everyone worries too much. Isn't that part of the problem? Fifty years ago, they gave kids toys made of scrap metal. Kids figure it out. She's at school, right? It's not like they forced her to be part of the urban farming teams."

"She's had outbursts, but never violent ones. I don't get it. I teach her that we fix problems. I try to figure her out but it's like she's locked away sometimes."

Krista's head cocked sideways at the last statement, which Rob didn't know if it was a good thing or a bad thing. Still, there was no worst-case scenario here. If she put up a wall or simply didn't care, it wouldn't affect anything. But if she *was* willing to help, well, Rob could use all the help he could get right now. "So I have to convey that at the hearing. That I know Sunny's troubled about something. I mean, it could be anything in this world, right? A kid is in quarantine between ages two and four, sees—" He stopped himself before giving away too much. What should he say? What could he say? Problem was, she was a stand-in, a practice run for the real thing. The school would be much more inquisitive. He needed to prepare. "Her mom is dead," he finally said. "That doesn't help."

"Listen." Krista's tone maintained the politeness from before but somehow the professional shield seemed to tone down, just a hair. "I got into fights at school all the time. Shitty family, stupid parents, the works. Look at me, I'm a perfectly well-adjusted adult. Though I do have one suggestion."

"A trick from the post-apocalyptic wedding planner's guide to wrangling flower girls?"

"No. Not quite." Krista visibly tensed up, and for a moment Rob wasn't sure if his dumb joke offended her. "But I know what *I* wanted when I felt like things went to hell as a kid. Try listening to her. Instead of fixing her."

Rob's face changed from tense and sharp to softer, sullen edges. "I don't know how many times Elena told me that. Hard to break some habits."

"Elena sounds like she was a smart woman."

"Yeah, she was. She definitely had that part down." He held up his phone, its screen coming to life briefly with the image of a smiling black-haired girl with bright eyes and round cheeks. "So yeah, can you help me practice?"

CHAPTER FIVE

Moira

The outage shut down a several-block radius, and by the time Moira got back to her office building, she saw a few PodStar employees leaving. She followed suit and started the thirty-minute walk across nearly two miles within the city's designated safe zone, soon crossing into the areas that still had power. And with that, broadcast voices coming from bars, restaurants, newstands, discussing two things over the air: President Hersh's upcoming speech and the waves made by her father in his search for MoJo.

The former should have been a big deal, especially with the reports of a flu outbreak in south Florida. But Moira couldn't focus on anything but her own past. Step after step, block after block; it didn't matter how tough she'd become living overland or how buried her identity was in this new world. The mere mention of her father's name, hearing a radio clip of him talking about how this was "a family affair," and Moira's body may have been walking in PASD-ridden San Francisco but her mind lived in London, almost a decade ago.

She was nearly seventeen at the time, sitting in the back of a limo through London's ceaseless traffic and smattering rain, a Coke in one hand and notes in the other. This was her first press conference, and though her dad taught her what to say, how to act, and—the most important point—how to smile, practice didn't match the real thing. The mere idea of cameras following her around, her image and words living forever in the internet age, turned her stomach inside out. For nearly her entire life up to that point, every moment was devoted to hitting a higher pitch, sustaining a note longer, or hitting dance cues with greater precision. She could do that. Her father *told* her she was born to do it, so much so that she'd been pulled out of school to attend a performance academy.

But in this limo, despite sitting next to her manager Chris, the very thought of discussing the debut single that had taken the UK by storm made her unable to take a sip from the cold soda can. "It will be fine," Chris said in his cigarette-beaten gravelly voice. He offered her some gum, his own admitted way for dealing with anxiety. She declined, and instead replayed her practiced answers in her head. He went on, "Listen, I know some of the journalists who will be there. I reminded them that this is your first presser and gave them some easy questions to use. You'll be in and out in fifteen minutes, I promise."

"I don't get why we're not just doing this on the phone like the other media requests."

"Maybe they wanted to see you in person. Your dad said he arranged it himself."

Nerves amplified with each step in her heeled boots, and though she moved carefully through the arena's loading doors to the small press area, her legs remained wobbly.

"I'll be right here. Just look at me if you get stuck, I'll mouth the answers to you." Chris smiled, his bright eyes and crooked teeth showing a confidence that she didn't feel in herself.

"Even with the gum?"

"Talking and chewing gum is one of my top skills. Oh," he said, looking down at the glowing phone in his hand. "It's your dad. Good timing. I'll be right back." He disappeared down the hallway, then someone with a headset motioned her through a curtain to a folding table. She sat by herself, the spot next to her with *CHRIS GORMAN* displayed in front of an empty chair. "Hi?" she finally said when the silence became unbearable. "I, um, not sure if we should be waiting for my manager. I'm kind of new to this."

Steel folding chairs squeaked as the half-dozen or so reporters adjusted, their faces hidden by the bright lights overhead. She tapped her fingers and drank from the free water bottle in front of her, and in between, she kept glancing over her shoulder at the curtain, waiting for someone to swoop in. If not for rescue, at least to tell her what to do.

Some time passed. She wasn't sure how much, though it felt like several days. Finally, she turned to the microphone.

Smile, she told herself. The MoJo smile, the one that she'd been practicing for years. *Remember, the eyes say as much as the mouth.* She pictured herself in the mirror, turning it off and on like a switch as she did daily. In the face of murmurs and silhouetted heads in front of her, the smile was all she could rely on. "I guess we should just do this? Do you lot ask questions now?"

One woman spoke up right away. "MoJo, given the inherent sexual overtones of your music video, do you feel you're appropriate for young girls?"

That wasn't part of the rehearsed questions.

"I'm...well, I, uh, hope everyone can enjoy the music. And the videos. It's, um, good fun, very artfully directed."

Even before her last word got out, someone else fired off a question. "How do you respond to allegations that you're not really singing on your album?"

"What?"

"Are you really singing on your album?"

"I…uh…what? Well, that's just not true. I've been singing my whole life." She took a drink of water, mostly because nothing else made sense in that moment. "I…where did you hear that?"

"What about the rumors that you refused to perform with Claudia Merrit?"

"What rumors? I don't even know where that comes from."

By now, her cheeks were a bright red, and she could sense the layer of sweat forming across her forehead—and it wasn't from the bright lights surrounding the podium. She wiped at it, though in doing so, her makeup smeared, the blue star drawn around her eye now smudged into a blur.

"Supposedly you're at odds with your father and that's why he's not here. Can you comment on that?"

"What? No! I mean…he's at some business meeting and my manager—"

Chris returned, moving in fast-forward, a dour frown matching deep creases on his face. "Excuse me," he said, pushing his way to the podium. He gave her a look and mouthed the words *I'm sorry* before turning back to face the press. "MoJo is running late for a previously scheduled event and doesn't want to disappoint anyone. So unfortunately, we'll have to end questions here. Follow-up questions can be sent to our publicity team and we'll try to answer them accordingly. Thank you." He put his arm around her, and as soon as they broke past the back curtain, tears flooded from her eyes. He tried to usher her forward, but she had to stop and sit, head in hands. Whatever makeup remained was now completely gone, a mess of ocean blue, silver, and glitter smeared across her fingers.

"That wasn't anything like we practiced," she finally managed to say.

"I know. I'm sorry," Chris said, kneeling down in front of her.

Each blink brought her vision steps back from a blurry mess until she was able to lock eyes with him, her breath calming back into a steady pace. "But you know what?" she asked, her voice still cracking but confidence finding its way back in. "I think I handled it."

Chris's cigarette-stained teeth flashed in a grin. "You did."

"I mean, I didn't fight back. I didn't melt down. I stayed cool—"

Before she finished, the phone in Chris's hand came to life. "It's your dad," he said, his voice popping with dryness following a heavy sigh.

"Johanna?" Her dad's voice barked through the phone. "I listened to a stream of the presser."

"I survived, yeah? Onward and—"

"What the *hell* was that?"

The air sucked out of the stuffy hallway, taking all noise with it except for her dad's voice. Except it didn't sound like the tinny transmission of a phone speaker; suddenly, he was there, standing next to her, glare disintegrating her posture and stealing her poise, his words like a megaphone against her eardrum.

"I'm..." she finally tried to say but the thought had no conclusion. Instead, it was a sound offered up in self-sacrifice, the bait for the stalking animal to launch into attack.

"I'll tell you what that was. That was someone who forgot *every single lesson* of PR training. You showed no poise. No confidence. No response. No, you rolled over on your back like a bloody scared mutt." His voice gathered in momentum and pace, and soon it began a line-by-line assessment of each question, each answer, what she'd said and what she should have said.

By the time it was over, her knees pressed against the concrete floor, her whole body in an uncontrollable shake. Tingling took over her fingertips as they tightly gripped the phone.

"And I *know* how you should have answered each and every question. Because I wrote them."

What little air remained managed to help her squeak out the smallest of questions. "You...what?"

"I wrote them as a test for you. Gave them to each reporter

with explicit instructions. Do you know how much money I lost doing that? Only to see you fail?" She heard the words but they didn't make sense. No response formed as she tried to comprehend and process what her father had just admitted, but it didn't compute, like if gravity suddenly stopped working. "And let me tell you something," he went on, "your mother was the world's finest pianist. She *lived* with that pressure. And the pressure of being an Iranian immigrant in a world of stuffy racists. She never once cracked. Always poised. Always ready to respond with a smile and a smart word. Never giving up a single inch. You think about that. And you think about how you handled today."

From the corner of her eye, she could see Chris's head in his hands, as if he heard every word.

Though he probably didn't need to. Her own response was enough.

"There's a car waiting for you. You're going to your hotel for emergency PR training before tonight's show. Hurry up. The consultant is waiting. But first, one thing I want to ask you."

Arena staff passed her by without even a sideways glance. Maybe this was normal to them? Did all pop stars have breakdowns in the hallway?

"Yes, Dad."

"Do you think your mother would be proud of how you did?"

Rather than bark out anything further, the line stayed quiet, only the sound of static and the occasional cough coming through. He wanted an answer. He wanted her to say it, to admit it.

"No."

"Then do better." The phone beeped as the line went dead, her father gone without even a parting word.

In that dim hallway, in the bowels of an arena, Moira handed the phone over to Chris, who could only whisper apologies.

But it didn't matter. That moment only confirmed what she'd suspected for most of her life: her father viewed her as an asset, not a child.

And if he was capable of that then, what could he possibly do after years of searching for his prized possession?

As she walked the remaining block to her apartment, the burst of autumn wind didn't bother Moira at all. She marched into the apartment she shared with Frank. It was thankfully empty, and she changed quickly into her workout clothes, then went to the bottom drawer of her dresser and pulled the whole thing nearly out of the frame. Her fingers felt to get to the folded hunting knife taped underneath.

The handle fit against her palm in perfect muscle memory, jagged ridges near the hinge remaining from the one time it took a bullet for her while she crept through Cedar Rapids on a mission to scavenge winter clothes.

Her phone chimed with two texts, one from Frank saying he had to work late.

The second was a long reach into her past, from a time before San Francisco, before living a normal life.

It was from Narc.

Narc, who'd led their band of survivors overland while the rest of the country hid, who founded a Reclaimed Territory commune by Sacramento after they'd survived a cross-country trek, who always seemed to know the right thing to say in the face of adversity or a hail of bullets.

Except when she'd told him that she was leaving their commune for a Metro. That had left him speechless, kneeling in farmer gloves and muddy overalls as he'd tried to pull a pesky yam from the ground.

Now he was reaching out.

I saw the news. You want to talk? it read.

The drawer back in place, Moira strode out and the door shut behind her with purpose. She stepped into the hallway, folded knife neatly concealed in hand. No talking right now. In a little bit. First, she needed to run.

It was what she did best.

CHAPTER SIX

Krista

Given Krista's circumstances, Rob represented very little to gain. With that wedding ring on his finger, he wasn't getting over his dead wife anytime soon, nor did he exactly come off as the big event type. And she was pretty sure that he wouldn't be able to help out in the search for MoJo, unless MoJo suddenly became a homebody or a teacher or baseball fan.

It would have been easy for her to shut down, play dumb, offer cursory input, and ignore him.

Yet an hour later, Krista concluded that Rob wasn't a bad guy. More importantly, he seemed to be a good parent. He clearly cared about Sunny—anyone who would practice the same speech over and over with a perfect stranger, even given the extreme circumstances, meant two things. First, he was willing to accept an outside opinion. Second, he worried enough about his kid to try.

Her standards admittedly stood pretty low on the parenting scale. But even though Krista's meter had been knocked into its own curve a long time ago, Rob's situation warranted her attention, at least while stuck in an elevator. "No, see, if you say 'I've tried to minimize' then you leave yourself open to interpretation. Try 'I know she's doing well.' Positive. And specifics. That's how you get through to people."

"Okay. Positive and specific." Rob blew out a sigh, his fingers aimlessly rolling the ring on his other hand. "How'd you get so good at this? I thought you were a wedding planner."

"Technically an event coordinator. I do stuff for businesses and communities too."

"Right. Well, you should be in human resources. You know how to nudge people."

Years ago, Krista's therapist had told her that children of alcoholics like her mother picked up on subtle nonverbal cues as a survival mechanism. She opted to *not* go there with Rob. "Comes with the territory."

"Damn it, if only I had phone signal, I could call one of the parents from Sunny's soccer team. I mean, we're not like buddy-buddy but at least it'd be one charac—"

A *clang* above interrupted Rob, then the lights overhead blinked to life.

Krista responded by shifting her weight from one half-numb side to the other. The grime from the stale elevator air permeated everything, though the feeling of being stuck felt more suffocating than any faulty ventilation.

"Are we gonna move?" Rob said. His laughter created an echo chamber as the elevator bounced and groaned before it made its way down. "We're moving!"

Krista snatched her boots off the floor, then looked straight up. Tiny spasms fired off in her back as she stretched; she should have done more yoga poses for her back instead of knitting. Damn her pencil skirt and its yoga-inhibiting design.

The elevator rumbled downward, and the door soon opened, ushering in the best-smelling parking lot air Krista had ever experienced. Rob stepped one foot out and held his position with the other. "Hey, look," he said, extending his right hand. "Thanks for talking me through this."

A handshake. Krista gave an internal sigh of relief; at least he wasn't a hugger. "Oh, I didn't do anything special," she said, taking his hand. "My ass is sore and I smell bad but that would have happened regardless of whether we talked."

Rob laughed; he obviously didn't know that Krista was being truthful. "I have no idea what I'm heading into." He pulled his phone out of his pocket. "Still no signal down here. So much for bringing a character witness."

"Good luck. And remember what I said about listening to her."

Rob took two steps out, then stopped. His head turned back and forth, and Krista could hear the very beginnings of words, though nothing formed fully. She started to move past him when his voice cut the silence. "Wait, please." They met eyes, his a mix of inquisitive with a tiny bit of desperate. "Hey, look," he finally said after several moments. "This is gonna sound weird."

"We've already established weird."

"Right. But..."

"But?"

"But..." He looked over his shoulder, presumably toward his car. "Look. This whole thing the FSB does, they wanna make sure you have like a hundred friends and do all these extra-curricular things and handle all the PASD stuff on top of that. And honestly, I just don't know that many people. We keep to ourselves. A lot of people do. You'd be surprised. But I can't just *tell* them that, I have to present something else. And I can't get a hold of anyone. So, um—" his hands gestured to accent his words "—based on what you learned about me and Sunny these past couple hours, would you be willing to act as my character witness? If you don't have something immediate to get to, that is. The school's over in Nob Hill."

"Rob, I hardly know you. And I've never met Sunny. My job makes me a good bullshitter but not *that* good."

"Yeah. Yeah. Okay, you're right. Sorry about making it weird. Thanks for helping me practice." He nodded and turned, took three steps away then turned back around, just as Krista had stepped out. "Look, what if I pay you?"

"Pay me?"

Those were the magic words. The envelope of cash in her purse flashed through Krista's mind, along with the necessary amount to fill the difference for tomorrow.

"Yeah. For a few hours of your time. What's your consulting rate?" Rob asked. The door dinged and slid closed behind her. From above came the rumbling of a car rolling through the garage. "I'll pay you. Whole day. Consider me a client. I'm desperate here. They want someone and I have nobody, and I'm already late."

Krista had taken on her share of strange client requests before, but this veered straight off into paid thespian tricks, something that she had zero experience with. On the other hand, bullshitting with clients and vendors, putting them at ease with little things like shaking her hand and breathing the same air as a total stranger, that *was* really what she did.

Because even when business was rolling, no one wanted to do that after a pandemic. Only problem today was that people stopped wanting to have any sort of large gathering thanks to PASD-induced paranoia. And unless Hersh's speech was "snap out of it and have a party, a wedding, or both," that didn't look to change soon.

She locked on to Rob's gaze. In another world, such a request would come across as, at best, bizarre and, at worst, offputting. But here, Krista didn't find it all that strange—at least he cared. At least he was going to show up and fight for his daughter, despite being two hours late. She pictured Sunny waiting for him, the little girl with black hair in his phone photos. Was she being grilled right now by the principal? Lied to? Or maybe just waiting, wondering if someone would come?

Krista knew that feeling. Some twenty or so years ago, she'd sat waiting at the windowsill of her mom's friend's house, yet another beg-and-plead set of weeks of couch crashing until they wore out their welcome. Things were unstable then, particularly when her dad randomly turned up for a short while before exploding again. That one afternoon raised the bar on chaos—and when the dust settled, she didn't dare turn around to look further into the state of a home that wasn't theirs. She'd heard the dishes shatter. She'd felt the walls vibrate when her dad punched them. The drunken slurs and screaming looped in her mind, despite things having gone quiet following her mom slamming the bedroom door and locking herself in. And it would all come to a head in a few hours when her mom's friend came home to a wrecked house, kicking off the cycle yet again.

In that house, Krista had sat with nervous anticipation, waiting for Uncle Dean to come back from medical school like he'd promised so they could go somewhere, anywhere, even for just a burger and fries. But he'd never arrived, and eventually she left the window, not to venture out, but as far as she could go inside: the bathroom at the back of the main hall. Door locked and lights out—most importantly, away from *them*—and her headphones blared while she sat against the chipped bathtub knitting the longest scarf ever made, at least until her iPod ran out of batteries.

Someone *caring* would have made a difference. Two people, even if one of them was paid, might have even changed everything.

Plus, Krista *needed* that Residence License. "Triple rate," she said. Double rate probably would have been good enough, but desperate times and all that. "I'll try my best."

Rob's sigh of relief seemed to fill the entire floor of the basement. He threw a thumbs-up, which Krista took in stride with a simple nod. "Thank you. Thank you, thank you. Follow my car, okay?"

From the Online Encyclopedia page on MoJo:

Johanna Moira Hatfield (b. July 14, 2000, Thorverton, Devon, England), better known as MoJo, was a British pop singer whose popularity peaked with the singles "Love This World" (#1 US, #1 UK), "Do You Remember Love?" (#5 US, #4 UK), and "We Can Win" (#1 US, #2 UK) in 2016.

MoJo was born to Evan Hatfield and Iranian-born child-prodigy pianist Tala Ahmadi. Hatfield and Ahmadi met at the Royal College of Music in London, England, where Hatfield specialized in electroacoustic music and Ahmadi pursued her career as a classical pianist.

Shortly after MoJo was born, Ahmadi was killed in a car accident in central London. Hatfield moved young Johanna to Manchester, where he raised her and began training her in voice and dance from a young age. Hatfield was often quoted as saying, "Tala would have wanted this for Johanna."

CHAPTER SEVEN

Rob

Halfway down the main hallway to the principal's office, second thoughts started to creep into Rob's mind. He hesitated, standing in an orange sunbeam filtering in from the dusk sky.

"You want me to just make up stuff?" Krista asked, as if reading his mind. Her face lit up with a smirk as he pondered the possibilities in the deserted school hallway.

"Let's keep it simple. How about you're doing an event for PodStar?"

"Well, I *am* planning a wedding for your coworker." Moira, the admin. She'd mentioned that as the reason why she was in the elevator in the first place. But right when she said that, her demeanor shifted into something inscrutable.

"You okay?" he asked.

"Nothing. It's nothing." Krista bit down on her lip and looked off. "Moira's getting cold feet, that's all. It happens. But it's fine. So one of your coworkers hired me and I've gotten to know you through her and you're totally socially normal. The end. Good?"

"Good."

They stopped a few feet outside the office door, and his hand shot up. "One thing," he said, his voice dropping low in case Sunny listened from inside, "just don't mention her mom. Elena."

Her mouth became a confused slant. "Why would I do that?"

"Just…don't. Sunny's…" Why didn't he think of this caveat earlier? Rob shut his eyes, thinking of the most delicate, least *weird* way to say this. "It's a touchy subject. Please don't mention her."

"Fine. I just know you through your coworker, remember?"

"Right," he said with a grin as he opened the door and walked in. Half of the room contained elementary school standards—photos of students and historical iconography—but sprinkled throughout stood various cartoonish safety protocols that applied only to the world that existed today. Rob had seen it all before, but there was still something disquieting about an anthropomorphized elephant giving tips on washing hands and putting on gas masks.

From the back hallway, the sounds of chatter stopped. "Sunny? There was a power—" Rob's musing was cut short by a bowling ball to the back of his legs, or at least that's what it felt like. His knees buckled, and he angled to see a little mop of black hair above a bobbing mess of fingers and elbows and backpack.

"Daddy!" Sunny's voice rang out, and as he took in his daughter, he noticed Krista wince from the volume. Ms. Eswara, Sunny's principal, trailed in, giving Rob a nod. She squeezed some sanitizer onto her hands, then passed the bottle along to both Rob and Krista.

"I'm Rob's friend," Krista said with too much niceness in her words.

"Sorry about being late. We got stuck from the power outage."

"I figured. It's all right," Ms. Eswara said. "Half the class pulled out early when word came down about the president's speech tonight. And no one stayed for after-school day care. People are worried."

Hersh's speech. Rob figured it would be about the headline he posted on the Metronet regarding the Miami fatality, but he had enough to worry about right now.

In the history of the world, Rob was sure a seven-year-old never hugged with the brute strength that Sunny did. Her arms wrapped around his squatting body, and he closed his eyes so that all he felt was her presence and Elena's memory. When he opened his eyes, Sunny's arms loosened up. She pulled back, but rather than a welcoming face, she greeted him with her mouth creased in a firm scowl.

"You lied to me, Daddy."

The words stole Rob's breath, though he kept looking straight at his daughter. No one at the school knew the exact truth about Elena, but adults could piece it together if Sunny said too much. "Sunny, what do you mean by that?"

"You said people always want you to tell the truth. But Noel laughed at me and made fun of Mommy, and you said—"

"Okay, let's back up a second. Noel, is he your classmate?"

"He's a poop face."

"Okay, now that's not a very nice thing to call someone. I'm sure he had his reasons. And besides, you're not supposed to talk about Mommy." Sunny crossed her arms, squinting with the realization that she'd been caught. "You know, a lot of people lost their mommies around quarantine, and so we have to be, um, sensitive to that." Rob didn't tap into any sort of prepared explanation, but he gave himself a mental pat on the back for conjuring something so quickly. "Maybe Noel did too, and he's just upset about it."

"Sunny." Ms. Eswara knelt down to her level. "I need to talk with your daddy for a few minutes. Can you stay here with…?"

"Krista Deal."

"Can you stay with Krista?"

Sunny shot Rob a look, which he forwarded to Krista. "I thought you'd want to talk with Krista?" he asked Ms. Eswara.

"If we have time, yes. The blackout's thrown everything off. But we need to speak first."

"It's fine," Krista said. "Don't forget, I work on weddings. Deal with kids all the time." Even though she said that, Rob felt her demeanor shift just slightly into something more tense. Still, they were all in too deep to pull out now. He watched as Krista dug into her purse for something, but Ms. Eswara interrupted. "Back here, Mr. Donelly." She started walking to the back office.

"Thank you," Rob mouthed to Krista before offering his daughter a reassuring smile.

Rob politely declined the disposable breathing mask offered by Ms. Eswara, then immediately second-guessed it. Was not wearing one a sign of lazy parenting? Was it a subtle test that would be a ding against him later?

Before he made peace with those questions, Ms. Eswara launched right into it. "Mr. Donelly, tell me about Sunny's home life."

This opened up another issue—what did Sunny actually say about Elena? Rob made an internal promise to keep the topic of mothers and their alive/dead state as vague as possible. He tried to recall the speech he'd practiced in the elevator, but under the scrutiny of a governmental decision, the whole thing vaporized, leaving him to wing it. "Well, she's happy. At least I like to think so. As much as you can be in this world. Her best friend moved to Reclaimed a few months ago and she doesn't quite understand that. I think that's affected her a bit. But really, I think we're all affected. And when you hear about PASD nonstop on TV, on the radio, in conversations, it's kind of hard to not let it just become part of you by exposure, you know?"

"Do you think she's affected by PASD? This is the third outburst in a short time."

"I know she misses her friend a lot. And sometimes we'll see bits of an old movie and she'll ask why things aren't like that, where did all the people go, that sort of thing. She's..." Rob searched for the right word. "Headstrong. She wants to do the right thing. She just gets ahead of herself sometimes. People told us that would serve her well as an adult."

Us. It'd been a while since that counted, maybe all the way back to right before the quarantine, when their friend Gail had told them that based on her child psychology background, then almost-two-year-old Sunny was a textbook high-energy child, and that high-energy children grew up to be leaders.

"And you? Are you affected by PASD?"

This was a delicate question. Too much chest-thumping and he'd clearly be lying. Too much self-pity and they might consider him a Greenwood-style risk. "I think when you see people you know, people you love wither away in a few days, it'll always affect you."

"I believe we recommended counseling, either in private sessions or PASD support groups, following Sunny's last outburst. Have you attended any? Has Sunny?"

"It's been hard to find time for that. But it's a priority." Each word came out with precision, a carefully crafted blend of contrite and excuse. "In fact, there's one right by my office at Pod-Star. Work's been really busy since the power outages started, and it's a high priority to keep the Metro government offices connected to the feds."

He sure hoped Krista was better at this.

"I see." It took Rob a second to realize that Ms. Eswara was shuffling papers on her lap, probably with these questions. Whether she purposefully hid them or not, he wasn't sure. "And we should discuss Sunny's mother."

Muscles tightened at the very question—his toes, his shoulders, his jaw. His whole body became a knot with no clear way to untie it.

Rob couldn't let the school or anyone involved with the Family Stability Board know that Sunny believed Elena to still be alive. Or that someday, she'd come home from "treatment."

"It's…not easy to talk about."

"I understand," said Ms. Eswara, her lips forming a thin straight line. "It sounds like today's altercation involved Sunny and her feelings about her mother. About missing her. Believing she'll see her again. I understand that belief in some form of afterlife or heaven isn't that common these days." The way Ms. Eswara phrased the question calmed some fears bubbling under the surface. Heaven. That was one way to interpret it. "And while we of course want to encourage the individual faith of any family, it's also important to consider Greenwood in context. Sometimes, these things go over the edge. Does Sunny mention her a lot? Does she miss her?"

"She…hardly remembers her. We only have a few photos left."

Few was a stretch.

In the early days of post-quarantine life, when the city itself was still being sectioned and families crammed into converted hotels for a year of transitional living, he'd hoped to recover things, including photographs, from their pre-quarantine home. But one morning, when it was Rob's turn to bus out beyond the reconstruction zone for Personal Item Retrieval, he turned the street corner to see the torched remains of the home they'd rented before MGS went wide. Charred-black beams and jagged edges opened up its left side with seemingly surgical precision, leaving enough of a gaping hole to peer inside. But the space left standing wasn't affected by water damage and the elements as much as brute force. Smashed chairs, collapsed dressers, remains of books and papers everywhere, and on the bottom floor, at the center of what must have been the fire's radius, was a metal garbage can.

Rob had peeked into the burned metal cylinder, a clear heat source for squatters, only to find the ashen remains of photo albums used as kindling. As he did, the sound of breaking glass came from the upstairs, followed soon by the sound of footsteps dashing away, fading laughter trailing it.

He didn't bring anything back that day, and never mentioned it to Sunny. Even to this day, this moment, the sight of urban decay and the sound of breaking glass instantly stopped his breath and strangled his attention.

"Do you feel you've been able to move on?"

Every answer he'd given so far had come out as a calculated response, a statement designed with a specific purpose. But for this question from Ms. Esawara, nothing strategic emerged, just a blank stare.

The cap of her pen tapped against the desk corner. *Tap. Tap. Tap.* He had to say *something.* Something was better than nothing after pausing for thirty seconds or so.

"I wish I could tell her more about Elena," he finally said, words rolling out without any filter. "I wish I could *show* her. And I wish Elena could *see* the wonderful little person Sunny's become. If that could happen, I swear Sunny wouldn't have any outbursts. But it's not possible. That's not the world we live in now." He looked Ms. Eswara in the eye, telling himself to regain composure and connect with her. Suddenly, the lines he'd practiced with Krista came flooding back with clarity. "I shouldn't complain. I know others have lost everything and everyone. I have my daughter. That's a miracle in itself. This world isn't easy. But we keep trying. And I believe I do right by her. I try, every day."

Rob drew in a breath, the last few sentences draining him to the point of exhaustion. But at least it was done, and if he was going to fail, at least he failed telling his personal truth.

Ms. Eswara didn't respond, instead scribbling down far too many notes for Rob's liking.

CHAPTER EIGHT

Moira

Code Polka Dot.

It sounded silly, but that was intentional. Narc had invented the term when they pushed through the battleground of Pittsburgh. Most of the major cities they'd encountered at that point had become urban ghost towns; Pittsburgh, though, offered different levels of shattered buildings and violence, all neatly sectioned by the city's rivers into gang territories and none of which were going to be friendly to their crew. Back then, Narc's boyfriend, Santiago, had just started training Moira and the band of fifteen or so overland survivors in parkour. Scaling walls, leaping from great heights, vaulting over obstacles, climbing barbed wire fences. He'd talked about how it'd get them *through* the city instead of around it, speeding things up and making it easier to scavenge supplies. With the downtown completely overrun by a bloody turf war and their caravan desperately low on car supplies, they decided as a group to risk it and go on a supply raid while rival factions fought each other.

Polka Dot was Narc's code for a status of heightened caution. He'd originally called it that to bring a tiny bit of levity to the situation, as "humor calms the nerves," he'd explained. Moira still put herself in Code Polka Dot once every few weeks when she left the safety of the reconstruction zone and pushed herself through the outlying areas—the same path every time through the remains of Haight-Ashbury, a shortcut through Golden Gate Park's converted farm sections, and into blocks of urban decay, the long rows of homes that would probably fail any eventual repurposing inspections—and that didn't even include the bullet-ridden cars and other remaining scars of a quarantine-period gang war over San Francisco.

She propelled further despite her burning lungs, mind in a heightened Code Polka Dot state. Every sense tuned in to her surroundings. Shifting shadows meant someone or something moved inside a boarded-up house. The smell of burning meant someone was trying to stay warm. Voices meant squatters nearby—and their tone told a lot.

And in her hand, the handle of her hunting knife. The blade folded outward and pointed down. She opened the weapon once she left the reconstruction zone and mentally entered Code Polka Dot, though in her six months or so of doing these runs, she'd found the squatters here were nothing compared to the anarchy she'd faced traveling overland. Still, she maintained Code Polka Dot, taking the least conspicuous routes and staying on her guard the whole time, leaping through the boards and concrete of burned-out houses and scaling over battered cars that once probably got used for a defensive structure of some sort. Over and through, quickly and quietly until she hit Ocean Beach, with about an hour of sunlight remaining.

The stillness of dead neighborhoods gave way to the lapping of ocean waves and the blend of pinks and golds in the sky. The wide, flat beach remained bordered by man-made walls holding back what used to be a parking lot; she jogged out to the edge of the wet sand with plenty of visibility around her.

The blade of the knife folded closed with a click. And she was out of Code Polka Dot, with nothing around her except nature partitioned off by the failures of humanity.

Moira pulled out her phone and stared at it, the corner icon showing full signal strength despite technically being in a reconstruction zone.

She'd texted with Narc from time to time, given that bursts of text characters often got sent more reliably than an actual call these days. So she expected Narc to give her grief when she reached out. Yet when he picked up, resentment didn't color his voice. "Moira!" he said with palpable excitement.

Typical Narc.

"Narc. How are you?"

"I know these connections aren't great these days but I swear that's an American accent I hear."

"Yeah." She spun around, making sure she was still alone in every direction. "Sorry. Sometimes I forget which one is the default these days." The American accent had started during the cross-country trek as a joke, but became the go-to since arriving in San Francisco.

"You grow your hair back?"

She had, in fact. A neat bob cut, typically matched with muted work attire and light makeup. "Shaved head is more of a wasteland look," she said. "I do miss the convenience though. You never have to worry about it when it's shaved."

"Blending in, huh?" Narc asked.

"I prefer 'life incognito.'"

"And that accent is some real uncanny valley shit there."

"Uncanny what?"

"Never mind. It's an admirable effort in covering up who you were. Say 'you know you need unique New York.'" She could practically see his grin from the beach.

"Theater dork," Moira said, returning a laugh. "'You know you need unique New York,'" she repeated, emphasizing the Americanized *R* sound for his benefit. His reaction, a jovial full-bodied chuckle, triggered a rush of memories, and though they'd fought through life-threatening situations together, the brightest memory was a simple one of Narc giving a monologue from *As You Like It* in front of a fire. She thought that was the play, though she was never really into Shakespeare. "All right," she said, reverting back to her native northern English accent. "More normal for you?"

"Yeah. It's not as jarring."

"How's the farm?" The farm being the Reclaimed Territory community that Narc led on the old UC Davis campus some one hundred miles east of where she stood, up by Sacramento. More of a college-sized off-the-grid commune than a farm, the "reclaimed" part of the name coming from reclaiming existing infrastructure and buildings into something new. Though farming was still a significant part of it.

"Oh, you know, it's fall. Days are getting shorter. But we had a good haul this summer, and we're selling well with the Sacramento Metro. They have a great farmer's market." His voice shifted into seriousness. "I saw the news. Are you all right?"

"Oh, I'm sure Hersh's speech won't be a big deal. I'm not as worried as a lot of the people here. Don't tell me you're freaked out about it."

"Come on, Moira. I know you. If your dad sent a single Reunion Services agent to find you, that'd be enough for you to dig ten miles underground. But this production? Tell me you're okay."

"I'm okay, Narc," Moira said, forcing a brighter tone than the hurricane of emotions inside her. Then it hit her: if she couldn't be honest with Narc of all people, then who? "No, I'm not."

"You're welcome to hide out here if you want. We're a long way from any Reunion Services agents. And if any of these outbreak rumors are true, we're self-contained enough to run our own quarantine."

She could theoretically do that. She could get in her battle-worn Jeep, the only sliver of her life that she'd kept from her overland days, and make the trek out there, drop it all, and start over yet again.

Maybe that would be easier. But not the normalcy she longed for.

"I'm not sure. There has to be a way to just erase my identity."

"Sure, it's simple. Everything rebooted when quarantine got out, right? Records are still fluid, no one knows which are accurate and which are leftovers from those who died. Get on the record with a common last name and you'll disappear. You're still Moira Gorman right now?"

Moira gave a "mmm-hmmm" into the phone, giving a quick silent thanks to Narc's friends who'd hacked into records to create that name.

"So you'll want to establish a new identity. Restart the paper trail. Preferably with a name like—"

"Smith?"

"I was going to say Jones." Narc chuckled. "But Smith works too."

"Well, good news. I'm engaged to a Smith."

The line went silent and Moira checked to make sure the signal didn't drop. Around her, the last of the afternoon sun began to duck down beneath the low cloud layer, dulling the colors that had been lighting up her view. "You're engaged?"

"For a few months now."

"You didn't tell us? This seems newsworthy. I'm..." Narc's voice trailed off and his hesitation said enough about how he felt. "Can I tell Santiago?"

"Yeah." Moira blinked the tears that suddenly arrived at the mention of her old friend Santiago, reminding herself to stay on guard. The beach was mostly harmless these days but she had to stay safe. Getting caught up in nostalgia wouldn't help anything.

"Well." Narc took in a deep sigh. "That would do it, I think. Marriage or birth records are better than, say, a bank account. Government seems to value those like gold now. I suppose Santiago and I should probably get on the record as married one of these days too. You know, that's one of the nice things about the government in this world. They don't care if you're queer as long as you get married. 'Can't make a baby? Adopt one or three!'" Narc caught himself right away. "Sorry, that's a bad joke. I shouldn't make fun of the orphan epidemic." His voice tilted back into his usual Zen self. "It's just nice to be accepted. It only took an apocalypse," he said with a laugh. "Anyway, sounds like you're set, then. Does your hubby know about our time together?"

"No. Not at all. That's why I didn't tell you about the wedding. I didn't invite anyone on my side. All the guests are his family. As far as he knows, everyone I know died. Pandemic is a pretty good excuse these days."

"You're serious, huh?"

"I told you I wanted a clean break when I left," she said, kneeling down. The butt end of the knife handle dug into the sand. "I still do. I need to be in a place where no one knows who I am."

She expected one of Narc's usual nuggets of wisdom, a piece of Zen that hit the target much better than his ability to shoot a gun. But he didn't offer any of that. Instead, several seconds stretched into a space that seemed larger than the hundred miles between them.

"Well, then," he finally said. "There you go. Guess I'll let you off the hook this time." Another hesitation, and for the first time all conversation, Moira couldn't picture his face. "But when Santiago and I get married, I expect you to make a cameo. Moira Smith-that-speaks-American. You can even bring Mr. Smith."

Moira opened her mouth, ready to spill everything over the past twenty-four hours, including the decision to meet up with Krista to call off the wedding and Krista's request for her to think about it. Narc was filled with wisdom, he always knew the right thing to say to defuse a situation. Which helped when everyone was starving and looking for supplies, or in less dire straits like this. Yet, the words didn't want to come out. This time, the silence was all Moira's fault. Not even a polite chuckle at Narc's joke made it out.

From the parking lot beyond the beach, Moira heard a car door slam.

"Narc, I gotta go. Code Polka Dot."

"Polka Dot? I thought you were in the Metro?"

"I'm on the outskirts." She scanned over, looking for anything, but the silhouettes didn't give away any threat details. "Past the reconstruction zone. I wanted to run tonight."

"Okay." Suddenly, they were both all business. "You know the drill."

"Right." Moira popped up on her feet, momentum carrying her forward. "I'm glad we talked." With only minutes of sun left, details started to get obscured in the shadows. Best to get home.

"Don't be a stranger. One phone call a year won't kill you."

"You're right," she whispered. "Gotta go. Love to Santiago."

Another car door slammed. Moira shoved her phone into the pocket of the body belt she wore under her workout gear, then ran parallel to the parking lot, identifying the origin of the sound, sprinting past it before cutting over to the wall, obscuring herself from any possible angle. She pushed herself, calves and lungs burning for a good quarter mile at top speed before getting to a dilapidated concrete structure that somehow meshed in with a natural stone wall. Moira vaulted up it, legs catching footholds and using all limbs in unison to balance and scale up until she hit the street level. One look down saw four silhouettes in the distance standing by the car, now barely the size of her fingernail. But it didn't matter—Pittsburgh had taught her you can never be too cautious. She opened up her knife and held it blade down.

She moved, a light jog at first as she tuned back into the environment, scanning for threats and risks. It was time to head home.

Getting married. Tying off loose ends. Shutting the door on the past. That meant no more runs to Ocean Beach, no more making up excuses about why her hand was cut or scraped from climbing over stuff. And definitely no more parkour.

She wouldn't need those skills anymore.

A new life. A new identity. And then she could stop running.

Someday, the city would rebuild this neighborhood. But for now, she sealed it off in her memory, then started a full-speed sprint home. And in the morning, she'd start figuring out where she could possibly go from here.

CHAPTER NINE

Krista

Ms. Eswara had disappeared before Krista managed to get a business card out of her purse.

So much for that.

"You're friends with my daddy?" Sunny looked up as the question lingered, her blue eyes wide open without blinking. Funny how this was plain creepy when adults did it, but Sunny seemed to infuse spirit into her every word. Amused as she was, Krista reminded herself that she was getting paid for this whole excursion, and to treat it like a gig.

A gig that veered into babysitting.

"Sure," she said. Krista and Sunny lingered in the small waiting area of the office. Outside, hurried voices discussed President Hersh's upcoming speech, though their hushed tones gave away where their minds were at.

It was easy to direct young kids around when it was for a wedding or party or whatever. Usually, she'd have to remind them to follow their parents' directions about germs and masks, then stand in a certain spot and wait for the adults to talk. This was a little different. "So, uh, what did you learn today?"

"We're reading maps."

"Maps. Oh, that's good. Learning to get here from there."

"Uh-huh. Did you know there used to be cities *everywhere*? Big ones and little ones. My friend Rory says a lot of them are haunted now."

Haunted might be a stretch. Krista had driven through a bunch of the deserted suburbs just south of the Bay Area to clear her head, and while no ghosts popped out at her, the abandoned cars and squatter-ruined homes probably hid something. "Yeah, there were a lot of cities. Well," Krista said, grasping for any kid-friendly responses, "sounds like you're learning a lot."

"I drew a map to get from home to Los… Los… Angels."

"Los Angeles?" California's largest Metro was also an absolute mess of broken infrastructure and bickering politicians, and their Residence Licenses were even more expensive than San Francisco. Krista seriously questioned the teacher's choice in crafting this map example.

"Yeah. You turn left from our house, then take the second right and stay there to Van Ness…" Krista tuned out as Sunny spouted out detailed instructions on getting down to the City of Angels; she figured the teacher probably didn't mention the large stretch of wasteland or the looter gangs that controlled the remains of Fresno or the theme-park turf wars. Last she'd heard, the SeaWorld ruins were a battleground for the Connis and Enzor gangs. "Can I ask you something?"

"I don't know. I'm not an expert at maps."

"It's not about maps. It's about Daddy." Sunny stepped forward, and she offered as much seriousness as a seven-year-old could muster. "He's sad a lot. You're his friend. How can we fix that?"

More fixing things. Rob definitely passed this idea forward. "He needs to get laid." The words came out before Krista's brain-to-mouth filter could catch it, and her cheeks burned with a fast flush.

"What's laid?"

Sunny's question showed that at least Rob kept his language clean, so that scored one point on the parenting meter. "I mean, your dad is very tired. Being a single parent is difficult." Krista tapped into her inner kid-logic translator. "Not that it's your fault. I just mean that, you know, he could use a little more sleep. He's busy at work."

"Do you work with him?"

Krista's conversations with ring bearers and flower girls usually didn't contain this level of inquisition. "Me? No, see, I don't work with him, but one of my clients does. I plan weddings and I was visiting her." She opted out to leave the other side gigs she'd taken on to try to maintain her Residence License: Reunion Services agent, elevator therapist, pretend babysitter.

Peak social normalcy.

"Oh." Sunny adjusted her backpack, then shuffled her feet as she grimaced in contemplation. "Did you plan the wedding for my mommy and daddy?"

Shit. How was she supposed to know that telling Sunny about her job would bring up Rob's dead wife? Krista's teeth clenched behind her forced smile. "No, I didn't. That was before I met your dad."

"Daddy once showed me pictures of their wedding. It looked fun. And Mommy was pretty in them. He says they're very special and we have to keep them safe."

"Weddings are usually pretty fun. That's why people have them." There. A nice, simple, very clean answer that followed Rob's weird rule and didn't mention Elena, either by name or implication.

"I liked seeing Daddy so happy. And I think Mommy wants him to be happy. He's sad without her. But when I ask him he says it's not that and he won't say what."

"Right. Um, I'm guessing she would want him to be happy. But, uh, maybe you should try to help him do things that would make him happy." The half statement, half question worked to dance around Sunny's Elena comment.

"See, look." Sunny pointed over to Rob. Even through the slight visibility of the office door's window, his crossed arms matched his grim face. "He needs to stop looking like that. I wish he'd just get over it."

Krista's ears perked up.

Did this little girl just spout Krista's favorite bit of wisdom?

"Get over what?" she asked, her tone filled with a little extra innocence to lead Sunny's response.

"Get over looking like that." A smirk crept over Krista's lips, one that became a full beam, followed by a laugh. She'd worked with whiny kids, precocious kids, kids that seemed cute in their kidness, but never had she heard one use full Krista Deal logic in a conversation. "Don't make fun."

"I'm not," she said, kneeling down to Sunny's level. She put her hands on Sunny's shoulders and looked directly at the girl. "I'm really not. You know what, Sunny, I think I like you."

"I like you too, Krista. You're cool."

"Well then, I think that makes us pals." Her smile dropped as her phone buzzed. She pulled it out to see a notification from Reunion Services.

Her eyes went wide. "Holy shit."

Finder's reward for Johanna "MoJo" Hatfield established: $15,000.

Fifteen grand? How the hell was that even possible? Maybe the UK hadn't consolidated the financial assets from the population—alive or dead—the way America had. Because she was pretty sure that absolutely no one in the San Francisco Metro—possibly even the state of California—had that kind of money. That was easily a hundred grand or more in pre-pandemic times.

All that for a missing pop star.

Sunny inhaled sharply. "You swore."

"Right. Right, I'm sorry. Bad words. You shouldn't say that." Krista bit down on her lower lip, rereading the message.

"Now *you're* looking like that. I don't get grown-ups. You need to get over it too."

"Sorry, it's this thing. There's this singer named MoJo and—"

"Oh!" The girl's eyes brightened with her outburst. "You like MoJo too?"

"Uh…not quite. You know her?"

"We have her DVD. Have you seen it? It's *so* cool."

"Oh, so could you recognize her if you saw her?"

Sunny didn't seem to hear the question, as she broke out into an impromptu version of what Krista assumed was a MoJo song. "I want to get married to that song." Sunny's proclamation came with a grin large enough to back up its sincerity.

"I can arrange that. Here." Krista reached into her bag and pulled out a card. "Call me in twenty or thirty years, okay?"

Little fingers promptly snatched the card out of her hands, and Sunny studied it with an intensity that made no sense. "You plan weddings."

"That's the job. No gas mask required. Though I have a degree in graphic design. Not that it helps much these days."

Sunny's eyes seemed to follow an invisible bouncing ball as she tracked from left to right in thought, her expression evolving from curiosity to epiphany, a joy in discovery that only came from being too young to be jaded—PASD or no PASD. "You can help me. I need to plan a wedding," Sunny said. Down the hallway, a door opened and Rob's voice came through.

"I suppose all girls dream of their weddings."

"You can plan mine too, later."

"Wait, whose wedding—"

"We can go," Rob said before Krista could finish. The little bell tied to Sunny's backpack rang as he patted her shoulder, and then she dashed ahead of them. "Hold up, Sun."

Sunny stopped in place, though she remained facing out the door.

"Ms. Eswara, I didn't get a chance to properly introduce my friend Krista. She comes by my office sometimes." Rob glanced at Krista, the pleading request in his eyes a bit too obvious.

Professional performance—Krista's inner switch flipped. She lived for this stuff. "I am *so* glad we have a chance to talk," she said. The principal's brow rose, either skepticism or surprise or perhaps a little bit of both. No bother, though. Diffusing that was part of her job. Krista strode forward, stopping to use the hand sanitizer on the counter again, based on Ms. Eswara's affinity for modern germ protection, then reached into her purse to pull out a business card. "I imagine teaching in this environment can be difficult, especially since the Greenwood incident. You're doing a great service. I plan weddings, and one of Rob's coworkers is a client. We just gradually got to know each other from that. I was with Rob when the power went out, but when he told me you could use a character witness I wanted to come by." A pleasant smile came through, the one typically saved for city officials or hotel workers or people who weren't at ease being in groups or public places. "Did you still want to speak?"

"Actually, though I do appreciate you coming by, we've had to cut it short. The power outage has thrown everyone's schedule off." A glance at the clock showed that it was pushing six o' clock. "Mr. Donelly, I'll file my recommendations to the board right now and you'll be getting an update within twenty-four hours. I'll note that you brought a character witness and Sunny seems very engaged with her."

A subtle chain reaction of glances unfolded, first Rob to Krista, then Krista to Sunny, then Sunny meeting her eyes. "Of course," Krista said. "If there's anything I can do, don't hesitate."

Triple rate? Krista could do this all day.

★★★

"Nice work back there," Rob said when they hit the parking lot minutes later.

"Thanks. Everything all right?" Krista asked, her voice low.

"Yeah. I just can't believe how schools think they know everything these days."

"Daddy, guess what?" Sunny's pep cut through the bitterness in her dad's voice.

"What's that, Sun?"

"Krista's going to plan my wedding when I grow up."

Krista forced herself to keep looking straight ahead, even though she knew he looked her way, a coy glance just within her peripheral vision. "Well, that's awfully generous of her."

"She also said Mommy wants you to be happy. Why aren't you more happy, Daddy?"

Even from the side of her eyes, she could see Rob's entire body stiffen up. Strands of hair whipped her cheeks as she turned in midstride. "I didn't say anything," she mouthed.

"Get in the car, Sun. Lemme talk to Krista a second." He hit the unlock button on his key ring. Just ahead of them, a blue SUV beeped a greeting.

Sunny ran to the car, a blur of gray hoodie and jeans, and opened the door, backpack zippers jingling a scattered melody. She jumped in, giving the car a slight bounce, and Rob shut the door behind her. "Did she bring up Elena?" he asked, his voice a few clicks above a whisper.

"I just told her what my job was." Krista's tone and volume matched his. "She brought it up. I offered to tell her about my college major but she didn't seem interested."

"Wait—what did she say?"

"She said that Elena wants you to be happy. I agreed with her. What was I supposed to say? 'Excited about Hersh's speech tonight'?"

Rob looked into the back window and motioned for Sunny

to buckle up. His chin rumpled with a frown, and he pulled up the handle on the car door, leaving it just slightly ajar. "It's all right. I'm sorry she bothered you about it. I appreciate all your help today. Mail you a check?"

Krista considered saying her usual spiel about how she preferred cash, and in most cases, only took cash. But given the swing of the day, following Rob around while he got some money would be more trouble than it was worth. "Cash please," she said, handing Rob a business card.

"Okay. And if there's anything you need, I owe you big-time."

"Tomorrow. I'll come by your office in the morning."

Rob nodded and said something lost in the wind as Krista walked to her own car. It beeped as she tapped her key ring, and she looked over one more time.

Not at Rob. At Sunny's grinning face and waving hands.

Krista showed Sunny a full, reassuring smile in return. She didn't even have to force it.

Official tally of individuals presumed missing due to the Fourth Path cult:

San Francisco Metro: 3, including Kay Greenwood

*Sacramento Metro: 2**

Santa Cruz Reclaimed Territory: 4

Monterey Reclaimed Territory: 19

Fresno Metro: 37

San Luis Obispo Reclaimed Territory: 8

Los Angeles Metro: 55

San Diego Metro: 92

*Various Looter Gangs: 68***

**It is uncertain if Kay Greenwood led her followers north to Sacramento before heading south or if these individuals were visiting the San Francisco Metro when the movement began.*

***Number is estimated based on anecdotal evidence from known California looter gangs.*

CHAPTER TEN

Sunny

A knock came on the door, then it pushed open a little bit. Light from the hallway came through the opening, and Daddy's head poked in. "Sun, I gotta talk with you about something." Sunny felt the bed sink as Daddy sat on the edge.

Something. He probably wanted to talk about Noel. And Ms. Eswara. And all of the bad stuff from earlier today. "Daddy, I said I was sorry about hitting Noel." She gripped the blankets tight between her fingers. "But he deserved it. He said Mommy was dead."

With the light behind him, she could barely see Daddy's face mash up, like he smelled something awful. Sunny waited patiently for him to say something, remembering the school lesson on speaking and listening. "Right. Well, see, this is the thing about Mommy..." His voice faded away and he looked down at the floor.

Sunny took it as her turn to speak. "Did you call her tonight?"

Daddy let out a *hmph* sound. His hands patted his knees several times before resting, and he rocked back and forth a few times. "No," he said after a moment. "Sunny, I couldn't talk with Mommy because—"

"How come the doctors let you talk to Mommy, but not me?" The words came out before she could stop them. She knew better than that. That was rude. She pulled the blankets up to her nose.

She'd wanted to ask that for some time now. At least it finally got out. She hoped it didn't upset him.

Daddy rubbed his face, and she saw he was frowning again, even without any lights turned on. "Well, it's because…" The edge of his knuckle pressed into his lip, pushing on his nose. "Look, there's something I have to tell you about Mommy. You see, sometimes people make the wrong choice—"

The wrong choice! "Is it because I do things like hitting Noel?" The question came out fast. She couldn't help it.

"What? No. No, Sun, it's not that at all." Daddy smiled gently. That made her feel even worse.

"I said I was sorry." She couldn't stop the feeling. The question about Mommy, she'd wanted to ask it for so long, and she thought she'd feel better after asking it, but now she just felt bad, everything felt bad. It made no sense. Her eyes felt hot and wet. She blinked, trying to slow things down, but the tears started to roll down her cheeks. "I said I was sorry."

Daddy reached over and pulled her in, her head now buried against his chest. He took her hand and gave it a squeeze. Sunny remembered what he always said about giving a firm handshake and squeezed back much harder. "Sunny, Mommy's very proud of you. I promise. She just doesn't want you hitting people. You have to talk about your problems."

"But Noel wouldn't believe me. I kept telling him that Mommy was getting treatment."

"Some people just won't believe the truth. And it's up to you to be the better person in the argument. Lies catch up to them eventually." She leaned back, first sitting, then suddenly feeling really tired, her head went back down to the pillow and Daddy kissed her on the top of her hair. "It's been a long day, hasn't it, Sun?"

"Yeah," she said, pulling the blankets back up to her nose.

"How about we get some rest? Start fresh tomorrow?"

"Okay, Daddy. I love you. And I love Mommy too. I can't wait for her to get better so I can see her."

Beneath the blanket, she was smiling. The room was still mostly dark, but the way he nodded, she bet Daddy was smiling too.

CHAPTER ELEVEN

Rob

Rob had considered telling Sunny the truth about Elena before, but never as seriously as tonight. The fact that he was pushed to this point, not by her own need to know or his willingness to tell, but by the Family Stability Board…

It certainly didn't make him think he'd been taking the high road this whole time.

Either way, things were going to get worse before they got better.

Elena had said that once. It applied now, pondering the possibilities of another outbreak, the conundrum in the form of his daughter, and the email he'd just received from the Family Stability Board. It applied back in quarantine, another moment when Rob stood by and watched Sunny sleep.

They'd sat alone in their prison-cell-turned-bunk, a cot on the floor for them and folded blankets in a large cardboard box for the then almost-two-year-old Sunny. Elena looked over, her usual long hair cut short ("less water, less shampoo") and now tied back into two blond pigtails. She held up her fork, offering the slice of Spam his way. He shook his head no, not that he had anything against Spam. His Japanese mother used to make Spam sushi, something that his father—a European mutt of the truest sense—used to joke about.

But it wasn't about salty canned meat. They had a protocol with rationed food: first Sunny ate, then Elena, then Rob took whatever was left over. Rob insisted, given that Sunny still nursed about half of her nourishment from Elena. Given the quarantine's limited resources—even more critical since overland looter gangs started hitting government supply convoys—they tried to keep Sunny on breast milk for as long as possible.

Sunny, however, seemed to have her own opinion on things, and was starting to refuse mother's milk.

"There's another distribution meeting tomorrow," Elena said.

Rob nodded. Everyone had a role in quarantine, whether it matched their pre-pandemic job or not. Rob fixed computers, kept the network running with a small team of three other people, and that morning as they worked on Wi-Fi stability, all talk had focused on the supply distribution meeting.

"We should go." Elena looked squarely at him and gestured to the meat on the fork again. "Both of us."

"I'll go—" Rob started but Elena shook her head at him.

"Sunny's weaning herself. It happens. We need more food. We both need to go."

"I'll ask for rations for two."

"They'll never go for that. The population is restless as it is. You saw the fights that broke out last time. You ask for a second portion and you'll get punched." Elena took Rob's hand. At first, he thought she was merely being affectionate, but then she opened his fingers up and put the fork in his hand. "Sunny's not nursing as much. My body doesn't need the extra fuel. Take it."

Elena's eyes somehow remained bright, despite the nights of bad sleep, the dank and cramped living conditions, the limited food supply. Her mouth broke upward, a tiny curl that projected a sense of calm out to him. How she remained an optimist, even living in a converted prison, he never knew.

The tough meat was the second thing Rob had to eat all day after an apple from the jailyard orchard they'd help plant months ago. He chewed it quick, swallowing and putting the fork into the small sink next to their cot.

"Everyone will be there. We won't be able to find a sitter for Sunny." The distribution was at 10:00 a.m.; it might have been possible to adjust her nap schedule so she'd be sleeping during that time. He considered the possibility of locking their cell and leaving her, but their quarters weren't exactly childproofed. No one had that luxury now.

"I know."

"The crowds, they might get rowdy."

"We'll protect her." Elena's voice radiated conviction.

Rob stood up, a dull ache radiating from his lower back down his legs to the pins and needles attacking his toes. He stepped over to their sleeping daughter, her would-be crib a large shipping box reinforced with duct tape, folded blankets forming a mattress inside. Her black hair was wildly long, outpacing the toddler's growing body. Her little fingers curled around a small pink dog, a toy donated by one of their quarantine neighbors. How the population of Quarantine CA14—a good five thousand or so survivors—could be so unified and fractured at the same time, he didn't understand.

"What if she sat on my shoulders?" he asked. "Above it all."

"That's why I married you. Always coming up with ways to fix things." Elena walked up behind him, her arms wrapping around his waist. They stood together, watching their sleeping daughter, the second hand from the cell's wind-up clock ticking away.

In the shadows of her bedroom, Sunny stirred, the subtle shifts under blankets pulling Rob back to this house, this doorway, this situation. And unlike that moment in quarantine, he watched his daughter alone.

Things were going to get worse before they got better. Elena said it, but she also told him to be good to himself.

Maybe it was finally time to do that.

Rob closed Sunny's door, then walked to his room and collapsed on the bed, the day's events bowling over him. His shoes hit the floor with a *thunk,* and he fired up his email again on his phone, the Family Stability Board message that he'd only skimmed some fifteen or twenty minutes ago loading line by line for about thirty seconds.

To: Rob Donelly
From: SF Metro Family Stability Board
Subject: Report #10213

Dear Mr. Donelly,

This notification is to inform you of a report from Kavita Eswara at Westerberg Elementary. As you may know, the Family Stability Board requires teachers and caregivers to report any incidents that may endanger the emotional or physical health of a child in the post-MGS landscape. As Ms. Eswara indicated emotional concerns, you are required to attend a social normalcy audit set for October 17 at 1:30 PM. At that time, the FSB will review all data and inform you of its findings at a later date. Failure to comply with the audit will result in the FSB assuming temporary custody of the child into the FSB housing facility.

The audit was devised as a community safety net for our children in this new world. It is vital to our society's well-being that we address any emotional or mental health concerns before they impact our next generation.

You may file social normalcy verifications and testimonials early by sending the appropriate forms to *fsb@sfmetro.gov*. These will be given equal consideration to the in-person hearing. Please contact us if you have further questions.

Temporary custody. FSB housing facility—where orphaned children in the End of the World and its PASD fallout wound up. Underfunded, understaffed, undertrained, and the last place in the world he'd want for Sunny to be. The adults in this world were screwed up enough, their boarding school for the familyless created media stories more horrifying than the Fourth Path cult, despite the best intentions. There were the success stories, the ones released to the Metronet featuring happy adoptions or reunifications after parental rehabilitation through therapy. But those masked what everyone knew about overwhelmed staff who battled their own PASD.

For some, it was the only thing they had. But that wasn't the case here. Sunny had Rob. And he wasn't going to let her go without a fight.

Rob opened up his phone's web browser, selected the San Francisco network rather than the impossible-to-load national search, and typed in *passing a social normalcy audit*. Only a few results arrived from terrified parents worrying their single mistake meant either losing custody of their child or leaving for Reclaimed Territory before it happened. Some even claimed to call the FSB's bluff, stating that presenting evidence at the meeting was enough to bypass the overtaxed agency staffers. Rob's day job crept into his mind for a moment, and he wondered if the lack of information stemmed from the internet's general instability, leading to the death of forums and social media, or if the FSB initiative was simply too new to have many discussions about it yet.

Living in a Metro may have had the shiny facade of the old world, but Residence Licenses and their strong-arm family guidelines showed that governments were as worried about it all falling apart as the people were.

Rob read and reread the posts, making a mental checklist of what supposedly satisfied the boards. Written testimonials from friends. Therapy and support group receipts. Evidence of dating.

That all lined up with what Ms. Eswara talked about. Asking him if he'd been to a support group. Bringing in a character witness.

Asking if he'd been able to move on.

His attention deviated, moving to the platinum ring on his finger. It stuck when he tried to loosen it; it needed a good twist to get it moving. The ring pulled up to midknuckle, cutting off the circulation below until another effort pulled it fully off.

He moved his fingers around, noticing the difference of not having a piece of metal rub up against them when he made a fist or even just wagged them back and forth. The ring made a slight *clink* as he placed it on the nightstand.

He hadn't slept without the ring since the night before his wedding. But for tonight, just as an experiment, it'd be interesting to try sleeping without its weight on his left hand. He could put it back on in the morning. Because even though he didn't want to move on from Elena, from the memories that lay burned up in the disintegrating remains of a house several miles from here, he might just have to in order to protect his daughter.

It seemed everyone needed the truth these days. But especially her.

Rob considered turning on President Hersh's upcoming speech but opted not to. He had enough on his mind.

CHAPTER TWELVE

Krista

Despite the school only being a few miles away from her apartment building, Krista had taken the long way home—on Highway 280 down into the foothills, past the suburbs-turned-government-farmland and back. Even with the high price of gas, roaming the roads with too-loud music was often a better—and more economical—option to therapy sessions that wouldn't work anyway. She'd stopped when the highway got too dilapidated around Half Moon Bay, then turned around, her mind mostly purged of the day's weird vibe. Between Moira's almost-departure and two hours stuck in an elevator *and* a stint as a babysitter, the quiet of the open road was better than any PASD support group could offer. As she got back into San Francisco's city limits, she decided to check in on the state of the world.

After all, everyone seemed to be fretting about it today.

The radio came to life with anticipation of President Hersh's speech. Host voices bantered the usual stuff about rumors, staying strong, goodwill toward humanity, all in a very business-like fashion. "Will President Hersh address the recent rumors of another outbreak? With us now via satellite are Lou Amberdine of the Modern Patriots political party, and Dr. Dean Francis, head of the communicable diseases department at Seattle's St. Vincent General Hospital and a leading researcher—"

Dean Francis. The name stirred nausea in Krista's gut, and she hit the shuffle button on the car's media player before Uncle Dean could say a word. The familiar post-punk stylings of Joy Division's "She's Lost Control" blared through the speakers and she increased the volume to drown out any sentiment toward her high-and-mighty uncle, Mr. Famous Researcher, for the rest of the drive.

Mick greeted her upon her first step inside the apartment, his round gray head and white whiskers rubbing up against her ankle. "I know, I'm late," she said. "Come on, you're self-sufficient. Here." She reached into her purse and pulled out the unfinished patch that she'd knitted mostly in the elevator. "Something new."

He sniffed the awkward rectangle and looked at it sideways before turning and mewing. "You big baby." They'd been doing this greeting routine for almost a decade now, since New York City after college, through quarantine, and now here in San Francisco, and yet every time Mick acted like she'd never come home. She scooped the cat up, giving him a kiss on the nose and whispering nonsensical affections to him. With both of them satiated, she put him down, and his hanging belly swung back and forth as he trotted to the bedroom. "Don't blame you. Elevator stink isn't cool." The TV came to life, an attempt for benign white noise as she thumbed through the mail. A news anchor appeared, a bland man in a gray suit and red tie. "...and as Russia remains mostly closed off to outside communications, reports have cited a return to a militarized state. In related news, protesters representing the Reclaimed communities continued to occupy state capitals today. Leaders in the Native American community issued a statement in support, stating, 'We stand in solidarity with the Reclaimed community, and while they operate on many of the same post-MGS principles as our Nations, they do not receive the federal recognition or benefits we do, and that must change.' Reclaimed protesters…" The news reporter droned further before cutting to an interview of some guy who looked like he hadn't bathed since getting out of quarantine.

Krista turned to the stack of mail in her hand.

Bill, bill, coupons, flyer for a free PASD support group, and another flyer for a business mixer from the Chamber of Commerce. That one stuck out.

"It's not just here. Governments around the world think they can tax us," the Reclaimed resident said. "We're survivors, not capitalists or socialists. We live *with* the land, not off it. We pay sales tax for our materials. If all our resources go into our crops, our supplies—produce we provide for the Metros—what else is there to tax? We're not waiting for the feds, the states control everything now."

Krista flipped over the Chamber of Commerce flyer—the organization struggled, at least in the San Francisco Metro. Maybe other Metros did booming business, free from post-apocalyptic agoraphobia and unsettled feelings. Here, they were lucky to get a single body to show up to an event.

"But government officials note that Reclaimed communities often aren't wholly self-sufficient," the TV reporter said. "While most focus on self-sustaining farming, many sell produce to nearby Metros, and they take up a large portion of satellite communications bandwidth. Despite that, thousands are giving up their Residence Licenses to join Reclaimed Territory."

This flyer, though, looked different. *The San Francisco Chamber of Commerce presents* Hope and Business: A Friends And Family Event. *Join San Francisco's leading business minds in a family-friendly mixer at Last Splash Cafe.*

Dangling a PASD therapy session in front of business owners? That just might get people out. But family-friendly, Krista would stick out like a sore flu-ridden thumb there. Maybe she could bring her cat?

Graphics flashed and music rattled beneath a compilation of ads for free PASD support groups. "Up next, the search for MoJo continues. As MoJo-mania sweeps the UK, in the United States, all eyes are now on the San Francisco Metro with the most recent statement by Evan Hatfield."

Krista looked at the TV for the first time since turning it on, half listening to the bloviating man talking about the release of unearthed recordings and other such trivial bullshit, all with the grand announcement that he'd narrowed MoJo's location to the San Francisco Metro. Further details fell by the wayside, and instead her mind bounced between the idea of the business mixer and the MoJo search. With everything else seeming to slip through her fingers, this felt like fate telling her to take back control of her life. She'd done it before, several times in fact. But that first time, just the mere idea of steering her own destiny was such a simple but *profound*—and new—idea that it burrowed deep into her core, synthesizing into her very instincts to this day.

Freshman year of college at Hofstra University and there she was, somehow roped along to a frat party by the people on her dorm floor. It was only one month into the school year, and though she ultimately gave in to the nonstop "you should come" urging by her dorm-mates, Krista clearly wasn't having a good time.

"Krista!" her roommate yelled over the din. "They're playing beer pong!"

Krista pretended not to hear, and instead wandered through the sweaty air and mass of humanity. To her left, a couple was making out like they needed to repopulate the planet right then and there. To her right, a girl sat, knees pulled up to her chest, eyes puffy and hair matted while one of her friends insisted that she drink some water. Noise seemed to waft above that, a horrifying mix of bad 1990s music and pop singles from the late 2000s, all jammed in with wave upon wave of voices. Talking. Laughing. Yelling. And a lot of screaming of the word *fuck*, all blissfully unaware that in a few years more than half of them would be dead. In that slice of time, though, all that mattered was the euphoria of being young and dumb.

Except for Krista. She wandered the house, wondering if she should walk back to her dorm, but decided against it, just in case her roommate drank too much and needed help back. Instead, she found an empty corner and sat against it. For about ten minutes, no one seemed to notice her.

Not even the guy who'd been standing next to where she sat. Tall and lean, the purple and pink lights of the party glowed off his brown skin and clear eyes. He glanced down and they met eyes, though she didn't match his brief smile.

"Don't bother asking if I want a drink," she said.

Rather than reply, his arm shot up, showing what looked to be an X tattooed on the back of his hand.

"Am I supposed to be impressed with that?" she asked.

"It means I make my own choices," he shouted right when someone yelled about beer, his English accent barely noticeable.

"You chose to use a magic marker on your hand. I can see why Hofstra accepted you."

"Look." He sat down, not to a creepy space-intrusive level, but to point across the room at the silhouette of a skinny guy drinking beer down a hose. "See that dumb arse doing keg stands? That's my twin brother. He can't resist this shit. He's visiting me for the weekend from London and wanted to go out. So I'm here to indulge him. But fuck that noise. I don't need it. I'd rather be in control of my life." He held up his hand again. "Straight edge."

Krista knew the term, the Minor Threat song that it came from, and the whole idea of a no drugs/no booze punk lifestyle. Suddenly, a flush came over her cheeks and she was glad they were in a dark room with sporadic party lighting; she should have recognized the symbol given her almost encyclopedic knowledge of punk.

"I know what that means," she bit out sheepishly.

"So, don't offer you a drink. Nailed that one."

"I don't need Minor Threat telling me to do it though." Krista told herself that she wasn't name-dropping or showing off, not using a hard-core punk band's name as some kind of secret code word to test this guy. But she knew that was all a lie. This guy was intriguing. "I made that choice on my own. So are you one of those anti-everything people?"

"Anti-fascist. Anti-capitalist. The usual bad stuff."

"The anti-capitalist is hanging out at a frat party. Okay, that makes sense," Krista said. She didn't even know why she said it at the time, though looking back later on, she'd eventually recognize that verbal kickback was her best attempt at flirting.

"The anti-capitalist still loves his brother. Even though said brother makes dumb choices." He glanced back at his brother and laughed, shaking his head. "My name's Jaswinder. But people who like Minor Threat can call me Jas."

"Krista. And they're okay, but Ian MacKaye's better band was Fugazi. And they both pale to The Clash."

"So, Krista, you come to a frat party and you're not drinking *and* you know your punk bands. What's your story?"

"My mom is an extraordinary fuckup." The statement came out so fast, so firmly etched into existence that it surprised her. Until that point, she'd never fully admitted such a thing. Now, to a stranger at a frat party, hundreds of miles away from her childhood, the door finally cracked. "That kind of explains everything."

"Ah. Well, um..." He searched for the right reply, and though she played it cool, she couldn't help stealing glances here or there while he was in thought. "I'll be honest," he said. "I don't have a snappy response for that. Though you seem to make good choices. Better than these people."

The *meaning* of Jas's words probably carried more than he intended. *Good choices.* For her whole life until then, she'd been told pretty much every message possible except those, so much so that the sheer possibility of that seemed out of reach.

But it was simpler than that. She *was* in control. She *could* make good choices.

"Hey," she said loudly over a sudden charge of drunken applause and chanting.

"Yeah?" he yelled back.

"Your brother will be fine," she said. "My roommate will be fine. Everyone here is an asshole. Let's get some air."

And they did, starting a debate about The Clash vs. Black Flag that lasted years, so long that it wasn't even resolved the last time she saw Jas right before college graduation. For a split second, she considered the resources made available to her as a Reunion Services agent, and maybe she should look up Jas, see if he was still alive.

But no. Nostalgia wasn't going to overrun her sensibilities. She had bigger things to get to.

She switched off the TV, silencing more talking heads with a fifteen-minute countdown to Hersh's speech. Then Krista picked up her phone and typed out a text to Rob.

You know how you said to get in touch if I needed anything? I need something. Some help from Sunny, if that's okay.

Rob's reply came quick. That's good. Because I've just been asked to be socially normal, so maybe we can trade? I'll pay for your time.

Getting paid. Getting to meet potential clients. Getting an

expert eye for hunting MoJo, though she told herself to keep that part close to the vest. It was a long shot but too much was at stake.

On it. I'll come by your office first thing tomorrow. Don't forget the cash.

Krista's finger mashed the Send button on her phone.

She was back in control.

And she wasn't going to lose it, not now. She considered turning on Hersh's speech, but opted for a glass of wine and a bath instead.

Jas would have found that amusing.

CHAPTER THIRTEEN

Moira

Moira studied Frank's face, waiting for it to break. A small part of her found some amusement in that. After all, he had been lucky. He and his immediate family went to quarantine in the first wave—one of the nicer ones, the setup that took over the whole Alcatraz island and offered scenic views and ocean walks to go with the rationed food. They missed the brutality that came with people waiting up to a year to go to quarantine, and though he'd known people that died, everyone he knew seemed to escape unscathed. Parents. Sister. Closest college friends. As if he was the hub of immunity against contracted illness, random violence, and sheer bad luck. He mourned and suffered like billions of others, but his conscience didn't seem to have a constant weight tied to its waist.

He never had the same look that Moira saw at support groups, not even a hint of it.

Until now.

"You want to cancel the wedding?" he asked.

"Not cancel. Just see if we can move it up," Moira said gently. "For tax purposes. So we can get the newlywed credit this year. Next year, the quota drops and we may not get it in time."

"The wedding's in February. You really think it'll be filled by then?"

"I do," Moira said, aware at the irony of her sentence. "With all these rumors, I think it's going to make people want to get married as soon as possible. I mean, look, Hersh's speech is on in five minutes? Imagine what people will be doing if it's really something."

"I don't know." He leaned forward on the sofa, one hand rubbing his cleft chin, the other the back of his dark brown hair. "I mean, that's a lot to rearrange. What will people think?"

"I think after a pandemic and quarantine, people would enjoy *any* wedding, whether it's one month or five months from now."

"But getting married is huge. It's life-changing. It's not just a legal document. It's a commitment. It's not something you sign and shove into a file cabinet." Frank sighed into his hand, then turned her way. "You're worried about something. I can tell."

From her toes to her shoulders, Moira tensed. Another rare Frank reaction—confrontational. Still gentle, still *Frank*, but this must have really done a number on him. "I'm not worried about anything." That was a lie. Through it all, from walking home amidst a power outage to her run outside the safety zone to her call with Narc, the throughline was simple: her father and his shitshow of a hunt. Of course he would put it on TV. Of course he would make it public. She knew him, how he thought, how he was *still* trying to make money off her, even when she'd escaped him. "I'm fine."

"No, I can tell. The way you pronounce stuff is a little different when you're stressed. It's like a nervous tic or something." He adjusted on the couch, moving a few inches closer until their hips touched and his arm settled around her, pulling her into his athletic frame. "Are you worried about wedding costs? We can scale back—"

"I'm not worried about money."

"The ceremony? Being in front of people? Being among people?" Frank's eyes lit up, like he really believed he was onto something. "I know gatherings scare a lot of people. But we'll have everyone undergo the usual safety precautions. I mean, we can all wear breathing masks except maybe during the vows or something. Look." He straightened up, little creases of concern marking his expression. "I know you don't like talking about your family and your past. But *something* happened to you. No one has zero people coming to their wedding—"

"I don't want to invite anyone to the wedding. The people we know together, that's all I care about." This time, it was Frank's turn to tense up. Moira looked out the window, a single plane hovering over the skyline to San Francisco International, perhaps one of only a handful of flights coming and going today. "I leave the past in the past."

"You just clam up is all. Maybe," Frank's words slowed their pace, tiptoeing on a mine field of vowels and consonants, "it'd be worth it to try counseling. Or a support group. They have free ones, you know."

The edges of Moira's mouth curled upward. He was trying. He didn't suspect her daily routine of going to a free PASD group by her office.

A new idea sparked, one that would perfectly riff on all this. There may even be a kernel of truth in it. "It's not just the tax benefits."

She let the sentence hang on purpose, and she watched as he followed the bread crumbs she'd laid out. "Health costs. You want the better family rates for private counseling."

"The thought had crossed my mind. But, you know, just consider it." The couch squeaked from her abrupt stand, and she turned off one of her favorite Andrews Sisters songs, creating silence while she walked to the kitchen. "I could even talk to Krista soon."

Light hit the glass of the microwave door at the exact right angle for Frank's reflection to appear. Moira lingered, pretending to thumb through junk mail and other papers while keeping one eye on his reaction. He sat still, deep lines worn into his brow to go with a tense stare of deep thought. Not angry. Not frustrated. Just thinking.

Mission accomplished.

Moira grabbed the TV remote and clicked the screen on. It came to life, greeting her with her own face, just about a decade younger, with a wild hairstyle and face paint. "...whose career peaked with her debut album, has been missing since the night quarantines were announced. However, her father hasn't given up hope—"

"Oh, her," Frank said nonchalantly. "I remember her. My best friend in high school had such a crush on her."

Moira's fingers lacked poetry in their movements; her dad would have been so disappointed at this type of performance anxiety. Instead, the simple act of changing the channel to something, anything else became a mess of button mashes, activating the TV menu, increasing the volume, and changing the channel all at once. The image blinked, and she no longer saw the ghost of herself, and instead it was President Hersh sitting at a desk in the Oval Office.

"My fellow Americans," she started. The president's close-cropped hair sat neatly back, her mouth in a neutral line, bright blue eyes staring straight ahead. She glanced quickly offscreen, then re-centered into a serious-yet-pleasant demeanor. "I am speaking to you tonight to address rumors..."

Frank didn't say another word about MoJo. Moira had suspected age and face-paint would create a reasonable separation from any suspicion, but her breath remained static as she observed his reaction. But he didn't care about MoJo. Instead, he sat up, hanging on to every word from President Hersh.

Moira stayed quiet, mind alive as it searched for a solution.

Excerpt from President Tanya Hersh's speech on the first post-quarantine fatality:

My fellow Americans. I am speaking to you tonight to address rumors that you've no doubt heard by now. For the past several weeks, reports out of the Miami, Florida, Metro have discussed cases of flu-like symptoms. In Europe, a similar situation has evolved, particularly in the southern France region of the Marseille Metro.

In the case of Miami, I can confirm the first fatality due to these symptoms.

That is a fact.

However, another fact is that ever since the end of quarantine four years ago, the global scientific and medical community has worked together to stay ahead of the curve when it comes to MGS mutations.

I must stress that there is no imminent threat, there is no need for fear, there is no need for panic.

Caution should be exercised, as with any situation involving fatalities. Both Florida and France have agreed to a transportation lockdown in and out of the region. Foreign visitors wishing to return to their native Metros will be quarantined for six days to ensure no symptoms arise, then they will be free to make travel arrangements home. The region will also experience weekly rolling blackouts except for medical facilities to conserve local resources. The Miami Metro will also enact its own travel and security measures to limit risks for the southeastern United States.

Now, how does this affect you, the American people? In short: it doesn't. This doesn't change a thing for you or me. We will continue to live for today, appreciate the life we have as MGS survivors, and continue to support each other during this difficult rebuilding period.

I hope this has calmed your fears, answered your questions, and dispelled any rumors you may have heard. In the meantime, we send our thoughts and prayers to the residents of the Marseille Metro. God bless them, God bless you, and God bless the United States of America.

PART 2:

PARTNERS

CHAPTER FOURTEEN

Krista

Krista hoped no one at Last Splash Cafe saw her cringe.

Beside her, a pair of local business owners sat at a table, holding hands and openly weeping. Next to her, a woman quietly nursed her baby. And most of the handful of residents who had come to this friend-and-family mixer stared at the TV above, replays of President Hersh's speech intermixed with various commentary. And interviews. So many interviews about the death out of Miami. People who knew the dead. People who thought they knew the dead. People who were freaking the hell out. People who didn't know how to react except to cry because *something* might be happening.

Not exactly the type of thing that was gonna generate business.

And then Uncle Dean popped up on the screen. The text below his face read *Dr. Dean Francis, Lead MGS Researcher.* Though the TV volume was set low, Krista could still hear the timbre of his voice, the way he drew out "uh" every three or four words, the even-keeled tone with which he responded to *everything.*

He even did that the last time she saw him—which was two hours too late. Krista had planned it on her last day of summer break right before senior year of college. Jas offered to come with her, but she insisted it had to be family, just her and Uncle Dean. She'd sent an invite to her shithead dad, but he didn't show up. He didn't even reply to the text.

That was expected. Uncle Dean's flakiness, however, was not. After spending three straight days with her mom, forcing laughter and smiles to keep the peace despite the sheer stupidity of her mom's "I need a drink or six to unwind after work" logic, she'd planned for Sunday afternoon, right after her mom got off her shift at the local drugstore.

Krista sat on the beat-up sofa in her mom's small apartment, the threads tearing apart at the corners of the cushions, minutes ticking by on her phone's clock. Uncle Dean was supposed to arrive at three. Her mom wouldn't arrive until around four thirty, giving them plenty of time to rehearse intervention speeches one last time.

It was textbook. They were supposed to catch Krista's mom at the front door, before she had a chance to pop open whatever she picked up at the convenience store on the way home. They'd tell her they loved her, that they were concerned about her, that they were losing the person they once knew—which was bullshit, from Krista's perspective. She'd never known her mom to be anything else, but that statement translated into the *potential* of who she might become.

Then they'd offer to take her to rehab, right then and there. Uncle Dean volunteered the funds. Krista would drive her. The administrative paperwork was ready. All she would have to do was say yes. And if not, they would both cut her off.

That was the plan. But it required two people and a credit card. Uncle Dean's credit card, to be exact. Three became three thirty, then four, then four fifteen. Uncle Dean didn't pick up his phone or answer his texts. Every time a car slowed in front of the apartment, Krista's hopes surged.

Then the footsteps came. The slow, trudging footsteps, the crinkles of a plastic bag, the muttering under breath about Shimmer, the "goddamn cat" across the street. Jingling of keys, then dropped keys and more cursed muttering, before the door finally opened.

"Krista? I thought you were leaving after lunch."

But without Uncle Dean, half her ammunition was gone. The speech about brother sister childhood, the dreams they had growing up, all that stuff evaporated. The financial means, poof, up in smoke. Instead, Krista stumbled through her part, mental shields up and active as her mom's venom unleashed itself, going full volume at Krista for even *daring* to suggest she had a problem. By the time Krista's mom cracked open the first can of shitty beer to "show" Krista that she could stop at one, numbness began to set in. She couldn't even fully recall what she'd said, just that she'd needed to get out of there and back to Jas as soon as possible.

And in the parking lot, right when the key cranked her car's ignition, Uncle Dean came up. He walked up to her window, shoulders shrugged. "How'd it go?" he asked. Like it was a freaking dental appointment.

"It didn't. I'm done." The words came out as a mission statement, reflective of the epiphany she'd just had: she could only march forward. Never back.

"Krista, I've thought about it a lot. And I don't think it's our place to get involved this way."

"Not our place?" The weight of her foot gradually pressed on the accelerator until the car was roaring in place. She eased off it, a big wall of blank in her mind rather than any snappy retort. "I don't even know what that means," she said through the open car window.

"It means that Kristen needs to make this decision by herself. Not as my sister. Not as your mom. We shouldn't *threaten* her, we're all she has."

"Bullshit. Every single goddamn pamphlet and website says we draw the line."

"Krista," Uncle Dean said, a long pause between his words. "I can't get involved."

Krista shifted the car into reverse without even looking at Uncle Dean after that. As the car rolled back, she yelled through the open window. "I made a promise to myself. And I'm keeping it." And she meant it—the promise to herself to never speak to either of them again.

That also extended to paying attention when Uncle Dean was on TV.

No. Only forward. Never back.

And definitely never paused.

Krista approached the only person she hadn't met yet, a woman probably about her own age but with lines stenciled further and deeper across her face. Krista put on the most sincere-looking insincere smile in her arsenal, then took several steps forward, business card in hand. "Hi there," she started. "Krista Deal. I'm the founder and owner of Atmosphere Special Events."

The woman pulled her breathing mask down just enough to show her lips. "Hello."

"I'm a complete event coordinator. Handle all of the meetings, pickups, organization—all the face-to-face so you don't have to." She held her card between two fingers. The woman pointed to her own stack of cards, then gestured to the other side of the table. Krista set her own card down in the blank space, then picked one off from the stack. "Thanks," she said, smile projecting again, though the woman didn't seem to notice; instead, she took Krista's card and put it in a small wallet before spraying sanitizer over her hands, her fingers showing the dryness and wear of cleaning too often.

So the first part of this visit was a bust.

Then there was Rob. Sitting with Sunny, as part of the "family" part of this whole "friends and family" business. Sunny reading a book and Rob with steaming tea, taking the occasional business card and acting, as he joked, socially normal. In fact, it sounded like Sunny didn't even hesitate when she heard about Krista's suggestion to go as a group to the mixer at Last Splash. Everyone agreed that it was win-win: Krista would do her thing, Sunny would have a noteworthy interaction, and Rob would even be able to get some bonus social normalcy evidence in the form of business cards and an event flyer.

The mood of the place finally told Krista to pull the plug on trying to socialize and return to Rob's table. "That was rough," she said, blowing out a breath.

"So much for friends and family mixing, huh?"

"Not quite. But at least everyone here came with someone else, so no one looked at me sideways. New business initiatives."

"Happy to help. Hey, Sun," he said, "go give the book back, okay? We're gonna take off soon."

The girl hopped off her chair and dashed over to the Chamber of Commerce attendant, book in hand. He took the book, then brushed the entire outside surface with a disinfectant wipe, then put it in a separate bin labeled *Returns*.

"Here," Rob said, handing her cash while Sunny was off. "Three hours of your time."

"And I'll email you a witness testimony for your audit." Krista eyed the bills, doing a mental count for accuracy. No risks given the Residence License deadline tomorrow.

"Let's get a few more socially normal *things* in before the audit if we can. Apparently speed dating is popular right now?"

Krista knew exactly what Rob was talking about. A PASD world hobbled normal dating situations, and the lack of high-speed connectivity meant that online matchmaking had disappeared. In its place were events that threw a bunch of traumatized people in a room together with the premise of trying to hook up. Feast or famine, really; in her experience, people either latched on to the first person that wasn't repulsive or they ran out crying and/or screaming. "It is. That's how most of my couples meet. It's the fastest way to get hitched these days." At least, when people actually wanted to get married. "You should look it up."

"It sounds kind of...horrifying. But maybe I'll do it, just to show the Board how socially normal I am."

"Well, one thing at a time. I've got some errands to run tomorrow. She can tag along. Sound good?" Krista asked. Rob gave a nod as Sunny ran back to them. "Hey, Sunny, ask your dad if I can buy you a snack."

"Daddy, can Krista buy me a snack?"

"Sure," Rob said, "but remember what we do with food."

"Make good choices," they said in unison.

The two of them marched over to the counter, Krista scanning the room the whole time. If MoJo was in San Francisco, she might have been *anyone*: Staring at the TV in the corner, coffee in hand. Consoling her partner at the table, stack of business cards in front of them. Writing in a notebook while eating a pastry. Hiding behind a mask, earbuds drowning out the world. About twenty people sat in the cafe for the mixer, and Krista figured that based on age, five of them could possibly be MoJo.

"Hey, Sunny," she said, pulling the girl's attention away from the glass case of snacks. "Let's play a game for a second."

"Okay!" Sunny replied with full enthusiasm.

"Take a look around." Krista knelt down to get to Sunny's eye level. "See the different women in here?"

"Uh-huh."

"Okay, now take a good look at them." Krista opted not to point out the ones she specifically thought might be MoJo. "Think real hard. You know that singer you like, MoJo? Does anyone here look like her? Think about how she looks from her concert and picture her a little older."

"Hmmm." Sunny's lips pursed and her brow crinkled in thought. She turned gradually from left to right, focus passing over everyone at Last Splash, including one confused glance from Rob. "Maybe her," she said with a point. "But I don't think so."

"No?"

"No. Her eyes are different."

"Okay. You know the cool thing about this game is you can play it anywhere you go. And if you see someone who looks like MoJo, you tell me. Okay?"

"Okay!"

"All right. Now, what are we getting here?"

Sunny didn't hesitate, immediately pointing to what must have been a Rob-authorized snack: a plastic cup of carrots and celery sticks. Sweets would have been cheaper, what with the fresh produce limited to the Metro's urban farm initiative, but given that the night was profitable, Krista considered this would be a tax write-off. "Look, Krista. Yums."

Krista gave a quarter to the man behind the counter. He nodded, the bob of his head catching light off the glittery stickers on his silicone mask, then he handed over the snack cup.

"Yums indeed," Krista said. "Let's go show your dad." Sunny pulled out a carrot and dipped it into the little cup of ranch dressing, then sprinted over to Rob. Was that safe for kids to run and chew? Probably not, but Rob didn't say anything, so Krista opted to not get involved.

"Everything okay?" Rob asked.

"Sure," Krista said, leaning over to examine the one woman who might have been MoJo. From what few photographs she'd found of the pop star, she was pretty sure Sunny was right. "We're just looking around."

CHAPTER FIFTEEN

Moira

Rumors. Speculation. If those were enough for President Hersh to make a speech last week, then they were also enough to bring the entire city out to support groups.

Or at least the people in the immediate vicinity of Moira's office building. The weekly Survivors Anonymous group at the abandoned-church-turned-community-center overflowed, standing room only. Well, standing room for this world. That still meant people kept their personal space and most of them wore masks. Attendance had gradually grown as rumors swirled, but this was unprecedented. Perhaps people didn't outwardly panic, but a spike in PASD support group attendance meant that *something* stirred in the public consciousness. She angled her way into the doorway, mask-wearing attendants backing away when they realized that she didn't have one on. Del Fuego, the moderator, gave his usual opening speech about how it was an open forum, identifying yourself was optional, the first half of the hour was open sharing and the second half would be a led discussion on this week's particular topic: anxiety upon hearing the name of a dead loved one.

The shares, normally a mixture of teary confessions in between silence, seemed rapid-fire this time. Moira did what she always did: linger near the back, consider raising her hand and finally telling *somebody* about those early days, and ultimately deciding not to, leaving right before the session's second half began.

Maybe she should ask if anyone knew anything about getting married in a civil ceremony. That was her new idea to try with Frank, something she'd just hatched this morning. She even considered going to City Hall and just getting the paperwork. Surprise Frank, see what he'd say.

With a Reunion Services bounty on her head, it couldn't hurt to ask.

Her patience for the group hit its usual limit and she turned, sliding sideways between the cluster of people blocking the exit, when a voice caused her to stop.

"My name is Rob. I'd like to say something."

"Share."

"Right. I'd like to share."

Rob. Moira craned her neck back, looking through heads and shoulders. She didn't have to see his face to know it was the guy from work; they'd never really talked at work other than the usual office stuff about printers. But even without Code Polka Dot, she'd grown a keen ear for identifying voices through the din.

"Hi, Rob," the crowd said in a mix of voices.

"I'm… I'm not sure why I'm here. Now, I mean. Years after everything happened."

"You're welcome anytime," said the moderator, a fit tan man who might have been a surfer if he wasn't leading a support group. "Tell us what's on your mind. This is a safe space. Nothing leaves here."

"Well," he said, huffing out a sigh, "it's strange. I feel like I'm kind of the opposite of what I've heard today. There's, you know, this *fear* running through people. You can feel it. It keeps everyone guarded, shut off. The news we hear, the rumors spreading, it makes it worse. Everyone is talking about fear. Even in this meeting. It's all fear. But why? Why hide behind that?"

Why hide behind that? The question burrowed in Moira's mind, refusing to let go. Security. Stability. Comfort in an uncomfortable world. A thousand answers flooded her thoughts, and before she could question the validity of those justifications, she shut it all off.

Or at least tried to.

Around the room, voices murmured.

"I've…thought about things recently. I… I have a social normalcy audit coming up. Because my kid has acted out." Moira's ears perked up and her attention tuned in even finer. "Thing is, I wonder if it's dangerous if we let PASD set the rules for everything. We live a stable, boring life. I have my head on my shoulders, I'm not going Greenwood, you know? But I can't just say that. I can't be honest that she's having a hard time because her mom isn't around. But it's so obvious. And instead, there's all these hoops and barriers we're jumping through. Instead of being real about who we are, where we are now."

The moderator nodded. "Thank you—"

"Wait. Just one more thing."

A few feet ahead, Moira heard someone whisper, "Get on with it already." She looked in the general direction and made a loud *shhhhh* sound. When a woman turned her head to see where it came from, Moira locked eyes, her icy glare unmoving.

"I guess I'm just tired of feeling like I'm hiding behind something. But it seems like everyone else is and no one's being honest with themselves about why. Why can't we face rumors and everything with something other than fear? Someone told me the other day that it's like we've paused as a society. I wonder if she's right." Rob looked around the room, and though

Moira couldn't see details from her perspective, his reaction said enough: his eyes squinted, darting around the room for several moments, like he searched for something that wasn't there. About a minute passed in silence, and he finally sighed; she wondered how many people caught his tiny head shake. "That's it. That's all I had to say."

"Thank you, Rob," said the moderator before asking for further shares. Moira didn't have a share, but she did have a question that wouldn't go away.

Moira waited, scrolling through the Metronet articles on her phone. *Evan Hatfield announces weekly live broadcasts in search for missing pop star MoJo.*

He wasn't letting up. On the contrary, he seemed to be going even harder. Moira knew him, the way he thought. Always planning several steps ahead. Manipulating all the pieces to get the outcome he wanted.

She just couldn't figure out if he really wanted to find her or if it was more lucrative for him to keep searching.

Blood slowly returned to her face, offset by the brief dizziness of fear. Her phone shoved back in her purse, her focus turning up, around, anywhere but what was just in her palm. Person after person shuffled out of the exit, most wearing masks while passing Moira with hardly a glance. But with nerves settling, her mind turned to different thoughts, curiosity mixed perhaps with a little bit of jealousy. When the familiar face came and went, she reached and tapped him on the shoulder.

"Rob?"

She'd debated this. Saying something, even revealing that she'd been there, would open herself up in ways that nobody ever saw. Especially not Frank. He wouldn't understand.

He simply couldn't.

Rob turned and locked eyes with her; a few seconds passed until recognition sparked in his eyes, which shifted into an uneasiness over his entire face. He stood long enough that he bumped shoulders with another attendee, leaving both with irritation painted on their expressions. "Moira. Hi. Were you..." The small rubber band on the back of his mask snapped as he lifted the whole thing over his face. "You, um, heard all that?"

"I did. I'm sorry you have to go through that."

"It's okay. It's..." He took in a heavy sigh. "It is what it is. You've been to these before?"

Moira nodded. "They get the job done. The price is right too." All types of support groups existed, from the free twelve-step ones to the groups that camped out in the woods, screaming at the wilderness for several thousand dollars—a hefty price before the End of the World, and much more extreme now given the post-quarantine global economic deflation.

"My first time. I mean, I read a couple books on PASD, but never went to anything in person before. Seems—" Rob shook his head, then glanced behind him "—a lot less welcoming than I expected. Maybe I *am* doing it wrong."

"People are scared."

"Yeah. I picked up on that." They stood, the noise around them dwindling as the final attendees left, leaving only awkward space between them. He gestured down the street. "Heading back to the office?" Moira nodded, and the two began walking in silence under the gray Bay Area sky. "It must be weird hearing your coworker has to go through a social normalcy audit."

"It is," Moira said after several steps. "But only because I didn't know you had a daughter. Otherwise, you hear everything in here. It's not the strangest thing."

"She's not in danger with me. She's a good kid."

"You don't have to convince me." Moira tried her best reassuring voice, though this all felt new. Her dad had been possessive, manipulative. Chris had been supportive, kind. Narc, Santiago, and the rest of that crew—things had been stuck in survival mode for too long to shake out anything therapeutic.

And Frank… Frank had it easy in this world. So many people would kill to be living life on Frank's curve.

Rob, though, carried a different vibe.

They continued walking, not a word spoken for the next block. Rob inhaled sharply a few times, like he had something lined up, but nothing materialized. Moira felt the same thing, though her curiosity powered the words finally through. "Do you think you're right about everyone?"

Rob stopped midstep on the sidewalk. She followed suit, turning to meet him face-to-face. "What do you mean?"

"About everyone hiding behind something. You think that's what this is?" She gestured a gloved hand to the recovering metropolis around them.

His arms crossed, brow turning into jagged lines. "For the longest time, I felt differently. I felt afraid. Anxious. But with the way Sunny's been, with what's happening, I just thought back to what my wife told me. I mean, she was dying and she told me to be good to myself. These were the words she'd leave the world with. And they didn't make sense until you face losing everything. Not to a virus, but to fear. All this fear, it just seems like that became a…a…" He shoved his hands in his pockets, foot tapping the cracked concrete beneath them. "A trophy almost. We can be better than that. I want to be. And not just because of the audit. Though," he laughed, "that *is* part of it."

For the first time in their conversation, their eyes connected, a look that said more than two random people who happened to work together.

"I think you're right. If it makes you feel better. We shouldn't be afraid of where we are now. Sometimes it's just hard to do." The sentiment tumbled out of Moira, like it'd been primed forever and only needed something to trigger it. *Tell him. Tell somebody*, her mind screamed out. And she could. She could reveal her identity and by doing so, she'd take it all back from *him*.

Until the inevitable flight to America. And the TV cameras, and press, and publicity.

No. Better to keep it under the rug.

"I used to feel guilty thinking about what my wife said. But now feels like the right time."

"To be good to yourself?"

Rob nodded, though that was his only response. They walked several blocks in silence, though she caught his gaze turning to the boarded-up houses on the edge of the reconstruction zone. Rob's face subtly shifted, from being completely inscrutable to a sudden collapse as they got closer. She traced his eyes to one specific building, the top floor a burnt husk of its former self, leaving only a burnt frame and spray paint. She swore she caught him blinking back tears as he stared across the way.

Was that socially normal? She considered the question as he seemed to stifle feelings away for the final block. Maybe not. But it seemed real.

She opened her mouth to ask if he was okay, to check in and see what was real, what he was feeling.

But she couldn't. Silence continued as they made it through the building's revolving doors, to the elevator, and all the way up to the PodStar office on the fourteenth floor. "Are you going to tomorrow's meeting too?" she finally asked.

"Yeah," he said. "You?"

Would she? Most likely. She'd tell herself that she didn't need to go, that they didn't understand or that this particular moderator took it in the wrong direction or some other thing like that. But then she'd get the itch to sit in a room of strangers, consider saying something, then remain quiet while others poured out their emotions—for better or worse.

"I think so."

"Cool." The elevator dinged and they stepped out together, afternoon sunlight coming in through the far office windows. "See you then."

CHAPTER SIXTEEN

Rob

"And remember, everything will be fine," Del Fuego had said to close out the Survivors Anonymous meeting. "We have each other."

Everything will be fine. Such a common phrase, a *trite* phrase, the thing people said to each other as a catch-all response for pretty much anything. Rob had attended eight meetings now, and Del had closed each one with that phrase. Yet today, the words clawed deep into him as he walked with Moira away from the people shuffling out of the meeting.

That phrase. Every single time, that phrase reminded him of the moment his life diverged. Without it, he wouldn't be at the meeting. He wouldn't be next to Moira. He wouldn't be facing an audit.

Because he used that phrase back in quarantine, six hours after Elena died. "Where Mama?" Rob had sat alone on the cot he used to share with his wife, Sunny at his feet. At one and a half, she grasped that *something* was not right but lacked the context to understand the magnitude of it. She managed the plastic spoon in her hand, feeding herself applesauce made from the quarantine's small courtyard farm. Her little question, two words in the mangled enunciation of a tiny child, froze him. What could he tell her? What would she comprehend? In the few days since the riot that put Elena in the quarantine trauma ward, he'd barely slept, barely *lived*, everything going on autopilot. Sunny asked again, impatience coloring her voice. "Where Mama?" She stomped over to him, tugging on his pant leg. "Where Mama?"

"Sun..." he said. This would have to end. In quarantine, they'd spent some nights apart due to different volunteer shifts, but a day, day and a half most was the longest Sunny had gone without seeing one of her parents. As if she sensed the lack of an answer in him, her fingers pressed into his jeans, pulling the blue fabric like it would make Elena magically appear. "Mommy's not coming home."

"No! Mama now! Want Mama!" Desperation had taken over the child's face, eyes pooling with the whiplash turn of raw emotions. She tossed the plastic spoon across the prison-cell-turned-living-space, her voice ramping up in volume and intensity. His arms wrapped around his daughter, even though she punched at his thigh in frustration; he held her as if she was the last thing in the world.

Rob blinked as the realization came to him. She was.

His home, his old life was gone. His parents and brother, killed by MGS. Their friends, their community, scattered and ravaged. And now Elena gone too.

Sunny was all he had left.

His chin rested on her soft hair, eyes catching sympathetic glances from people in cells across the hall. Her voice screamed into his chest, heat radiating off her whole body. "Mama now! Where Mama?"

Rob shushed and whispered gibberish in the form of generic words of comfort, words that ultimately meant nothing.

Nothing except they were truly alone together. And he couldn't lose that.

"Sunny. Sun," he said, trying to get the toddler's attention. "Sun, Mommy's not here right now. She needs you to be brave." Maybe it was the soothing tone of voice. Maybe it was the word *mommy.* Maybe she'd just naturally worn out her feelings, ready to swing in another direction after burning bright. Whatever it was, Sunny seemed calmer, focused, enough so that she stepped back from Rob and looked up at her dad.

"Mama come home?" she asked, her voice calm but direct. "Want Mama now."

"I know. I know, I do too. I want her back too. I can't..." His voice cracked, raw nerves exposed to the world. No, he couldn't, not now, not in front of Sunny. He needed a cover. "She will. You just need to be patient," he blurted out.

Sunny's demeanor instantly changed, like the word flipped a switch in her rapidly developing brain. "When Mama?"

"Not now, but someday. Someday everything will be fine."

Moira's voice snapped Rob back to the present. "What's wrong?" she asked.

That was the thing about Moira. From their first encounter to now, she looked at Rob like she could instantly read him, for better or worse. And even if it was for the worse, like this time, it still rooted in a tiny drop of reassurance, a single thread tethering to the rest of humanity.

The only other person who could do that was Elena.

"I get the feeling this isn't about Miami," Moira said, a gust of wind kicking out strands of her black hair. "Do you want to tell me?" She walked in time with him, her hands shoved in her jacket pockets.

"I do," Rob finally said as they waited for a crosswalk that led to the community center. "I just need to tell someone. I need to tell someone why they might take Sunny away."

Moira looked at him. She didn't say anything.

They missed the crosswalk as Rob revealed *almost* everything. The recent outbursts, fight at school, the Family Stability Board, social normalcy audits, getting evidence and testimonials. The ultimate truth crept up to the surface, so close to hitting daylight. But he couldn't; not now, not to Moira or anyone else on the planet. That bit remained buried, guarded as much as his remaining photos of Elena.

"So that's why you're looking at speed dating," Moira finally said.

"Yeah. Honestly, I don't even know if I'm ready for it. But I have to go, just to get it on the record. I barely talk to adults outside of work, so I can't imagine what trying to do speed dating will be like. They should offer a practice round."

"And that's why you started going to this." Moira thumbed at the entrance to the support group.

"Yeah."

"Is that," she hesitated, "why we walk together?" Though nothing he'd explained about Sunny seemed to trouble her, this question obviously did. Her brow wrinkled and her eyes looked past him, mouth taking the slightest of dips—not quite to a frown, but just past neutral to show the weight of what she asked. "To get someone else to write a testimonial for you?" she finally finished, still frozen in the same pose.

Several seconds passed before Rob responded. "No," he said, the answer arriving in a short breath before turning her way. "Not just that. You're someone I can talk to." Their eyes locked into each other. "I miss having that."

He promised himself he'd tell her everything when this was all over.

Someone he could talk to.

Such a simple thought, and yet the sentiment seemed revelatory for the two of them, so much so that Moira beamed a grin that gave way to laughter and a shake of the head. Here they were, both wanting someone to talk to and suddenly they were speechless.

"Come on," Rob finally said. "We have a few minutes before the meeting. I've got an idea."

"What?" she asked, following him across the street, eyes tracing over to the lingering people outside of the building.

"Let's speed date. Right here. I need to practice this." He hesitated, as if the request surprised himself. "Say something so I don't feel stupid."

"Spontaneous. I like it," she said, nodding to a bus stop bench. They sat below a pre-apocalypse faded sign, its big out-of-order red-painted X looming over them. "Hi, I'm Moira Gorman." She stuck out her right hand.

"Rob Donelly." He took her hand in return with a solid grip.

"So, Rob. Tell me about yourself. Don't be shy."

"Well, I have a daughter. Sunny. And I work at PodStar doing network stuff for the Metro," he said, eyes tracking skyward. "I'm a baseball nut. I can't wait for it to restart. I, um, do day trips for hiking and camping. We're waiting for the state to finish restoring access to Yosemite."

"Oh, really? So you like outdoors stuff? Do you run?"

"Yeah. It's been a while, but yeah, I do. Did. Cross-country in high school."

"I love running. It's so freeing." She grinned, then looked away. Something about it looked different from the way she usually smiled. "I'll go for a run just to relax. Running. And singing. Real singing. Old tunes from the forties. Billie Holiday–type stuff."

"Oh, really? Maybe you could sing a tune." They locked eyes again, this time with Rob in full-on smirk mode. "Don't be shy. Isn't that what you said?"

"Singing." Her mouth twisted, front teeth biting down on her lip. She glanced all around, then pointed to the small alley next to the community center. "All right. But away from anyone. Stage fright."

"It's okay. I was just playing along."

"No, no, it's fine. Staying in character, right?" They walked over until the shadows of adjacent buildings made the space dimmer, sunlight drawing a clear barrier between the alley and the sidewalk. Moira stood against the light, her back to the public and facing him. "*Living for you,*" she sang, her voice low but the tone steady, "*is easy living; it's easy to live when you're in love, and I'm so in love.*"

The final note hovered before fading away, and staccato claps rang through from Rob. Moira glanced back over her shoulder several times, then seemed to relax when passersby seemed more interested in adjusting their silicone masks than her brief performance.

"Support group speed dating," she said with a laugh. "We should sell this concept. Make a fortune."

"Split the profits. Hey, time out," Rob said, forming a T with his hands. "Do you really do all that, or are you just pretending? Running and singing and stuff."

"I'm pretending—I'm in character," she said, her fingers making air quotes for "character."

"I'm much more boring. Now—" she pointed his way "—not that bad, right? You've got this whole speed dating thing down."

Rob motioned back to the front entrance of the building, the regular attendees shuffling in. "It's nice," he finally said. "Who knew adults didn't just discuss PASD or the End of the World? We should have recorded that for the audit. You make it easy. Can't you just be my date at this thing?" His head shook while he laughed, the sheer ridiculousness of what they'd done, why they'd done it, how trivial it seemed against the idea of gaming a social normalcy audit, all of it causing the most unexpected laughter.

For a split second, Moira's demeanor changed, though it might have been the burst of cold wind suddenly blasting both of them. It kicked up the back of her head, blowing her hair forward and into her eyes; a flush came to her olive-toned cheeks and her posture became a rigid line, though maybe it was a cold shiver.

It disappeared, and as she brushed the hair back out of her face, she flashed a polite smile, holding up her left hand, and waved her ring finger, diamonds sparkling in sunlight. "Sorry. Already taken."

Before Rob could respond, his phone buzzed. He pulled up a text, apparently sent en masse to parents of students.

We regret to inform you that for the foreseeable future, school days will end at noon. The recent news has affected many of us, and we have recently lost several staff departing to Reclaimed Territory. In the meantime, if you are interested in a teacher or administrative position, please contact the San Francisco Metro's education department.

Excerpt from *Before the Fourth Path: Kay Greenwood and Unlucky Faith, New World Magazine*:

Kay Greenwood always wanted the American Dream. Before quarantine, she worked tirelessly to support her husband Thomas's music shop while raising young Freda. When they emerged from quarantine intact—mother, father, and daughter—friends say she became obsessed with another type of American Dream. "She talked a lot about 'their miracle,'" said Kim Dando, Kay's cousin. "Her old drive for traditional ideals, that belief changed into the idea that a nuclear family was the goal." Despite modern society's apathy to organized religion, Kay found solace in the fledgling church community. "Family wasn't just family, it now had a purpose, I think that's what drove her to the church." Thomas dismissed post-apocalyptic religion, instead considering Reclaimed beliefs, and that drove a wedge into the family dynamics.

CHAPTER SEVENTEEN

Moira

"I'd like forms to get married in a civil ceremony," Moira said. The woman at the county clerk desk nodded without a word, and simply stood up and walked to a filing cabinet in the corner of the room. Before the End of the World, this task probably would have been a few taps on a computer keyboard followed by the hum of a printer. But now, they'd reverted to something a little more old-fashioned, the hinges and drawers of the file cabinet squeaking as it opened and shut as the afternoon sun filtered into the small office.

The woman returned, papers in hand. "Fill these out to apply for a marriage license. Then look at the appointment book," she said, and pointed to a binder sitting on a small table across the room, "and sign up for a time."

"That's it?" Moira asked.

A simple nod was the only response from the woman before settling back into her chair. In the office—a room off the second floor in San Francisco's City Hall—voices murmured behind her, and Moira glanced at the line behind her. Several couples stood, some in masks and others standing with faces revealed. But none of them looked happy to be there. Instead, they all carried neutral expressions and tired eyes, as if they'd almost resigned themselves to go through the process of filling out a form.

When she became Moira Gorman, changing her identity was also a form—and a hacker friend. News had just come through that the quarantine was winding down and humanity would be released to live back in cities once the military had secured the urban centers from occupying gangs and the persistent reach of nature. The revitalized Metro sector would apparently encompass the central part of San Francisco, with the goal to eventually expand and reach the whole city. Pockets of Silicon Valley would be part of it, with the government building fences along freeway corridors as part of the new Major Highway Safety Program, as protection for commuters from any lingering looter gang activity, though most gangs had been driven out to stretches of wastelands with recent military efforts. Even parts of wine country would be involved across the Golden Gate, used for protected farming initiatives. And where Moira and her crew were, newly set up on the UC Davis campus, going east for an hour would see a smaller Sacramento Metro initiative.

That was the grand plan mentioned by government releases. But the reality was messier, which meant that for anyone with the means and the skills, hacking a new identity became an exercise in diligence, technology, and a little good luck. Moira stood on the gravelly rooftop, the tallest building on campus at some nine stories high—not quite skyscraper material. But enough for Fred, their resident hacker, to get some hardware that tapped into high-speed networks across satellites still used for communication between state and federal governments.

"Try moving around," Fred said, sitting cross-legged with a laptop resting across his knees. She carried the transponder, some sort of signal booster that Fred had mined out of the engineering labs on campus, and walked around in an ever-widening circle, extension cord trailing like a tail. "Stop, stop, stop. Right there. Put it down."

"Here?" From that very specific spot on the rooftop, the edge of the city's abandoned downtown was visible, along with the rows of cars their crew had moved in line to use as blockades.

"Yeah." He clicked away at the keyboard, the sun reflecting off the computer's shiny chrome case. They'd salvaged an entire pallet from a wholesale warehouse some fifty miles north, carefully avoiding the military efforts to secure sealed goods—while the canned food and clothing were picked over long ago, looters didn't seem to care for technology when no one was sure whether the entire electrical grid would return. "I think I'm in. And...yep, I'm in. So now we know the governments haven't been working on cybersecurity during quarantine. Fill this out." He slid a clipboard over, pen sitting atop a photocopy of handwritten form fields: birthdate, birthplace, height, weight, and other identifying information.

"You got the copier working?"

"Yep. Mass-produced forms are back, baby." He pointed over at the rack of solar panels clumsily installed across the roof. "As long as those hold up, we'll be able to make as many documents as we want. Letters to make *Happy Birthday* signs. Scan some of Narc's art. No asses on the copier though. That's gross."

Moira laughed, then glanced at the panels, the mere look of them making her shudder with the thought of lifting those up flights of stairs again. "You know who we should recruit from these new Metro communities? Professional movers to lift things up stairs for us," she said, adjusting the rifle on her back.

"I go for electrician. General contractor. Because getting shocked by those," he said, "was not fun. Okay, let's birth you into this 'post-MGS identity database' they're setting up. Standard asset distribution and all that stuff. You want a college degree?"

"Sure," Moira said when the walkie-talkie on her belt squawked with a burst of static. "What's a catch-all degree? Like business?"

"Business it is. Oh, hey, I'm an idiot. Forgot to add name to the form." Fred's voice shifted to a deep, official tone. "What is your full legal name, ma'am?"

"Johanna Moira Hatfield," she said, bitterness painting her crisp English diction while she rubbed her close-cropped hair, which was finally growing back in after several years of shaving it on the go. Her fingers found their way to the scar on her cheek, a short diagonal slash about an inch long. Funny how they'd made it that far, through gunfire and broken glass, twisted rebar and decaying buildings, and yet the only facial scar she bore came from falling on a beach when she was a toddler.

Right when she said that, her walkie came to life again. "Moira! Our lookout spotted gang riders on Highway 80! They could just be passing through but we'll need some water tower support just in case."

"They could just wanna buy organic produce from our farm?" Moira replied into the walkie.

"Hopefully. Tell them we only barter for now. No cash and definitely no cards. But stand guard just in case they're not grocery shopping."

The water tower. That was a good mile away. About a seven-minute sprint normally, longer with the rifle on her back. "On it," she said, before turning to Fred. "Back in a bit. Gotta save the world."

"Maybe it's just the government installing those automated gas pumps? I hear they're putting in those to open up travel. You know, so it's not just scary violent assholes between us and the Metros."

"Let's hope so. It'd be nice to trade supplies with the Sacramento Metro." The rifle clicked as Moira checked the load on it, then patted her belt to confirm extra ammo. "Have fun giving birth."

"Right. Oh. Birthplace? You're American now?"

"Yeah," Moira said, turning on her not-quite-there accent. "Uh-mare-eh-can."

She'd returned an hour later after a relatively uneventful watch from the campus water tower. Looter gangs by that time had begun congregating in the long stretches of nothing between communities, fighting themselves over turf more often than attacking Reclaimed communities for vegetables. By then, Fred had created her identity as Johanna Hatfield, not realizing she'd been joking. That one ill-timed slip probably created the lead that drew Moira's father to San Francisco. He scrambled to add another entry but by then found he didn't have permissions to delete Johanna. "Shit. I'm sorry, I didn't realize you were kidding around," he said on the rooftop at the time.

"It's okay. I just never want to be Johanna again. Make a new record." Moira spoke the whole thing in her American accent, the one that would have to be her normal speaking voice when she drove out to the San Francisco Metro in a few months. "Let's call her Moira Gorman."

"Gorman? *G-O-R-M-A-N?*"

"Yeah." Moira pictured Chris, his tired eyes, red cheeks, and constant gum chewing. "Gorman."

That was how Moira Gorman came to exist. But other than one bank account and one credit card, she didn't have the true set of traceable roots that authentic identities did.

But she would soon.

Moira stood, echoes of footsteps and voices surrounding her in City Hall, then she opened up the scheduling binder for civil ceremonies and scanned for available dates: the first one was next week. She hadn't told Frank about this yet, and given his reaction the other night, she imagined it'd be a mixture of confusion and resistance. But looking at the hanging TV screen in the corner, even now her dad watched over her shoulder. There he was, standing in front of a podium somewhere out in Manchester, holding up a press photo of her with the MoJo makeup and MoJo hair and MoJo smile from nearly a decade ago.

She wasn't going to play his games anymore. This was a clean break.

CHAPTER EIGHTEEN

Krista

City Hall wasn't exactly the most impressive place in San Francisco, even after the End of the World and subsequent reconstruction. Clearly, Sunny had never seen anything quite like the building's central hallway, with its sprawling central staircase and domed ceiling. The place supposedly suffered significant damage during the quarantine period, but from the look of it, it had been restored exactly the way Krista remembered it when visiting the Bay Area as a thirteen-year-old. During that visit, she didn't quite have the wide-eyed stare that was on Sunny's face, though it did trigger a mix of emotions in her. For every happy memory of being able to breathe easy, an entire country apart from her mom, there also remained the complication of protective lying every time her grandparents asked her how she was doing.

"It's so big." Sunny took in a deep breath, as if some of the building's majesty would rub off on her. Hydraulics on the door behind them gradually brought the front entrance to a close, its tinted coating dulling the afternoon sunbeams into a muted yellow glow.

"Yep," Krista said, and she jolted when Sunny took her hand. Still needed to get used to that.

"So, I have to go to an office on the second floor there—" Krista pointed up and around "—and pay a bill. That's it. But you can look around while I do that."

Were seven-year-olds allowed to wander by themselves at a building like City Hall while adults ran errands? Krista ground her teeth, unsure of what was normal for that sort of thing, either before MGS or after. Better to go with the safer route. "Actually, stay with me while I do that and then we'll check it out."

"Like over there?" Sunny pointed to a small cluster of people by the hallway adjacent to the main stairway, their heads and shoulders blocking the sign for some exhibit tucked away in the corner.

"Yeah..." Krista angled her neck to decipher the letters explaining the exhibit. "*H-O*... 'How' something. Well, we'll check it out. Hey, what game are we still playing?"

"'Does she look like MoJo?'"

"You got it." Hands still clasped together, she led the little girl up the stairs and through a back hallway. They weaved through, getting the occasional side-eye from mask-wearers as they stepped through and around pockets of people. Sunny gave oohs and ahs at the tall photos showing snippets of San Francisco's past, though she stopped halfway down the hallway.

First came a tug on the arm. Then the quiet words, her cheeks bright with an excited smile. "Krista!" she said just above a whisper.

"What's up?"

"She looks like MoJo."

They'd done this game at a few places. This was the first time Sunny made that proclamation unprompted.

A flurry rippled through Krista's stomach and her senses all turned up. Noises got louder, colors became brighter, she was suddenly more *present* and grounded despite the musky air of the corridor. Her fingernails dug into her palms as she scanned the handful of people in the hallway. Most were either too old or too young to possibly be the pop star, but then her eyes stopped on the short black hair of a woman leaning over a binder. "That woman?"

"Yeah. With the binder."

Was that…?

All of the excitement tempered, its wings suddenly clipped. That couldn't be MoJo.

"Okay, so don't say anything. That's, um, part of the game."

Krista waited until the woman snapped the binder shut and looked up to talk to an attendant in the office across the hall. The neat posture, polite gestures, the way she held a smile a fraction of a second more than necessary, it all instantly screamed that the woman standing there was her lone remaining client.

Not a pop star. Just Moira.

"Are you sure?" Krista asked.

"I *think* so."

"Well, see, that's—" The phone in Krista's back pocket began buzzing, and she pulled it out to see a text from Rob.

Do you mind watching Sunny a few more hours? Paid of course. Found a speed dating event tonight. Should be done by 7. Just please don't tell Sunny specifics, she won't understand.

Some people married for love. Some for stability. Some for money, or at least they used to. Rob apparently was in the market so he could prep for a meeting. An important meeting, of course, but still. This must have been the new world's version of getting married for a green card.

No problem. We'll hang out, Krista texted back.

The Send icon floated onto the phone's small screen, then

vanished. Krista looked up only to find Moira gone. Not at the binder, not farther down the hall, not at the water fountain next to the large canvas print of the Bay Bridge, nothing. Her head swiveled back and forth, eyes scanning for Moira, but she was nowhere to be seen. "Did you see that woman leave?"

"Uh-huh. She went that way." Sunny pointed out to the main hallway. "I swear, she looks like MoJo."

"Okay. Let's keep that in mind," Krista said. They walked down the hallway to the Residence License registrar, slowing down only to read the sign by where Moira had stood: *Office of the County Clerk.*

Some twenty minutes and one renewed Residence License later, Krista and Sunny made their way downstairs after touring the entire second floor of City Hall—something that, when you got down to it, really was just a bunch of offices with nice stone tiling on the outside. Downstairs, the small crowd of people still lingered.

Krista's phone buzzed, and pulling it out revealed the usual Reunion Services message about a pending local contract, except this time Krista recognized the target's name: Donita Finch, a woman who'd hired her last year. "Hey, Sunny, go check out the exhibit over there for a second. I have to handle this but I'll be right here."

The girl nodded, and as she trotted off, Krista yelled, "Don't forget to play the game." Whether she heard her or not, Krista couldn't tell; Sunny disappeared into the space, though Krista kept glancing up from her phone to make sure she tracked the girl's mop of black hair. Her contact list loaded up, and she scrolled to the name *Donita Finch.*

A perfect match. This would be easy. Someday, when citywide phone directories or even old-school phone books returned, an entire industry would vanish. For now, this was money in Krista's pocket. She entered in her Reunion Services agent code as a reply to the notification text, though her finger hesitated to hit Send.

Echoes of her last reunion attempt rattled her mind, the woman's desperate pleas asking her to do anything but connect her with her brother. "Tell him I'm dead. Tell him you couldn't find me. You don't know these people, this family. Let me escape." There was a reason, the target had explained, why she'd never reached out. Krista understood that all too well.

Did she really want to confront that again?

On the other hand, the stark reality of losing her Residence License tickled different memories, the sheer urgency that came with every breath when her mother searched for some place for them to stay. No, she needed a home of her own, some place she controlled. She wouldn't go through that again. And that meant taking on easy money.

Krista hit Send and a reply message appeared about fifteen seconds later.

We're sorry, this contract has been claimed. We look forward to working with you soon.

Claimed already. Probably by someone who didn't hesitate. Her attention returned to the exhibit, to catching up with Sunny, who'd moved past the crowd to examine a series of photos lining the room perimeter.

"Why's she sleeping?" Sunny asked of the image, an oversized picture of a woman sleeping on the floor of an airport terminal.

"Maybe she missed her flight. They used to have a lot of them."

The next one featured what looked like a makeshift stage of some sort, performers using sewn-up blankets as costumes as they stood in a courtyard in front of a small group of children.

"Those are weird costumes," Sunny said.

"I knew theater kids in college. It's probably some sort of interpretive thing."

After that, a woman and a child laughing, their clothes dirty from soil as they knelt next to a rooftop garden. And after that one, a man sitting at a table, lines of concentration bored deep in his face, clipboard in one hand with stacks of canned goods around and behind him. And even farther, the weathered face and fragile hair of an old man, standing by himself but holding up a photo of a teenager, a long line of people running from left to right behind him.

With each progressive image, Sunny grew quieter and the discomfort unfurled in Krista, first from the feeling that this was some sort of artsy fartsy photo exhibit to the grueling realization that they'd walked into a PASD trap.

Then the next one: a group holding hands around a makeshift grave, the domed walls of a stadium in the background.

Not just a stadium. A stadium turned quarantine. Tension returned to Krista's shoulders, though in a different way from the creeping dread of losing a Residence License. This was sharp and immediate, prompting her to arch her neck to finally see what the exhibit was called.

How We Remember: Life in Quarantine.

This couldn't be good for anyone's PASD, and yet here they were. "You know, we should probably go. Sunny?" But Sunny still stared at the image of the prayer circle around the grave, and Krista could practically see the little gears churning in her head. Krista scanned the scene for the quickest way out when her eyes landed on the next photo: a swarm of people pushing each other during ration handouts—in the middle, a toddler with a mop of black hair sat on her father's shoulders as he was shoved out, his hand reaching to a woman falling to the ground.

The man struck Krista as familiar, from the lines around his mouth to the wide-eyed stare. Between that, the child on his shoulders, and the tumbling blonde woman, puzzle pieces fit into place. She reached down and grabbed Sunny's hand just as the girl began to step to the next image.

"We should go."

"Are we done here? We didn't even look for MoJo."

"Yeah. We really should go."

The image seared into her mind, even the tiniest of details, while her legs pumped at full speed to get back into City Hall's main lobby. The way the little girl had one hand on the father's shoulder, the other covering her ear. The way the man's wide eyes screamed desperation, panic, and horror all at once.

The man was Rob.

Krista found her jaw locked up, teeth pushing so hard against each other that even her cheeks ached. She tried forcing the picture out, pushing it all away or at least far into a corner of her mind where she could bury it under trivial things. Like remembering that today was supposed to be about business, or the fact that she needed to pick up cat food on the way home.

Her focus finally shook free when her phone buzzed again. But instead of Rob texting about his speed dating, it was, of all people, Moira.

I have a question about civil ceremonies at City Hall. Can we talk?

Suddenly, the county clerk's office made sense.

"So what were all those pictures about?" Sunny asked. "Was that the quarantine?"

"Hold on one sec." Krista looked back at the photo exhibit, the people standing in solemn observation of the photos, their quiet demeanor and serious expressions making far too much sense now, then down at her phone, the name MOIRA in all capital letters on the primitive pixelated screen. "Did you really think that woman upstairs looked like MoJo?"

"She did! She had MoJo's eyes! And smile!"

The images of MoJo in her pop star regalia buried the real person under makeup and glamour. But eyes and smile, that would never change.

Krista smirked to herself.

They needed something to do while Rob was at speed dating. This was a hell of a something. "I've got an idea," she said as she typed back to Moira.

How about we drop by your place?

CHAPTER NINETEEN

Rob

A large banner greeted Rob when he walked into House Tornado Wine Bar; its reflection bounced off the mirrored decor to create infinite *Welcome Love Solutions Daters!* He held the door open but waited to step inside while he took a closer peek.

The women appeared to be between their midtwenties to midforties, and the men seemed to be five or ten years older as a group. Difficult to tell these days; depending on how people handled PASD, some appeared wearier than their actual age. And surprisingly, none of them wore masks. Instead, a sign stood at the entrance. *Please remove your masks so we can get to know you better! Hand sanitizer is provided at each table.*

Rob adjusted his tie and stepped in, the glass door behind him coming to a close.

"Hi!" A tall, skinny blonde woman approached, clipboard in hand. "Are you here for Love Solutions?"

"That's right."

"All righty, then. Many of our singles have already arrived

and are enjoying our free appetizers and drinks. Just fill out this form, then I'll give you your name tag and information packet."

Rob nodded, and the woman disappeared, leaving him with a single sheet on a clipboard. Men and women littered the bar, but the PA system overpowered their voices with the horns and brushed drums of jazz from nearly a century ago. The soundtrack made for a safe choice, given the dire mood of today's music and the potential emotional baggage songs from a decade or two ago might trigger—though Rob couldn't help but think of Moira and her impromptu alleyway performance. The chaos sprawled all around him, forcing him to retreat into the bar's lone quiet corner.

He worked his way down the form from the obvious contact info to the more open-ended questions probably used for marketing surveys. *Why did you choose Love Solutions?* Little check boxes sat next to "A friend referred me," "Advertisement," "Coupon/special," and "Other," which Rob marked and noted "My dying wife told me to be good to myself" in the blank space next to it.

That truth was better than "I meet the Family Stability Board soon."

"All done," Rob said, handing the clipboard back to the excitable blonde woman.

"Fan-TAS-tic!" She bent down over her little table and scribbled *ROB* on a name tag, then pasted it on his chest with a hearty push. "We'll go over the instructions in this packet together, so don't worry about it now. Here are your two free drink tickets," she said, handing him square scraps with the Love Solutions logo. "Go ahead and mingle. You never know who you might run into."

Mingle. Rob chose the path of least resistance, walking over to the thin Asian woman standing closest to him. Her black pixie cut had a dark red tint in it. "Hi," he said, reminding himself why he was there. "I'm..."

But before he got any further, the woman turned and stepped

away. Rob scanned the room, but outside of people asking the bartender for drinks, it might as well have been filled with statues. Men and women stood in various frozen poses, looking everywhere except at one another.

If the hostess's enthusiasm was intended to be catching, it failed miserably; instead, Rob found himself trading his free drink coupon for a bottle of beer and then blending into the corner, watching the TV news: first a report on the surge of people moving to the Silicon Valley extension of the Metro despite resource and power limitations, then a look at the repurposed Benicia oil refinery plant that now acted as a processing-and-distribution center for pre-MGS unopened products, then finally talking heads arguing about Miami and whether another outbreak was even feasible given the scattered population centers and flight travel limitations. No one else seemed to notice.

"Hello, and welcome to Love Solutions—where the solution is *you*." The bar's noise level didn't change beyond its mix of low murmurs, so the hostess clapped her hands, and the few staff members around her did the same.

"I don't need a Love Solution—I need whatever happy pills she's taking," the woman next to Rob said.

He turned and surveyed her up and down; her dark brown skin was complemented by thick red lipstick and a modest but flattering black dress that rose to her collarbone while showing off athletic legs. He took in a deep breath and reminded himself that he was here to be socially normal. "I think she's used more than her two free drink tickets."

The woman smiled, an inviting type of smile with warmth and grace, the kind that Rob didn't see much, or maybe he just hadn't noticed. "I would too if I had to organize this. It's like a middle school dance where no one talks to anyone. A great sociology study, at the very least."

Rob leaned in to take a sneak peek at the woman's name

tag—Zoe, it said. "We're all just animals trapped in a cage. With free drinks."

"And at least there are free drinks. I think I need about ten more to get through this."

"See, that's why the host's so happy. She's probably getting a cut of the bar sales."

"Ah. Good call. You're pretty smart..." Zoe angled to see the name tag on his shirt. "Rob."

"Okay, people," the excitable host said, clapping her hands again. "Find a table and we'll start the rotation. One guy, one girl, one table, okay?"

"Thanks..." Rob paused, pretending to look at her name tag. "Zoe." He inhaled sharply while he considered the next thing to say. "Shall we?"

"Sure. First impressions of this mess and each other."

Rob slid onto the tall stool across from Zoe. She was tall—much taller than Elena—and the light glowed off her dress's subtle shimmer.

Maybe this whole excursion wasn't just for the Family Stability Board.

The hostess clapped her hands one more time—how raw did they get after every event? She shouted above everyone. "Okay, folks, your seven minutes start now. Go!"

"Where to start, huh? Just tell me about yourself." She reached over and squeezed his hand. "I won't bite."

"Okay, I'm Rob Donelly," he said with a nod. "I'm thirty-one, I work at PodStar Technologies. I, um, help us stay connected to other Metros. And pull headlines from those regions. Mostly."

"Employed. And you must have a Residence License. Good start." Zoe's laugh rose over the other talking couples; it rang out with audible fireworks, releasing all of the tension Rob stored up in his shoulders. "What did you do during quarantine?"

"Pretty much the same thing. Helped keep the networks up,

fixed people's laptops. Kinda sucked when you couldn't order new parts. You?"

"I tapped into my waitressing days from college. Not much need for a tax lawyer during quarantine. So, tell me more, Rob the IT analyst."

"I have a daughter. She's seven, and her name is Sunny. And… uh…" The blank slate reappeared, stealing any other possibly interesting items about Rob; he became "the guy with the kid" despite all his attempts to be *more* than that. "Oh, and I'm a baseball fan. My whole life. Can't wait for it to start up again. And I used to go hiking and camping a lot, but I don't anymore, although I really should again. I should take Sunny." He blew out a sigh, followed by a quick laugh. "That was tough."

"You did great. I don't know about baseball, though. Too slow for me. I'm a hockey girl, grew up in Boston. Live and die with the Bruins." The joy suddenly disappeared from Zoe's face, everything falling to neutral. "I shouldn't say that, huh?"

"What?"

"Live and die with sports. That's silly. We have a new definition of life and death now." She bit down on her lip, leaving a tiny hint of lipstick on her front teeth. "I'm being a buzzkill. Go on."

"Oh. Well, um, that's basically it. How about you?"

"So, I'm Zoe. Zoe Reynolds. I'm thirty-four, I work as a tax attorney, which is as exciting as it sounds. Too many new laws to learn, Residence Licenses and everything. Always need a lawyer, even after the world ends, right? And I'll just say it. I returned from Reclaimed six months ago."

That was a first. Rob never heard of anyone coming back to a Metro. "Wow. Really?"

"I didn't see anything scary. No Fourth Path cult–type stuff. It just wasn't for me. Living out there. It's too quiet. I need to feel like I'm in society, you know?"

"Well." Rob straightened up and tried his most charming smile. "I'm glad you're here."

"I'll always be a Boston girl, it's too bad New England is struggling to rebuild. That last winter storm really reset reconstruction. Still, I think I could live in San Francisco forever. It's beautiful here."

"Yeah. We like it. Even now, there's so much for Sunny to see and do. Do you have children?" Even before he finished his question, Rob knew it was the absolute wrong thing to say. He might as well have asked, "So, which family members of yours died during the End of the World?"

"One." Everything about Zoe fell, from her eyes to her posture to the air around her. "I had one. My son."

"Oh, shit. I'm so sorry. I didn't mean to—"

"No, no. It's okay. We all have this, right?" Her hand covered her mouth, and lines formed around her eyes as they shut, tears leaking out each side. "I thought I could do this."

"Zoe, it's fine. We're all going through it. I have to meet the Family Stability—"

"I'm sorry." She stood up, reached over, and clasped his hands. "I'm sorry I wasted your time, Rob. I hope you find what you're looking for. I'm just not ready."

Rob slouched over, rubbing his temples, while Zoe bolted out the door and disappeared. The host, who must have lost her excitability away from the spotlight, came over. "Don't feel bad," she said, "this happens all the time."

"I bet."

"Here. For your troubles."

Rob stared at the slip of paper. "A free drink ticket?"

"Oh. I think I've got more to hand out over there. Hang tight, we'll be switching tables in—" she looked down at her watch "—two minutes and thirty-four seconds."

"Sure," he said, taking a sip. Two more people left, one woman and one man, both wearing Zoe's pained expression.

Dating was hard enough *before* PASD. Factor in the scars of five billion dead people? Rob took another drink and cursed the odds.

"Okay, people," the host said, doing her hand-clap, "you've got ten minutes to write down who *you'd* like to connect with. And if they'd like to connect with you, then we've got a match—and that's your Love Solution!"

Rob pulled the sheets out of his packet: three pieces of paper, one form for names, one for a feedback survey, and one advertisement for Love Solutions: New Year's Eve party. Staff members delivered golf pencils for everyone, and he stared at the two-columned sheet—the left side for the name of the person, the right side for optional notes about what made them so darn wonderful.

Rob reviewed the past hour, trying to remember what, if anything, stood out about the four women he'd met besides Zoe. Hallie presented herself as a nature girl, living at her estate dorm rather than get a Residence License; she offered a stern lecture about why people needed to quit their frivolous jobs and join the 30 or 40 percent of Metro population working at the urban farms. Maxine seemed like Krista without the snark, handing out business cards and talking about possible contacts across various Metros, from thriving ones like Portland to struggling ones like Minneapolis. Roberta explained the great international government conspiracy behind MGS strain 140-85, even breaking down her supposed hidden meaning for the virus's full name ("multi-generational syndrome, one-hundred-forty-day half-life, eighty-five percent kill rate") and why governments would possibly want to unleash it ("all the governments are participating in Project Preservation, which absorbs the unclaimed funds from casualties to reset the world's finances"). And Maria jumped over the border into religious zealot; Rob respected people's faiths, but the idea of "worshipping Jesus" as a favorite hobby and "team Jesus" as a favorite sports team didn't quite work for him, though he gave her credit for keeping religion when so many others had lost it.

He scrawled two big *X*s on either column, though the thought of noting Zoe's name crossed his mind. She was, after all, beautiful and genuine and smart—well, he assumed smart since the only people he knew who went to law school were pretty smart. But her scars tied her down, holding her so tight that even a few sentences were too much.

He should know, after all. He'd felt that way a handful of weeks ago. But today, he understood a tad clearer; even if he took a few small steps forward, the rest of the world might not be so willing.

"Maybe some other time, Zoe," Rob said, jabbing the sheet with one final dot before leaving it at his table. He took a few papers to prove he went.

One mission accomplished.

From the Online Encyclopedia page on MoJo:

Though MoJo was primarily marketed toward preteen and teen audiences, several notable controversies made her occasional tabloid fodder:

In March 2017, MoJo left her hotel with a backup dancer the night before a show at Toronto's Air Canada Centre. Cell phone footage captures her apparently inebriated and dancing within a circle of flames caused by burning several backpacks and T-shirts with her image on them.

In December 2018, MoJo gave mostly one-word answers during a pre-show press conference. Reporters noted that she appeared "hazy" and "glassy-eyed" during the event. For the last set of questions, her answer each time was "ask my dad."

In April 2019, two months before her final show, MoJo was asked if she was worried about the emerging flu epidemic. She answered, "At least I won't have to wear this shit anymore." One day later, she apologized for an "inappropriate and insensitive joke" in a press release.

CHAPTER TWENTY

Moira

Despite standing in the bathroom, Moira heard the familiar click of the front door opening. She shut the blow dryer off even with her damp hair still pressing against her ears and neck, and leaned into the small hallway.

Frank offered a quiet greeting. Then Krista said hello.

Then a third voice. A little girl?

Moira closed her eyes, focusing on the voices.

"I'm watching her for a friend. She's cool," Krista said.

Moira positioned the weight of her feet equally to keep her steady, as if she was back in a deteriorating building with questionable structure. It was instinct now, it would always be instinct whenever she shifted her mind into scanning and listening. The afternoon sun came through the apartment's windows down the hall, and as she opened her eyes, it took several seconds to adjust. However, even though he was out of view, Moira could picture Frank's every gesture and pose as his quiet words filtered her way.

"I heard you were bringing a helper today," Frank said. From the squeak of the floorboards, and sound of footsteps, he must have motioned them in. "Moira's just finishing her shower." Then the sound of a bag slapping on the kitchen table. A light bag, so probably the one from the little girl. A squeak came, the familiar sound of the kitchen chair, the one on the back left that always made that noise when anyone sat in it, then the sound of unzipping. "So," his voice now a few levels above a whisper, "Moira asked me today about scheduling a civil ceremony. Did you talk to her about this?"

"Not specifically, no."

"Didn't it seem a bit...out of nowhere to you?"

Krista took in a breath. The girl remained quiet. "Brides freak out at times. I've stopped trying to figure it out. Sometimes it's because they have cold feet, and sometimes it's because they have unresolved issues." Her tone remained even. Steady, professional. "I mean, PASD affects everyone these days."

"I'm not getting any of that from her, though."

"What did she say to you?"

"She said she thought it would be good for tax and insurance reasons. The newlywed tax credit, I think they're trying to drive the economy with it. She'd mentioned the other day moving the date up, and now this." He hesitated, and Moira practically saw his bushy brows forming nearly a single line. "This is all so sudden. It's completely out of character. I'm worried about her."

"Well, we'll talk about it. She asked me to explain options."

"Yeah," Frank replied, his voice going even quieter. "Don't tell her what I said, all right?"

"Don't worry, I'm great at keeping secrets."

"Right. Okay." Frank sighed, probably arm up and hand rubbing the back of his head. "I'll go get her." The swish of his pants legs meant that he was coming this way.

Before Moira ducked back into the bathroom, she picked up

Krista's voice, though it was quieter. "Subtle," she said to the girl. "Do you know what *subtle* means?"

"No."

"Like, um, sneaky."

"Oh. Sneaky. Got it."

Moira didn't have time to ponder what this meant before Frank turned the corner. She stood in front of the mirror and grabbed the hand towel, rumpling it as if she were in miduse. "Are they here?" she called out before poking her head out into the hallway. "Oh! God, you scared me," she said at Frank's proximity.

"Sorry about that. Krista's here. And she brought company. You all right?"

"Sure. One sec."

She let Frank get halfway down the hallway before following him, keeping an even trail behind. Both Krista and the girl looked up at him by the time she'd turned the corner, Krista still standing and the girl at the table, unpacking a Ziploc of crayons and a coloring book. Her parents or guardians or Krista or whoever must have gotten it from the new Benicia distribution center. They had pre-MGS manufactured electronics and furniture, why not coloring books? The girl sat quietly, the colors in front of her all neatly sketched within the lines of a bear wearing a hat and pants. Thankfully, the coloring book was of pre-pandemic cartoon characters and not a MoJo one.

Moira's dad hadn't been shy about merchandising money all those years ago.

"Thanks for chatting on such short notice." Moira came out of the dim hallway barefoot in jeans and a tank top. "I wanted to talk with both of you about—" A sudden squeal cut her off.

"MoJo!"

The blood drained from Moira's face and her heart began to pound so intensely that it might have ripped out of her chest. She blinked and told herself to steady her composure. Fortunately, both Krista and Frank now looked at the girl rather than her.

Moira tried to read Krista's face, but it remained inscrutable.

"Oh!" The girl's voice dropped to a whisper, hand over mouth at Krista, her words quiet enough that Frank probably missed them. Moira, though, had taught herself to tune in when people whispered about her. She'd picked those skills up years before the End of the World. "I mean, it's MoJo. She looks like MoJo. She has the same line on her cheek."

The scar. She saw the scar.

A tiny laugh came out as Krista knelt down, getting to Sunny's height. She whispered something inaudible to the girl, then pulled back. "We're here to work, remember?"

"MoJo?" Frank said. "That singer in the news?" He squinted, then looked at his fiancée sideways. "Heh, I guess there's some resemblance."

"Frank, you don't even know what she looks like," Moira bit out. Frank's stunned expression showed that her forceful tone let her anxieties get the best of her.

"Sorry for the outburst," Krista said, her tone calm and words coming out a little slower than normal. This must have been where her professional experience came into the mix. PASD, the past, dead spouses, all of that *had* to interfere with emotions at family gatherings, even corporate events. Probably the first time teen pop stars came up, though. "Well, let's talk about civil ceremonies. The pros and cons. Moira, this is Sunny. She's my helper for the day."

"Sunny..." Moira said, her voice fading away, but her eyes darting back and forth. The name registered. Seconds later, her mind connected the face with the photo on Rob's desk. "You're...Rob's daughter?" She noticed Krista watching her with a sudden inquisitiveness. Sunny nodded her reply, an enthusiastic bob that made her black hair shake up and down. "I've heard about you. Her dad works at PodStar," she said to Frank.

“Small world,” Frank said with a chuckle that came out a little too forced, probably trying to reset the mood in his own way.

“Hi, Sunny,” Moira said, shaking out of her stupor to also come down to Sunny’s eye level. “My name is Moira. And this is Frank. You’re helping us talk about our wedding, right?”

“Are you MoJo?” she whispered. “Can you sing ‘Love This World’? I know all the words.”

“Sunny,” Krista started, slight exasperation getting into her tone.

“Hey, maybe we should pretend and turn you in,” Frank said. “We’d be rich.” This time, it was Moira’s turn for a forced chuckle. Her whole body was tense, and she let out short, subtle breaths, trying to relax one part at a time. “You should have been a pop star.” Frank stepped behind her, giving a squeeze on the shoulder. It was probably meant to be joking, affectionate. But given the state of everything, Moira had to contain her overland instincts to elbow anyone who approached her from behind, then follow it up with a turn and a kick to the crotch. “You have a great voice. I don’t know why you don’t sing more.”

“Oh, I couldn’t do that.” Her words came out clipped, probably only on a level that she knew. “I hate being the center of attention.” She met Sunny’s gaze, though something about the girl’s bright blue eyes grounded her. “I *can* sing, but I’m not who you think I am. I’m Moira.” She added extra sweetness to her voice, though this wasn’t manipulation. Despite Sunny striking a nerve, the earnest question colored over her inner discomfort.

“But you look *just like her.*”

“Hey, Sunny.” Krista put her arms on the little girl’s shoulders. “Remember we’re here to help them talk about civil ceremonies. You know what that is?”

Sunny shook her head no.

“You can get married all sorts of places. Civil ceremonies are at City Hall.”

“Where we just were?”

They were just at City Hall also? Moira had hurried out of there so fast she didn't pay attention to who was around, especially with that quarantine exhibit going on.

"That's right. Different office from where you pay Residence License fees. So let's help them out. You said you wanted to learn about weddings, right?"

"Uh-huh. Because they make people happy."

"Yeah." Krista's whole demeanor changed when talking to Sunny—the professionalism softened, the smile came out more often, the tone lightened. Moira wondered if she acted this way around all children, flower girls or whatever. "Best thing you can do to help out right now is to color each of us a really cool picture. While the grown-ups talk. Sound good?"

"Okay!" Sunny turned back to her coloring, stealing an occasional glance up at Moira. Each time, Moira caught them with a smile, sometimes even a little wave.

Twenty minutes later, Krista continued to play referee between Moira and Frank, particularly when Moira revealed that she'd already booked a date for next week. "So, that's really it, then," Krista said. "It's paperwork. You don't even have to tell any vendors. Nothing changes except your status with the government. You'll qualify for the newlywed tax credit, you'd be able to share married health care rates. It's a formality."

Moira kept her facade neutral, but tracked Frank's reactions the whole time. One of the issues with being engaged to a guy who was *so* normal, so relatively unaffected by MGS, was that it informed his entire worldview. He sympathized but failed to empathize. He'd never been through it. "What I'd suggest is think about it for a few days. I understand your hesitation," Krista said to Frank, "but it doesn't have to define how you move forward. So, think it over, let me know what you're comfortable with."

"I checked City Hall's cancellation policy." Moira handed the informational sheet to Frank. "You can cancel within forty-eight hours. So think about it."

"Well, while I *am* here—and assuming the ceremony is still on—is there anything you wanted to go over?"

"I had some questions about guest travel accommodations. Can you arrange the interstate permits?" Frank asked. "And we had some cancellations."

"We" wasn't entirely accurate, given that Moira had zero guests on her side. Frank was too polite to belabor that point. Pandemic offered a good excuse for any sort of family quirks, or lack thereof. "Lemme load up my email. Back in a few minutes."

Frank disappeared into the bedroom, and soon the familiar *beep* of his laptop powering up came through. Moira waited until she heard him shuffling through some papers to grab Krista. "There's something else I need to talk with you about." Her voice was hushed, hurried, low enough that she knew Frank wouldn't hear. He wasn't anywhere close to her level of hypervigilance or awareness.

"Well, let's give Frank—"

"No, it's not about that. Well, it is and it isn't." She had to, right here and right now. Sunny not only suspected who she was, she'd identified the facial scar that could prove it. Trusting anyone was a risk, but the risk/reward calculation made sense. "It's about *everything*." She took in a breath, then glanced back at Sunny. "I am MoJo. I used to be. I ran away during the outbreak. Lived overland. I was with a Reclaimed group before I moved here. And I need to keep my dad far away from me. He's coming. He's looking for me, there's a bounty, and he absolutely cannot find me. Even if he knows I'm here, even if I refuse to speak to him, he'll turn it into some publicity thing. I will *not* be pulled into his orbit again. That's why I need to get married soon. To officially establish my identity. Because Moira Gorman is fake. But if I can make her real, I have an alibi. I can deny. I can disappear."

"Got it," Frank announced from the bedroom.

Krista looked back and forth, bouncing between Moira and back at Sunny.

"Please don't let Sunny tell anyone. Not even her dad. Just... contain it. Please," Moira said.

Krista nodded, but that didn't give Moira enough time to enjoy the tiny shift in her favor. Instead, she straightened up, giving Frank a welcoming look, her edges rounding into something softer, less on guard. She smiled, attempting a genuine expression of affection—or at least appreciative friendliness at a future of stability, security.

But it came out as it often did under duress, the same burning cheek muscles and weary jaw that came with the MoJo smile she'd learned over a decade ago.

CHAPTER TWENTY-ONE

Krista

"Knock, knock," Krista said, pushing open the front door. She didn't see any scantily clad women hanging around the living room, though if the speed dating went well, maybe they hid upstairs. If Rob managed that, she might just beam with some level of pride.

"In the kitchen."

"Meet anyone who needs a planner? Or babysitter?"

Sunny's backpack landed on the floor with a light *thump,* and she sprinted into the kitchen before Rob answered. "Daddy, Daddy, guess what?"

"What's that, Sun?" Rob said.

"We saw MoJo."

Apparently, "respect Moira's wishes" went out the window with Sunny. Though in a way, a touch of envy struck Krista. What must it be like to be able to tell your parents *anything*?

Rob's skeptical look prompted Krista to respond as she entered the kitchen. "Sunny thinks that Moira looks a lot like MoJo."

"It's her, Daddy. I swear."

"Now, Sunny," Krista said, inviting her up to the stool next to the kitchen's island, "remember what we talked about. She says that she is not MoJo, so she isn't."

The discussion flew over Rob, barely registering in his eyes. Good. Not that she wanted Rob to deal with the Family Stability Board, but that preoccupation did mean one fewer potential competitor. He had bigger things to worry about, leaving Krista solely with the decision of what to do with the information from tonight—not just the truth about MoJo, but the unexpected *fear* in Moira's eyes. Enough for Krista to slow down and consider the situation.

"She was good?" Rob asked.

All the MoJo business pushed aside the photo exhibit for a few hours. But as Krista met Rob's eyes, the image from the quarantine riot shot to the surface, so much so that she couldn't look at him and instead she pulled out her phone, reloading the Metronet for no reason at all other than to buy a few seconds of reset time. "Not bad," Krista managed to say. "How was speed…er, your thing?"

"It was…interesting. Hey, Sun," he said, giving his daughter a squeeze on the shoulder, "I'm gonna walk Krista out, then we can talk about your big day, okay?"

Sunny hopped down from the stool she'd just got on, then gave Krista another one of her bearlike hugs. "Okay, Krista. I like it when we hang out."

Rob's smirk reappeared, and as they left the kitchen, her pace picked up across the living room. The front door closed behind them, the words spilled out as the latch clicked into place. "What's with that look? You think I did a bad job with Sunny or something?"

"On the contrary," Rob said, leaning against the door frame. "I think you did an excellent job. You even talked to her like, you know, someone who cares."

Krista realized her fingers started fidgeting, which she stemmed with tight fists while thinking up a response. "It's fine, I mean, you're paying me."

"You're welcome."

"Yeah. Right. Thanks." Krista readjusted the purse on her shoulder and glanced back at a passing car on the street. "So, how was Love Solutions? Did you find a solution to love?"

"No. Not at all. But I got stuff to bring to the Family Stability Board."

"Were all the people ugly or something?"

"No. It was..." Rob's expression changed to the thoughtful opposite of his previous look. "It was actually quite...sad."

"So the people *were* ugly."

"It's not that simple. No, these people, they were all affected by PASD. Angry. Scared. Still in mourning. It all came out in different ways. But I don't know, maybe the world isn't ready to date yet." He rubbed his cheeks, his hand casting rigid shadows across his nose and chin from the dim light overhead. "Maybe you're right. That's the next evolution of dating. We've rolled backward a century or two, arranging marriages for security and safety."

"I check that the flowers are delivered on time. Not that the bride and groom are in love."

"And I'm sure you've never met the right person."

Memories poked through, like an involuntary reflex in her cerebral cortex, those brief moments when Jas sure seemed like he fit the bill. Not just the strong cheekbones or brilliant eyes, or the impeccable taste in music or the hint of Punjabi dialect across his London accent. He *got* her. Even at her most explosive or defensive, he always knew how to defuse the situation, reconnect with her.

Well. Almost always. But Krista slammed the door on that memory before it could ignite any *other* feelings in her.

"Actually, I have met Mr. Right."

"Your cat doesn't count."

"Not my cat, I'm referring to Mr. Vibrator, and he never lets me down."

"Okay, too much information." Rob's hands shot up in mock protest. "Thanks for watching Sunny. You're a far better babysitter than you think. Five stars. Well worth the money. She loves it, you know. I know we're doing this to help us all be 'socially normal' but she's having a good time with you."

"I won't say anytime, but…" A softness crept its way past Krista's defenses. "You know my hourly rate." She fought the urge to finish with something sarcastic and hustled to her car before Rob said anything further.

She had to rush because a wave of *something* hit her, a queasiness that sank to the pit of her stomach. Unexpected tears surfaced, and as the car roared to life, Krista struggled to ignore the question suddenly refusing to leave her mind.

If she could care for Sunny in such a short time, how come her own mother never cared the same way?

CHAPTER TWENTY-TWO

Rob

Nothing was supposed to come out of speed dating. The whole thing should have been a simple checklist item, something to show the Family Stability Board that he could go out in public and engage with other adults per acceptable standards.

He wasn't supposed to actually be interested in someone. And yet, there he was, sitting at his workstation, one of the rare high-speed connections in the San Francisco Metro, and ready to use it to look up Zoe's law firm. For the first time since getting caught in the elevator, something else occupied his mind besides audits and consequences. He hadn't even been to a bar since before the End of the World.

The last time, in fact, was on the night the quarantine announcements unfolded, the night New York City exploded into rioting and chaos on the other side of the country. In San Francisco, it came out at a quieter pace. That night, people stood with their drinks, TVs lit up while chatter and music formed an incomprehensible soundtrack. But the mood back then carried a different air, one of baseball fans having a post-game drink, enjoying themselves with some semblance of normalcy despite the previous weeks' unfurling news.

Rob still felt the way Elena usually held his hand, her first three fingers gripping tight while the pinkie almost always remained loose. That afternoon, Rob's parents watched Sunny as a belated birthday gift while he and Elena went to the interleague San Francisco Giants/Oakland A's game.

The game was significant, not because of statistics or standings, but as the final contest before Major League Baseball went on indefinite pandemic hiatus from restrictions on travel and large events. East Coast teams had already shut down. Unofficial death tolls sprinkled through internet chatter—Rob had seen claims as low as one million and as high as forty million—but Rob and Elena agreed not to talk about *it* tonight. Most seemed to agree, and the game itself went on with the usual drunken revelry of watching professional sports.

Ten minutes after they walked in the bar and ordered, all the various TV networks switched to footage of a concert, that teenybopper singer that Elena liked and Rob despised. Apparently, a riot had broken out there, and while he stared at the screen and sipped his beer, his eyes squinted to read the scrolling text along the bottom.

"Government...quarantine?" Elena's voice was barely audible over the din of the bar. At least at first; soon conversations faded out, and within a few minutes, there was only the sound of clinking glasses. One of the bartenders turned the volume up on the feed, and Elena took Rob's hand again, except this time all her fingers squeezed hard.

"...an international quarantine with unprecedented agreement across the globe. On a national level, controlled rollouts will unfurl from East Coast to West across an eight-week period. Emergency teams have been dispatched to large remote facilities, and though quarantine specifics aren't available yet, the preliminary list appears to include the indoor facilities of at least seven hundred thousand square feet such as large arenas, indoor shopping malls, and fulfillment warehouses, as well as standalone facilities such as airports, prisons, and military bases. Individual and corporate assets will be frozen during this indefinite period. Insiders suggest regular waves of quarantine enrollment across the next ten to twelve months. To date, the farthest west reported fatality is out of Las Vegas two days ago."

"We should get home," Elena said.

Rob nodded, wordless, and put his full glass on the bar. Heads down, they shuffled out with a handful of others while most remained glued to the screen. "It's bullshit," one woman said, "it hasn't even touched out here."

"Preventative measures," her friend said.

"Still bullshit."

Their debate continued while Rob and Elena went outside, where it appeared everyone within the San Francisco ballpark's vicinity was trying to hail a cab. That night, they agreed to walk the five or so miles home rather than search for transportation. A light rain began sprinkling over them with their first steps, and Rob looked back at the bar, uncertain faces still visible through its front windows.

He hadn't been back to a bar until last night. And the juxtaposition of that last night out with Elena against that brief connection with Zoe… Rob wasn't sure if it felt right or ironic or just like some sort of karmic balance. Maybe all of it. Maybe none of it at all.

Or maybe the universe was just giving him the okay to take a step back into the world.

He stared at Zoe's photo and law firm title on his computer screen, an image that took a good minute to load despite its low resolution; even his connection hiccuped from time to time.

The gap between Zoe's corporate headshot and the broken, beautiful woman he'd met seemed too wide to cross. But those few minutes they talked, that felt worth the risk. He picked up the phone off the cradle, then hesitated, playing out scenarios in his mind.

Say Zoe responded. Say they went out for coffee, lunch maybe. Say it became a proper date.

Then what would he tell Sunny? How could he possibly explain that first, her mother was dead, and second, he was dating someone new?

The phone's receiver went from a dial tone to a recorded message asking him to please hang up the phone, and then the line went silent. Rob's eyes drew to his calendar, a big red *F* marking the upcoming Family Stability Board meeting.

Worrying about all that could come later. They wanted him to be socially normal, then he'd try his best and figure out the rest when he had to.

He reset the receiver until a dial tone came back, then punched in the numbers.

"This is Zoe."

"Zoe, hi. This is Rob." He straightened up, as if she could see his good posture. "Rob, from the dumb speed dating thing."

"Rob. Oh. Oh, wow. Hi. Um..." The crinkle of papers shuffling came over the phone. "Hi."

"Look, I know things seemed a bit awkward, but I thought we had a bit of a connection. I'm hurting and you're hurting, but that doesn't mean we can't, you know, take a step back into the world."

"Rob. Listen. You seem like a really nice guy—"

"Uh-oh. You called me nice."

"No, I mean it. It's really just not the right time for me right now. The other day made me realize that I need to work on myself. Go to one of those Healing Hope seminars or something."

"Would it help if I said I was a shrink?"

"I thought you were in IT."

"I am. Bad joke. I'm sorry to have bothered you. I..." The

inside of his lip stung, his teeth digging in while he considered what to say. “I hope you feel better.”

“Thanks. I hope someday I’m as strong as you. Maybe then we can get a drink. That is,” she said with a small laugh, “if some beautiful woman hasn’t scooped you up by then.”

Some beautiful woman, he thought as they said their goodbyes.

Maybe he *was* ready to take a step back into the world. But fate—or everyone else in the world—didn’t seem quite ready yet. Rob’s eyes set on the big *F* on the calendar again, not as wayward happenstance, but direct focus. Only a few days remained. And all he could do was present the best case possible, to show he didn’t fail Sunny—or Elena.

That, and hope. He could still hope.

Message recovered from Thomas Greenwood's email:

To: Portia Wiggs
From: Thomas Greenwood
Subject: Re: Need to vent

I can't get through to Kay. It's like she's so hell-bent (ha) on church life that she can't see that the Metro system is weakening. I mean, what are we paying Residence Licenses for? A power grid that doesn't work, streets with potholes, and crummy jobs? You remember how we used to camp for days on end as kids? I was an Eagle Scout, I know how to do those things. That makes more sense now, but she doesn't get it.

I've tried telling her that Reclaimed is the way to live with the land. It's not perfect, but I don't see any other path. I mean, you know me, I've always thought religion is stupid, but I even tried "it's more godly out there." Like, Jesus would want us to live in a commune. She won't listen. And it's driving Freda even further away. I'm not sure what to do.

P.S. Is it true that Reclaimed toilets work like a dream? Because this weekly clogging from low water pressure is not cool.

CHAPTER TWENTY-THREE

Moira

This afternoon was the social normalcy audit at the Family Stability Board.

And now that it was here, Moira knew she was going to kind of miss it.

Not the audit, or what it represented or the stress that it caused Rob. None of that was good or welcome. But every day, she met up with Rob and they walked to Survivors Anonymous together. The twenty minutes there, the twenty minutes back, talking the whole time. Sometimes, they didn't even go into the meeting, instead opting to sit on a bench outside and discuss Rob's speed dating nerves or the latest rumors out of Miami or how Sunny was doing. Rob didn't bring up MoJo at all, so she assumed Sunny kept her word (and in turn, Krista kept hers). But even without that, Moira nearly told him the truth several times.

Now it was gone. She would continue to go, but his need for it would be done, and then…what? That one hour a day where she felt honest, without the guard that was so necessary around Frank, what would happen to that?

For now, there was only one way to end this. Moira stood up and walked over to Rob's cube and saw him sitting with tense brow, fingers tented against his chin. "It's almost time, huh?"

"Yeah." He stood up, grabbing the coat sitting over his chair, and blew out a breath. "Still a little early. But better than sitting and waiting."

Her posture went from casual to serious. "Are you ready?"

"Probably more than I was for speed dating."

Her head bobbed, though it quickly became a shake and a sigh. She could see right through the words: Rob wanted to downplay the awkwardness, the weight of the moment. He looked at her again, this time his mouth trembling in slight movements, as if a question were just on the verge.

"What is it?" she asked.

"Look, I know it's imposing a bit. But I could use all the help I can get. Krista's watching Sunny right now, but she gave me a written testimonial. I just, I thought if it's not too much, you might be able to come and say a few words."

Two weeks of going to daily support groups together, two weeks of peeling back the layers of each other's defenses to arrive at an honesty that no longer seemed to exist after five billion people died.

And now this.

This person, a coworker who was nothing more than a name tag and a title a few weeks ago, now faced the unthinkable. And he asked if she'd fight the fight with him.

Moira responded in a way that seemed to completely surprise Rob.

It caught her off guard too.

She hugged him.

"Of course," she said, squeezing him tight, as if she could funnel any good karma she'd earned over the past few weeks into the battle for his daughter, MoJo and her dad be damned. "Sunny's a good kid. You're a good person. It'll be okay." They separated, though they stayed at arm's length.

Rob smiled and no further words were necessary.

Several minutes later, the Bay Area wind whipped around them during the long march to City Hall. They passed by the edge of the reconstruction zone, tall buildings formerly offering posh hotel space now showing the wear of being government housing for non-licensed residents. Everything from the paint to the signage to the structure itself seemed to exhale, though it was a smaller building several spaces past it that caught Moira's eye.

Not so much the building but the glow coming from a partially exposed front wall. And the smoke trailing to the sky.

"What the—" Rob jogged several steps forward before stopping. Moira joined him, the smell of burning stinging her nose. "Is that house on fire?"

Suddenly, the front door opened and a man—no, boy, no older than a teenager—stepped outside, with a hurried look and concern on his face. His long coat over ill-fitting clothes gave away the fact that he probably lived on the outskirts, surviving from day to day. But he didn't call for help or run toward them or do anything to stop the flames. Instead, he spotted them across the street, his eyes lit with the panic that only implied guilt, and began running down the alley next to the building.

"Hey!" Rob yelled, a sudden burst of speed propelling him into the street. A lone car blared its horn at him, and Moira caught a quick glimpse of his eyes. They were wide, wild, a fury in them that seemed impossible for Rob. "Hey! Get back here! That's someone's life you're burning!"

From the alley came the sounds of clanging garbage cans and broken glass. Rob dodged one oncoming car, then stopped, first staring at the runaway would-be arsonist. Moira ran too, and her body naturally assumed Code Polka Dot, pushing faster than others should have seen her. She caught up with him easily.

"That goddamn kid," he said, an anger fusing deep into his words, "that *kid*. What right does he have to do this? Those are people's memories in there."

Moira turned and spied two citizen patrol officers down the block. Arms up, hands waving, her gestures caught their attention and they began sprinting over, one on his phone. Their whistles blew, and she then pointed down the street past Rob, in her head noting that she probably ran faster than they did.

"Rob. Cit-pats. They'll get the fire department. Rob?" Rob stood quiet and still while the glowing fire from inside began to eat up the house's frame and ceiling. She went around to look at him, only to see his eyes squeezed shut.

"Hey," she said, voice laced with sudden concern. "We should get going. The Family Stability—"

"My home was just like this. Burned up by looters." His eyes remained shut. "They used my photo albums as kindling. They trashed our belongings. Our lives. Our home, gutted and destroyed. We put our lives on hold for quarantine and we come back—*I* come back—to find it looted. Burned." Rob's voice was dry, giving his words a gravelly rumble. "They must have been raiding that house. They're getting bolder, reaching farther into the cities."

"I don't think real looter gangs are brave enough to raid Metros. They're just dumb kids. They probably slipped through the adoption cracks or ran away from the FSB dorms and this is how they deal. I mean, in a way, maybe we should feel bad for them. Who knows how long they've survived this way?"

"So many places to live in this world, and they just take from others. Even now." His eyes opened and he pointed up at the now-visible flames. From behind, the sound of a fire engine approached. "No one thinks of what's left behind when they're told, 'Go to the bus *today* or you'll miss your turn.' You just fill up one suitcase and go, you hear the reports and rumors and you hope it doesn't hit you when you get out. All I have are some old pictures and the wedding album we brought to quarantine. That's it. Everything else, it's in here," he said, tapping his temple. "I can't bring anything else back."

"I'm sorry. Rob, I'm so sorry. God—" She stopped, further words failing to materialize in her mind. "I need something else to say, huh?"

"I wonder how many of them kept on looting. Like those guys. Or did they return to normal when everything cleared? Back to their cars and their TVs, their little *Mad Max* adventure come and gone."

What Moira would have given to bleed her thoughts and memories into Rob's head, to show him that for many, looting meant survival. Winter clothes. Food. Medicine. Rope, backpack, hydration, sometimes while being chased or shot at or atop buildings so fraught with water damage that the floor had rotted away.

But she couldn't say that. She may have been honest with him about her feelings, but those experiences had to stay hidden. Protected. "I know it's not much consolation, but everyone was just trying to find a way. Some chose the government way, some chose the overland route. No one knew what would happen. You have the right to be angry, but you can't hold a grudge against everyone. It'll eat you alive. You have to move on," she said, her deep breath louder than the gust of wind that blasted them. "We all do."

Across the street, the fire engine parked, its brakes squeaking, and people in yellow overcoats poured out of it. "This is how my first speed date went—" he turned to Moira "—except I was on the other side and poor Zoe had the meltdown. She didn't almost get run over, so I one-upped her."

"Come on," she said gently. "Your meeting."

Rob nodded, then shook his head, laughing to himself. "Sorry you had to see that."

"It's okay. We all deal with PASD. But better you get it out of your system now. Shall we?" They walked, quiet but at ease. So many moments created an uncomfortable silence, but Moira wondered if there was such a thing as a *comfortable* silence.

"Hey, wait," Rob said halfway down the next block. They turned to face each other. "I really like how we're honest with each other. There's not enough of that. So don't take this the wrong way, but I have a personal question. Is that okay? Don't worry, it's not bad. Or it won't be bad. I just want to know."

So much for comfortable.

Sunny must have said something. Moira's defenses immediately went up, all types of fake backstories coming to her mind, from the things she'd told Frank to all new ideas sparking.

But after a moment, all of those seemed unnecessary. This was Rob. This was what they talked about on their walks.

"Sure."

"Sunny thinks you're that pop star in the news. MoJo. She says you smile like her. I told her we shouldn't bother you about it and I'm not going to pursue any reward. I just…wanted to know." In the distance behind them, the *putt-putt-putt* of the fire engine was still audible. "It's just funny because Elena loved MoJo. That song 'Love This World'? I heard it so much. Elena sang it to Sunny as a lullaby. It's like she passed it on. Now Sunny loves it. I wanted to know because, well," he gestured around them, "it'd be kind of funny how this all works out, you know?"

Simply hearing the name MoJo lit the spark. Reflexes began to twist her facial muscles into a scowl, something she fought to reset, all while batting away a flutter of fast-arriving memories. Lights. Recording booths. Her father yelling "One more time!" Empty booze bottles shoved between hotel couch cushions.

All of it got pushed down, far down, and Moira managed to turn to Rob. "She's a smart girl."

"It's all right. I promise you, I won't do anything about it. And you definitely look better without the face paint. And with that hair. We're all hiding something. God knows I am. But—" he grinned out of nowhere, despite the weary lines around his face "—it's nice to know the truth."

"The truth," Moira said, tracking a pair of birds flying into the broken windows up above them. "The truth is I hate all of it. I've been trying to forget about MoJo for half my life. Even when I *was* her, I tried to forget about her. Teen stars have pretty easy access to drugs. I go by Moira Gorman now. Gorman is the surname of my old manager, Chris, the only adult in my life who actually looked after me."

"Don't worry. I won't tell Sunny."

"Honesty, right?" She motioned Rob forward, and they began walking again. "That MoJo smile. It's like a reflex. My dad, he made me practice it all the time when I was a kid. I hate that bloody thing. And now I've done it so much, I have no control over it." Images flew through her mind of a mirror's reflection, practicing for hours on end. "You've been right all along, you know," she said, looking straight at the passing sidewalk lines with each step. "About being honest. I'm sure the Family Stability Board will see that."

"I'll keep your secret," Rob said, hand landing on her shoulder. "I promise, no one's going to turn you in. Some secrets have to be held tightly."

"I appreciate it."

Moira knew that they walked another six blocks to City Hall, though her vision seemed to show two parallel worlds. In one, it was all streetlights and plants crawling through abandoned buildings and the same wind that haunted San Francisco autumn afternoons years and years before mutant viruses. Blended over that came images she'd long pushed away, buried underneath years of another life, another identity. Singing lessons. Dance training. Tour buses. Handlers. Greenrooms and endless backstages, one after another, first small and then bigger and bigger until the biggest in the world.

Yet, the two lives seemed to intersect into a single thought by the time they reached the office.

"I was thinking," she said right when they got to City Hall's front door, "can Sunny keep a secret too?"

"If you tell her to keep something quiet, she will. It just depends on how you position it."

"Okay. This can't get back to Frank. He doesn't know about that life. But if MoJo really means a lot to Sunny, I'd be willing to sing a song or two for her. In private."

Secrets built upon secrets. This should have been a house-of-cards idea, a flash that came and went, collapsing under the weight of ill-formed logic. But while Moira awaited his response, she found herself rooting for it to be a go.

Something felt *right* about the simple act of singing for a little girl, like that would burn away all of the poison music had done to her long ago.

CHAPTER TWENTY-FOUR

Krista

Krista had gotten to know Sunny well enough by now that she understood when something occupied the little girl's thoughts. Sunny's lips would purse and she'd look away, only occasionally glancing back for eye contact before dropping again. "What's on your mind, Sunny?"

Sunny's piercing eyes locked on to Krista's, and though her voice was small, its direct intensity easily cut through the noise of the diner they sat in. "Are you sure Moira isn't MoJo?"

Though Sunny's school was still running on half days, today's pickup had seemed strangely empty and hushed. Even the teachers got out of there quick. Krista didn't spend too much time on it though, because right when she got to Sunny, she knew that Rob would probably be prepping for the audit.

He didn't seem to know what would happen or how long it would take. His only request was that she take Sunny somewhere "fun" while he dealt with it. In turn, Krista went on a news-and-business blackout. Just for one afternoon. She even let Sunny bring along her MoJo CD, which was as terrible as she'd expected—probably the reason why the pop star still lingered in Sunny's mind.

"Moira is just Moira. I'm sure of it." Which was a gigantic lie, the complete opposite of truth. But given that the last day had given Krista enough time to weigh all the possibilities—and the fact that she absolutely refused to lose her home—calming Sunny's curiosity was the easy way out.

Especially since tonight, after she dropped Sunny off, Krista planned on turning Moira in.

"Chicken fingers and fries," the waitress said, putting a small red plate in front of Sunny, "and a bacon patty melt with onion rings." A larger green plate landed in front of Krista with a clink.

The End of the World claimed all but the biggest fast-food chains, but thankfully throwback diners still existed. Not too many displays of life from the modern era worked into everyday life, but the diner's 1950s decor must have been otherworldly enough to be acceptable. "Thanks."

"Your daughter is so cute. She's got your eyes."

The statement left Krista speechless, so she went to her go-to impulse for such things: avoidance. "Sunny, dig in. This diner is great."

The next five minutes passed in silence while Sunny ate her chicken fingers at a deliberate pace, politely dabbing with her napkin every three or four bites. Krista considered matching her level of neatness, but hunger overrode that idea. A few minutes later, Sunny's plate was picked clean, except the fries had all been shoved to one side. "Something wrong with those?"

"Daddy won't let me have fries."

"Oh, I won't tell Rob. See," she said, pointing to the fries, "we had salad for lunch."

"I don't see a salad."

Krista's small laugh couldn't be heard above the noise of the diner. "I won't tell your dad that you're having fries. I'll tell him we shared a salad."

"But that's lying. Lying is what bad people do."

Sunny would soon learn the world wasn't so black and white. Especially when losing a Residence License was the result.

"Well, yeah, but it's just a little white lie. It doesn't hurt anyone. Don't you know about the one-a-year rule?"

"What's that?"

"Once a year, you're allowed to tell a little white lie. The kind that doesn't hurt anyone." Krista congratulated herself for her ability to make up crap on the fly. "So, I'm going to use my one little white lie today so you can have fries. Okay?"

"Okay. But fries will make me sick."

"No, they won't. They're great. The best fries in the world are..." Krista stopped herself before finishing with "better than sex."

"The best fries in the world will make you happy. They won't make you sick."

"You promise?"

"I promise. Try it."

Sunny grabbed one of the smaller fries and took a tiny nibble. "I don't feel sick."

"You see?"

"I like this a lot," she said, grabbing a second and a third.

"I can't believe Rob won't let you have them." A tiny part of Krista admired Rob's apparent dedication to health, but it got quickly overshadowed by the horror of a world without fries.

"He says they're bad for you."

"All right, look. See, fries are like...well, look at this." Krista pointed to her bacon patty melt. "If you had this every day, you *would* get sick. And you'd probably be all sweaty and gross and stuff. So you can't have it every day. That *is* bad. Every now and then is okay. In fact, it's more than okay. It's good for you. I usually have smoothies for lunch, but sometimes you need more."

"It makes you strong?"

"In a way, yeah. I mean, it's never good for you from a diet perspective, but it's just so good that it's like…it's like, you know, okay to occasionally break the rules. It, um, keeps things balanced. And sometimes the rules aren't the best thing. Like in history, did you learn about George Washington?"

"Uh-huh."

"So he broke rules against England, but that was a good thing. And now we're sitting here in this diner because of him."

"So…" Sunny's eyes narrowed, and she paused in midbite. "Sometimes you *should* break the rules. But how do you know when?"

Krista considered the question—not the literal interpretation, but the fact that her response would somehow nudge this little girl's path. The weight of such responsibility bore down on her, making any words hesitate in their formation until she told herself to get over it; clearly she overthought such a trite request. "I think you just know."

Sunny resumed attacking her fries, losing the restrained pace she'd used with her chicken fingers. "So, Sunny," Krista started. Her teeth dug into her bottom lip, each word carefully selected. "You know how I've been hanging out with you a lot lately?"

"Yeah. It's fun."

"Right, so here's the thing. I was helping your dad out." Krista skipped the part about getting paid. "But his, um, work stuff is finishing up. So when that's done, I'm not going to be around as much."

Sunny stopped in midbite, half-eaten fry in hand. "Are we still friends?"

"Of course. Of course we are." Krista spoke quickly and emphatically, so much so that it surprised herself. Her gut suddenly ached, and it had nothing to do with diner food. "I'm, um… I'm sure we'll get to see each other sometime."

"Oh! My school project. Will you help with that?"

"What school project?"

"We get to talk about what we want to be when we grow up. And I wanna plan weddings. Like you."

A flood of excuses came into Krista's mind, all the ways she could tell Sunny that she wasn't getting involved. Time wasn't a factor, not with the way business was going. And as for money, Rob's daily payments worked as a little bit of a buffer. And there was still the matter of Moira and that mega reward.

Sunny's bright blue eyes remained wide with anticipation, the half-eaten fry still in her hand.

"I, um, have to check my schedule. This is…unexpected."

"So…maybe?"

"Maybe."

"Cool!" The diner booth filled with the sound of her little hands clapping, her enthusiasm sprinkling into the air and even catching on Krista. Somehow, even the voice that told her to not get involved managed to quiet itself. It let a smile slip through, at least until Krista remembered the audit.

As Sunny cleared off the remaining bits of fries the waitress returned with the check.

"Oh," Krista said, "I have it right here." She handed a ten and a five over to the waitress. Somehow, dipping into her stash of Rob Donelly payments for this didn't feel steps away from financial doom. "We don't need any change."

"Daddy says cash is bad," Sunny said, brow narrowed in disapproval.

Jesus, what *else* did Rob say was bad? French fries were bad, paying cash was bad, was Mick bad too because he stunk up the litter box? "Why does he say that?"

"He says bad people steal cash, so you shouldn't use it unless you want bad people to take it from you."

"Ironic. I use cash so bad people can't find me."

Sunny responded with a twisted look.

"What I mean is that credit cards leave records that can track back to you…" Krista stopped before going into any detail about her family history. "What I *really* mean is that, um, cash is good."

"But what about the bad people?"

Krista mulled an answer—she'd never been mugged, but that didn't mean it couldn't happen. "Well, you just have to know how to protect yourself." She shuffled out of the booth and motioned Sunny to follow suit. As Sunny gathered her things, Krista stood back and took in the scene: here she was, giving advice—no, being a mentor—to a young girl, and it all seemed so easy. Broaden her horizons? Check. Give her real-world advice? Check. Listen to her? Check. For someone fairly new to this whole kid thing, Krista gave herself an A or even an A-plus; who knew it'd come so easily?

Sunny grabbed Krista's hand as they ambled toward the exit, but stopped a few feet before the door. "What's that?" She pointed at a vintage photo booth.

"Oh that?" Krista said. "You sit—" As she turned, she realized that everyone remaining in the diner stared at their phones. This happened all the time before the End of the World, but with the slow-loading Metronet, such a sight was an artifact from another age, much like the photo booth that caught Sunny's attention. "You sit inside it and it takes pictures of you." Murmurs rippled through the diner's space, prompting Krista to reach for her own phone.

"Can we do it?" Sunny squeezed Krista's free hand, pushing three of her four fingers so hard the knuckles pressed against each other.

The news could wait. She wanted to give Sunny a good time. If a photo booth stemmed the tide of whatever lay ahead, who was she to judge? "Sure." They settled in, the machine eating up a quarter and spitting back a nickel and a dime before its screen came to life, showing Sunny's beaming face and Krista's amused smirk. It counted down: three, two, one, then took four photos in rapid fire. Within seconds, the machine whirred and several photos dropped out in the tiny slot below.

Sunny grabbed them, their developing colors still coming in. "I love it!" she said, waving it in front of Krista. Krista took one and studied it: Sunny's bright eyes and wide smile sat next to Krista's expression, which didn't come out nearly as bemused as she'd expected.

In fact, it was kind of nice.

CHAPTER TWENTY-FIVE

Rob

Dorms.

The idea repeated over and over in Rob's mind. If he failed, Sunny would be shipped into Family Stability Board dorms. The thumping in his chest may as well have been a jackhammer. A thin layer of sweat formed on his forehead, and his fidgeting fingers kept finding *anything* to do while he sat.

Something covered them, a steady warmth that sent a calming sensation up and down his body. Moira's hand squeezed on top of his, and she stole his attention despite him staring at the clock above the door. "It'll be fine," she whispered.

"Thanks," he said, the word more instinctive than considered.

In the background, the news shifted from some sort of incident in Detroit to an exposé on how Japan and China reflected polar opposite states in the post-MGS world. Rob heard the broadcast, he comprehended the sentences, but none of it felt like listening.

"You know what," Moira said, her voice stronger. "I only said that because that's what you're supposed to say. Or what people think you're supposed to say. But we're past those kind of fronts, you and me. I don't know if it'll be fine. I hope it will. All I can say is that knowing you as I do, I believe it *will* be fine. I hope that helps a little."

Rob's eyes broke from the clock as he turned to her. He took in a breath, nerves barely able to take the air in, though he settled enough to get a genuine thought out. "It does."

"We'll get—"

The door opened and a man's voice called out. "Rob Donelly?"

"Here we go," he said, and as they rose together, Moira's hand lingered on his enough for one more squeeze to echo through his body.

"I'm Bernard Langston, Family Stability Board advisor. And the first thing I tell people is to not worry. Our goal is to strengthen families, not tear them apart."

Rob nodded as he scanned the office. So much of the economy was driven by restoration work, and even though they were only a few years removed from quarantine, government offices must have been remodeled at least twice by now. How else could they explain an office as pristine and modern, all interactive screens and furniture at sharp angles?

"I'm sure you've heard stories over the past year. Greenwood, the Fourth Path, all of that. I wish the media would stop talking about that, it makes it worse. Even parents taking their children to Reclaimed Territory against their children's wishes. We believe the pillar of society is the bond of family. Newlywed credits, the expedited adoption program, support for LGBT couples wanting to adopt orphaned children, the highway and transportation projects. These encourage people to come into the Metros, to stay in the Metros, to keep the infrastructure of society together. So don't worry. In fact, we're often told that parents feel better about things after a social normalcy audit."

How long did it take for these advisors to come up with that spin?

"Now, your daughter—Sunny. She had an incident two weeks ago. And it looks like she's been having some behavioral issues as reported by her school. Of course, there are many reasons why children—and parents—have problems in this landscape. We're here just to make sure none of them become extreme. Shall we begin?"

Over the next twenty minutes, Bernard grilled Rob on family history, quarantine life, Sunny's upbringing, and Elena. Receipts and forms followed, along with Krista's written testimonial, then explanations of his various attempts at social normalcy. Those topics seemed obvious, and Rob retorted practiced answer after practiced answer, even remembering when to take emotional breaks between statements.

It wasn't that easy. Speaking to a mirror was one thing, but saying them to another person, with Moira next to him, that turned the volume on emotions up.

"Mr. Donelly, you seem like a straightforward person," he finally said after scribbling in a notepad.

"I like to think so."

"Do you have any theories about why your daughter has been acting out?"

The hallway TV was loud enough that its broadcast bled through the walls and wooden door of the office. Rob's lips pursed as he considered the question—not so much the answer, he knew that, but how much of it he should actually say.

He could hide the fact that Sunny thought Elena was alive. Or come up with a twisted version that tried to plausibly tie it all together.

Or he could tell the truth. That he made the wrong choice.

Once the idea appeared, a wave of relaxation hit him, nearly causing him to sink back into his chair, a full-body exhale that broke his inner-pressure release valve.

The truth. Hadn't that been the focus of all his conversations with Moira?

The words came out before he could consider the consequences.

"Sunny thinks Elena is alive."

Bernard continued writing, as if he'd heard such a thing before. Beside him, Moira gasped, then sat straight up.

"I like to think—used to think—that I'm protecting her, but a lie is a lie." His hands clasped in front of him, an unintentional prayer pose. "And the stupid thing is I *know* it's wrong. I've tried to talk with Sun about it a few times, but it's, well, not exactly something that just comes up in conversation."

A tremor ran through his voice, and he blinked quickly over wet eyes, fighting back against what desperately wanted to come out. "That's it. Sunny thinks Elena is still alive. Sick, in treatment away from us, but still alive. And the constant battle that comes from that lie, I think that's why she's been acting out." He cringed, though in his peripheral vision, he could see Moira's posture soften.

That subtle gesture was almost enough to tell him that he'd done the right thing.

Bernard clicked the pen's top button twice before putting it down. He took off his glasses and looked at Rob without giving anything away. "Why did you do it?"

"Sunny was so young when it happened. Elena died in quarantine when she was almost two. Not from MGS. A riot happened in our sector when they were handing out weekly rations. It was a year or so in and supplies ran tight, they prioritized people with children. We'd get all sorts of offers to trade our supplies but we tried to keep to ourselves. That night, a riot broke out. She got knocked over and kicked in the head. Over and over. No one knows if it was intentional or not, it just happened. Mob mentality. It happened all over the world, usually when rations were low. I actually saw a documentary on it last year, people pieced it together from cell phone photos and videos. And Sunny, she doesn't really remember it now, but she screamed and screamed. I wouldn't let her see Elena on life support. Not with the swelling and her skull knocked in. How do you explain that to a child?"

His hands pushed against his temples, rubbing back and forth. Moira's chair squeaked next to him as she shifted.

"I don't think there's a right answer to that question," Bernard said.

"I had to do something when they removed her from life support." The words came out low and dry, drained of energy or feeling. "I had to say something. Didn't plan on it. It just came out, and Sunny believed it."

"You wanted to protect her from the pain instead of sending her into it," Moira said, her first interjection of the meeting.

"I don't know how much kids retain at that age, but that's the story I put out and I stuck with it. She's so sensitive. I'm not sure how I'm going to break it to her. But I need to. Sooner rather than later."

Bernard repeated his line of "mmm-hmmm," and Rob studied his every move while he finished his notes. Was his neutral face from desensitization, hearing too many of these stories? Or was apathy a necessary protection against family stories? "I'm sorry," he said, turning to Moira, "your name was..."

"Moira Gorman," she said, then spelling out her last name while Bernard wrote on his pad.

"We typically want testimonials in writing but I'm happy to listen to you now, if you'd like to speak."

"I would."

"Please tell me how long you've known Mr. Donelly and your assessment of his situation."

"Well, I work with Rob at PodStar Technologies. A year now, I think? We..." She blinked a few times in thought. "We go to the same lunchtime support group. We walk there together every day. We talk on the way." Moira looked over at Rob. "We talk. We talk about this world. Sometimes about nothing at all. But I can say this: we're honest with each other. Which is rare these days. And I think that says a lot about someone. He'll do the right thing. He made a mistake, but really, who doesn't have a decision haunting them these days? Rob loves his daughter and he'll do right by her. That's really all you need to know."

The muffled scratch of pen and paper ran at a furious pace until Bernard looked back up. "I'm afraid we're out of time. But thank you both for your input. Mr. Donelly, you can expect a response soon."

"What does 'soon' mean? I mean, in a week you could just show up on my doorstep and take her away?"

The pen landed on the desk with a click and he tented his fingers. "It's not that simple. There are many steps here. Next week's response is our assessment of the social normalcy audit to determine if there is any imminent emotional or physical risk to the child. Then there's an appeal process." He looked at Rob and Moira, back and forth. "Things like the Greenwood incident sometimes come out of nowhere."

The pounding heartbeat returned, Rob's nerves tangling his feet in the chair beneath him as he tried to get up. He turned to leave when Moira caught him midstep.

"I just need to say something. Not about Rob, but what you're doing." Her voice turned from polite to harsh. "I get it. I understand what you're trying to protect against. But you have to understand, there is nothing worse you can do than rip a child out of her home at Sunny's age. Nothing. Things may not be perfect, Rob may have some things to set straight, but rehoming will never replace that. I should know."

Moira's words drew Rob's focus to her.

"My dad sent me away to an academy when I was eight. I learned to be the best at everything. I *excelled*, I practiced, I did everything that was the opposite of normal. And I hated every minute of it. I wanted to be home with my family. And instead, I was pushed into something else. Don't ever take that away. If you think there's a danger, be absolutely sure that there *is* a danger. You don't get to undo this. And there is no danger with Rob and Sunny."

The impact of Moira's words—simple, straightforward words delivered with a force more powerful than anger or rage could have—made Rob want to thank her and carry whatever pain caused it in her away. But instead, they both remained quiet, waiting to see if her speech resonated the same way with the man who held Sunny's future in his hands.

Bernard sat still, not taking any notes, until his phone rang. He glanced over, a look of surprise on his face, and then picked up the receiver.

Rob couldn't tell what was being said but based on Bernard's body language, it wasn't good. Rob looked at Moira, exchanging uncertainty when the phone hung up. "I'm going to have to end this," Bernard said. "We will be in touch."

From the hallway, a door slammed and a rush of footsteps whizzed by.

"What's happening?"

"I'm not sure. But our offices are closing. We've been told to go home."

With that, Rob and Moira shuffled out into the main thoroughfare of City Hall, the lobby area now completely empty except for two people.

A large older man standing with hands on hips, eyes scanning the space. And in front of him, a younger man holding a camera up.

The older man pointed up the stairs and started walking.

"Oh, *fuck*," Moira said. She pulled Rob into a corner with a strength that shocked him, then wrapped her arms around his waist. "That's my dad. He's here. I *knew* he'd come," she whispered into his ear. "Act natural." She pulled back, then shot a look over her shoulder. "He's gonna pass us. We need to get past him, get out of here."

Rob tried to not be conspicuous as he continued holding her back. "What if we duck into a hallway?" he whispered back.

"He's got a cameraman. We can't let him catch my face on it." Still locked together, she angled so that her back was directly against the stairway. "How far is he?"

"Halfway up the stairs."

"I'm so sorry about this."

"What are—" Rob started until he was cut off by the force of Moira's lips pressing against his. He sank into it, realizing what she was doing, and kept one eye barely open to gauge her dad's distance. They remained, an intensity to the act that was different from passion, until Rob tracked him safely at the top of the stairs and away.

"He's gone," he said after pulling back.

She nodded, then without a word grabbed Rob's hand and pulled him to the exit.

CHAPTER TWENTY-SIX

Krista

By the time Krista pulled up to the Donelly house, she recognized the beat-up Jeep parked in front of it. For such a *together* woman, Moira sure drove a clunky car, one that even had symmetrical holes on the door frame, like something used to be bolted on there. Car manufacturing hadn't restarted, but plenty of recovered and scavenged vehicles were available, most with high-MPG options, so why choose a gas guzzler with fuel prices so high?

More importantly, why was she even here? The mere sight of the vehicle chipped away at the resolve Krista had been building up.

But no. She was going to make that phone call. Her home, her whole *life* depended on it.

Krista opened the unlocked front door. "Knock, knock," she said. She met eyes with Rob, who'd only sent a vague text about the audit being done. Moira sat next to him, though something on her expression read off.

"Hey. We just got here. Sunny?" he asked. His daughter jogged over to the couch, eyes trained on Moira the whole time. "I brought someone who wants to see you. You remember Moira?"

"I..." Sunny said as she stood still. Her lips pursed, and she glanced back at Krista.

"It's all right." Moira took Sunny's hand and leaned in. "I'm going to let you in on a secret. A grown-up secret. Can you keep one?"

Krista's eyebrow arched up.

Was she really going to go there?

"I can," Sunny said.

"Okay, you can't tell your friends or your teacher or even Frank. You remember Frank, right?" Frank? She was bringing up Frank?

Sunny nodded, and Moira sucked in a heavy breath. "When I was around your age, I started singing. I practiced and practiced, and eventually I started to perform in shows. And when I was fifteen, I met some people who wrote music, and we decided to work together. They gave me the name MoJo, and we recorded two albums, but after the quarantine, I started a new life and put that behind me."

"Quarantine?" Sunny's focus shifted for a moment before she snapped to attention. "Oh. Before everyone got out?"

"Right. After everything got better, I had new things to focus on. So I haven't sung MoJo songs in years, but I came here to sing some for you. Would you like that?"

"Daddy, did you hear that?" Sunny said, her shoes clapping on the floor as she jumped up and down.

"I did, Sun. What do you say?"

Sunny straightened up, hands behind her back and chest pumped out at full attention. "Thank you, Moira."

"No problem, Sunny. Remember, you can't tell anyone about

this." She turned to the adults in the room. "You guys want to hear this too?"

"No offense, Moira, but I heard these songs enough in the car." Krista looked at Rob and mouthed the words *How was it?* straight at Rob.

"Let's talk. Kitchen." He stepped past the living room couch, squeezing Sunny's shoulder as he passed her and whispering "Thank you" to Moira.

"Everything okay?"

"I'm not sure." Behind him, Moira started singing, her full voice expanding out to all corners of the living room. "I was honest. Moira came along. She was honest too."

"I can see that."

"She said she told you?"

"Yeah." Krista turned her eyes to the living room, the pull of the reward tugging at her mind.

"We ran into her father at City Hall," Rob told her.

"Oh." She battled back the urge to ask if the reward had been claimed.

"He didn't see us. But she was pretty shaken. I've never seen her like that before." The statement caused Krista to avert her eyes; they pulled away from the image of Moira and Sunny sitting side by side and fell straight to the floor. "The meeting ended abruptly. They said we'd know something 'soon.'" His fingers formed quotes with the last word. "Which could mean anything. I think Moira feels bad for Sunny. She wanted to give her something kind."

"I bought her fries," Krista said, finally looking Rob in the eye. "She deserved it."

"Yeah." Rob nodded. "She does." They stood quietly, only Moira's singing bleeding into the kitchen. "Something weird happened at City Hall. I'm gonna look it up," he said, stepping to the computer set up in the kitchen nook.

Krista pulled out her phone and loaded the latest Metronet

stories. "Hersh is giving a speech in an hour. Doesn't say what it's about."

"I have access to other Metro news feeds. Austin is the most connected city now, maybe they have more info. You guys don't get the whole picture."

"What's that mean?" Krista considered what he'd just said, then shook it off. "You know what, never mind." She turned and leaned into the doorway, watching the scene unfold in front of her. Moira and Sunny laughed, their voices meshing together as if nothing could possibly trouble them: no Family Stability Board, no father hunting around the globe, no upcoming presidential speeches.

At least for them. For Krista, questions remained. Promises and commitments digging at her under the surface, the way they always did when things kicked at the careful life she'd built for herself. In fact, no one had quite encroached on her sense of self-sufficiency the same way since Jas did years ago.

In that moment back in Jas's dingy Long Island apartment, Krista had stared at him, wondering if he really had said what he actually said.

From his lack of reaction, the way his eyes zeroed in on hers, calm but inquisitive, she knew he was serious.

"Uh-oh." He offered a familiar grin, half playful and half caring, usually meant to cut through the bullshit and ground their situation. "It's that Krista Deal *thinking* look."

"I'm, uh..."

"C'mon, we've been together since freshman year. I know when shit freaks you out."

"I'm not freaked out."

"The word *married* came out of my mouth and it's like an alien took over your body. Seriously, you should see yourself." Jas laughed, and she knew from his tone that he wasn't making fun of her but instead trying to bring a bit of levity to the situation. He stood up, setting aside the unplugged electric guitar that he'd been picking at, then came across the room to her, putting his arms around her waist. He kissed the top of her head, his facial scruff scratching her forehead. "I finally did it. I made you speechless. Fuck yeah."

Speechless wasn't the issue. They'd talked about their future now that they were on the cusp of graduation, Jas set to go to medical school in Boston and Krista with a job lined up in New York City. Of course they'd make it work long distance, neither of them feared that. After years of going to punk shows, late-night studying, road trips up and down the coast, they stepped and thought and *felt* in sync, even if Krista still couldn't convince him that The Clash was better than The Misfits. It seemed like nothing could tear them apart.

Nothing, that was, except marriage.

That was the first time the word had been used. It caused Krista's entire body to seize up, like strings pulled her muscles taut while walls closed in on her.

"Hey," Jas said, "now I'm worried. You never act this way when we talk about the future."

Is that what things came down to for Jas? Was it that simple? Flames erupted in Krista's cheeks, and suddenly every decision over the past years became a question in her mind. Marriage. What kind of old-fashioned horror was that?

"I can't believe you're talking about marriage." Krista looked for something to hurl or smash or throttle. "Marriage doesn't work. Marriage is…is…a patriarchal construct. Something designed to take away our identities."

"Whoa, whoa, whoa. We've talked about *dying* together at age ninety-nine and eleven months. How is getting married counter to that?"

The very *word* rattled Krista, firing off a torrent of memories, all involving her mother slurring about some new guy she met or getting back together with her dad or so many other bad choices. Krista was *not* going to be like that.

She was above that.

"Krista, it's a piece of paper that gives us tax breaks."

"I don't need tax breaks. Is that what you see this as? Money?" He didn't, of course. She knew that. But he put himself in a vulnerable position, which, given the prickly nature of the topic, left *her* feeling exposed. And her instincts would not have any of that. She was *not* going to let herself be cornered.

"No, that's not what I mean. It's just, like, one of the benefits of it."

"So you *are* thinking of it that way. And that's bullshit."

At that point, Jas had his hands up, perhaps unconsciously, and his voice shifted to total bedside-manner tone, probably textbook performance from his pre-med classes. "Let's reset a second."

"Nope. You unleashed this, not me. You know how I feel."

"No, I don't! I love you. You love me. People get married when that happens! Why is that *word* so hard to swallow?"

"I told you. It's a patriarchal construct."

"Okay, fine. Ditch the word. Life partnership. Or legal commitment. Whatever you want to call it. It's me and you. Will you let me pledge that? I just want to be with you."

"If that were true, you wouldn't need a goddamn document to prove it. What are you so afraid of?"

Jas followed this with various forms of defusing and reaching out, but by then, his words bounced off her layers upon layers of defense. "Oh, no. I can't believe I've been a sucker for so long," she finally said. "If you're going to surprise me with this, what *else* don't I know about you? Huh? What else are you hiding?"

"Okay. Okay, I see I hit a nerve. Look, I just want to be together." His voice was calm, steady, though the inflection from his native Punjabi held a greater presence, as it always did when his emotions stirred. "However we file the paperwork, whatever works… I mean, come on. It's us. It's not like we're gonna break up."

"Look at you. You just *assume*. Listen, I've never relied on anyone my whole life and I am not going to start now." Images flashed through Krista's mind, not of her time with Jas, but something buried far deeper: her preteen self, one hand blocking the errant batting and shoving from her half-conscious-but-still-drunk mother, the other hand wrestling a towel to soak up the soiled mess underneath her so-called parent. The memory came and went, only slipping through the cracks because someone she dared to trust snuck past her defenses. "Fuck this."

"That's not what I meant—"

"No way. You're not off the hook that easily." Krista scanned Jas's bedroom. A hoodie. A T-shirt. A pair of shoes. Her old iPod. *Her* stuff. Not his. "I think we're done here."

"Agreed. Let's talk about this tomorrow—"

"No. That's not what I meant. We are *done* here. You can't walk this back. This isn't some dumb debate about bands. I am not going to be subject to your control."

"Control? What? Jesus, Krista, you know me better than that. I am not your mom—"

"Don't you *dare* talk about my family. What do you know about them? You've never even met them." Krista grabbed a grocery bag on the floor and began throwing her stuff into it. "This is *bullshit*."

"Krista, wait." He trailed her as she stormed through the apartment, ignoring the horrified look on Jas's roommate's face. "Wait. Just wait a—"

"Don't call me," she yelled before opening the door. She stepped through, slamming the door hard enough that the impact echoed down the hall. Jas had the good sense not to follow her to the elevator, where she hit the button, then tried to hide her tears as some people passed by.

They talked after, of course. She apologized for exploding. He got it, he understood, but something had changed. Every time he tried connecting, those same feelings came up, so much that she kept him at arm's length, and didn't even respond to his farewell text when he left for Boston.

In front of her, no one was asking for that type of legal commitment. They wanted something simpler than that. Sunny was asking for a friend. Rob, through all of this, though he *did* pay, was asking for honest support.

And Moira. Though her voice filled the room, Krista suddenly only heard her plea from the other night, the urgency of her request. And though her eyes were closed in song, Krista only saw the fear in them as she pleaded to keep her secret.

Did Krista look like that when she paid for a faked death certificate to be sent to Uncle Dean after quarantine? That moment had *felt* like bravado, like control, but even now Krista understood that same fear had driven it, even if she hadn't worn it on her face.

She watched as Sunny held her eyes on Moira, whose voice reverberated across the entire room. Sunny sat captivated, and Moira, through all her stiff interactions and strange politeness, now she seemed like a whole person.

Krista couldn't take that away from Moira. Or, maybe more importantly, from Sunny.

She'd figure something else out.

Moira held out one last note, imbuing the pithy musings of a pop song with a soul that seemed to come out of nowhere, then went quiet. Sunny bopped up and down with her clapping, then Moira did a double take at Krista. Moira's cheeks flushed, and her posture straightened. "Something the matter?"

"No. Not at all," Krista said. "Sunny, I just realized that I'll be able to help you with your project after all."

Right when she said that, Rob's chair rattled on the hardwood floor. He stood up, arms crossed and face ashen, and walked into the room. Moira's beaming smile fell when she read Rob's expression, and Krista turned to him.

"It's happened. MGS has spread. In Los Angeles. In Detroit. And here." Rob's lips pursed, and though his eyes flashed briefly to Sunny, they quickly filled with concern as he looked at the adults. "It's in San Francisco."

Excerpt from President Tanya Hersh's speech on the mutated MGS 96 strain:

My fellow Americans. I realize that not too long ago, I addressed the first fatality out of the Miami Metro. I had referred to it as a cause for caution, not alarm. I still believe that we should approach with caution, and in the face of recent news, that level of caution should be upgraded.

It is clear that something is happening. There are documented fatalities in Miami, Los Angeles, San Francisco, and Detroit now. In addition, severe symptoms have been reported in Chicago and Dallas. Our friends north of the border also have reported symptoms in Montreal. Those are the known red-zone locations. Any other cities are purely hearsay and I ask that you keep a level head to not spread rumors.

With this news, the international community has agreed on steps to contain these outbreaks. We recommend you stay in your homes as much as possible. Wear masks when going to work. If you feel any sort of flu-like symptoms, stay home and call your Metro Emergency Health Line.

In addition, inter-Metro travel will be halted within the coming week. This is done to contain the spread of the virus and ensure we as a society get a handle on it. Details of this will be announced by individual Metro governments. At the same time, a global coalition of scientists and doctors are continuing their tireless efforts to understand and stay ahead of this new strain.

Don't give in to panic. Don't give in to fear. Many, many people are putting in a round-the-clock effort for the betterment of humanity. And humanity will prevail, I promise you.

PART 3:

ENEMIES

CHAPTER TWENTY-SEVEN

Krista

The last time news of an outbreak and government-mandated restrictions went public, panic had carried through the air. Who needed a killer virus to ruin things when people let themselves devolve into sheer assholes? From the third story of the shared Brooklyn townhome Krista lived in back then, noises had spiked through walls: breaking glass, car horns, and bursts of yelling. Between Krista's ankles, then two-year-old Mick didn't seem to be bothered by the noise, his tail curling up and around her legs as he did figure-eights, a reminder that the dying boyfriend in the bed shouldn't preclude her from opening a can of cat food.

Krista hadn't loved Anthony. She knew that, and had no intention of staying with him long term, but in those college-graduate days, she had found him a total palate cleanser after Jas: nice and attractive, charming at times, and the sex was good, but he was more of a passing fad, a trend, a fond memory tucked away for later. The best part about him? He didn't matter.

At least until the last few days, when he'd fallen ill, first with sniffles, then a fever that topped out at a hundred and eight, and then his sweat-covered body convulsed, his mouth uttering unintelligible sounds, coupled with the occasional whimper. Had she not seen the rapid deterioration with her own eyes, Krista would have never believed such timid, sorry noises could have come from a former college hockey player.

Anthony wasn't long-term material but that didn't mean that she wanted him dead. Krista dialed 911 again, only to hit the brick wall of a busy signal.

Downstairs, the front door slammed, reverberating through the house. Had the looters finally gone past the markets and shops and attacked the neighborhoods? Beneath her T-shirt-turned-germ-mask, sweat trickled down her cheeks and she cut the lights, shooing Mick away for the moment. Her fingers reached to the nightstand next to Anthony's barely breathing body and wrapped around the metal form of a rusty box cutter, thumb pressing down to slide the blade open.

Beneath them, most likely on the second floor, a door shut. Whoever it was failed the subtlety test. Krista flipped the box cutter so it sat blade down, like she'd seen in so many spy films. She grasped the doorknob when a voice broke through the silence.

"Wai Lin? You here? Come on, we got to go."

Male voice. And Wai Lin was the guy with the room across the hall. Krista opened the door and stepped out, shutting it behind before Mick could wander into the hallway. "He's not here," she called out behind her mask, knife behind her back.

Footsteps echoed as the silhouette of a man trotted up the stairs to meet her, and though the light was dim, his details still came through. She must have gotten used to seeing in the dark after a few days of candlelight and unstable power. Deep bags set under his eyes, and he looked like he had a naturally skinny frame and dark skin. If this had been two weeks ago, he probably would have been fashionable, his jagged haircut styled up, his body at a healthy trim size, lean and fit. But the man who stood before her looked dialed down several notches, from the tired eyes to the slanted chunk of dirty hair that poked out from underneath his hood. "You his roommate?" he said, the *r* curled in a Puerto Rican accent.

"Yeah. I moved in two weeks ago. Met him like twice." Krista glanced behind her, her fingers flexing against the box cutter's handle. "Haven't seen him since this all began."

"Me neither."

"You his friend?" she asked him.

"Sometimes. Sometimes more. Sometimes less."

"Well, he's not here. I think," she said, adjusting her posture to appear taller, "you should probably go. We're holding things down here."

"Go? That's what I'm trying to do. The buses for the Staten Island quarantine are scheduled. Running hourly out of JFK. Who knows when the next quarantine block will be? Could be tomorrow, could be weeks."

"You can't get there now. The road's blocked. It's been chaos. This is what happens when a pandemic coincides with a stupid pop concert."

"No, you don't drive. You run there."

JFK Airport. That was six or seven miles across normally quiet neighborhoods, though the past week had been anything but quiet, including the fires at Ozone Park—the last area she'd heard riot reports from. "You can't run through there. You'll get killed."

"You can. If you know the way. I'm heading there now." The man pulled back his hood, his unkempt hair swishing in a bunch of directions, though it couldn't hide the bloody gash across his scalp. "I'm Alejandro."

"Krista."

"Look, I know Wai Lin was mad at me last week, but that shit doesn't matter anymore. I'm grabbing anyone on the way and getting to quarantine before *la monga* kills me. Or the people. They're worse." His shoes scuffed against the floor, toes kicking into the thin carpet. "You alone?"

The blade remained behind her, though trembles started to take over her arm. She couldn't actually use it, could she? "No."

"More roommates? Friends?"

"My boyfriend."

"Get him. Let's go. I'll show you how to get to the quarantine buses."

Krista knew how to read bullshitters. She'd seen them her whole life.

Alejandro was honest.

"I can't."

"He doesn't want to go to quarantine?"

"No. That's not it." She lowered her mask, its sweaty knot resting now against her neck.

"*La monga.* Sorry, 'the flu.' How long?"

"Fever hit two days ago."

Alejandro groaned, low at first before becoming loud enough to bounce across the small hallway, his head shaking the whole time. He looked up and locked eyes with her. "It's too late. You should come with me."

"What do you mean it's too late? They said stay in bed, stay hydrated. It's not necessarily fatal. Some people break out of it."

"Some. Not many. They're trying to stop panic. Like, people-killing-each-other-in-the-streets panic. You really believe it? You honestly think he has a chance?"

Krista closed her eyes, picturing Anthony's purple lips and pale skin, drained of color even by candlelight, the only sounds coming from the occasional blood-sputtering cough or unintelligible gibberish.

"Death toll's already at two billion worldwide. You won't hear that on the news, but it's true. Asia, Eastern Europe are decimated. I've heard rural China is basically gone. Like totally gone. Think about where you were two months ago when this was just a *thing* in the news. And now, look around. It's coming in waves and each wave is getting bigger. Look at how fast it's spread. Look at *him*." Alejandro pulled his phone out of his pocket, briefly illuminating the hallway with its clock before putting it away. "Quarantine. It's the only safe place to go. They say everyone is welcome but that can't be true. There's only so much space. Punch your ticket now."

Behind her, Mick's meow came through the door, followed by a quiet scratching sound. Alejandro didn't appear to hear it.

"Look, you don't have to trust me. I'm just offering you a way out. Stay with your boyfriend if you want. I'll get going."

The scratching intensified, a rhythmic push-and-slide against the door's thin wood. "How do you know that I don't have it?"

"You've been around your boyfriend for two days and you don't have a fever. You're good for now. Don't ask why, just say *gracias dios*. Because if you don't go to quarantine, you might get it later. I've seen it."

They stood in silence, the only noise coming from Mick's incessant door-scratching and a sudden screaming outside. Alejandro looked down the stairs, then at her, then back down. "All right. Good luck, Krista." He turned without hesitation and trotted down the stairs, his legs going from zero to sixty instantly.

"Wait."

Alejandro's silhouette stopped halfway down.

"Give me a minute."

"You saying goodbye?"

"No." Krista opened the door and picked up Mick in one motion, shoving him face-first into the cat carrier sitting in the corner of the room. She tossed a stack of wedding magazines off her backpack—not material for life with Anthony, but research for her job at a lifestyle web magazine—and unzipped the top pouch. She stuffed in an extra pair of jeans, some T-shirts, her phone charger, and a few bottles of water. She dumped kibble onto the floor in a rattle, shrinking the cat-food bag to about half-full, just enough so she could roll it up and force it into her backpack. She threw open a desk drawer and grabbed her wallet. Underneath sat a small pile of emergency cash, and as her fingers wrapped around the bills, she wondered if credit cards would work in quarantine.

Probably not.

Across the room, Anthony mumbled in his delirious sleep, nonsensical words coming out through his raspy throat.

She'd figured it was just a fling. But knowing this would be the last time she'd see him, that the *world* would see him, the very notion took hold of her, frightening her in a way that she hadn't felt in years. The urge to scream and cry battled to release, and she stood, hands shaking at her side, shoving it all downward as quickly and thoroughly as possible.

From the corner, Mick started to meow in his carrier. She closed the box cutter, put it in her back pocket, and grabbed the cat carrier's handle. Her other pocket buzzed, a reminder that the world's satellites still worked, and she took a moment to check.

A text.

From Jas.

The world is going to shit. I wanted to make sure you're not going down with it. Let me know you're OK. Things are better with Krista Deal running the show.

Her fingers had moved reflexively on the phone's screen, powered by the relief of knowing that Jas was still out there, still thinking of her. I'm here, she typed, going to quarantine. Make sure to bring some good music.

She hit Send on her phone, but a big red *X* kept flashing—no signal. She didn't know it then, but that would be the end of cell phone calling for some time, the infrastructure for commercial communication would also pause. In the moment, though, all she could do was resist the tears born out of frustration. Crying was weakness, vulnerability, giving the outside world—or her family—the upper hand.

But the feelings welled up. Not looking at Anthony. Not contemplating his mortality, or the fragile nature of the outside world. But Jas checking in with her when chaos was overtaking everything—that was enough to trigger something in her, even for a blink.

Krista closed her eyes, waiting for the moment to pass. Then she shoved the phone into her pocket, made sure Mick's carrier was locked, and headed down to meet Alejandro. That night, they ran, Alejandro leading her through roads and alleys filled with torched cars, smashed storefronts, and street brawls, all toward the quarantine buses, the black sky capping a glowing orange from the ravaged city skyline.

It had been the start of chaos.

Tonight's outbreak was more civil. The world seemed to be on much better behavior, at least from the view of the Donelly living room.

"They're just repeating the same thing now." Krista adjusted her weight, her left leg and her butt asleep from sitting on the floor. Nearly three hours had passed since they'd sat down together, Rob and Moira on the couch and Krista on the floor, knitting the bulky yarn she'd had in the car. Sunny came and went, heading upstairs to play before coming back down and finally crashing, her head in Krista's lap. Perhaps the rhythmic clinking of the knitting needles put her to sleep.

"West Coast states haven't made a statement yet. Maybe that's a good thing?" Rob said.

"Or the feds are withholding information. Trying to take back some level of authority. I bet all five political parties are in on it." Moira's governmental disdain came with surprising tangibility in tone, though when Krista looked at her, she just leaned back into the couch and stretched, face betraying nothing.

"The local Family Stability Board has set up emergency intervention hotlines in hopes of preventing any Greenwood-type incidents. And we've got breaking news," the TV anchor said. He'd been on the air for about two hours without commercials, in addition to however long he'd worked before they switched the TV on, and even the magic of lighting and makeup couldn't conceal the layer of sweat forming across his bald dome. "The Center for Disease Control is making a statement. Now let's send you to the CDC's Laurie Martinez."

The screen cut to a woman standing behind a podium, the sound of cameras clicking in the background. A muffled voice came over the TV, asking an incomprehensible question. "The appropriate response is to limit travel there," she said. "This new strain, which we've identified as MGS 96, works slower than the original virus." The woman frowned, then adjusted her microphone. "We've seen it in action, and the reason we believe travel lockdowns are appropriate is that the symptoms appear within 24 hours and can be easily identified, though death occurs in fifteen to twenty days, much longer than the 85 strand. If someone had it, they wouldn't be able to travel."

"Well, that's good news," Krista said.

Rob looked her way and huffed out a sigh. "This is no time for jokes."

"Who's joking? We know that none of us are infected because we're sitting here and not suffering from an impossible fever. Isn't that good to know?"

"She has you there," Moira said. Krista leaned over to nod at Moira, but she didn't even notice; she was too busy nudging Rob with her elbow.

"Is it true that federal agencies have known about a potential outbreak for months? Possibly years?" a reporter asked.

"I'm not at liberty to say."

"First Miami, now all over—"

"I can't confirm that they are all directly related."

"The Chicago Metro's website network was reporting a number of cases there before all traces of the articles were removed. Has the federal government assumed control of each regional Metronet?"

"I won't comment on rumors or speculation." A clamor of questions created a wall of voices, which finally stopped when the woman held up her hand. "I'm going to turn this over to my colleague on the phone. Dr. Dean Francis is one of our leading researchers and is working on a potential vaccine with an international team."

"Oh, Jesus," Krista said, jolting upward. "Not this asshole."

Both Rob and Moira straightened up. "Krista!" Rob motioned toward the sleeping Sunny in her lap as he shot off a disapproving groan.

"Sorry, sorry. That's my uncle. He's an ass—he's a jerk." Krista stared at the screen, as if she could reach through and slap Uncle Dean via electronic signal. Maybe she'd even probe him to see if her mom was alive. Purely for informational purposes.

"Jerk or not, he's working on a vaccine."

Uncle Dean's voice came over the TV, and the woman at the podium was quickly replaced by a stock photo of him. Even there, he seemed like an asshole. "We are working with medical teams all over the world. We're all sharing data as I speak. Internationally, governments—including ours—have granted us access to high-speed satellite networks for this. We're moving much faster than what you experience on your home computer."

Sunny stirred, possibly from Krista's movement a second ago. The little girl stretched, blinking away her sleep. "What's going on?"

"Sorry, Sunny. My uncle's on TV," she said, pointing to the screen.

"…and keep in mind, my staff in Seattle are some of the finest—"

"Oh, god, will he ever shut up? Turn it off, please."

"Krista, I really want to see this," Rob said.

Moira nodded in agreement, and both of them watched the biggest jerk in Krista's extended family, at least until a vibrating sound got their attention and Moira pulled out her phone. "Oh."

"What is it?"

"I'm…" Moira's mouth offered a pleasant smile, though her eyes offered something different, almost hesitation. "It's good news. I guess everything happening motivated Frank. He's agreed to the civil ceremony."

"Okay, then," Krista said. "That's in two days. There's not too much to these things. I mean, you don't even really need me unless you want me there."

"My dad is in town. With the travel lockdown, he might be around awhile. I could use the second set of eyes," Moira said in an almost deadpan tone.

So Moira would be getting the stability and new identity she wanted, and Rob should be happy for his coworker/kind-of friend. Really, Krista hadn't quite figured out *why* they were so chummy—but maybe they did a lot of corporate bonding exercises together. Yet instead of being celebratory or at least a mild high-five, they turned back to the TV, both looking like they smelled something terrible.

There was, though, the whole world-imploding business going on, but somehow Krista figured their reactions weren't quite about that.

"We'll talk tomorrow, then. After I help Sunny out with her school project." The knitting needles clinked again as Krista cast off the final row of her impromptu scarf. "Hey, look." She held up the short blue-and-green scarf she'd knit in one sitting. "I made it for you. You can wear it to our class presentation."

Sunny took it, her eyes still while examining the wool creation in her hands. "Pretty cool, huh?" Krista nudged.

"I like blue."

"Awesome. Well, there you—"

"But I don't like green," she said, putting it on the floor.

"Oh." The words came out with a frankness typical for seven-year-olds, but something about it stunned Krista. In fact, that short sentence seemed to carry more weight than all of the words coming out of the TV in that moment.

CHAPTER TWENTY-EIGHT

Moira

The soul of a city came from its din, and San Francisco was no different in a post-MGS world. Horns beeped, people talked, dogs barked. All of that, the whooshing of distant cars going onto freeway on-ramps or the squeak of brakes as they activated a little later than they should have, those were the heartbeat of a city. Even the areas left to decay outside of the urban farms and reconstruction zones had their own vibe.

Today was different. Despite the fact that the president, the CDC, and even Krista's uncle told everyone to do normal things, San Francisco doubled as a ghost town during Moira's morning: an empty bus ride into work, the lonely vibe of the office, even now during her walk to the support group. It wasn't a calm before a storm. The silence felt more oppressive, an invisible gag order, and even though Moira kept her ears open with each stride, barely anything broke the quiet, which made it all the easier to obsess over the thing she'd seen an hour ago.

Her father. On the local news, talking about how he felt he

was close to locating MoJo. Clips of him walking through City Hall, the urban farms, the Financial District. He must have worked with the broadcast team on a whole production, including clean concert footage that not even she'd seen.

Maybe the local channels wanted to drown out the fear from the death in the San Francisco Metro. Because details of it evaporated, and now only rumors pinpointed every possible variation of the victim's details, none of them in agreement.

Though the eerie quiet of the once-bustling city allowed her to stew on things buried deep beneath layers of lies and truths, it bubbled closer to the surface with each step, waiting to exhale at a support group.

Except rather than the usual shuffling of people toward the converted church, the building mirrored the rest of the city: still, quiet.

Lifeless.

Instead of a gathering of support, a single note was taped to the front door.

My friends, it has been my privilege to guide you through the pain of PASD. With the recent news, I have had to assess where I am and who I am. I have concluded that I am a free spirit and no virus can take me.

I have turned in my Residence License and packed my things. I will be driving somewhere, no destination. Perhaps a Reclaimed settlement or my own little patch of land. Don't worry, I'm not going to become a Fourth Path–style victim. Maybe I'll finally explore this country from coast to coast. Either way, if a new outbreak takes me, then it'll have been on my terms.

Stay healthy. And remember, everything will be fine. You have each other. I hope all of our paths cross again. —DF

Moira read and reread the last part, wondering where Del might go. Several years ago, she'd told Santiago that the Metros would be where the homes were. He laughed back then, simply replying with his crackpot Zen wisdom, something about "home is wherever you're alive."

She'd given him grief back then about his PhD in philosophy coupled with his farmer upbringing. But maybe there was more to his little sayings than mere quips.

"Moira," a familiar voice called out. She turned to see Rob coming her way. So he'd come in to work after all. Or maybe he skipped that part and came straight here. He nodded at the closed doors. "People don't want support on a day like today?"

"I think they're either hiding or running." Her fingernail tapped against the taped sheet of paper. "Del's gone. He left."

"What about you?"

"Me? Business as usual. I have a job to do. A civil ceremony to prepare for." *A long-lost father to evade.* "You?"

"Still waiting on the Family Stability Board. Maybe this—" he gestured to the buildings around them "—is getting in the way. You all right?"

"You saw?"

Rob nodded, mouth a solemn line. "It's on the Metronet. Directive from above. Put up anything that's *not* about the deaths or the pending travel lockdown. Sorry. I argued against MoJo posts."

Moira nodded, a reflex more than anything else. "I understand. It's okay, if it's not there, then it's on TV. But tomorrow it'll all be over. New identity. New name. New records. A final reset. If anyone asks, I have the records to prove I'm me. The new me."

Rob's face told two different stories. His mouth and cheeks were all comfort, smiling mouth and soft jaw. But his eyes, one glimpse and she couldn't meet them anymore. Something else lingered behind the irises, but it did her no good to think about it.

"Shall we walk?" Rob said after several seconds.

The lump in Moira's throat came out of nowhere, along with the stinging heat in her eyes. Her foot twisted in place, the heel of her shoe grinding against the worn city pavement, and her heart sank as she looked back at the closed doors. Wind kicked up, biting at her cheeks with its briskness. "Yeah," Moira said, "let's go for a walk."

She took a step forward, then stopped when she realized Rob was digging in his back pocket. He pulled out his phone and the color drained from his face.

"It's the Family Stability Board," he said.

CHAPTER TWENTY-NINE

Rob

One of the benefits of Rob's job was the ability to check his email on a high-speed connection.

Today, though, that was a curse.

Because if he was on a standard Metro network, he would have had another minute or two, the load time leaving him willfully ignorant before receiving the Family Stability Board's audit assessment. At PodStar, though, the text loaded up in a snap.

The call had been simply a recorded message, telling him that the full report would be available via email. He waited until he got back inside to load it up. Moira stood behind him as his breath shook on its way out, and a heavy weight pulled on his eyelids, the feeling of fight-or-flight in the face of the unthinkable suddenly draining all his energy. He forced himself to straighten up, focus, and reread the message.

Dear Rob Donelly,

Thank you for your participation in the Family Stability Board's social normalcy audit. Following the in-person discussion with

Bernard Langston, the FSB has determined that Sunny Donelly is at risk due to elements of PASD that have affected a number of issues, including:

- Her mother's status and whereabouts
- Violent behavior at school
- Difficulty processing the loss of friends to Reclaimed Territory
- Lack of support system

It is the decision of the board that in order to remain a San Francisco Metro resident, Sunny should be rehomed and supervised in the FSB dorms by Union Square. An appeal and extension may be filed up to 30 days following this notice. Any appeals must include significant testimonials from previously unheard sources. Quarterly hearings will assess the situation to determine if it is safe for the child to return to the parent's living situation.

We understand that this may be difficult to process. Our counselors are available around the clock to discuss the matter (note: counselors are only available for emotional support and cannot affect audit decisions).

Rob knew he had work tasks to accomplish, things to do to keep the Metronet updated and connected and stable. But none of that mattered right now. He sat, head in hands, unable to comprehend what he'd wrought by telling Sunny a lie five years ago. A lie that was supposed to protect her. A gentle weight landed on his shoulder in the form of Moira's hand, but he couldn't find any solace in the gesture.

Excerpt from "The Most Dangerous Gun Incidents Following MGS," *Counting Backward Magazine*:

Though the Metros offered a sense of stability, many found their biggest benefit to be infrastructure rather than security. That translated to a lucrative black market for guns. Technically outlawed in the Metros as part of the Populace Entry & Community Safety Agreement, dealers sold from caches miles outside of Metro borders—buried or booby-trapped or both. Despite the lack of firearms within Metro borders, occasional gun violence still found its way into communities. One of the most famous cases in the years after quarantine has become known as the Greenwood Incident. Since then, activists argue that the Greenwood Incident was preventable and gun smuggling requires greater oversight in a PASD world.

CHAPTER THIRTY

Krista

Krista had hoped that the announcement of deaths, travel lockdowns, and all the other stuff that triggered the wrong type of flashbacks in most of the population would at least mean a lot of sudden engagements. She was partially right.

Not that people needed her to run around and coordinate with a bunch of vendors and venues. But many people seemed to be taking the lead of Moira and Frank, and in a time when fewer people wanted to engage with *anyone* in the outside world, they asked Krista to go into the fray—or at least into City Hall to get paperwork and sign up for available times—on their behalf.

It wasn't much, but money would at least change hands. Once Krista finished dealing with elementary school kids. Sunny glanced up at her, big grin on her face but no blue-and-green scarf around her neck. Rob had originally been slotted in for this presentation, but Krista was apparently deemed cooler. So there was that, at least. Krista sat on a too-small stool, waiting for another adult to finish talking about her job as a manager on the urban farming initiative, when her phone buzzed again, displaying an unknown number. "When it rains," she said to herself, excusing herself to step into the hallway. "Atmosphere Special Events, this is Krista."

"Krista Deal?" a woman's voice asked.

"Speaking."

"Krista Deal of Rochester, New York, graduate of Hofstra University?"

Did outbreak anxiety amp up the amount of client vetting? Despite annoyance tickling at her sensibilities, Krista reminded herself to be cool, professional, someone that the woman would want to give a giant wad of cash to. "That's me. What can I do for you?" she said, grabbing a pen from her purse and removing the cap.

"Ms. Deal, my name is Anna Haden. I work for a company called Reunion Services. We specialize in reconnecting people."

Reunion Services. Was this a gig offer? Something about Moira?

Or worse—someone from *her* past?

Krista looked at the phone's big red End Call button, weighing whether she should just hit it now. "Is this a job offer?" she finally said.

"Not exactly. I've been hired by Jaswinder Deshpande to see if I could locate you. I'll be honest, there were conflicting reports that you were dead. But Mr. Deshpande insisted we get the truth."

Jas. Alive. Though the odds of him having made it this far *did* seem favorable, seeing that he was straight edge, vegan, ran marathons, could carry a tune and play four instruments, *and* rock a five o'clock shadow on his great jawline. Nostalgia flooded over Krista, and it took all her strength to push it back and stifle it into a one-syllable response. "Oh."

"He contacted me last night. With your business licenses, it wasn't that difficult to locate you once I figured out you weren't in New York State."

"Yeah, Jas could be sentimental."

"It seems to be how people are reacting. I'm booked all day."

Clearly Krista had picked the wrong time to disable notifications for her account. Reunions and marriage proposals. The news reports earlier talked about runs on canned goods and food dehydrators, so however people were getting together, the food wouldn't be very good. "How did he know I was in San Francisco?" Krista asked, buying time to sort out her thoughts.

"Educated guess. In his notes, he said your grandparents lived out here. He has a message for you but instructed me to ask your permission first. May I play it for you?"

Jas asking for permission; the thought of it brought a smile to her face, one that she consciously tried to avoid. Of course he'd ask for consent. If Jas ever quit being a doctor, he should take over Reunion Services and make that company policy. "Sure. Why not? He's just a guy I dated in college, so, you know, whatever. Couldn't hurt."

"All right. One second." The line crackled for a moment, then beeped before a low hiss came and went.

"Hello, Krista." Nearly nine years had passed since she'd walked away from Jas, yet the way he spoke with his crisp but blended accent, it rolled into her mind like it had never left. "If these hired stalkers actually find you, then you'll be hearing this. Otherwise, I suppose I could turn it into song lyrics, except I don't have a band right now. Can't find a drummer and being a doctor is kinda busy. In any case, I know you're careful about your space and boundaries, so don't worry, I'm not trying to cramp your style. I just wanted to know if you're still alive. That's it. That's all I want. And if you're wondering why I'd blow money on such a binary piece of information, well, it's simple. Given everything that happened this morning and the fact that we don't know what will happen to us surviving two billion or so folks, I thought about it and somehow, I find the idea of Krista Deal taking charge in a world gone mad a bit reassuring. I thought that, and then I thought you might want to know. By the way, *Walk Among Us* is still a better album than *London Calling.* I listened to both tonight back to back and I'm sure of it. Take care of yourself."

Krista listened to the whole message without blinking, her body as frozen as her eyes. "Ms. Deal? Are you still there?"

"Yeah," she said, her dry voice barely capable of pushing the word out.

"Can I confirm with Mr. Deshpande that we connected?"

"Yeah." She cleared her throat. "Yeah, that's fine."

"Do you want to leave him a message or contact information?"

The question bounced around her mind, answered by what-ifs and could-have-beens, but she forced it all away. Jas got what he wanted and that was that. "No. I really have to go."

"All right, I appreciate your time. I'll text you Mr. Deshpande's contact information if you—"

The phone beeped, cutting off the woman as Krista hit the End Call button. As she slipped back through the door into Sunny's classroom, her phone buzzed again, this time with the icon of a text message. True to her word, the Reunion Services woman sent what looked like Jas's phone number and email.

"Whatever," Krista said to herself, promptly hitting the Delete button before any bad ideas could creep into her mind. Ms. Eswara, the school's principal-turned-substitute-teacher, glanced at her, then nodded at Sunny, who'd already begun explaining Krista's job with semi-accuracy. Krista walked up and stood beside her, blinking any thoughts of Jas away.

"And after she plans weddings, she likes ice cream and a bath," Sunny finally said. Little titters sprinkled through the watching group, and Sunny turned to Krista, as if their reaction didn't make any sense to her.

"And if you have any aunts or uncles or big sisters or brothers that are getting married, I can help them out." Krista pulled a stack of business cards out and put them on Ms. Eswara's desk. "Just take one of those."

"All right, thank you, Sunny," Ms. Eswara said from her chair. "Class, do you have any questions for Krista?" A boy with disheveled red hair raised his hand. "Okay, David, go ahead."

"Does they always kiss at the end?"

"Most of the time. Except when one has cooties."

The class let out a collective "ewww," and Krista checked with Ms. Eswara to make sure her level of sarcasm hadn't destroyed their potential academic careers. A girl with big blond hair and bigger glasses raised her hand, and Krista pointed at her. "Do you help the brides pick their dresses?"

"If they ask me to. Sometimes they pick it with their friends and family." *If they're not all dead.*

"Will you help Sunny pick the dress?" the same girl asked.

"Well, I think Sunny's a little young to get married. Unless," Krista said, raising a knowing eyebrow at the class, "one of you likes her."

"Not for her. For her mom."

"Excuse me?" The playfulness disappeared from Krista's demeanor, and she couldn't figure out if this kid was being stupid, cruel, or both.

Ms. Eswara stood up and walked over next to Krista. "Thank you, Lark, that's enough."

Lark apparently didn't think so, as she continued on. "When her mom comes back. Aren't you helping Sunny plan the wedding?"

"Lark, that's—"

"No, wait," Krista said. She turned to Sunny, who stared straight at the floor. "When her mom comes back from where?"

"From treatment. When she gets better."

"Sunny, what is she talking about?"

Sunny looked up, her bottom lip sticking out in full pout mode. "It was supposed to be a surprise for Daddy. And now it's not, *no thanks to you*," she said, giving Lark a death stare probably reminiscent of when she'd hit her classmate a few weeks back.

Ms. Eswara clapped her hands, drawing the classroom's attention back to her while the dots created by all of the different statements from Rob and Sunny began to connect in Krista's mind. "Class, take out your notepads, I want you to write down what you want your wedding to look like, and we'll share with Krista, okay? Right, Krista?" she asked, but Krista had already started marching toward the door, phone in hand. "Krista?"

"Be right back. I need to call someone."

The teacher's footsteps hurried behind her, tracking her out into the hallway. She grabbed Krista's arm, shaking her off balance, then met her with a wide-eyed stare, before shaking her head. "Don't."

"How long did you know about this?"

"Last week. Mr. Donelly told the board at his audit."

"And you didn't say anything? I thought teachers were supposed to be *more* involved these days."

"The school has a government directive to monitor for any potential PASD-related issues impacting the children. This does..." Ms. Eswara peeked in on her class, then focused back on Krista. "The board has issued a directive to Mr. Donelly. But it's not my place to tell her the truth."

The brown of Ms. Eswara's eyes maintained their calm poise, followed by her entire demeanor. But poise in this case meant inaction, and inaction didn't help anyone. Countless adults had failed Krista during her childhood through inaction, and that was one family tradition she fully intended on breaking. "Screw it. I'm calling Rob."

"Please. Don't."

"Fine. Then I'll tell her myself."

A hand grabbed Krista's arm, the grip so authoritarian that

she got flashbacks from her own elementary school days. "If you tell her, it'll cause a whole new set of problems. It's up to the primary caregiver to do it."

Ms. Eswara's tone seemed so *clinical* that Krista was reminded of the failed counseling sessions of her teens. One quick look around the school, with cartoon characters emphasizing safety and security up and down the halls, re-aligned her compass to the realities of this world. "This isn't like the Tooth Fairy. I mean, this is…" There weren't too many times in Krista's adult life when she was at a loss for words, but in that moment, standing outside of a first-grade classroom with the teacher of a little girl she didn't even know several weeks ago, no clever words came to mind. "This is fucked up."

The hand let go and Ms. Eswara laughed, her black hair twisting as she shook her head. "I know we all deal with this new life a little differently. You'd be surprised. I've actually heard worse."

"And you've managed to not punch anyone?"

"Barely."

Krista nodded, though it didn't mean that she agreed with Ms. Eswara. In fact, a certainty screamed out from her gut; she *knew* the right thing to do, of course she did, and better than Sunny's father or teacher. Maybe not right this second—it could wait a few hours—but soon, soon she'd look out for Sunny the right way—the way no adult in Krista's life ever had. No words came out, though unlike earlier this silence was by choice.

Ms. Eswara motioned her to come back inside.

Krista nodded, though her thoughts were elsewhere.

Only forward. Never back. And definitely never paused.

CHAPTER THIRTY-ONE

Moira

Though she'd originally planned on a quiet evening with Frank, Rob's news gripped Moira's mind, coloring her every thought. He'd left the office early, offering a smile but defeat locked into the air around him. Moira told him that he could call, that he *should* call if he needed to.

In the meantime, she needed to run. But not like before. She moved comfortably on autopilot. Her feet met pavement, her breath steady, but all the while she suppressed the urge to sprint off and climb through the urban decay that lay beyond the border.

That instinct was probably going to linger for a while. After they'd moved into the UC Davis campus, Santiago would tell Moira that she was getting soft, that her parkour skills were getting rusty. He'd offered to help her practice with nearly an entire city at their disposal. Yet she'd constantly turned it down once the real world started crawling back over the horizon. And now she would have given anything to take a hard left down an alley full of obstacles, and push her body to its limit.

But she didn't, instead completing her route, a five-mile dash by the businesses and homes that had settled into an eerie quiet. Though she couldn't stay in the apartment with Frank another minute, she at least remained in character, the new version of herself, reinvented once again to finally strip away any lingering traces of her survivalist self. Frank had offered to go with her, thinking it was a training run like they usually did on the weekends. She shut the suggestion down quick, though. No need for the additional burden of masking her thoughts. Run, refresh, then reboot her life tomorrow.

That was the plan, anyway, until she stepped into a corner market and looked up at the small shop's TV. It wasn't President Hersh again, or anyone who announced world-ending news.

For her, it was worse.

"Friends, I am here to tell you that the search for MoJo is almost over." The woman running the drugstore checkout register looked up in midtransaction, halfway through a carbon copy swipe. The man in front of Moira nodded, his face taking a curious turn. The ten or fifteen people lingering around all went quiet and gravitated toward the hanging television in the corner. Moira adjusted her posture, fingers gripping a sports drink as she wiped sweat off her forehead, the mere sound of his voice draining blood from her face.

"I am humbled and overwhelmed by your support," her dad said. The label on the bottom of the screen noted that the shot was live, and judging by the dusk colors behind him, that was true. "I can't say for certain who has earned the reward just yet. There are several tips that we're still finalizing. But I am *so* thankful that I made it to San Francisco before the lockdown commenced. I look forward to seeing my beloved daughter again."

From her back pocket, Moira's phone buzzed. She pulled it out, hoping it was Rob. But it was a text message from Frank checking in.

How's your run? Everything okay out there?

She was late. Too much time with her own thoughts.

The register dinged and Moira moved up in line. She put the sports drink on the counter and handed over two quarters. "Keep the change," she said. The clerk nodded, and Moira stepped outside, taking a long drink before assessing the surrounding area.

Like in the store, San Francisco appeared calm. No sirens blaring in the background, no fires lighting up the night sky, no sounds of broken glass ravaging the evening.

Things were normal, at least on the surface.

Good, she typed, just stopping for a quick drink. Be home soon.

The message fired off, and Frank's reply came in seconds.

Great. See you soon. Love you.

Moira finished off the bottle and took one more look around. Should she call Rob? Text him? Show him some measure of support? But she decided against it; there was such a thing as being too involved. He knew he could call her; she'd told him as much.

She slid her phone back in her pocket. She stretched her hamstrings for several seconds, then began a light cooldown jog back to the apartment, wishing the path had rubble or hurdles or something else to vault over.

CHAPTER THIRTY-TWO

Rob

Daylight had just begun its transition to the purple hue of sunset, tinting Rob's vision as he looked out the front window. A rumble came from down the street, and Krista's sedan rolled up, pulling alongside the sidewalk.

The overwhelming petrification from several hours ago dissipated as reality set in, leaving an uncertain path ahead. The core truth of it all was that he had one month to figure out how to win an appeal.

One month. A lot could happen in one month. But at the same time, keeping it from Sunny didn't seem like the best idea.

Look where deception had got them in the first place.

Should he tell her now? Should he wait until after an appeal? Who would even *help* an appeal?

"Before I left? I'm not going anywhere," Krista said, her voice audible as she helped Sunny get out of the car.

"Oh. I thought you were going to see your uncle." Sunny's

softer voice still came through, then Rob had to interpret the muffled sounds into words.

"Uncle Dean? Um, he and I don't get along very well."

"I don't get it. I thought you said you were going to see him soon—"

"Okay, I see. No, Sunny, I'm staying right here in San Francisco. I just meant that he'd be on TV a lot." They walked up the driveway, and Rob debated opening the door to greet them.

"Oh," Sunny said. She stopped just short of the porch.

Krista knelt down next to her. "You sound disappointed."

"Well, if you were going to see your uncle, I was going to have you ask him something. But that's okay."

"I don't want to talk to him. But you're welcome to call. St. Vincent's Seattle is publicly listed." Rob detected a sarcasm that Sunny didn't seem to get, judging by her pursed lips.

"Hey," Rob said as he opened the door. Krista shot a tense look his way. They'd just been at the school; did Ms. Eswara tell her about the audit findings? "Sun, I have to talk with Krista about some grown-up stuff. Can you hang out in your room for a little bit?"

"I was gonna show Krista my bunny."

"You can show her after. Okay?" He looked over at Krista, whose expression hadn't shifted from its harsh angles and unblinking glare. "I'll get you when we're done." Sunny grunted a reluctant approval and Rob nodded toward the kitchen. "I heard from the Board," he said quietly while they walked together. He leaned against the counter and waited for the sound of Sunny's footsteps all the way upstairs, then everything came out.

During the entire explanation, Krista's face didn't change at all. Sympathy, empathy, horror, none of it arrived. Just a silent fury etched like stone, only her eyes moving while she tracked him.

"So I don't know what to do," he said.

"I know what you should do. Tell Sunny the goddamn truth. Right now."

"I'm debating whether to wait after the appeal process—"

"Not *that* truth. The truth about her mother. What the hell are you thinking?"

Krista's words punched him. She *knew*. What did Sunny tell her? When did she know? "Shhh, keep your voice down."

"That's right," Krista said, her voice lowering but keeping its sharp tone, "we wouldn't want her to accidentally learn that her mom is dead. Dead, Rob. Elena is dead. Five billion people died, and Elena was one of them. Get over—" She stopped, her body lurching as if it took all of her strength to not finish that sentence. "This is really, really bad."

Her words took breath after breath away from him. "I know I need to tell her. I've tried. I tried again right after we met you, actually. It's not exactly easy to explain."

"You're the adult. You're supposed to guide her through it. Not just pretend like it never happened. You know why she thinks weddings are cool? She wants to throw a secret wedding when Elena 'gets better.' Cute, huh? It'd be really cute if it were true. So, you'll crush her twice—first, when she realizes that, surprise, her mom is *dead*, and second, this wonderful thing that she's been constructing in her mind to greet her mom will be all for nothing. Instead, she gets a double whammy of crap." Her response came at an unflinching speed, one that was so flippant Rob wondered if Krista even knew what she said. "All I needed as a kid was an adult willing to see the truth. How could you do this to her?"

He put his palm up. "I appreciate your concern," he said, his voice filled with the tone of a hostage negotiator, "but you weren't there in quarantine. You didn't have to make the choice."

"I am so tired of selfish parents. I've seen it my whole life. Is there a single goddamn parent in the world who does the right thing?"

Rob heard her words, but told himself not to get into a sparring battle with Krista's own projected demons. *I got into fights at school all the time*, she'd said in the elevator. *Shitty family, stupid parents, the works. Look at me, I'm a perfectly well-adjusted adult.* "Krista. I'm not your parents. Don't lump me in the same category—"

"You don't know a *thing* about my family. But I've seen people like you. Hiding behind whatever because you can't make the right decision. Tell her. Tell her *now* before your bullshit causes any more collateral damage."

"What the *hell* do you know about this? You just met us a few weeks ago."

"And *you* paid me to hang out with your daughter. So who's more fucked up, huh? At least I can tell right from wrong."

"Jesus, Krista, is everything so black and white in your world? Look around us. Look what's happening—"

Rob stopped when he heard the floorboards squeak. He turned his head, Krista mirroring his actions, to find Sunny standing in the doorway.

"Daddy, I wanted some water."

"Good timing." Krista walked over and gave Sunny a pat. She stared straight at Rob, then nodded at Sunny. "Now," she mouthed to him, though he shook his head no.

"Sunny," Krista said, her voice suddenly filled with professional calm. "I really think you should tell your dad about the wedding you wanted to plan. It's pretty…intense."

Sunny's defiant expression altered to wide eyes and dropped jaw before reversing, then finally a bitter frown and flushed cheeks. "You were *supposed* to be on my side."

"Sunny, I am. But I'm an adult, and *I* know the right thing to do." She fired a glare up at Rob "You really should tell your dad about it. He needs to know."

"No, he doesn't! It's a surprise! It'll make him happy!" Sunny ended the final word of each sentence with a stomp.

"Sunny," Rob said, "be polite. Krista is our guest."

"No, she's not. She's a poop head."

The term *poop head* was probably meant to be the worst insult Sunny could possibly conjure up; Rob had heard it before and told her that wasn't a kind phrase. Krista reacted with a reflexive laugh, one that she stopped right away, but the damage was done. The redness spread from Sunny's cheeks, and her bottom lip jutted out. Her shoulders bobbed from deep breaths, and she didn't blink.

"I'm sorry, Sunny. I didn't mean to laugh. Can you forgive me?" Sunny shook her head no, then continued the death stares at both of them. "Okay, look. Sunny, there's something you should tell your dad. Rob, there's something you *need* to tell your daughter. Right? Clear the air. And…go!" Her fingers snapped. "Go!" she said, repeating the snap, but no one moved. "Oh, Jesus, Rob. Now's the time. No more mommy secrets."

"Krista, don't." He knew she was right. She was right about all of it, how everything stemmed from one decision years ago, something that rippled outward as lie upon lie tapped against the trajectory of their lives, ultimately changing its course one degree at a time.

She just had a *really* terrible bedside manner.

"If you have any ounce of caring in you for Sunny, you will stop right now and let me figure out what is happening," he said.

"The world is going to shit again. Do you want to enter another possible quarantine with this on your head?"

"This is not the time. How can you not see that? How many kids have you raised, Krista? Tell me that."

"One." The word came out louder than it needed to be, and Krista's tough exterior cracked, a vulnerability in her eyes betraying the fury on the rest of her face. "*Myself.* And I know what I needed back then. Someone to speak the goddamn truth. All these people, going to support groups and the Family Stability Board and all that trauma crap? It's bullshit. You *fight* for it.

You stop being weak and you fight for every damn inch until people stop bullshitting you."

"The world is not so simple. Sunny is not you. I'm not your parents. Stop projecting your own issues onto—"

"Stop it!" Sunny's scream carried a force stronger than either of the adults in the room. "Stop fighting *right now*. Grown-ups should know better!" Sunny marched upstairs, each step an exaggerated stomp causing a vibration to ripple through the hardwood floorboards. A lifetime of silence seemed to pass after Sunny slammed the door upstairs. Rob's lips turned inward and flattened into a colorless line.

"Sunny," Krista called, turning to pursue her.

"Don't. You can't talk to kids like this. They need time. Jesus, have some common sense."

"No, I'm doing this *now*."

The sheer stubbornness triggered something in Rob, the single grain that caused an internal implosion after weeks of the Family Stability Board, support groups, *fear* chipping away at it. And now this. "Stop." Rather than being a full-force attack, Rob's voice changed to an eerie low tone. "You need to leave."

Krista turned, flushed cheeks and flared brows. "Why, so you can fuck things up again?"

Any sense of calm evaporated. "Get out of this house, get out of our lives, and *stay away from Sunny*. You're not her parent."

"Fine. You're the one living in your fantasy world."

"Right, let me listen to the wedding planner on breaking devastating news to a seven-year-old. You're not always right. And you don't know everything." He aimed for the nerve. "You can't fix your own broken childhood, so you try to steal Sunny's?"

For just a flash, Krista's posture sank, her shoulders shivering, and she turned quickly when he noticed a welling of tears in her eyes. Then everything tensed up again, her words coming out at a quick clip, as if she wanted to say something for the sheer purpose of covering up whatever her truth might be.

"Forget it. I'm done. I don't need you guys. Thanks for the gig. Goodbye." Her heels clicked as she began marching to the front door. "You know what might have happened if your head wasn't so far up your ass? If you weren't so hung up on someone who's *dead*, you probably could have talked to Moira way before she met Frank, and maybe she'd be singing shitty songs to Sunny every night. Ever think of that?"

"Moira—"

"Stop." Krista threw her hand up. "Moira's getting married tomorrow. Something to consider when you think about why you won't take off your own wedding ring." She began to stomp out, nose in the air. The door swung open with a harsh brush of air, and she turned. Rob braced himself for one last parting show when something caused her to look up.

"Krista?"

The tiny voice stopped Krista cold, yanking her back. Sunny's anxious face stuck through the banister posts, and in a really strange way, one that Rob couldn't decipher, Krista's expression almost seemed *more* hurt. "I'm not getting involved," she finally said. "You don't need me. And I don't need you. It was a job."

Sunny called out her name again, but the words seemed to bounce off of her. "No. I am…not…getting…involved." Her eyes shut tight. "You understand? Both of you. Not involved. I don't care how many viruses are out there."

"But we're friends!" The words fell down the stairs and Krista shook her head, though Rob had no clue as to who that was meant for. Maybe she spoke to herself with that gesture.

"Get over it." Krista took quick, even steps out and slammed the door. Rob ran up to Sunny, and they stayed on the stairs for long minutes. That whole time, Rob didn't hear the sound of Krista's car.

Half an hour must have passed, maybe more, since the outburst. Sunny slouched off to bed by herself, insisting she wanted to be alone. Rob didn't purposefully avoid pushing further; he just didn't quite know what to say, either about Krista's behavior or her own secret wedding plan or the Family Stability Board or Elena. In fact, the one thing that made sense was *where* all of that had come from. Krista probably thought she was doing the right thing; she was only too stubborn—or damaged—to think otherwise, or even see that he'd agreed with her on telling Sunny, just not when.

That still didn't answer the question about what he'd say to her, though. His last attempt had been an ad-libbing disaster. How could a seven-year-old handle information like "Sorry, there is no hope that you'll ever see your mother again"? The thought unearthed a long-buried memory, a grudge that lasted several years and burned with the intensity of childhood over being told the truth about Santa.

This was going to be a little bit bigger than Santa.

Rob shut down that line of thinking fast before it could spiral out of control. In search of inspiration, or perhaps just nostalgic distraction, he sat at the computer in the kitchen nook, staring at the scanned images from his wedding album and remaining photos of Elena.

So many questions just waiting to be unleashed, the tenuous lid he'd kept on it now pressurizing in ways he could have never foreseen. If he told Sunny now, tonight, would that mean anything to the Family Stability Board? Could she ever forgive him for what he'd done? How long would it take for her to grasp the no-win scenario he'd been forced into?

Moira. Moira would know what to do. Of course she would; she was the only person whom he felt he could be truly honest with. And the whole escape-from-being-MoJo thing cut pretty close to the choices he'd had to make. He pulled his phone out of his pocket. She'd said he could call. But she was also getting married tomorrow morning. What kind of friend would he be, interrupting that?

No. He had to do this himself.

Rob stood up and began a slow, steady walk across the living room and up the stairs with nothing but a rough jumble of words primed up.

"Sunny? Sun, you awake?" Rob said, pushing the door open. The light from the hallway cast a triangular beam into the room, and his vision needed a moment to adjust to the dark.

"I can't sleep, Daddy."

"Rough night, huh?"

"I keep thinking."

"About what, Sun?" he said, the mattress bowing under his weight as he sat.

"Krista. She said 'no more Mommy secrets.' What did she mean by that?"

At the very least, Sunny was learning critical thinking skills. "Well, look. I need to talk with you about that."

"Mommy's mad at me, huh?"

"What? No, not at all. Why would you think that?"

The slit of hallway light caught Sunny's eyes, and from the irritated red in them he could see that she'd been crying. "Because she won't talk to me. She only talks to you. And now she's not coming, and Krista's mad at me. It's all my fault."

"No, no, no. Sunny, that's not it at all. There's something I need to tell you." Rob sucked in a deep breath, and he hoped that she didn't notice his pounding chest. "Krista's right. There's something you need to know. See, something happened a long time ago, something—" Before he could finish, the room filled with the sound of Sunny crying. He held his daughter, letting her sob into his chest as he considered his next move. At least he'd got the first part out.

"It's my fault. It's all my fault," she said through the choked sobs. "I made Mommy mad. I made you and Krista fight."

"No, Sunny. It's not your fault. It's not anyone's fault. Sometimes, things just happen. You know, maybe we should talk about this in the morning. Get some rest."

Sunny responded with a gradual slowing of her tears. Her voice remained quiet and strained. "Can I ask you something?"

"Sure, Sun."

"Is Krista's uncle treating Mommy?"

"Sun..." Rob's voice trailed off, unsure of what to say. Playing out any further complications wouldn't work, but her emotions deserved a break. "He's treating a lot of sick people."

"Maybe he'll let me talk to Mommy. If I could just talk to her, I know she wouldn't be mad at me anymore."

Years ago, Elena's friend Gail gave them one of those marriage survival guide books, the latest in modern pop-psychobabble. "Preventative measures," she'd said, probably referencing her own divorce at age twenty-four. Though many of the details eluded him now, he always remembered the nugget about how "don't go to bed angry" was bullshit since sleeping was how the brain processed and recharged, that going to bed angry was a good thing as long as you talked about it the next day.

He wanted to tell Sunny. He needed to tell her. But one good night of sleep might prevent it from going off the rails.

"Look, why don't we both get some rest? It's been such a long day. Try again in the morning," he said, though it could have been for himself as much as Sunny.

"Okay, Daddy. If you talk to Mommy, tell her I'm sorry I made her mad. And Krista too."

"No one's mad at you. I promise. Not me, not Krista, and definitely not Mommy." Rob leaned in and kissed her on the forehead, then adjusted the blankets, tucking them in around her shoulders. "Good night, Sun."

CHAPTER THIRTY-THREE

Sunny

Sunny's eyes were closed. But she couldn't sleep.

She'd tried counting, like Daddy suggested. Counting up while picturing monkeys walking by. Sometimes it helped. But not tonight.

She had been asleep, at least she thought. The clock said two twenty-one, which meant that…four plus two…six hours had passed until she felt this way. But then she had that dream about coming home to find Mommy napping on the couch, and she was about to wake her up, but then she woke up in real life.

Sunny had tried so hard to go back to sleep. But now her eyes opened. And everyone was still upset. She knew it.

Mommy wouldn't talk to her. Krista was yelling at Daddy. Daddy was yelling at Krista. And the man on the news made it sound like the *world* was upset. People wouldn't even be able to travel to different cities anymore.

What would make them all feel better?

Sunny's bare feet hit the floor. Usually, she only went to the bathroom at this time of night. But now she wandered down the stairs, careful to skip the sixth step down because it creaked, and got a glass of water. Even so, her elbow caught the corner of the nook desk, and the kitchen brightened as the computer monitor woke up.

Daddy must have been working. It was still on even though he always told her to save power and turn things off, and instead of work stuff, it showed pictures of Mommy. She sat in front of the screen, glass in hand.

There it was: a picture of Mommy, from behind, holding her as a baby. Walking down a path outdoors. Gray sky. Trees. Mommy's blond hair tied in a ponytail that hung over her coat's hood. Daddy had shown her this before. He said that they didn't have a lot of photos left, but this was one of his favorites.

She liked it too. She wished she looked at it more.

The longer she stared at the picture, the more questions came. She had to make them stop, so she clicked the other browser tab. It loaded to the main Metronet news and it showed Krista's uncle, the not-nice one who treated sick people.

Sick people like Mommy.

As Sunny stared at the words and pictures on the screen, a new idea formed in her head. How could she fix *everything*? She suddenly knew. And she didn't have much time to do it. Not with all the travel stuff in the news.

She checked the clock on the microwave.

Two forty-five in the morning.

She grinned, so much that her cheeks hurt.

This would make everyone so happy.

She typed Uncle Dean's name, then clicked Search and waited for the screen to load, results appearing line by line.

From the Online Encyclopedia page on MoJo:

Final Performance: On March 11, 2019, MoJo was scheduled to perform at Madison Square Garden in New York City in support of her second album Battle Cry. *The arena was by all accounts half-empty due to the media fervor over the previous week's outbreak. The order for transportation lockdown, stemming from the Center for Disease Control's findings on the MGS 85 virus, was made public in the middle of MoJo's second song. When the lights went up following the fourth song, a near-riot ensued as the attending crowd attempted to leave the building all at once. Staff encountered similar issues backstage.*

MoJo was never seen or heard from again.

CHAPTER THIRTY-FOUR

Krista

People had told Krista that they were fearful to go to City Hall themselves.

As she walked into the building, she reminded herself that "don't believe people" was still a general life guideline. The building was packed. Concerns about crowded places must have been outweighed by a desire to get hitched as soon as possible. Though after Krista took care of a handful of requests from yesterday's new clients, she was still stuck with the one that suddenly carried way more baggage.

She told herself to focus and put on her professional shell, a tight-lipped, straight-ahead stare that came with a steady walk and a polite nod to Frank, his parents, and his sister while they waited outside the county clerk's office, discussing the outbreak like it was no big deal. "Is Moira late?"

"I think she's in the ladies'," Frank's dad, Joe, said. "We've got time. They're delayed." Ever the gentleman, Joe probably got embarrassed saying that his future daughter-in-law used the bathroom. Frank's mom, Kelley, gave Krista a hug before she realized it, pulling her into her trim body.

"Oh, okay. Maybe I'll bump into her. I have to take a quick break too." She didn't, but better to run into Moira alone and resolve any lingering bullshit just in case Rob talked with her. She moved back into the main lobby, where crowds pushed their way around.

Focus. Do *not* think about Sunny or what she'd said to her last night. She had a job to do, after all.

Krista stopped at the top of the stairs, looking one more time at Frank's group. He might have been the only person in San Francisco, if not California and quite possibly the world, who had his entire immediate family survive. A snapshot showed smiles, laughter, his sister Leslie mock-boxing with him; it could have been a wholesome family from any pre-MGS year. They were a living time capsule, a miracle of smiles and life without the weight of trauma.

Krista wondered if that made them lucky or clueless. Maybe both.

She turned and bumped shoulders with Moira, causing Moira's bag to drop to the floor. She smoothed out the bottom of her midlength black dress, then stood at attention, as if Krista's collision didn't impact her at all. "Oh," she said. "Hello."

"Hey." *Did she know what happened with Rob and Sunny?* "You know, the past few days have been a bit strange. I'd like to just forget it. Forget all of it, really. I'm a professional, and I want today to be smooth for you. That's what you're paying me for." There. Simple, to the point, and not offensive in any way.

"Right. I wanted to say the same thing." The paper shopping bag on the floor crinkled as Moira picked it up by the handles. "I do think you're being a bit hard on Rob."

She *did* know. "You talked?"

"Texted. Late last night."

Did she initiate or vice versa? "I don't want to discuss this right now—"

"You're right, you're right. I'm sorry, I just… I have a lot of empathy for Rob. And Sunny."

"It's his life. He has to make these decisions. Not us. I'm not getting involved. I have more important things to do." Judging by the look on Moira's face, the words sounded convincing enough. Which was good, since Krista spent most of the previous evening telling herself that she really believed such a thing, that letting herself get even remotely attached to Sunny was a ridiculous idea in the first place.

Basically, get over it.

She repeated the advice to herself and turned before Moira could detect anything.

"Like this?" Moira's words lacked any of the typical bride enthusiasm found on wedding days. In fact, they landed somewhere between apathetic, disappointed, and annoyed, as if her mind was elsewhere.

Krista assumed the professional pose she'd carried with her to City Hall. "Like this," she said, as calm and straight as possible. The two women stood there, side by side, tucked away in the small hallway off the main staircase, and Krista glanced back at Frank's family. They smiled and laughed, joking and chatting like Krista and Moira could never return and they wouldn't notice. "They're so normal after everything that's happened. I mean, look at that. Mom, dad, sister, laughing and wearing sweaters. How is that even possible?"

Moira stepped forward and stared at her fiancé's family, not with adoration but with lips twisted slightly downward. "It's something, isn't it?" She gestured out at Frank's family, the bag in her hand caught in a light sway. The crack in the top revealed Moira's wedding shoes—a pair of white running shoes based on the couple's mutual love of running.

If Frank only knew.

"Families can sure be annoying, huh?"

"They're not. They're genuine and happy. And lucky. Almost to a fault. Not a trace of PASD."

"And apparently they're not that curious about your past either."

Moira's face fell to neutral. "No one pushes the topic. I've got the pandemic excuse. They're polite. Normal. The universe delivered them here unscathed. Who wouldn't want that?"

Krista studied Moira as she talked about Frank's family. Krista had been with countless couples by now, a few genuinely in love, some in lust, and most trying to desperately fill a void. But none of them had Moira's dispassionate attitude. "Everyone's got an itch to scratch, huh?"

"Isn't that why you care about Sunny?"

The question hit hard and low, and she refused to look at Moira, instead turning straight ahead out the hallway. She smoothed out her skirt and adjusted the purse on her shoulder. "They're waiting for us. I like your dress. And you brought your wedding shoes."

"Thought it'd be appropriate to wear. If this outbreak gets worse, we may not get our big ceremony. Just imagine the—" Moira stopped, and Krista tried tracing her gaze upward at the TV screen.

Evan Hatfield had been unavoidable on media, as much as Uncle Dean but for different reasons. But this wasn't a replay from the other day. This was him giving some sort of press conference in front of City Hall, the word *LIVE* plastered across the top and *Hatfield announces MoJo reward is imminent.*

Though the sound was off, the broadcast's captions scrolled across the bottom while he spoke. *My daughter is here, in the San Francisco Metro. By tonight, I will hand out the reward.*

"It can't be," Moira said. Her fingers grasped the handrail, the knuckles leaking their color away. "Did you turn me in?"

The question seemed to come more out of panic than suspicion.

"What? No, of course not." Though if this was going to happen anyway, Krista had the thought that she should have. The money would have helped.

"I can't deal with that now," Moira said, tugging on Krista's arm. "Let's get this over with."

Between singing songs for Sunny and requesting an immediate civil ceremony, Krista had stopped trying to figure Moira out. She sighed and followed her back down to the lobby.

"The line hasn't moved," Joe said, as they returned. Moira set her bag down and sat on the lobby's small bench next to Frank. Krista watched her client's expression remain as a controlled pleasantness, not too high or low. Krista kept craning her neck, scanning the people coming and going, though the masses appeared to only be seeking something from the local government, be it answers or marriage licenses. "They told me we could be delayed an hour, maybe two," Krista said. "Maybe they're figuring out how the state can afford all these newlywed tax credits."

"So much for our first-thing appointment. You all right?" Frank asked Moira.

She gave a silent nod, then a half yawn. "I'm just tired. That's all," she said, curling into Frank's arms. But for a flash, there was that look again: eyes wide and darting, as if she scanned the immediate surroundings.

"I've gone to a few civil ceremonies," Krista said, "and it's usually fast. You're in there five, maybe ten minutes. Something else is holding up—" The phone in Krista's hand came to life, its bright screen reflecting light around them. She read the caller ID aloud. "Rob."

"Rob?" Moira looked up.

"I'm not answering that."

"My coworker," Moira said to the puzzled looks surrounding her. "His daughter, she came over that one time. Sunny."

"Oh." Frank's head bobbed up and down politely.

The phone stopped buzzing, but right when Krista opened her mouth, it sprang back to life. "Jesus, Rob," she said to the screen ID. "Hang on, I'm going to get this really quick."

Krista stepped a few feet away. "Rob, I told you I'm out of your lives now. And in case you forgot, we're in the middle of something here."

"Krista. Krista, Sunny is missing." Rob's voice broke, his words clipped by an urgency that rammed individual words together into a mash of sounds without breath. "Her backpack is gone, she's gone."

CHAPTER THIRTY-FIVE

Rob

Rob had woken up at six thirty and filled the downstairs with the aroma of fresh-brewed coffee. Normally, his first task of the day would be to wake Sunny so she could prepare for school, but he decided to let her sleep in today. She hardly ever enjoyed that luxury, and besides, he'd already left a message at the school, calling in sick for her after a few minutes of negotiating busy signals. On most days, that'd pique his curiosity; today, he had bigger things to worry about.

He sat at the kitchen table with coffee cup and pen, crafting notes that would make some *sense* of the whole Elena situation. By seven o'clock, the front side of the sheet had filled up with stops and starts, sentences and words jammed together then struck through, little notes veering off left and right but nowhere near the right direction.

"It's no good," he said to himself. He'd tried to tell her gently twice now, but that twisted into something else. Only clear specifics would probably work now, and nothing seemed like the appropriate start for that, not jumping straight in or working into it, and certainly not opening with a joke. All of this had to fit into the vocabulary of a child, and maybe that was the right beginning.

"What would you want me to say?" he asked an invisible Elena.

He stared at the blank back side of the sheet, then sipped coffee, a police siren zooming in and out of range in the background. *I have to talk with you about something*, he wrote. *Sometimes, grown-ups have difficult decisions to make and not much time to make them. Then when they do, they realize later that it was the wrong one.*

The other attempts had prompted immediate reactions, laughter or groans for even trying. This one, though, somehow agreed. He crafted the sentences, considering the impact each word choice would have on Sunny's short- and long-term psyche.

After filling up an entire sheet, he thought it formed some semblance of what he wanted to say. Truth? Check. Apology? Check. Justification? Check. He held the paper firm, as if that would inject some confidence into the words, then read out loud. "Your mom was injured on a very bad night years ago." Though Rob read the words out loud to prepare for speaking them to Sunny, everything seemed outside himself, a disembodied voice talking to him rather than his own reading it. "I told you that she went to the hospital, and she did, but I wasn't honest about what happened. The truth is that she died in the hospital a few days later."

He stopped at that sentence, staring at the dried ink on the paper. He looked down to see what that strange rattling noise was, until he realized it was the pen jabbing the table in an uncontrollable tremor. The pen dropped, and he forced his fingers wide, placing them flat on the table before starting again. "I've led you to believe something else this whole time, that she was alive and getting treatment, that her return would only be a matter of time. But the truth is that she's never coming home. It's not your fault, and I'm very sorry I lied to you. If you want to know why I did it, it's because I love you, and I loved your mother, and I didn't want you to feel the pain of her loss. You may not understand it now, but I hope someday you will, and we can talk about it again when you're ready. I'm very sorry you'll never get to know her." The last few words stumbled out, followed by silence, the only sounds coming from passing cars. Rob propped his elbows on the table and began rubbing his cheeks, only stopping when his palms completely obscured his vision.

He sat petrified for a while, and the sounds from outside—voices, cars driving by, the occasional horn honk—all drifted into another space and time, registering but quickly disappearing.

The real world returned as Rob looked over at the clock. Somehow, it had gotten to be eight thirty-two. Even with sleeping in, this was a little late for Sunny; he folded the sheet into a neat creased square and slipped it into the pocket of the jacket hanging on the chair, then began a slow walk up the stairs to wake his daughter.

At the top of the stairs he gave himself a moment, studying Sunny's closed door. She might hate him forever after this, or she could just start her rebellious teen phase years early. Or maybe she might understand. Sunny didn't have the cognition of an adult, but she had the empathy of fifty, so maybe that balanced out.

"Hey, Sunny?" he said as he opened the door. "It's time to get up." She didn't rouse from her bed, instead staying burrowed beneath the comforters, head tucked under. "Sun, you gotta get up. I need to talk with you about last night. Sunny?"

Rob stopped, his hand touching the top sheet and comforter; it pushed all the way to the mattress, a stuffed penguin squirting out the side and falling to the floor. Panic gripped his body, striking everything from his toes to the top of his head with pins and needles. He threw back the sheet with a *whoosh*, and instead of Sunny he found half of her stuffed animals jammed together in a row. "Sunny?" he called out in a half yell. He stormed out, then checked the bathroom. "Sunny? Come on, kiddo, we don't have time for games."

The stairs sounded like drums as he rattled down them, and each time he called out her name, the frantic energy in his tone dialed up. "Sunny?" he fired out into their small backyard in a full-on yell. "Sunny, where are you?"

Rob sprinted back upstairs, then surveyed her room. Her shoes were gone, as was her backpack, and the scarf Krista had knitted for her was no longer draped over the side table. He opened the top drawer on her desk, and her kid-sized wallet was missing too. A half-folded sheet with a picture of City Hall sat next to the scattered toys on her desk; he picked it up and realized what it was.

Shit, shit, shit. Rob ran back down, then stood in the center of the living room. "Sunny?" he yelled out. "If you're here, come out. I'm not mad at you. I just need you to come out right now. Please."

A ten count gave way to a twenty count, then a full minute with no response, and Rob's shouts for his daughter soon degenerated into a nonstop roll of curse words he'd never want her to hear. He grabbed his phone and struggled to hit the nine and the one button twice, creating a gibberish set several times over until he got it right. "Busy? How the hell is nine-one-one busy?"

Rob turned on the TV, then put on the morning news in case anything came up about a missing child on the ticker. His hands continued to rattle, and pulling Krista's name out of his contact list became an exercise in slow, controlled movements. Just as he was about to dial, he looked up at the TV and paused.

"...confirming outbreak of what scientists termed MGS 96 has spread from Baltimore to Philadelphia and parts of Delaware despite the best efforts for a local quarantine. Multiple deaths have also been reported in Los Angeles. That news is breaking as of thirty minutes ago." The blonde woman reading the news didn't manage to keep her steady tone, and a little crack found its way into her trained reporter's voice. "Local governments have accelerated the lockdown schedule announced two days ago. Transportation lockdowns in all major government-support Metropolitan zones west of the Mississippi start tomorrow morning at seven a.m. The East Coast is already in full lockdown mode with a combination of CDC checkups and quarantine areas set up. President Hersh refuses to comment on the possibility of a full quarantine like the one that happened six years ago..."

The woman's voice went into a rattle of East Coast cities, and Rob shook his head, bringing him back into the moment. He'd done everything to fight the Family Stability Board, and now it was his own lie that lost Sunny.

His finger slammed the Send button, and the phone rang for Krista with no answer. "Goddamn it, Krista," he said, trying one more time.

"Rob," she said after the third ring, "I told you I'm out of your lives now. And in case you forgot, we're in the middle of something here."

"Krista. Krista, Sunny is missing. Her backpack is gone, she's gone."

A loud rattling sound slammed through the phone, followed by some shuffling, and finally Krista's voice again. "What happened? Sunny's just...gone?"

"Just gone. Have you seen the news? The outbreak has spread. There's all sorts of transportation lockdown plans happening way faster. I have to find Sunny before that kicks in. She had the civil ceremony brochure on her desk. Maybe she's on her way down there. You haven't seen her?"

"No. No, I haven't, but I hope it's that simple. She was really into the whole wedding thing."

"You're at City Hall right now, right?" He placed the building in relation to his house. "That's not that far. She could have walked there. I'm heading over. Okay? Go down to the lobby and tell security to look for a little girl."

"Got it." The line clicked off, and Rob tried nine-one-one again, only to reach the same busy signal. *San Francisco police. Find their direct number.* Rob's footsteps echoed off the hardwood floor as he ran to the desktop computer. The screen awoke, greeting him with the national hospital directory, one of the few items nationally mirrored on the high-speed Vital Information Server Network. Rob clicked through the page history, lists of different doctors and hospitals loading at pre-MGS broadband speeds, then stopped when he saw one familiar name: Dr. Dean Francis of St. Vincent General Hospital in Seattle. Krista's uncle. Sunny had asked about him last night, thinking he somehow had the key to speaking with Elena. How did he factor into all this?

Rob jolted out of midthought and told himself to just go. He grabbed a sheet of paper and scribbled a note down in case she came home, then taped it to the front door before running up the stairs to change his clothes.

Back in high school, Rob ran cross-country during his sophomore and junior years. That seemed like a lifetime ago, and any conditioning he'd had long since faded thanks to things like pandemics and parenting. He still pushed, reminding himself of the rhythm of it, especially when he tried not to trip while scouring the sidewalks for any hint that Sunny had been that way. The streets had devolved into bumper-to-bumper anger, random swearing mixing with horns, and the occasional person standing on a hood. As Rob hit the corner to turn onto Polk Street, he stopped at the small Asian market, its doors held open by boxes of vegetables, though shelves meant for beef jerky and dried fruit appeared mostly empty. The owner leaned over the counter, pointing to the TV screen and its images of international reaction, from riots in the Atlanta epicenter to mask-wearing Hong Kong citizens shuffling into prefabricated quarantine areas. "World going to shit again," the man said, pushing his glasses up.

"Have you seen a little girl? Seven years old, dark hair."

"She wear backpack and scarf?"

"Yes. Yes, that's her—a pink and black backpack with a scarf."

"She come by around five this morning. Bought two bananas. Paid cash. Took a bus schedule."

The urge to both punch and hug the man overtook Rob, but he did neither. Instead, he reminded himself to stay focused instead of screaming at the man for not calling the police. Could she interpret the Muni schedule? And where the hell did she get cash? "Do you know which direction she went?"

The man shook his head no, leaving Rob with little other than the fact that Sunny would get her daily potassium and she had cash. He began his sprint to City Hall, dodging the occasional person; despite the endless traffic jamming up one of San Francisco's biggest streets, the sidewalks were strangely clear.

CHAPTER THIRTY-SIX

Moira

As soon as the phone had left Krista's ear, the words escaped Moira's mouth. "What is it?"

"Sunny. She's missing." Krista said the statement aloud, and it took several seconds for Moira to process what it actually meant. Just minutes ago, she'd told herself to focus. This morning. The finish line. A new identity.

A hard wall of separation between herself and all her past lives.

And now, it all seemed so insignificant.

Moira's eyes widened. "No."

"She might be on her way here. I'm going down to the lobby." Krista stomped her way past the rows of people waiting for the county clerk, skimming by Frank's family and their dumbfounded stares.

Moira met their eyes, reading the confusion on their faces. "I'm gonna help look for her." It was the simplest thing to say. Something that explained the situation without any of how it all connected together. "Krista, I'll go with you," she said, her heels clicking with a light jog.

"Oh, and the outbreak's spread. There's some news about accelerating the lockdown," Krista said to Frank's family, causing them to start an incoherent blend of conversations amongst all of them. "I don't know the details, but you'll probably have to decide what to do."

Joe grabbed his son by the shoulder. "We have to find out what's going on."

"Moira, wait—" Frank reached after her.

Moira stopped as Krista held the door open to leave the county clerk's area, the same place that not that long ago had seemed like the answer to all her fears. "Frank, I have to help. She's only seven. Stay here in case she comes up." He nodded, as she expected. But before he could ask anything further, she took that moment and rushed off with Krista. "Where might she have gone?"

"She knows the civil ceremony is here. And she wanted to learn about weddings because of the whole crazy thing about Elena. So I'm guessing she'd look for us."

"And if she doesn't?"

"I'll look upstairs. Go meet Rob in the lobby, and take a look outside if you can." Moira grunted an affirmative, and for just a moment the two women stood back, the scene unfolding in front of them. News of the lockdown must have spread; rather than everyone jamming in and milling about, the main lobby saw streams of pushing and shoving. Moira stood poised, in case she even saw a *hint* of Sunny in the building, her legs coiled and ready.

"I don't get it," Krista said. "Why do you care so much? Your fiancé is over there, and there's been an outbreak."

"Frank's family is… Maybe they're just the lucky ones. Or maybe they're the people most in denial. I still haven't figured that out yet." Were they panicking about the travel lockdown?

Did they understand what might happen again? Or was it impossible for them to truly grasp the choices that could come from a world on the brink again? "But I do know that Rob and Sunny deserve to be happy. They've suffered a lot."

"So have a lot of people."

"Doesn't mean they don't deserve to be happy." Moira shot a look over her shoulder. "It's not an eye-for-an-eye world. I don't know if it ever was, but it certainly isn't now." She nodded, but the gesture wasn't directed at her wedding planner. "I'll be back soon."

She moved swiftly despite her heels, eyes scanning for the easiest path all the way through to the front exit. At the double doors, an older couple passed by, looking her way and making some comment about how the crazies had already come out.

Daylight flooded the hallway as Moira gripped the door's metal handle and pulled, only to see Rob leaping up several steps at a time. His toe caught on the top one, causing him to tumble to the ground. His hands pushed down on the cold pavement and he looked around, clearly dazed. "Rob!" Moira shouted.

"Did you find her?" he asked, pulling himself up.

"No. Krista's looking upstairs." Her mind activated, as if she was back in a dilapidated apartment floor, just her and Santiago with bags of supplies, eyes and ears poised to scan for movements or risks. But back then, she entered Code Polka Dot to survive. Now she funneled all her senses into detecting any sign of Sunny's familiar black hair. "I don't see her."

Moira finally noticed the sweat pouring down his face; he must have run here, and his body clearly didn't agree with his heart or mind at this point. "Krista!" Moira called out, waving her over. Krista came from the main staircase, lips pursed and head shaking.

"Any luck?" Krista asked. "There's nothing up there. All the offices are locked. I even knocked just in case."

"No," Rob said through heavy breaths. "There was a market owner. Back that way, he saw her. Backpack and scarf. It had to be her."

Moira caught an uncharacteristic softening of Krista's features at the mention of Sunny's scarf.

"Around five this morning," Rob continued. "She grabbed a bus schedule."

"Bus schedule," Moira said. "That's not good."

"But buses can't go anywhere in this gridlock." Rob stood up straight, then pulled his legs into a stretch. "We can call the Muni office—"

"Two problems," Krista interjected. "The streets weren't jammed at five, and people are freaking out now. How many Muni workers are still actually working?"

Krista's logic sank in, and the trio stood, tension tightening the space between them. Rob leaned back into the wall, his eyes loaded with emotions that no curse words could possibly capture. "I gotta think," he said. "I gotta think."

"Moira!" The clip-clop of footsteps came out from down the hall, and they looked over in unison to see Frank and his family in tow. Joe and Kelley marched, and Leslie, arm swinging the bag that contained Moira's ceremony shoes. "No children showed up. There's no sign of her," Frank said. "They're telling us to go home. Get indoors, away from public places."

"Are you the girl's father?" Kelley asked Rob.

"Yes. Sunny is my daughter."

"I'm very sorry, but we all need to get somewhere that's not public right now. The CDC has advised everyone to stay inside and avoid travel unless absolutely necessary to get home. They've put all types of limitations on—"

"Travel!" Rob's voice pushed past Frank's mom's words, catching everyone's attention. "Travel—she got a bus schedule at the market, but she wouldn't need that to get here."

"Would she try to go anywhere else?" Moira said, ignoring

her fiancé and his family. "Any hint about where she wanted to go?"

"Krista's uncle." The words could barely come out from Rob. His brow crinkled, as if dots connected with every passing second. "Your uncle. She looked him up."

"Oh, no, no, no." Krista bit down on her lip before beginning to pace back and forth. "Not him. Anyone but him. She asked about him, what he does. If I was going to see him." Her eyes flared as she turned to Rob. "She probably thinks Dean can cure Elena. That's what her whole wedding idea is about."

"You're getting married?" Frank's dad asked.

"No. My wife…my wife is dead."

"Right, his wife is dead, and he lied to his daughter about it. Goddamn it, Rob, see what you've done—"

"Krista, *not now.* I think she's gone one step further. I tried telling her the truth last night, and she got it all mixed up."

"Why weren't you just clear to her? 'Sunny, your mom is dead. *Dead.* No cure. Let's move on.'"

"No, no, no. Do you think that works on kids?" Rob adjusted, still stretching his thighs. "And why the hell would you tell her about your uncle?"

"Because she *asked.* And I didn't want to be yet another adult lying to her about everything." Krista moved directly in Rob's way, her arms crossed, though they might as well have been loaded for punching. "She's had enough of—"

"*Stop!*" Moira's yell rattled the entire lobby, catching the attention of just about everyone. "We can blame later." Moira flashed a cool expression first at Rob, then at Krista. "We're losing time." She tapped her forehead, as if it would speed up the already pounding connections in her mind. "Okay, we have to cover our bases. Best-case scenario, she's calling the hospital from somewhere in the city. Worst case…" She took a deep breath and tried not to imagine the possibilities. "Worst case, she's got a bus schedule, and she's trying to actually go see him up in Seattle. And if that's true, we have to find out before the transportation lockdown goes into effect."

"Muni doesn't go to Seattle. She'd need something else." Krista pointed behind them. "There's a bus station downtown, about two miles east."

"I know that one. It's by our office. Well," Moira said, "if she made it there, there's no way she'd be able to buy a bus ticket. Maybe they'd just hold her?"

"She has cash." Rob's palms came up with a defeated shake of the head. "I don't know where she got it or how much it is, but she has some. She bought bananas at the corner market."

"Oh, *fuck*." Everyone, from Frank's silent family to the other frantic adults standing by, looked at Krista. "I gave her cash."

"*What?*"

"I gave her cash in case of emergency. Forty dollars."

Rob's eyes went wide. "Why would you give a child that?"

"I was teaching her to be prepared. In case of another outbreak, which you promised her would never happen, but see the mess we're—"

"Blame later." Moira grabbed Rob by the hand. "We'll never make it by car in this traffic. It's two miles—thirty minutes if we walk, much less if we run. Can you run?"

Rob bounced from side to side, his movement a little looser than a few minutes ago. "I don't know if I can, but I'm going to."

Krista glanced down at her phone, her mouth forming a thin straight line. "Okay, you two go. I'm going to try to get through to Muni security in case they've seen her. And," she said, giving a slow blink, like her thoughts stuttered as they formed, "I'll call Uncle Dean. I'll try his hospital to see if she's called there."

"Thank you," Rob said, his volume pulled down by his solemn tone. "I appreciate it."

"Right," Moira said, her British accent slipping out, as it did occasionally under duress. She caught it and self-corrected. "If I'm going to run, I'm going to need these." She reached into the bag held by Frank's sister and pulled out the pair of white running shoes. "Might as well break them in now." Her heels landed on the floor a few feet away, and she started lacing up.

A small smile cut through Krista's flat look. "I knew there was a reason you wanted those."

"Wait, Moira, what are you doing?" Frank walked over and put his arm around his fiancée as she stood up from tying her shoes. "The CDC is telling us to stay inside. Our whole family is here—"

"They're a family too."

"But they're not *your* family."

"There's no time for this right now. But you have to understand, I'm more like them than anyone knows." She gave the laces one hard tug before looking at Rob. "I think we're all family these days."

Excerpt from Police Report #4ADSIRE:

Records show that Freda Greenwood acquired the pistol two weeks before the incident. During that time, neighbors reported Thomas discussing an impending move to Reclaimed Territory while Kay was seen spending more time at the local church. Freda's intent, as detailed in email and phone records, was to travel east after being recruited into the Rocks looter gang following Thomas's announcement that the entire family was moving to the San Luis Obispo Reclaimed commune. On the morning of the fourth, Thomas discovered the weapon and tried to confront Freda about her plan. The pistol discharged during a struggle, shooting Freda in the forehead just as Kay returned home. In distress, Thomas barricaded himself in the bathroom while Kay remained with the body of her daughter. Kay called her local pastor, and while on the phone with him, Thomas turned the gun on himself (timing of gunshot audio confirmed by pastor). Cit-pats arrived first to find Thomas's body still locked inside the bathroom door while Kay sat by herself on the kitchen floor. After her release from questioning, she left the San Francisco Metro. Her last known words were "There has to be another path."

CHAPTER THIRTY-SEVEN

Rob

"Can you keep up?" Moira's voice rose over the chaos, reaching Rob half a block back.

"Yep," he yelled in return, but the truth was that adrenaline had only carried him so far. What about those stories of mothers lifting cars to save their babies? That wasn't happening, maybe because he'd actually *considered* that adrenaline would restore his high school shape, he'd jinxed the whole damn thing.

Moira stopped at the crosswalk, but there really wasn't any need—cars inched along, if they moved at all. The cool San Francisco air didn't do anything to keep him from sweat-soaking his undershirt, and when he caught up, he bent over at the waist, hands on knees and pockets of air fighting into his lungs. "You all right?" she asked him.

"I call bullshit on the whole emergency adrenaline thing. I feel terrible."

"We have three blocks to go. Can you make it?"

"Just go ahead. I'll catch up."

"Okay. I'll meet you in front of the bus station. I'll peek inside and come back out. Otherwise, we might get lost in the mob." And just like that, Moira spun and floated off, deftly swerving around the few people lingering on the street.

Sunny. Push forward. Find Sunny. He took a few more deep breaths and stretched out his aching quads as he checked left and right; the main street offered complete gridlock, but the side streets showed signs of relief. *Just go,* he told himself, and his legs started moving again, the muscle burn reminding him with every step that he wasn't seventeen anymore. Rob couldn't even remember the last time he'd actually exercised; the quarantine softball league and driveway soccer with Sunny didn't count. When he looked up, the bus station now seemed *farther* away.

Moira returned when he still had a block to go. "It's packed. We'll have to push our way through."

Rob forced himself to sprint past the cross-traffic of random people, finally arriving at the bus station's front entrance. As he opened the door, a blast of noise nearly knocked him over. "Holy shit," he said to Moira. Even the air was thick from the dense crowd.

"Maybe a ticket agent knows. They'd have to remember a little girl buying a ticket."

Rob flashed a thumbs-up and began to slither his way through the labyrinth of men and women, a stew of body type, race, and height. The crowd surged and swelled, swaying with a regular rhythm as people bought their tickets and were released out to the waiting area.

"Look," Moira yelled in his ear, tapping on his shoulder. "Seattle bus leaving in fifteen minutes."

"Okay," Rob yelled back, and he snuck his shoulder in between two people and pushed himself forward.

"Excuse me," a young woman said, her angry volume betraying the polite words, "but you better not be cutting in line."

"I'm not buying a ticket. I'm trying to find my daughter."

"Right, and I lost my dog up there too. Get your ass back."

"Listen, I'm serious. My daughter is lost and I need to get through."

An older man, the pale lights reflecting off his dark skin and curly hair, pushed his own way between Rob and the woman. "Jesus, let the man find his daughter."

"He's full of shit."

"How do you know?" The man and woman soon ignored Rob and sank into the meaningless back-and-forth arguing that captured the vibe in the room. Rob kept his head low and shoulders sideways, slipping and sliding past people to the edge of the front counters.

Moira got there too, seemingly without any of the problems he'd encountered.

"Have you seen a little girl here today?" Rob said, yelling at the ticket agent who refused to turn his way.

"Sir, you're going to have to wait."

"Listen, I'm *not* here to buy a ticket. I just need to know if you've seen my daughter. Did you sell any tickets to a little girl today?"

"Little girl? How old?"

"Seven. Black hair. About this high," he said, waving his arm around his ribs.

"No, go to the back of the line."

Rising up on his tiptoes, Rob counted six ticket agents, each separated by about two feet, but in this place, it might as well have been a thousand miles. "Excuse me," he yelled, trying to get the attention of the next ticket agent over. "Hey!"

The crowd continued to push and pull, a dense beast in constant flux. "This isn't going to work." He turned to check with Moira, but she was gone.

Not lost in the crowd. Not arguing with a ticket agent. Instead, he caught a blur of movement over the counter, and suddenly she was on the inside, working her way through each agent.

Had she just done a gymnast vault over everything?

"Rob!" Her voice flew through the chaos, and she waved her arm over the third agent—a small, older woman with a bad perm, just like his own mom used to have.

Moira gestured for him to climb over. He planted his hands on the counter and propelled himself up as swiftly and quickly as he could, though he lacked anything close to Moira's grace. His feet tumbled into something or someone, and he repeated "Sorry" before landing in the employee's trench and dashing to her.

"You girl's father?" the ticket agent asked in a thick accent.

"Yes. Yes, I am. When did she come here?"

"About an hour ago. Buy ticket to Seattle."

"Why did you sell her that? She's seven!"

"She pay cash. Say she have to see her mom."

"We're getting somewhere now." Moira put a hand on his shoulder. "Do you remember what bus she took?"

"Think that one." The woman pointed at the double doors to the boarding area. "Leave in five minutes."

The crowd surged forward, pushing the first row of people against the counter, causing the computer monitors on them to shake. "Shit. How are we going to get through that?"

Moira looked at him, her face neutral, but not in the same way it was at work. "Meet me out front in five minutes."

"What?"

"Go. Just work your way out. I'll be there in five minutes."

"But the buses are over there."

"Just go." There was a calm in her eyes, and she tilted her head as if she saw something that no one else did. "I can do this," she said, though he wasn't clear who that was meant for. It didn't matter, because before he asked, she vaulted back onto the counter, made three quick, large strides, and jumped into the wall.

Except she didn't just collide with the wall like a bird flying into glass; her left leg compressed into it, then pushed out, propelling her sideways. She took two horizontal strides on the adjacent wall, then landed neatly on the other side of the crowd, crouched on the balls of her feet in front of the boarding area door.

"You friend is crazy."

"Yeah," he said, watching Moira disappear into the line of buses. "I think so."

Getting out proved to be much easier than going in—people were more than happy to release someone from the crowd. Four citizen patrol officers sprinted by while Rob waited, the familiar red vests with a big blue *PATROL* on them, though he couldn't tell if they were rushing to control the emerging chaos or if they also wanted bus tickets. The din created by people coming, going, or simply panicking pulled memories out of Rob's vault, aligning this world with the noise downtown San Francisco used to experience daily before quarantine. Moira finally emerged, and his heart jumped at what he thought was the shadow of a little girl behind. As the light crept into the open door, his hopes were dashed by the shape of a stranger's rolling luggage.

"It's no good," Moira said. "She's not on the Seattle bus. The security guard says he saw her about an hour ago. A different bus left for Seattle around then."

All the blood drained from Rob's face, quicker than Moira flying over the angry mob. "The transportation lockdown. When does that start?"

"Inter-Metro travel is cut off starting tomorrow morning at seven. And I'm guessing state borders are pretty guarded right now."

Rob's phone lit up with the time as he pushed a button. "It's about eleven. We can make it. There's still a direct highway there. How long of a drive is it?"

A rash of sprinting people blew past them, and a smaller group shortly following. "There," Moira said, nodding toward a side street. "We have to think this through."

"What the hell was that back there?" Rob asked when they got to the quiet alley.

"I had a friend who taught me how to do that. It's been a while." Moira looked at the shuffling car traffic. She shrugged as she leaned against the alley's concrete wall and brushed sweat off her forehead. "I should practice more."

CHAPTER THIRTY-EIGHT

Krista

Uncle Dean. Uncle Asshole or Uncle Dickhead or Dr. Jerk or any of the other names Krista had for him growing up. She assigned many nicknames for horrible relatives, but Uncle Dean got the worst of her anger. Not because he necessarily treated her the worst, not directly, but even though he'd actually managed to do something with his life, he didn't do anything for Krista's when things went to hell. Now, just like before, she tried to reach him as the world devolved into chaos, one far bigger than the shit of her childhood home.

Across the lobby, Frank's family had changed from a serene bit of Americana to a group of discordant talking heads. They each assumed a different personality trait like the fairy tale dwarves of panic: Frantic (Kelley), Confused (Joe), Mopey (Frank), and Drunk (Leslie).

"I know there's mistrust right now, but I can honestly say that scientists and doctors around the world are working on this," some important old guy said on the TV over Krista's head.

"You say that, but we've heard this before. What are you expecting? Days? Months? Years?"

"I'm not a medical person. I'm just saying please, don't panic, and be patient."

"Whatever," Krista said as she searched for Uncle Dean's hospital phone number. Even though hospital, utility, and government sites were supposed to load faster than the usual Metro stuff, the screen still greeted her with a never-ending loading icon. Outside, peace and love failed to prevail, with two fights already breaking out in the gridlocked traffic. A policeman came in, and his weary posture said enough about what he was seeing. She even saw a citizen patrol officer throw her vest off and disappear down the street.

St. Vincent General Hospital's directory finally loaded and Krista clicked on the Staff link, then again on Doctors, then one more time on Uncle Dean's bolded name.

His profile came up, with all of the fancy credentials and descriptions like "Specialist in Communicable Diseases" along with a small photo—same Uncle Dean she remembered, only with a little less hair up top and a little more gray. Just as she remembered for years and years, Uncle Dean didn't smile. His mouth formed a straight line across, like it didn't know which way to go.

Krista dialed and, without much surprise, hung up at the busy signal. Ten more times she tried, and ten more times she got a busy signal.

She shook her head at the absurdity of it; all this time, she'd stayed the hell away from Uncle Dean, not even getting in touch with him after the All Clear, and now a little girl changed everything. She scrolled down the screen, revealing another phone number at the bottom: the hospital's general line.

The line beeped four times to indicate a long-distance Metro call, then without ringing, the call changed to a chime sound, then a recorded voice. "Welcome to St. Vincent General Hospital of Seattle. If you know your party's extension, say it now or enter it, followed by the pound sign."

"Dean Francis."

"I'm sorry, I didn't understand your request. Please try again."

"I'd like to talk to my uncle Dean."

"I'm sorry, I didn't understand your request. Please try again."

"Uncle Dean. He's the big-shot who's always on TV."

"I'm sorry, I didn't understand your request. Please try again."

"Dean. Francis. He's a giant asshole."

"One moment please."

Well then, she thought, *maybe the computer system thinks he's a jerk too.* "St. Vincent General Hospital, can you hold, please?"

"Actually, no, I can't."

"Ma'am, we're in a state of emergency right now. Can you hold, please?"

"I have my own emergency. I need to talk to Dr. Dean Francis."

"You and the rest of the world. Dr. Francis is very busy right now. I'm even getting kids saying they need to talk to him."

"Kids? Was it a girl named Sunny?"

"Lady, I don't know. You're wasting my time."

"No, you don't understand." Krista straightened up in her seat, then looked out the window to see a pair of police officers dragging a handcuffed man away. "I need to talk to him right now. I'm his niece. My name is Krista Deal."

"His niece, huh?" The operator sighed, the sound of low murmurs and occasional screaming coming over the phone. "All right, let me see if he'll take your call. One second."

"Thank you."

A small mob surrounded the officers, yelling and screaming with a misplaced anger, blaming all of their traffic rage and possible dying relatives on two San Francisco cops brave enough to try maintaining some sense of duty.

"Listen, lady," the operator's voice fired over the line, "you're a real bitch to be pulling this right now. What kind of sick pleasure do you get prank calling a hospital at a time like this? I was going to hang up on you, but you deserve to know what a terrible person you are."

"Wait a minute. I'm just trying to talk to my uncle."

"Dr. Francis said that Krista Deal died years ago. So don't even try pulling one on me. I hope… I hope you *get* this new plague. I'm blocking this number."

The screen told her that the call had ended as Krista stared at it for options. Frank's family remained, their bickering silenced, grim scowls all around. "We should leave." Joe stood up from the couch, groaning with arms stretched overhead. "Instead of waiting around here. We need to get across the Golden Gate to Marin."

Frank crossed his arms. "I'm not leaving without Moira."

"I just don't understand how she could leave during an emergency."

"The real emergency is a missing girl." Krista's phone vibrated, the device buzzing against her palm. "I bet that's them," she said, pulling out her phone. "Rob. What happened?"

Even over the phone, frenetic voices continued behind her, heightening what Rob said. "Sunny's gone. She's on a bus to Seattle. We have to get there."

"I think she tried calling the hospital. The operator said a girl called asking for Uncle Dean. Who else could it be?"

"Okay. So at least we know. She's not picking up her cell phone."

"How do we get around the lockdown?"

"I'm not—" The sound of shuffling came through and Rob's voice disappeared. "Oh, wait, Moira wants to say something."

"Moira?" As Krista said her name, Frank's entire family stood, forming a half circle around her. Krista turned on the phone's speaker. "Moira, you there?"

"Krista, get the keys to my Jeep from Leslie. Meet us at the alley halfway down Howard Street, south of the bus station. I might have something that will work, but I have to call someone. I have a plan—you need to trust me."

"Whoa, whoa, whoa." Frank moved around Krista's hand and leaned over the phone. "Can someone tell me what is going on here?"

"Frank, there's no time. I'm parked in the underground garage. Traffic is starting to move. Take the side streets—it's faster."

"Right." Krista reached out her free hand toward Leslie and keys landed on her fingers. "Be there in a few."

"Wait!" Frank ran up next to her, attempting to match her determined stride.

"Sunny *needs* us," she said, her steps accelerating. "If you want to get involved, you'll just have to follow me."

By the time Krista got to the elevator and pushed the Down button, the rest of Frank's family had scrambled behind him. They waited for the elevator. No one spoke.

CHAPTER THIRTY-NINE

Moira

All around, noises burst into Moira's concentration. Police sirens. Screaming. Car horns honking. The occasional breaking glass.

She closed her eyes, trying to blank it out and focus. Rob's voice trailed back and forth, and despite shutting everything off, she pictured him as he spoke—phone up to his ear, concern stenciled across his face, posture hunched over, hoping against hope that the local police had seen her or some citizen patrol officers reported her.

And then another set of footsteps came in. Soft, almost subtle and tentative.

Moira opened her eyes and whirled around. She expected Frank.

But it was her father.

Moira caught herself before she could sharply inhale. Her mind fired off in a thousand different directions. She tried to picture herself from a few years ago: shaved head, covered in grime, sprinting across rooftops and climbing over burnt cars.

She willed that image up to shove anything from childhood aside, but it lost to the flood of rehearsals and studios. The mere sight of her father meant that the battle was already over, and rather than memories of overland survival, all she heard in her mind was a loop of his voice yelling "Again!" Her legs almost went instinctively into ready position to practice a dance routine one more time.

"Johanna." His voice came out in a grizzled British accent. "You're here."

Do something, Moira told herself, and she tried to stand up with a tall, firm posture, though everything felt crushingly small right now. "I don't know who you are, but now is not a good time," she said, perhaps overdoing it on the American accent.

"Let's not do that. Your hair is different. You've grown up. But it's you. Of course it's you. Any parent would recognize their child's smile. I guess some things never change. Look, the scar on your cheek, from when you fell at Dawlish Town Beach." His familiar grimace turned into a smile. "I've come a long way looking for you. You look exhausted, Johanna. Aren't you tired?"

Moira's mind blanked as the wind kicked up around them, blowing through the alley.

"You know what started all this? Chris. Chris and I were talking about everything. He had pancreatic cancer. Last year, after the quarantine. There we were, two old fools talking about you while he was dying. He wondered where you were. He wondered if you were alive, happy. I wish he could see you now. He passed six months ago."

Thoughts returned, though they lacked any coherent connection. Instead, a mix of memories and questions came to the fray.

"He told me to find you. That was one of the last things we discussed. And now I have."

"Chris..." Moira realized her posture was shriveled, her legs weak, even her tone was small. She straightened up, thinking about Chris and the mad way he used to chomp on gum, desperate to beat his nicotine addiction. The press conferences, the public search, the reward.

All this was for him?

"But then I got an idea." Evan leaned back, out of the alley, then waved someone over. A young man stepped into view, and Moira recognized him from the other day, the person with the camera. He pulled a handheld camera out of his bag and pointed it right at her. "The world *needs* MoJo right now. It needs music. It needs something bright and strong. Think of how we could uplift things. Even with this. Even with all of this. We could broadcast it to so many. Not just music but the *story*. All the people who listened to you, they've grown up. They want you back."

The words, the tone, the *ideas*, it all created a familiar creeping tension that locked up her spine and stole her breath. It took Rob putting a hand on her shoulder to break it and ground her back to where they were, what was at stake. "Every emergency line is busy," Rob said in a calm even tone, as if he understood everything unfolding. "We need to go. We need to do something."

At the other end of the alley, the familiar *putt-putt-putt* of her Jeep rolled up, then shut off, followed by several slamming doors.

"The San Francisco Metro's broadcast group is ready for me. Right now. This is the perfect time. Look at all the attention we've gotten. An outbreak is happening and we're still the lead story. Just look into the camera, say you're MoJo and you're back to sing for the world. Right there." He pointed to the cameraman.

Sets of footsteps trailed forward, along with Krista's voice. "I can't get a hold of my uncle," she said as Rob let go of Moira and greeted her. "But I think Sunny called the hospital."

"She's there," Rob said. "That has to be it. We need to go."

"I—" Krista started. Though Moira continued staring straight ahead, she heard a quiet conversation behind her, along with Krista's barely audible "ohhhh."

"I know who you are," her dad continued, seemingly ignoring

the people behind her. "I found Moira Gorman weeks ago. All this buildup? I have an agreement with the BBC. They weren't sure about it but I promised them it'd captivate the world. And it has. People want something to believe in right now. They want a good story. We're here to give it to them."

"Moira?" Frank called out, approaching. His family followed, though they kept their distance from the scene playing out. "What's happening?"

"Listen. It's not just the BBC. We've got agreements here in the United States and Canada. They've all sponsored this. There's no reward at all because I already knew who you were," he said. "We've even negotiated contingency plans in case of another quarantine. They've learned from the last one about the importance of morale and entertainment. I've got it all mapped out. Come with me and you'll be safe from all of this. The chaos, the survival, you'll never have to worry about that. Food, medicine, shelter, all of it guaranteed, no matter what happens. Your talent, your story, it will finally be rewarded. All you have to do is say yes."

Her dad's words rattled around, a magnetic force that nearly crushed her own thoughts and pulled her back into his orbit. His logic crept at her self-doubt, tugging on little strings sewn into her consciousness since birth, muscles and thoughts trained to exclusively listen.

Everything she'd done, everything she'd built up since dashing out of Madison Square Garden, it all seemed to shrivel away. Of course the world needed hope. Of course the world needed music. Maybe he was right.

Around her, the sounds of chaos amplified, like that first night all over again. Cold nights searching for food overland or sprinting from gunfire, Rob's stories of the quarantine and the reckless mob that killed his wife, the sheer *uncertainty* of it all. Could it get that bad again? And yet, here was one simple escape, one way to shield herself from the dangers of a world struggling to find its feet.

"Moira." Rob's voice was quiet but even. "You said you have a plan. Help me find Sunny. Please."

Rob's voice shook her free, and she looked around at him.

"Go on," her dad said. "Tell him who you are. Tell the world." He signaled to the cameraman, who stepped forward. "They want to know."

Moira turned in a circle, slowly taking in the faces. Her father, ready to pull her old life into the new world. Krista, an almost *angry* look on her face, but beneath that, the slightest touch of sympathy. Frank, whose expression evolved from the wrinkles of confusion to the wide eyes of disbelief, puzzle pieces locking into place.

And Rob, a quiet determination coming through with steady breaths and sharp eyes.

"I know..." she started. The words pulled everyone in, each presence leaning closer as if the world depended on what she said next.

Maybe it did. At least the world that mattered.

"I know someone who can help us." Moira's chin jutted out just slightly as she looked over all of Frank's family. "He lives off the grid. Up by New Sacramento."

Frank broke forward out of their small semicircle. "Off the grid? What are you talking about? Who *are* you?"

Butterflies tore through Moira's gut, the chaos of the city pale in comparison to the tug-of-war she felt. Her past. Her present. Her future. They all fought for control. "I owe you the biggest apology." Moira turned from Frank, unable to meet his eyes. Stability over love. In that moment, she wished she'd never bought into such a thing. "Because I'm not who you think I am. I never was."

"You are my daughter." Evan Hatfield's tone shifted, filled with creeping irritation that would soon turn to fury. He was right: some things never changed. "Look at everything around you. The chaos, the fear. The *world* needs MoJo. It needs you."

Moira's body shifted as she faced her father. If Narc was here, he'd tell her it was Code Polka Dot. Not from a collapsing building, not from wasteland gang members and raiders, but from what was at stake, what needed to be done.

Sunny. Sunny was who needed her. "We need to go," Moira said. "It's about noon. We can get to Seattle by early morning if we leave now."

Everything went quiet, as if all the chaos and noise around them got put on mute for a minute. Her dad stepped forward and took in a breath. "I understand," he said, a gravelly tear to his voice.

Moira looked up. Had she been too quick to judge him?

"Sounds like your friends need your help. It'll be the perfect way to start your comeback. I'll announce that I've found you today. And once you've sorted that out, you can tell your story—"

"No!" Years of suppressed rage, all the things that he'd built into her to keep her in line, manage her responses, they finally broke through with an outburst that caused Frank and Rob to wince. "You will not use me anymore."

Krista, though, didn't seem surprised.

"And I'm not hiding anymore." She took in a deep breath, blowing it out slowly as she closed her eyes. "I used to be Johanna Moira Hatfield," she said, her voice taking on its full native English accent. "Before the End of the World, they called me MoJo. But I left that life at the first chance I got." Her attention turned to Frank. "I tried to start a new one. One without any connections to the past. And, Rob, I'm sorry to say this, but to get there, I lived overland during the quarantine. Narc, the man we need to see, is an old friend. He taught me how to survive during that time—"

Rob's face fell into quiet shock, his voice lowering to a level barely audible above the city chaos around them. "You were a looter."

"Yes. Rob, I looted as we made our way to California, but we were survivors. We did what we had to. I'm sorry, Rob. I know how you feel." She put a hand on his shoulder. "That was a long time ago, it doesn't matter now. Narc lives on the remains of the UC Davis campus. He can get us what we need to travel north."

"You lied to me," Frank said, his voice broken and gravelly. Behind him, little sobs came from his mother, head in hands.

"I lied to everyone," Moira said. She looked over at Krista before lingering on Rob. "In one way or another. I wanted to live another life—a normal life." She turned back to Frank. "You're the most normal person I'd ever met. That's a compliment, it really is. But I need to be the real me. At least for now. Not who you thought. Not the Johanna *he* wants. Someone different. Someone who's going to help find Sunny." A short laugh escaped, and Moira felt her cheeks burn. "It's funny how easy it is to turn off my American accent."

They stood, seemingly divided into teams, Krista finally breaking the stalemate. "We're wasting time. Even if we get to Seattle, I don't know how the hell we're going to get to my uncle."

"We'll take my Jeep to handle the off-road parts. It'll also look less conspicuous to any looter gangs." Moira pulled Rob toward her. "Rob, we are going to find your daughter. We're going to get help and find Sunny and everything will be fine. Okay?"

He twisted to look over the people around him, meeting each one eye to eye. Krista responded with an assured nod, and despite the uncertainty facing them, his lips curled into a smirk. "Sounds like a plan."

Moira moved around to the driver's side, and while she put up a brave facade, the shouts from her dad, the cries from Frank's family, all of it chipped away until she sat down, buckled in.

She rested her forehead on the steering wheel. A sharp inhale caused her to straighten up, and she looked right at Frank, who walked up to the still-open door. "Frank, you can hate me now, but I have to do this." Her fingers tugged at the ring on her left hand, moving fast enough that the swift motion of handing it to Frank happened before she could think otherwise.

"Moira, don't go." Frank's rage disintegrated, swinging his tone into desperation as he took the ring. "Let's talk about this."

"It's really simple. This isn't about me. It's about finding Sunny before things get worse. I'm sorry, Frank. I really am. But I need to do this." She slammed the door shut and cranked the engine to life.

"We should stop by my place first," Krista said.

Rob and Moira gave inquisitive looks her way, though she didn't meet either of them. "I have a large sum of cash. It might come in handy."

Moira nodded, then released the parking brake.

Moira had run to Narc before, years ago. Like now, she went to him for help, for a way through the chaos.

Back then, she just hadn't met him yet.

As she left Madison Square Garden's loading area, people burst in all directions around her, trying to find their way home or to loved ones or whatever they considered safe.

Moira—Johanna as she was known then, or the even more repulsive MoJo—did the opposite of that. She didn't run to the hotel where her family and hired help stayed, she didn't run to closed quarters; she flew into the chaos, past breaking windows and crashing cars and open flames, as long as it meant going *away* from the life she knew.

She'd kept going, sprinting to walking to jogging in every possible combination, reaching into destroyed storefronts to grab layers of clothing or bags of chips or the miracle find of unopened vodka. The hours counted past, an aimless direction moving her farther and farther from the massive arena until dusk broke. The purple hues of the morning turned into daylight, the ugliness of the previous night failing to subside when the sun cast a spotlight on it all. Twelve hours became sixteen became twenty became a blur when her phone gave out.

She'd been awake for well over a day at that point, exhausted, drunk for at least a quarter of that time, and nourished only on a diet of salt-and-vinegar chips, a Snickers bar, and an orange. Sometime in the afternoon, she'd found a quiet spot in an alley next to a barred-up Chinese restaurant, the soundtrack of blaring car alarms, police sirens, and distant yelling singing her body to sleep. She knelt down, back against the hard, cold wall, then slid to sitting, eyes unable to stay open anymore. Everything went into shutdown mode.

She didn't even hear the two men approach, or when one of them flicked open a knife.

They didn't say a word, other than a whispered "You think the cops will help you right now?" The knife's blade pressed up against her neck, and a forearm braced across her shoulders. "Why do I get the feeling you're one of those rich kids?" the man said, pulling rings off her fingers. He was probably unaware that her ensemble consisted only of costume jewelry she hadn't bothered to remove. "How rich are you?"

Inside, everything wanted to fight back. Her will pulled to scream and scratch and claw, punching and kicking, a lifetime of pent-up rage ready to explode. But her body wasn't willing. It'd been awake too long, pushed too far, drank too much, and all she could muster was a meager push against the pressure.

Shutting down mentally and emotionally wasn't anything new. She closed her eyes, awaiting the worst. Except it didn't arrive.

Instead, she sat dumbfounded as something flew over her, vaulting across an adjacent Dumpster and landing with enough force to swiftly knock the two assailants down. A few blinks later and she registered a new person, a man about ten or fifteen years older than her, Latino complexion, black hair as filthy as her own, T-shirt stained dark.

And pointing a gun. Not at her, but at the two men he'd just taken out.

"You two don't need to do this," he said. The pair looked at each other, then at him; they both put their hands up and backed away. "There's a big city fighting out there. How about you boys go join it?"

Within seconds, the men disappeared.

"You all right?"

"I don't need rescuing," she said, though her exhausted body told her otherwise.

"I'm not rescuing anyone. This is a shortcut. The other alleys are blocked." He gestured around them. "Just doing a good deed while passing through. Here, have some water."

"I'm fine. I'm fine." Her shoes scuffed the pavement as she shuffled to her feet. Fatigue tried to drape her eyes shut, but she told herself to focus. "What was that? The…" She lacked the words to describe what she'd just seen, instead mock flailing her arms and legs.

"Ah. Jiujitsu. Well, the second part, anyway." He mimicked her arm gestures. "And parkour."

The terms meant nothing to her, other than saving if not her life, then her physical self and what little sanity remained. "Thanks. Guess I owe you one, yeah?"

"British. You on vacation here with your folks? Or studying?"

"Little bit of both. Kind of." She exhaled, and it felt like it had been building up for years. Despite being sweaty and grimy, the man's eyes flickered with something so rare in her life that it took several seconds for her to recognize it.

Honesty. Almost enough to disarm her. Almost.

"Look, um, I don't know where you're heading—" he started.

"Nowhere. Leave me alone."

"I thought you said you were with your folks."

"Doesn't mean I'm going back to them."

"Ah." The man's lips pursed, as he turned to examine the string of police sirens that whizzed by the alley. "They fell to the flu?"

"I don't know."

They stared at each other for a good twenty seconds. She felt certain he wasn't going to harm her, though given the group of people usually paid to accompany her, perhaps she wasn't the best judge of character. Still, nothing compelled her to run—and even if she did, her body may not have had the remaining strength to obey such a command.

"Okay." The man broke the silence, sliding the gun into his boot. "Okay, look. If you want to stay here, that's fine. If you want to try and get into quarantine, that's fine too. But you're welcome to come with me. My friends and I have decided. We're standing our ground. No governments. No quarantines. We'll live off the land. Either here or somewhere else."

Live off the land. Up until that moment, the only options seemed to be quarantine with her dad or quarantine without. Or death. An alternative seemed so distant, so unlikely, that it had never materialized before.

"Did you hear about the shite going down at Madison Square Garden?" she asked.

"*Shite*," he said, a playful lilt in his mock accent, "is going down everywhere."

"Right. Well, there was a concert when things went bad. I was onstage."

"You? Are you like a pop idol or something?"

"In some ways." Her eyes fell to the uneven cement of New York City pavement beneath her. "They call me MoJo."

"Hmm. Sorry," he said, checking his watch. "Never heard of you."

That moment burned in her memory with a frightening clarity: the grime on her hands, the sweat-stuck clothes, the pain in her feet, the aching sense of dehydration tinted with hunger, the burning in the air mixed with manhole stench. All of those details stitched permanently in her mind as the background to one single event.

She pulled the hood off her head and, on the ground, caught a distorted view of herself in a hubcap lying against the concrete wall. Slanted, pulled, out of proportion, the image blurred everything except for the eyes: they were tired eyes, but something seemed so unfamiliar, unique about them, despite having seen them in the mirror every day of her life—usually when prepping for a show or rehearsal.

Freedom sat beneath them.

She finally smiled.

"It's okay if you don't want to come. I'm just offering. But you have no reason to trust me." The man looked down, then behind them, then down again before reaching and pulling out the gun. He grabbed it by the barrel, then held it out to her. "I should get going. Take this."

"I don't like guns."

"Me neither. But with this?" He gestured around them. "It's not a bad idea." His logic made sense, but other fears ran through her mind. Bodyguards and limos and security had protected her all this time. A gun? She wouldn't even know how to use it.

"I'm not sure."

"About the gun or about coming along?"

She kept silent, eyes bouncing between the weapon and the man.

"What do you want? Maybe you should ask yourself that," the man said, popping the clip out from the handle. He held it sideways, and though her gun experience amounted to zero, even her tired eyes recognized an empty clip. "You want to head to quarantine? Because the busing stations are that way." He pointed in a direction that meant nothing to her.

"I want to be no one. For once."

The man studied her for what felt like minutes, though that might have simply been the exhaustion and dehydration taking over. He finally nodded, putting the clip back into the gun's handle and offering it to her. She clasped her fingers around it, the weight of the weapon surprising her. "You're a teenage girl in a world going to shit. A gun looks better on you than it does me. Even if it's empty."

"Will you teach me to use it?"

The man let out a quick huff followed by a smile, nodding to no one in particular. "I'm not the best shot. But I'll try. Like I said, I hate guns. Come on." He propped her up. "We'll meet up with my friend. He's organizing a group to get out of New York. Everyone calls him Narc. I'm Santiago, by the way. What's your name?"

"Jo—" she started before catching herself. She cleared her throat and stood up straight despite the overwhelming weariness. "Moira."

"Moira." Santiago reached into his backpack and pulled out a plastic bottle, cap still sealed, and handed it to her. Water had never tasted better. "I like it. Much better than MoJo."

For years after that moment, she'd hidden behind the name Moira, using it to deflect from her past. But now, with Frank and his family shrinking in the rearview mirror, her dad's shouts *still* audible, the chaos of the city swirling around them, and a family to reunite, the name Moira was no longer a shield.

It simply was who she was.

Excerpt from President Tanya Hersh's speech on the accelerated lockdown window and spreading MGS:

Barricades have been put up in most of the major cities by now with controlled entrance and exit checkpoints established by the end of the day. Certified citizen patrol officers will be monitoring secured highways to minimize looter gang activity. We urge all citizens to avoid gang conflict zones if they are traveling home. Travelers are reminded that a valid photo ID is required for entrance into a state using supported highways, and only people returning to their home address will be admitted. International air travel is permitted only for those who are returning to their native countries. This window will close in two days.

I understand that there will be questions about a quarantine state. Please know that we hear you and that there are no active plans for quarantine. Our focus is on resolving the situation at hand, not uprooting everyone's lives again.

As our resources are limited, Reclaimed Territory groups will be left to plan their own response to this emergency.

PART 4:

FRIENDS

CHAPTER FORTY

Moira

For the first hour, the drive out of San Francisco was calm and quiet.

But not now.

Krista was yelling. So was Rob.

Moira knew this, though she couldn't understand what they were saying. The throttle roared, and her boot slammed the brake, enough to break up their pace as she turned the wheel and slid across the four empty lanes of the highway.

The last time someone had fired a gun at her, adrenaline pumped through her body and each step seemed like another inch toward victory—victory over what, she didn't know, but some sort of self-affirmation, a point where her physical abilities to climb and leap matched her attitude. Maybe she only wanted to impress Narc, Santiago, and the crew through the beaten remains of Reno's main strip on Sierra Street. She didn't consider it much back then—in fact, at that point, she didn't think about anything except getting to California right before civilization trickled out of quarantines. Something—a bullet, shrapnel, whatever—grazed her bare shoulder during that sprint between a valley of casinos, slicing into the flesh enough that Santiago tore a strip off the bottom of his shirt while in mid-stride and ran beside her to tie it.

The pain felt almost good then, a challenge to be alive. There was no panic, there was nothing to lose, and they'd seen so much on their cross-country trek that that felt like one more test before getting through.

The distinct *pop-pop-pop* of gunfire, the echo of bullets bouncing off the pavement. It sounded the same today, right now, but speeding down the highway with Rob and Krista, it *felt* different. There was no bravado in her actions. In fact, only one thought remained.

We have to get to Sunny. The line repeated itself from the instant they left Frank and his family, from gathering supplies at Rob's to a pit stop at Krista's for a ridiculous pile of cash and to set up Krista's cat with her neighbor, all the way to the brief call with Narc before leaving the San Francisco Metro phone coverage zone. It kept her focus when they escaped across the Bay Bridge—with shocking ease; by the time they set out, traffic had died down. Either people had given up or they'd got through—past the checkpoint of the government-supported zone at the Benicia Bridge, and into the wilderness of Highway 80, surrounded only by the Major Highway Safety Project's protective structure and the occasional automated fill-up station.

When a pair of looter gang vehicles appeared on the opposite side of the highway, it was still at the forefront of her mind.

"Holy shit," Krista yelled, ducking her head down as the ceiling pinged with a bullet. "Those assholes are trying to *kill* us."

"Hang on." Moira's voice was steady. Calm. But not fearless. "Warning shots," she said, though she didn't necessarily believe it.

"Stop the car!" a megaphoned voice called from outside. "Give us your shit and you can walk home."

"Don't think so." She glanced at the straight stretch of Highway 80 eastbound, a mostly empty expanse, dilapidated despite the barbed-wire fencing of the MHSP on either side. She could see the government barricades blocking the next off-ramp. In the sky, two highway patrol drones hovered, watching passively from above, similar to the pair they'd passed about twenty miles ago.

"You totally jinxed us," Krista said to Rob. "You just had to say, 'Oh, at least it's an MHSP highway.'"

"The *only* two cars we've seen turn out to be looter gangs," Rob yelled, holding their bags down in the back. "Who are these guys?"

"Die Urbans." At least, that's what Moira thought. Her memory of looter gang signs was a little shaky, and she'd only gotten a glance of the spray-painted X-U on a truck on the opposite side of the highway before it flipped a U and started running parallel to them down the wrong way. "They don't usually hit MHSP highways. They're alone. We can lose them."

"That's a really, really, really—" Krista's comment got cut off as Moira jerked the car suddenly to go wide of an abandoned truck sitting in the middle lane. "That's a really weird name for a gang. Are they German or something?"

"Dunno. Narc might know."

"We have to get to Narc first," Rob said.

Moira nodded. She glanced over her shoulder across the highway divider. Two Die Urban vehicles, one truck and one beat-up sports car, continued racing just steps behind them. If there was anyone driving westbound on Highway 80, it wouldn't end well. She told herself to focus, and maybe if they kept this distance for a bit, the pirates would get bored and go off.

The Jeep jolted forward with Moira's foot jamming the accelerator, the car's cage rattling.

"I think—" she started until a static squawk interrupted her.

"Moira," a voice said from the dash's CB radio. "Moira Gorman, is that you causing trouble on the highway?"

Narc.

She snatched the microphone from the dash. "Narc, are you gonna just sit and watch?"

"Well, yeah. I've got the highway drone feed up here."

"Thanks," Moira said reflexively, unable to add much sarcasm in it.

"But I'm sending some help. We've had a few Die Urban scouts down here over the past few weeks. We know how to scare them off."

"Narc, they are *shooting* at us. Like, right now."

"I can see that. Help is on the way. Just don't run into them."

"I think we'd be happy to see them."

"No, literally, *don't* run into them. It took us forever to build those cars."

"Come on…" Moira's voice trailed off as a black speck popped out of the horizon, flying in an arc over the highway divide. She tracked it as it hovered over the westbound side, followed by two more drones. Smoke began to plume out of them, falling onto the pavement below, and the drones, barely visible through the dense vapors, zigged and zagged to blanket the opposing lanes while trying to keep up with them. Moira pressed the accelerator, the Jeep's engine rattling as it pushed its limits.

The CB came to life again. "I think you're good. But just for good measure…"

Right when Narc said that, the rearview mirror lit up with a geyser of flames reaching up some twenty feet in the air.

"Jesus," Rob said. "Did we drive into a war zone?"

"Looks good," Narc said, as if he could hear Rob's question, "but it's pretty harmless. The Die Urbans are turning around now. Too much trouble for just one car. They were probably on their way to raid the convoys coming out of the Benicia warehouses. You'll be coming up on my friends soon."

Moira saw it. On the far shoulder, tiny blocks resolved into three parked SUVs, each trimmed with fashioned bits of armor drilled exactly where she remembered it: one patch for each door frame, another one reinforcing the back panel, and double plating over the gas cap and tank. The bolt points were still on her car from years ago, something that had occasionally prompted Frank to suggest that she get a new car.

"I see them," Moira said into the CB. They slowed as each of the cars came to life, engines turning over and taillights activating.

"They'll escort you in." The vehicles built a formation around them, one on either side and another lagging shortly behind her. Rob eased back into his seat, a look of relief on his face while Krista sat tensed in the passenger side, constantly looking from side to side. "Welcome home, Moira."

Despite only being a few miles off Highway 80, the old University of California, Davis, campus was nearly inaccessible. The off-ramp still existed, but it looked different from the last time Moira had seen it, some two years ago. When she'd left, building materials and dead cars formed a checkpoint of sorts, watched by a row of guards.

But now, the path was cleaner. Someone still kept watch, though only two people guarded the main highway exit. Perhaps the further society came to returning, the less everyone needed to be ready for attack or defense. Moira followed the escort, each car peeling off one by one until Narc himself guided her to a meeting spot off of Russell Boulevard.

"He's converted a frat house," Rob said.

"I never need to go in one of those again," Krista said.

The Jeep jerked when it came to a stop, and Moira hit the parking brake. Rob stepped outside and stretched in the afternoon sun. "He's got solar panels?"

"Yes, we do. New Sacramento took almost all of the remaining wind turbines but factories produced tons of solar panels before the outbreak. They power most Reclaimed communities. Plenty for us to use." Narc's voice cut through the air, and Moira's body reacted with the same speed as when she heard her dad. Except this was opposite in every way. Instead of fear, there was excitement. Instead of dread, there was warmth. Instead of wanting to run away, she dashed forward and threw her arms around the man who'd saved her life in so many different ways.

"Narc, you lovely bastard!" Moira yelled with a distinctly English lilt, leaping out of the driver's seat and giving him a big hug.

"I thought you swapped trouble for Metro life. Bad timing with the Die Urbans. Ever since they opened up the processing center down 80, shipping convoys are getting hit."

"Glad you kept an eye out for us." They let go and stepped back, Moira unable to hold back her grin. Same Narc: tall, broad shoulders, thin glasses, and a welcoming laugh to go with neatly cropped brown hair and smile lines that gave away his age. Maybe he was embracing the hippie Zen master thing more these days, based on him standing barefoot on the front lawn.

"Nice accent," he said. "No longer incognito?"

Moira caught Rob's look, lingering for a moment before hopping to Krista, then back to Narc. "I don't know right now. That's not important."

"Right, right. This isn't a social visit." He walked over to Rob. "I'm very sorry to hear about your daughter. I hope I can help." He gave Rob a gentle shoulder squeeze, almost fatherly, and Moira could see Rob relax. Inside, she laughed to herself.

Narc had that effect on people.

"Come on. We'll be quick," Moira said, trotting up to join her former mentor.

CHAPTER FORTY-ONE

Krista

Krista leaned over to Rob while they followed Narc to the house. "Where's his army? With cars like that, I thought we'd walk into spikes and guns."

"Me too," he said.

"These old college campuses are great for Reclaimed communities." Narc gestured around them, then began pointing at various things as they walked. "So much of the infrastructure has remained intact. We have five hundred people here, fifty or so joining in the last six months. A dozen in a trial period. We can defend ourselves if we need to, but looter gangs usually aren't big enough or organized enough to take on a community. Besides, all we have here is vegetables. They'd rather steal resource convoys or commercial transports or just fight each other. Those pyrotechnics we used? Homegrown. We have a former chemist here. Running water," Narc said, nodding to the kitchen as they walked through his home. "I installed a new water heater myself. Plenty of supplies to grab in the ghost town stores."

Krista watched the strangest thing unfold in front of her: Rob cringed at Narc's last sentence, and Moira responded by shooting him a look. In some other circumstance, it might have come off as pithy or scolding, but her action didn't carry any expectation or weight to it. Instead, it felt more efficient, a coded shorthand between two people beginning to understand each other. He fired off a nod, and she ended the silent conversation with a short, warm smile.

Those two. They'd better hold on to Krista's business cards.

"I have my printers back here." Narc led them into a room filled with printing equipment, walls lined with paintings that were more random splotched colors than art to her. "Your IDs won't be perfect, but they'll get the job done. Just give me a few minutes."

"Won't they inspect them closely?" Rob asked.

Narc laughed, not a condescending laugh but a short, friendly one. "You give them too much credit. Think about what's happening—it's going to be overworked police or military and cit-pats who aren't trained to spot a fake ID. They can't even get manufacturing going again, let alone infrastructure or law enforcement. You'd probably get scrutinized more getting into a bar. Let's take some quick photos."

Krista stayed back while Narc talked through the smaller printer's settings with Moira, then positioned her against a blank backdrop. "What do you think?" Rob asked in a low voice.

"I don't trust him yet," she said, matching his volume.

"You don't trust anyone."

"Neither do you."

"Some people. I trust Moira." His head tilted, offset with a tiny upward tick coming to his lips. "I might even be trusting you. Just a little bit."

"You told me to stay out of your lives."

"And you said you weren't getting involved."

"Yeah, well, I think I figured something out."

"What's that?"

Krista hesitated. Uncertainty tugged at her thoughts, but it wasn't the anxiety of the situation that caused it.

Instead, her stomach jumped at the *newness* of it all. "I care about Sunny." She knew that Rob turned to her, though she couldn't fully gauge his reaction from her peripheral vision.

The sentence replayed in her head several times over. When was the last time she'd said that about *anyone*?

"How about that, huh?" she asked, quiet enough that Rob might not have even heard the question. It didn't matter since it wasn't intended for him.

"You're an interesting one, Krista. I'll give you that."

"Now you two." They stayed quiet while Narc ushered them through the process of creating ID cards of their era—no fancy holograms or embedded details anymore, instead a return to the days of sturdy cards and lamination. Minutes later, Narc presented three fresh fake IDs in hand. "State of Washington. Rob Donelly, Krista Deal." The cards still felt hot from the printer. "Oh, and Moira Donelly. I thought it would look better if two of you were married."

Moira pulled a ring off her right hand and stuck it on the ring finger of her left hand, the same place Frank's engagement ring had sat just a few hours ago. "Seems like I'm always switching who I am, huh?"

"When you get to the hospital, I'd try the front door first, of course. But with everything happening, you never know how tight security will be. So, just in case, hospital scrubs." Narc opened a small metal cabinet and pulled out one set of green, one set of purple, and one with cartoon kittens on it.

"Dibs on the cats," Krista said.

Narc nodded and continued. "I use them to keep clean with art projects, but it'll look better than walking in wearing jeans. Oh, and a lab coat. It might have some metal shavings on it, but again, better than nothing and it *looks* like a doctor's coat. No hospital IDs, though. You're on your own for that."

"Well, I hope my Uncle Asshole will see us, then."

Moira opened her backpack and shoved the clothing inside. "Anything else?" she said.

"Follow me." Narc led them down a cramped hallway lined with canvases and odd sculptures.

"Is Santiago still living with you?" Moira said while they walked into the garage.

"If you ever bothered to call, you'd know that he lives about a half mile from here. A converted two-story dorm."

"Oh, I'm sorry."

"Sorry about what?" Narc pulled a box down and began rustling through it.

"Sorry that you guys broke up."

"Actually, it's not like that at all. Santiago's place is next to a big field—he's expanding the farm. With so much going on, it's just easier if he keeps his things there. New Sac is a bare-bones Metro, honest living. We sell our produce there, and I guarantee you it's better than anything produced in a converted Metro park or skyscraper farms. It's calmer out here than San Francisco. A little quieter, a little more wild. Someday, this place will really be up and running, and who knows, maybe we'll finally get around to getting married. There's just not enough time for all that right now."

Both Moira and Rob looked at Krista. "What?" she finally asked. "I'm not a cartoon character, it's not like I have business cards ready to fire out."

"Krista's a wedding planner," Rob said.

"Event coordinator."

"Actually," Narc said, a thoughtful shift coming to his face. "That might not be a bad idea. A little party for our corner of the world. I'll talk with him tonight about it." He pulled out a small black box with a mess of cords hanging from it. "Here we go. Binoculars. Police scanner. And adapter for car power."

Krista took the scanner from him, wrapping the cords around its metallic square frame. "You think we'll need to worry about the cops?"

"Speeding isn't exactly a concern for them when the world's going to shit. And you can bet that at least some of the police have skipped out to be with their families. No, this will just give you a heads-up if anything happens. Citizen patrols use the same band, so you'll hear everything. Though taking MHSP-protected roads should be fine. Most looter activity is in SoCal and Nevada right now. The Die Urbans are mostly up by Chico," he said as he pushed his glasses up the bridge of his nose. "Go load up, and I'll meet you out front with one more thing."

Krista had seen this before. Not the exact couch in the exact living room as Narc's setup, but something that looked remarkably similar to the night she met Jas—same formation, same architecture, just with no drunk people and bad music.

Krista blinked, then blinked again, refusing to acknowledge the sudden irritation in her eyes or the way this *room* brought back that night in alarming clarity, so much so that she couldn't ignore the question taking root in the corner of her mind, one that had grown a little every hour since Jas reached out.

How dare he make her feel regret like that.

A click followed by a squeak caused her to leap off the couch and she shut everything off, compartmentalizing her emotions like she'd learned to as a kid. Narc walked through the door, box in arms. "Oh. Thought you were out front."

"Sorry. Just taking a moment."

"Don't worry about it. It's comfy, huh? That was here when we found this place. Reupholstered it myself." Krista nodded, though her eyes continued to draw back to the room at large, little details seemingly pulled out of a time warp. Even the guitar in the corner made her wonder if she could remember the chords Jas taught her one late night. "Something the matter?"

"No. Just reminded me of someone I once knew. That's all."

"Ah." Narc's voice dropped in tone, a softness mixed in with its dry grate. "You never know when those moments will come. I still get them. Friends and family who got sick and died, they just pop up in the strangest places."

"Oh, Jas isn't dead."

"I see. The other kind of lost." His chin dropped but a small smile came to his lips. "Those are good too. And at least they're out there for a second chance." Krista's whole body stiffened, enough that Narc seemed to notice as he spoke quick. "I mean, if you're looking for it."

"Why do you live here?" she said, deflecting the subject. "Away from where everyone else is."

"Why do you think?"

"Because people are assholes."

His laugh filled the space, reaching all the way up to the vaulted ceiling. "No, of course not. I love people." His head slanted as he studied Krista. "Is that how you feel? I thought you worked with people."

"Doesn't mean people aren't assholes."

"It's too easy in the cities. I have friends in Austin and Denver, they tell me that they've got the best tech restoration initiatives in the country, that it's almost like it was before. That actually sounds awful to me. The noise, the pace. No thank you. I like New Sac, it's the perfect place for us to trade with, and they appreciate what we do. But we're barely two hours out of San Francisco, and city dwellers think it's a wasteland. It's not. It's beautiful, a little rough around the edges, but we work together. We're our own family, this community." Narc's eyes brightened as he spoke. "We're not disconnected out here. I read about the whole Fourth Path thing. You know, the saddest part, Kay Greenwood's pursuit of something that doesn't exist anymore, that idea is what caused the whole thing. I'm out here *because* I love people, and that's the American Dream today. We mourn, we rebuild, we respect the things we have. We're self-sustaining. And I think that's the way it should be."

"So you *are* a hippie."

"If you want to call it that, sure." The box rumbled as he steadied it in his arms. "I like to think of it as not taking anything or anyone for granted anymore."

CHAPTER FORTY-TWO

Rob

The words on the building across the street caused Rob to squint: something "Hall," but the name was missing a letter or two, and an overgrowth of vines had taken over the wall. They had ghost towns, so what was this, a ghost college?

"It's weird, isn't it?" Moira came over and stood next to Rob, then pointed at the row of buildings across the way. "They're still standing. Just empty. No one to fill them."

"I think I've stayed in San Francisco for so long that I forgot it was like this out here," he said as he turned to her. "You been back to England?"

"Nope. This is my home now."

"You're not curious about if it's any different?"

"I've seen the statistics. It's just like here. Most of the remaining people stuck to major cities. London, Manchester, Liverpool." Moira's words came out matter-of-fact, neutral, almost like she was back at work. "It's like that everywhere."

"You all right with that? I mean, you haven't really said much about it."

"I'm fine." She let out a hefty sigh, and it dissolved into the silence around them, bringing forth a smile—not the MoJo smile, but one with bright cheeks and glowing eyes.

"I really am. I don't doubt that Frank thought we were a good fit. It seemed reason enough to marry because Moira Gorman needed something official besides pay stubs and credit card bills to go with the falsified records. I figured if he was happy, then I could make it work just being safe and content. Everyone else married for that comfort. Why not me? I mean, plenty of people did that before the End of the World." Her voice cracked as the words fought their way out. Rob read everything underneath her tone, the cadence of her speech. Regret, shame, all of that stuff. No matter how it got dressed up, it was still the same in the end. "That's wrong, though. Every single one of those people, all of those people marrying for stability. They're selling themselves short. We're better than that."

"There's a better way to rebuild," Rob said. He looked at her, the purple and orange beams of the California sunset lighting her from behind. There wasn't a drop of irony or cynicism in his statement. "More than survival. If we're the only two people on the planet that realize that, well, you gotta start somewhere."

Rob thought back to the FSB meeting, how Moira seemed to believe down to her bones that her testifying would be the help he needed. But standing there together, the simplicity of it all, he realized that maybe they'd both done the right thing in a different way.

Because on that afternoon, together, they opened up their real selves to someone else.

"Security is why I left Reclaimed. I've wanted comfort my whole life," Moira said. "I thought now was my time." He watched her shoulders slump, each word seeming to drag her down. "Then *he* came poking around. It was going to come together so fast. No more Johanna Hatfield. But that's not really necessary now, is it? Everyone knows, and now I'm here. Frank needs someone better than me. I led him on. I thought it was okay, like the social norm. But it's not. I owe him a huge apology."

"Things will work out," he said. "We all—" He stopped, dropping the thought as he pulled out a buzzing phone.

"It's Sunny."

His hands shook, a finger barely able to swipe the screen.

"A text."

Never before had a single text message brought so much relief.

He'd sent texts to her phone, the one he gave her for emergencies, every twenty or thirty minutes since San Francisco. With limited cell coverage outside of the Metros, it wasn't clear how many—if any—got through. "'I'm okay, Daddy,'" he read, "'see you soon.' Sent an hour ago." The pace of his words picked up, the anxiety turning into excitement. "She probably passed a Metro in Oregon and it just processed. I'm not getting anything else. I must have caught a hiccup of Sacramento's coverage." His whole body shook with a laugh that reached the sky, eyes squeezed and a grin that spelled out so many different kinds of emotions, all culminating with arms wrapped around her. "She's safe. She's safe, she's safe."

"She is," Moira said, returning the gesture. In their embrace, he wasn't sure who held who. Maybe they held each other. "We'll find her."

"Okay." He pulled back slightly, though they remained eye to eye, her arms still around his waist. "Okay. We can do this. For now, she's okay. We just have to get up there."

"We will," she said, with a fierce determination beyond its quiet volume, as if her voice connected directly to his ears.

They stood at arm's length, eyes locked, the calm of the Reclaimed community leaving them only with each other and a world of possibilities, including the invisible pull that suddenly drew them closer together, so close that they nearly—

"I think this is it." Narc's voice called across the space, a door slamming right after.

They separated, heat flooding Rob's cheeks, and Narc came out, box in hand and with Krista a few steps behind. "A few more goodies for the road," he said, planting the box at their feet. He lifted the cardboard lid and pointed. "Carrots. Apples. Pears. A few bottles of fresh-squeezed lemonade." The lid fell flush, and he patted its top. "Hopefully you'll be enjoying them with your daughter tomorrow."

Rob glanced at Moira. Everyone seemed to be all business now. As they should be. "I got a text from her. As of an hour ago, she's safe," he said.

Krista beamed.

"Well, then you guys should hit the road and catch up with her," Narc said.

Moira took the box and put it in the open trunk of her Jeep. "Santiago grew these?"

"Yup. From our family to yours." Moira slammed the trunk gate shut and gave Narc a big hug. "You're welcome to visit when there's not an emergency, you know," he told her.

"Let's get through this first."

Narc nodded and let go of Moira, then shook hands with Rob and Krista. They bounded into the Jeep, Moira behind the wheel, Krista in the back, and Rob up front. "Oh, one more thing." Narc reached behind him and pulled something out with a glint of black. Rob blinked to make sure he saw it right from the passenger's seat.

"Is that…a gun?"

"Yeah. Metro gun ban still in place?"

"Sounds like it. Probably even tighter now that there's unrest."

"Keep it for safety on the road but hide it. Don't let anyone see it, especially police or cit-pats. I wouldn't recommend using it unless you have to, but you never know what you might encounter. Don't forget that citizen patrol officers only carry Tasers. Can you still shoot?"

Moira nodded as she took it. She held it up, checking it from side to side, and put it under her seat. "Not very well."

"Then be extra careful. Keep the safety on at all times, and promise me you won't use it unless you absolutely have to."

"Believe me, I don't want to use it."

"Okay, then." Narc leaned over, poking his head through Moira's window to look right at Rob. "What's your daughter's name?"

"Sunny."

"I hope you find Sunny."

"Hey, Narc," Krista said from the back seat. "Why does Moira call you that? Were you a cop before everything? Or a drug dealer?"

"Nothing that exciting. My last name's Narcizo. Narc for short." He tapped the metal roof, and Moira gave the engine a roar. "Good luck. Maybe we'll be planning a wedding soon. And Krista," he said, waving through the open driver-side window, "don't give up on people, okay? Some deserve a second chance."

Rob turned to look at Krista. She stared straight down and said nothing as the car began to move.

Excerpt from *Walking in the Dark: An Oral History of the Fourth Path*:

"She said she was a traveler, that she'd walked all the way from San Francisco and made friends along the way. And she wanted nothing: not food, not shelter, nothing. People watched as this silent mob marched with her. She spoke just once, right before they headed to Los Angeles.

"She didn't blink. When I asked her if she was okay, she just smiled but it didn't look like she saw me, like she saw something else. She talked about how people had gotten it wrong, that the Metros were the old way that failed, that Reclaimed still traded in commerce, that gang life abused humanity and the planet. The Fourth Path, she said, is to go where the land takes them."

CHAPTER FORTY-THREE

Rob

The California-Oregon border checkpoint was smoother than the ride up. The Jeep off-roaded through the wasteland to get to the remains of the old Highway 113, monitoring the police scanner the entire time for reports of looter gang activity, though the majority of conflict areas remained far south of their location. They pushed forward, all the way until they rejoined the MHSP-protected Highway 5, and the journey itself proved uneventful. At the checkpoint, the path narrowed to two lanes, a uniformed soldier on either side. They flashed their IDs, faces still behind breathing masks, and were waved along without any hesitation. In fact, the three of them were specifically instructed *not* to touch the soldier in any way, even to hand over the ID, presumably because MGS 96 was contact-transmitted rather than airborne.

Rob had eagerly taken over driving for a leg of the journey, but maybe Krista was right about him jinxing things, because the moment he'd thought about how smooth things had been since getting Sunny's text, he noticed the engine's temperature gauge rising. He glanced over at Krista, who'd been staring silently at her knitting while the needles clicked a regular rhythm for the past twenty minutes or so. Behind them, Moira slept horizontal, with a jacket as a pillow.

The car *felt* fine. Best not to say anything about it right now. He already had his ebb and flow of panic, the last thing he needed was to get the others worked up about potentially nothing. He turned the radio on for something to fill the quiet beyond Krista's knitting. It came to life with a pop and a man's voice came through the speakers. "We have confirmed reports as far west as Denver, Colorado, and Houston, Texas. On the line with us is Dean Francis…"

Krista's face formed an immediate scowl and Rob lowered the volume, keeping it loud enough to hear the update while giving Krista some space. "Don't you want to hear the update?" he asked.

"Not from Uncle Asshole. It's hard enough knowing I'm going to probably see him when we get to the hospital."

"You ready to give him a second chance?" Rob said, staring straight ahead.

"I'm doing this for Sunny. If that means talking to him, then I'll leave it at that. Who said anything about second chances?" Krista threw a sideways look at him. "He's never earned that."

"Sorry. I thought Narc mentioned something about that."

"That wasn't about Uncle Dean," Krista said.

The temperature gauge continued creeping up, segment by segment. He eased off the accelerator. Maybe his poor stick-shift skills had caused this. "Should I even ask?"

The car rumbled along, their voyage framed by the endless line of MHSP fencing around them. "His name is Jas," she finally said. "Something at Narc's reminded me of him, that's all."

"'Is.' Not 'was.' Still alive?"

"Yep." The knitting stopped, and from his peripheral vision, he could see Krista stare out at the black landscape all around them, some four hours having passed since the last rays of sunlight. "You know, I don't actually like knitting," she said after a few minutes. "It just helps me think. The rhythm of it. I learned that about myself early on."

"You're, uh..." Rob selected his words carefully. "Not knitting now. Do you want to—" He stopped halfway through the question, his focus stolen by a puff of steam rising out from the hood. A thin line fanned out into a plume, visible enough for Krista to sit up before calling to Moira in the back.

A voice from ages ago played in his mind: his own dad, almost fifteen years ago, jabbing him for not taking auto-shop in high school. *You're gonna need it someday. Don't make me say I told you so.*

The car veered onto the dirt shoulder, all the while with Rob cursing himself for jinxing the trip. He forced his mind quiet and watched silently as Moira said she'd see what she could do.

They gathered in front of the open hood, Krista and Rob an audience while Moira inspected the situation with a flashlight. She held without a word, then moved to the passenger side, her fingers tracing along the area adjacent to the front wheel well. "Damn it," she said. "Die Urbans. This shot got through somehow. I never should have taken off the armor plates." The flashlight swung out as she moved back to the hood. "The coolant tank. It nicked a crack in it." She motioned them over; Rob squinted to see a line in the plastic about two inches from the tank bottom. "It's about an inch long, splinters about an inch wide. We'll need to patch it. Get some coolant too, or at least water."

Patching a leak didn't sound like a huge problem. Rob had helped out a bit with all sorts of plumbing work during quarantine, some big and some small. The issue here was the actual supplies.

And time. Every second they were stalled, Sunny got farther toward Seattle, and who knew what shape *that* Metro was in.

"I'm assuming Narc didn't give us anything for that," Krista said. "Unless apples work."

"No, but…" Without another word, Moira jogged over to the top of the small hill some thirty or forty feet from the highway, her silhouette breaking the skyline of stars against the moonlight. "There," she called out after a minute. Rob gave Krista a look of uncertainty; she shot him one back. "It's about a half mile down. You can see it from the off-ramp." They joined Moira atop the mound of earth but Rob didn't see anything except darkness, even after his eyes adjusted to the lack of light. "It's an old exit stop. Gas stations, convenience stores. Probably a Denny's. Come on." She set out on foot with barely a wave for Rob and Krista. "Maybe we'll get lucky."

Lucky, Rob thought to himself. He moved forward, following Moira, and as he did, the small complex came into view—shadows of rectangular buildings and unlit signs, all forgotten as days turned to months turned to years. Would they find a treasure trove of supplies inside? Or would everything useful already be gone?

Moira ran ahead to scout out their options, then motioned them over to a small service station. While he jogged to catch up, Rob's mind wandered to what these places were and what they'd become. The Denny's to the left, it should have been filled with weary travelers and drunken college students. The pharmacy to the right, perhaps the only one for a few miles—the place people relied upon when they were sick.

Both now lifeless shells, transformed by a world that didn't need them to be those things anymore.

But perhaps that was the thing with the post-MGS landscape. There was Moira, who'd broken with civilization only to come clawing back. There was Krista, who played by rules only she understood, but pushed her boundaries to be here. They confronted their own demons, not just because they cared about Sunny, but because it made *sense*, particularly in this world, whatever it was now. Though Krista probably wouldn't admit that, at least not to him.

And now, it seemed right for him to do so too. Looters, rules, all that stuff, they existed in someone else's definitions. All that remained were the things that gave him hope.

Like looting an old service station.

Not looting. Surviving.

There was a difference. Rob was beginning to see that.

As he followed Moira in, Krista a few steps behind him, any queasiness in his stomach or uncertainty disappeared.

They were here on a mission.

"Look, finally a break." Moira tossed him a box. He held it up to the sliver of moonlight and read *Plastic Tank & Radiator Repair Kit*. "Come on, let's see what else they've got left." Though it was near-dark, she seemed to move with an uncanny swiftness. "Flashlights over here. Two of them, I think. And a roll of duct tape. You can always use duct tape."

Rob nodded at her selections, though he wasn't sure if she actually could see it. "Narc taught you to survive overland?"

"Mm-hmm," she said as she led him down each aisle. "The world collapsed, and it was the first freedom I ever had in my life. I chose to spend it drinking. A lot." The tone of Moira's voice softened. "I probably wouldn't have made it past a few months without Narc and his friends. We formed our own family. For a lot of us, it was better than our real ones."

"You need family to survive," Rob said, his voice just above a whisper.

"There were others like us, and we'd go on supply runs together. I mean, yeah, people took, like, a board game or a book or something for entertainment, but most of it was just what you needed. Food, water, supplies." She reached out and grabbed what Rob thought were packs of batteries. "You did what you needed to do to push forward." Moira's silhouette tilted, angling a little closer. "Isn't that why you told Sunny what you did?"

"I suppose so."

"And don't you think that's why Krista's so…Krista?"

"You realize I'm one aisle over, right?" Krista's voice came in from behind the two of them.

Rob laughed and turned back to Moira, only to find her with one hand outstretched holding what looked like a small piece of paper.

"Is that…" Rob squinted in the darkness "…cash?"

Moira's silhouette nodded. "I know how you feel about looters. I know learning that *I* looted wasn't exactly pleasant. So I thought maybe we could leave a twenty on the counter."

Rob reached up, fingers and thumb closing on the paper currency. But rather than take it, he guided her hand down. They stood, hands still linked. "You know, all of us, it doesn't matter how we got here. MoJo or Uncle Dean or Elena. The important thing is that we're here. And we get to Sunny." The sound of opening boxes and crinkled plastic wrapping came from the other end of the store, though Rob and Moira seemed to exist in their own space. "How about we hold on to it for now? I don't want to jinx anything, but I doubt the manager's coming by anytime soon."

Though Moira's face was buried in shadows, he could tell her cheeks rose with a grin. She tucked the cash back in her pocket and stepped forward, close enough that he could feel the heat coming off her in the middle of the cold empty aisle. They nearly came nose to nose when she gasped and broke to the side.

"Oh, wow," Moira said. "This is a sign." She took something off the bottom shelf, and as Krista caught up with them, the moonlight revealed the forgotten treasure. "Look," she said, holding up a backpack. "See what happens when you're famous?"

"Now I totally get why you hate your dad," Krista said.

Rob traced his finger over the vinyl patch on the backpack's main pouch, outlining a stylized image of Moira, younger with wild hair and microphone in hand, with the MoJo logo below it. "Can we give it to Sunny?" he asked.

Moira opened it and began putting the supplies inside. "That's a great plan."

CHAPTER FORTY-FOUR

Sunny

Sunny's chest pounded so much it hurt.

Boom. Boom. Boom.

She put her hand over heart, like she was saying the morning Humanity Pledge. Except this wasn't a morning at school. She did it because it felt like the beats would thump right out of her body.

The nice couple next to her, the ones who'd asked her why she'd boarded the bus alone when she sat down next to them, began to wake up when the bus driver announced they'd got to Seattle. Sunny wasn't sure when exactly the road became the city, just that the long view away had glowing lights in the shadows.

"Do you know where to go to find your mom?" the woman asked with a yawn. Betty was her name maybe, Sunny thought, but she couldn't quite remember and it wasn't polite to ask again. Instead, Sunny nodded and pulled a stack of folded papers from her backpack. She remembered how Ms. Eswara showed them to color a symbol on the back of the papers to see which was which. She thumbed past the square (bus schedule), circle (map to the bus station by their house), triangle (phone numbers), all the way to the heart.

The map of Seattle, with a line drawn from the bus station to Uncle Doctor Dean's hospital.

The woman's mouth turned sideways. Maybe she was still sleepy. She *had* been sleeping for the past hour or so.

"Sunny," Ivo said. She remembered his name. His voice was soft, like when Ms. Eswara announced that Juliana had left for the Reclaimed place. "I think this map is to the hospital."

"Mm-hmm."

"Is your mommy..." Maybe-Betty's voice trailed off. She looked at Ivo before turning back to Sunny. "Is your mommy sick?"

"Mm-hmm. But Uncle Doctor Dean is going to make her better."

"And your dad, he's still back in San Francisco. But your uncle's here with your mom?"

"Mm-hmm." Sunny nodded when she said it because they didn't look too sure at her answer.

Both maybe-Betty and Ivo did that heavy breathing thing that grown-ups did. Ms. Eswara did it sometimes after she talked to the students. Daddy usually did it after he put her to bed, right after he stepped out the door. Krista seemed to do it a lot when she looked at her phone. It seemed to mean that they were thinking hard.

"Well," he said. His voice went quiet when he turned to maybe-Betty, but Sunny still heard what he said. "If she can't get through, what do you say about taking her there?"

"Do you think it's safe to be out?"

"She's just a kid. Her mom's sick."

The woman looked out the window, lines forming around her face. "It's really early. Maybe it'll be quiet. The roads look clear."

Ivo took his phone out. "Looks like we're back in the signal zone." He tapped on his screen. "I'll text Gil and let them know we're going to be another hour." After his screen blinked, he looked back at Sunny. "Sunny, listen. We have to meet up with my brother, but we have some time. We'll help you follow the map, okay? Get you safe to your mom and uncle."

Ivo's phone reminded her, she should check hers too. The signal bar was a big X for the longest time, but now it finally had a few bars. Seven more texts from Daddy. It looked like it sent hers earlier too.

Except the battery bar said it only had 1 percent left.

She skimmed Daddy's messages, questions about how to get in touch and instructions on staying in one spot. This whole thing took longer than she thought it would and she didn't want him to worry, even though she had a surprise in store for him. I am safe, she typed. Some nice people are helping me.

She couldn't help the big grin on her face as she typed the next sentence.

I have a big surprise for you.

A notification appeared to confirm the sent message, then Sunny's phone shut down.

CHAPTER FORTY-FIVE

Krista

The checkpoint into the state of Washington wasn't going to make it into any tourism brochures. Krista spied cones across lanes on both sides of the highway with police cars and barricades funneling traffic into a single lane each for north and south. In and out. At two in the morning on a typical day, there probably wouldn't be enough traffic to fill it up. With nationwide travel restrictions happening, Moira's Jeep was the only vehicle.

A uniformed police officer stood to the side of one barricade, his breath rolling out into the cold night air. Krista steadied herself in the back seat as Moira lowered her window and removed her mask. "Evening, officer." Moira's voice had reverted back to its American accent.

"Evening, folks. Heading home?"

"Yep. Back to Seattle."

"All the way from California, huh?" The officer tugged on his thick jacket with gloved hands, and even from the back seat Krista saw a hint of tremble from the cold.

"My husband and I work there, but we want to be at our real home just in case." For appearances' sake—at least that's what Krista figured—Rob grabbed Moira's hand. "Be with our families."

"I understand. And you, ma'am—" he looked over at Krista "—you're their friend?"

"More like coworker," she said, figuring the appropriate level of relationship would make it seem more natural. "But I think we've become friends during this. Long drive."

The officer gave a tired nod in return. "I hear you. That's my new best friend on the other side there," he said, thumbing to the citizen patrol officer in the southbound lane. "Actually, he's a dick. Takes his authority way too seriously. All the cit-pat volunteers do. I think most of them are in it for the power trip." Their heads bobbed in unison, and Krista made sure to laugh too. "We'll get you rolling quick. IDs, please. And please remove your breathing masks."

Three hands handed three fake Washington IDs over, and Krista felt a little bump in her chest as she watched the officer study them. He took each one and held it up to a flashlight. "I'll be right back," he said, before disappearing into the squad car behind him.

"Goddamn it, Narc," Moira said below her breath.

"Let's not freak out." Krista's words came through gritted teeth. "Nothing's happened yet."

"Could everyone please step out of the vehicle?" he called out, half-inside the driver's side of his squad car.

"There goes that thought," Krista said.

"Shit. Okay, everyone just be cool." Rob turned his head around as he got out, though if he saw a way out his reaction didn't give it away.

"Good idea. Don't freak out." Krista pushed the lever to throw the seat forward. "I really mean it because he's got a gun."

"So do we," Moira said as she undid her seat belt. "We can't let him search the car."

The officer's deep voice came in a clear half yell. "Stand by the back, please." They lined up, Krista in the middle, and she looked over at the other side to find the citizen patrol officer standing at attention, seemingly absorbed in monitoring his half of the path rather than what was happening there. The cop walked slowly over to them. "Mrs. Donelly, what's your address in Seattle?"

"Six nine two Doolittle Road." Moira spat the address out just as they'd practiced in the car. Krista loaded up her own fake address, ready to recite.

"Uh-huh. And what's the cross street?"

Moira's left side tensed up with her fingers curled into a fist, brushing Krista's hand as she did it. "You know what, officer, I'm just blanking right now. It's been a few years since we moved down to San Francisco."

"If it's been a few years, why are your licenses all valid? Shouldn't your current ones be California IDs?"

"We come home a few times a year and renew when we need to. It's easier legally to manage our rental property." Moira spoke the words with real conviction; Krista didn't know anything about managing rental property or if the location of a home address would affect that, but it *sounded* good.

"I see." The officer looked at the IDs, holding them like a poker hand against the flashlight beam. "So, you have your rental property. Is that where you manufacture your fake IDs, or is that down in San Francisco?"

Krista repressed the urge to curse and kick the officer in the shins; Moira let out a sigh while a bead of sweat rolled down the side of Rob's cheek despite the night chill. Various desperate scenarios played out in her head, but before she could judge which had the least potential for disaster, Rob stepped forward. "Look, officer, I'm going to level with you. You have to believe me when I say that my daughter is lost up in Seattle." The officer held up his hand, and Rob took a much slower follow-up step. "We would love nothing more than to be back in San Francisco waiting for good news about a vaccine, but we have to make it to Seattle before the travel restrictions come down fully. Can I show you a picture of her?"

"Slowly," the officer said as Rob reached into his pocket. He held his phone up, then began tapping on the screen after the officer nodded to him.

"See? That's her." He flashed the lit screen toward the officer. "And there and there. I guess pretty much all of my pictures are of her."

The officer leaned in and squinted at the screen. "I remember her," he said quietly. "Start of the shift. Five, six hours ago?"

"You saw her? Was she okay?" Rob's eyes widened; if the officer doubted his sincerity before, he couldn't now. "Who was she with? How did she even get here?"

"She said she was alone. But then the couple sitting by her, they said she was with them, that they were taking her to family in Seattle." He shook his head. "She didn't have ID. Said she was going to see her mom. I'd seen weirder stuff and they vouched for her so with this going on," he gestured around, "I wasn't going to deny her entry for lack of ID." The officer heaved out a heavy sigh as he surveyed the three of them in the dim light. "You know, sir, I feel for you. I really do. Hopefully she's probably already there with her mom now. But the law is the law. I can't let you pass with a fake ID."

They looked at each other, a mixture of desperation and fear in both Moira's and Rob's eyes. Krista thought and thought, her muscle for reading people going into overdrive as she stared at the officer, trying to find *something* they could use.

One idea came through. And much to her own surprise, she didn't hesitate to do it.

"Officer, if I may." Krista stood up straight, trying to project as much confidence as possible. "We're being completely honest with you, but I think we all understand that you've got your duty. On the other hand, I've got eighteen hundred dollars in cash in my back pocket. Now, I'm sure the government isn't paying you overtime in an emergency situation like this, so how about we cover your overtime expenses and you let us go find his daughter?" After the officer nodded, she reached into her left back pocket and grabbed the wad of neatly folded bills.

"Are you trying to bribe me? That's a federal offense."

"It's more than a bribe. It's more than cash. It's a chance. I have carried this with me ever since the quarantine. I've kept it safe, hid it away, but it was always there for me. I knew, I *knew,* that whatever happened, I always had it as a safety net. I could restart my life with it, keep my independence." Krista stared at the cash in her hand. A stack of printed paper or a sum of currency. No, this was something different. "It was the parachute for my life."

The officer nodded, and for the first time, she noticed the deep bags and weary lines etched across his face. "I'm facing eviction," she continued. "My business is dying. I barely renewed my Residence License." In her peripheral vision, she saw Moira and Rob look at each other. Guess they never put it together before. "I thought about taking this cash and just rebooting my life with it. But instead, I want you to have it." Krista held it out, the weight of stacked money resting against her palm. "It's a trade. You do whatever you need to do in your life. We do whatever we need to do for Sunny, because she's *not* with her mom. You get a chance. We get a chance." She looked back at Rob and Moira.

The officer looked each of them over, then checked out the cit-pat, who waved over at him. "Just one second." He returned with some horizontal hand gestures, which hopefully meant "all clear" rather than "arrest these jerks," and the cit-pat returned to his original position.

They stood in silence, neither of them moving a muscle until a tiny speck in the distance grew to approaching bright dots to actual headlights. "Sir, was that really your daughter?"

"Yes, officer. I'd… I don't know how else to say it, but I'd give anything to prove that to you."

"All right," he said. His gloved hand wrapped over Krista's as he took the cash. "Go before things get worse. I hope you find her."

"Thank you." Rob let out a full body sigh, one that deflated everything from his shoulders down as he spouted off four more thank-yous.

They gathered into the Jeep, and the engine roared to life. The officer stepped back, waving as they passed. They drove in tense silence. When they crossed the state line, Rob let out a sigh that filled the entire vehicle, hands on the dashboard. "I thought we were screwed for sure."

"What a team, huh?" Moira's native English accent returned with her short sentence. "Rob sets them up, then Krista bribes them."

"See?" Krista adjusted to sit with her legs up across the back seat. "That's why I use cash for everything. People love cash. Though—" she shook her head "—I should have kept some of it, huh? My big dramatic speech got ahead of itself."

"We're going to need one hell of a bake sale to get that back to you," Rob said.

A tiny part of Krista panicked at the thought of losing her safety net, especially with such uncertainty in the upcoming days. But that part seemed smaller than even she expected, and the closer they got to Seattle, the more her anxiety shrunk. "Some things are more important than money," she said. "But you're right. All forms of payment accepted."

They pushed forward for another mile, a sense of relief taking over the car the farther it got beyond the state border. Rob's phone illuminated the car's interior. "We must have hit a coverage pocket." His voice had a shake in it. "More texts from Sunny. All timestamped a few hours ago. I've got one bar of signal."

"What do they say?" Moira asked, but Rob had already put the phone up to his ear.

"Voice mail. Her phone might be dead now," he said while the car navigated a wide curve around a hill. "Sunny, it's Daddy. If you get this, find a spot and stay still. We're coming to get you, okay? Just be safe." He locked eyes with Krista in the back seat. "We're coming."

CHAPTER FORTY-SIX

Moira

The front door didn't work.

Since crossing the Seattle city limits, they'd seen pockets of protesters and unrest appear, but nothing like the dense group that was standing outside of St. Vincent General Hospital. Signs touted things like *Reclaim Our Country* and the less-friendly *The Cure for Tyranny*, and while some of the people looked like the typical Reclaimed crowd, Moira noted the appearance of masked individuals the closer they got, and they'd donned masks to fit in with the crowd. "Hey!" Rob yelled to the closest security guard. He braced himself against the wood barricade and Moira jammed in behind him, with Krista's shoulder leaning into her back. A bright light came out of nowhere, and after her eyes adjusted, she saw that it had nothing to do with guards but rather a TV news crew lurking by the hospital doors. "Security?"

The officers stood in full riot gear from shields to helmets with no sign of certified citizen patrols around. Perhaps volunteers only got road duty while official law enforcement duties stayed with the big boys. Regardless, the officers either ignored Rob or didn't hear him.

"It's not gonna work," Krista said, her voice muffled by her mask.

Moira gauged the chaos around her, from the unruly crowd on all sides to the armored guards ahead. Going through meant somehow getting past layer upon layer to get to the front door. Narc was usually right, but not this time.

Rob pulled his mask down; it hung by its rubber string from his neck, his full face exposed. "Security!" he yelled. "I need help!" That little touch of humanity must have worked, as the nearest officer broke his frozen stance and stepped their way. "We need to get inside," Rob said to the security officer as he leaned in to hear over the chaos. "My daughter is somewhere in there."

Moira barely heard the response over the growing furor. "Sir, this hospital is currently closed to public admittance. City orders. All medical emergencies are being redirected to County General in—" His sentence got cut off by the sound of breaking glass, first a few feet past the officer, then another directly in front of them as a bottle bounced off his helmet. The TV crew's lights and camera swung in their direction, blinding her vision for a second; when it cleared up, it looked like the lone officer multiplied into a dozen, all with face shields down. More bottles and debris flew overhead.

They had to go. "Come on," she yelled, grabbing Rob's hand with one arm and pushing Krista back with another.

The farther they got to the back of the crowd, the louder the noise grew behind them, as if someone sprinkled pixie dust of aggression over the unruly hordes. By the time they broke free and began back to the car, the sound of police bullhorns demanding order battled the crowd's yelling and screaming.

"These aren't the Reclaimed people I knew." Moira sighed

when they returned to the Jeep. "Narc and Santiago would never do that. These are anarchists looking to blow stuff up."

"Damn it. He was *right* there." Rob's fingers balled into fists, eyes turned skyward. "Plan B?" Rob asked.

Krista punched the air in front of her. "Run over all those jerks and storm the door?"

Moira opened the trunk and rummaged through the things that Narc packed for them. "Maybe this will help," she said, pulling out the police scanner. It squawked to life, spitting out static and random noise until she twiddled some knobs and hit some buttons. Voices passed through, pouring out sentence after sentence of technicalities.

"…and it's just getting worse out front," a male voice said out of the scanner. "If it keeps going, we may need the tear gas. I subdued one who tried to break into the entrance."

"Copy that," a female voice responded. "Suspect is in custody now?"

"That's affirmative. He keeps shouting about how the government is refusing to help the Reclaimed community, so I may need earplugs."

"Copy that. Did you ask if he paid taxes?"

"Negative, but I should. We have the side and back entrances sealed off, though we're low on manpower right now. Sarge said protect the front entrance and the pharmacy wing. We're always running low, even without any looter raids. Leave the loading dock alone for now, the barbed wire and gate will do."

"Copy that. I'll pass that along to the captain…"

Moira turned the volume down and closed her eyes, plan forming in her head. "Loading dock. That sounds like our way in."

Krista marched over to the trunk and shortly after hospital scrubs flew out. Moira snatched hers out of the air, things moving in autopilot. They changed into their disguises quickly, right there by the Jeep. Krista's serious expression seemed out of character for her. Rob carried an equally grim look, though his focus remained on the large hospital building, probably wondering where in the structure his daughter might be. Despite his maintaining a calm exterior for much of the journey, Moira knew him well enough by now to tell that his nerves were on fire this close to the finish line. He shifted, meeting her eyes. She smiled, the warmth coming so easily she wondered how Mo-Jo's plastic expressions had ever overtaken her natural instincts.

Moira did a mental check of everything in the backpack hanging off Rob's shoulders: duct tape, flashlights, binoculars. They left what little cash remained in the car, though Moira saw Krista shove her business card holder in her pocket.

The backpack also held the gun. Unloaded, ammo clip in a side pouch. But still, it was an illegal firearm, and even though she had experience with them during her overland days, being near guns unnerved her. From the expressions on Krista's and Rob's faces, they felt it even more.

Moira led them along the perimeter fence, keeping their distance at first until the loading dock angled into view. From a small hill, they were able to survey the situation: one gate in and out and a long chain-link fence around it, all topped with barbed wire—basically, security for a hospital in a post-pandemic world, one that might slow an angry mob but nothing that could truly keep out individuals who really wanted to break in.

She'd dealt with worse though.

Farther in, a dim orange glow came from the loading area's light, lighting the outline of a man, puffs of smoke trailing behind him. Moira pulled out the binoculars for a better look. The smoking man appeared to be someone on break, not security. One camera was visible, but it lay on top of the door—a door that had a badge reader for security.

"We're gonna need to get that guy's badge. And it looks like that delivery gate's chained up. We need to move fast. He's only on a break." She checked for lighting around the perimeter, as well as any hiding spots. "There." She pointed to a spot with a tree on the outside of the fence and a Dumpster several feet from its interior. "That will hide us. Come with me."

The plans, the instincts for movement and concealment, all activated in ways that felt as instinctive as speaking in an English accent again.

Maybe more.

"Okay. Rob, find a safe spot to grab the barbed wire by hand and pull it down here. Krista, do the same thing there." She gestured about four feet away. Rob was able to reach from his tiptoes though Krista needed toeholds on the fence to give her extra height. "Hold it tight. Do *not* let go," she said. Before they could grunt affirmatives, Moira was up, then swung her leg over the pulled section of barbed wire and dropped to the ground.

She moved to Krista's side and grabbed the same spot in the barbed line. "Krista, you're gonna need to climb too."

Krista's eyes went wide as she looked at the gap of about four feet of depressed barbed wire. "Fuck," she said under her breath. "Yoga does *not* train you for this."

"Just be careful when you swing your leg over. Jump down, I'll catch you."

"Jesus, Moira, how strong are you?"

"Just trust me, we did this all the time with Narc."

Krista scaled the fence, slower than Moira and producing much more noise than she would have preferred. Moira kept glancing over her shoulder at the smoking man, but the noise didn't seem to catch his attention. "Okay, drop," Moira said, and she angled herself to absorb Krista's fall, her arms catching under Krista's shoulders.

Krista looked back at the fence with her feet on the ground. "Let's not do that again."

"Oh shit," Rob said. "He's putting out his cigarette. You guys go before he heads back in."

Moira assessed the situation, from the position of the man to the probable range of the security camera to the equipment in the backpack. "Krista. Run as quietly as you can that way. In the shadows. Then about halfway down the fence line, limp out and call to him for help."

"What are you going to do?"

"No time. Just go."

A grimace came over Krista's face, but she still departed at a brisk pace.

"Rob, slide the backpack under the barbed wire." He did as told, the backpack's straps briefly catching on the top of the fence line but making it into Moira's hands.

"What's the plan?"

"Just wait here." From the distance, Krista made her fake cry for help. Moira set the backpack on the ground, then ripped the zipper open. Rob made an audible gasp when Moira pulled out the gun. "And trust me."

She stepped out from the safety of the Dumpster to see the man approaching Krista, who hobbled on one leg toward him. Bits of their conversation broke through, and Moira had to hand it to Krista. Maybe it was the training as an event coordinator, but she sold her excuse about going on break for a walk before catching her leg on cracked pavement. So well, in fact, that the man didn't realize when Moira began approaching him. She swung her track wide just to make sure they were out of camera view, then held the gun up.

"Don't move. I've got a gun."

The man inhaled as his hands popped up in the air. He glanced back at her, his eyes widened with panic. "Walk slowly to the Dumpster, and you won't get hurt."

"Listen." The man's voice cracked as he stepped forward. "I'm not involved with politics. I mean, I'm registered with the Centrist party, we kind of agree with everyone, you know? And I know nothing about what's happening, I only work here because all the jobs are in the Metro."

"Get the duct tape," Moira said, tossing it over. Krista grabbed it, eyes still filled with uncertainty as they moved over to the far side of the Dumpster. From their angle, Rob was still on the other side but not visible. "What's your name?"

"Jim."

"Listen, Jim. I've got a friend. He's actually just over by the gate. We're not anarchists, and we're not here to hurt anyone. But for now, you're going to have to stay here. On your knees, and stick your hands behind your back." Moira nodded at Krista. "Tape his ankles and wrists."

Krista unfurled the tape with a sharp precision that caught Moira's attention, and maybe that had something to do with setting up events. She moved quickly, though she checked in with the man on occasion, asking him if it was too tight or if it hurt. While Krista finished up, she looked over. "Grab his keys and badge."

Krista frisked the man, then pulled out what Moira requested. "Does this badge open up the loading gate?" Krista said as she released it from his belt loop.

"No. A supervisor has to do it."

"Damn it. But it'll get us inside?" He nodded and Krista gripped the massive key ring, then hooked it onto her belt. "That'll do. I'll figure something out for Rob. One more thing," she said, staying down on his level. "Have you seen a little girl in the hospital? Seven years old, black hair? Earnest in a cute kind of way?"

The creases along his mouth softened and his eyes tightened. "I think so. I saw security walking with a girl about two or three hours ago. She had a scarf, kind of this ugly blue thing." Moira caught the faintest hint of a smile from Krista. He craned his neck around to the two women. "Is that what this is about?"

"It is," Moira said. "And I'm really sorry we're doing this to you. But you're going to have to sit tight until we find her. Cover his mouth. We're not going to hurt you."

"I'm sorry," Krista said, pulling the duct tape over his mouth.

She held the gun up, turning it at an angle to show a hollow bottom. "Never loaded it." From afar, the sounds of police sirens came whirring in, probably at the front of the hospital. "I don't know how much time we have. If you found your uncle, would he talk to you or would he call security?"

"He'd talk. I'm sure of it. I just have to do my part and not yell at him."

"Okay. I'll get Rob over. Let's badge you into the back door, then leave it with me. I'll text you when we're in. Remember, it's a hospital, not a prison. Even with the military around, people will probably still act fairly normal. Act like you belong and you'll blend right in."

"You sure you don't want me to help you get Rob over?"

"There's no time. We don't know how things are going to play out." Moira pointed over to the back entrance and the women began jogging over. "Good luck," she said, as the badge caused the door to beep and unlock.

Krista swung the door open, then handed the badge back to Moira, who shoved it in her pocket. "The first time someone flips out, I'm blaming you," Krista said. Before Moira could come up with a clever enough retort, Krista disappeared down the hallway and the door shut behind her.

From the Online Encyclopedia page on MoJo:

As with many celebrities of the era, the official record for Johanna Hatfield states that she is "missing, presumed dead."

CHAPTER FORTY-SEVEN

Rob

"Is everyone okay?" Rob asked. He tried to position it as innocently as possible, but the fact that a gun was involved and everything was out of view rattled his nerves. "I heard you guys talking but I couldn't make out what was being said."

"Yeah. I'll explain on the way in. He's fine, though. Just tied up." Moira flashed the badge out of her pocket. "Krista's already in. Let's get you up and over." She hopped up on the chain-link fence, then pulled the barbed wire down. "There's a little less space with just me holding it down. Take your time, be careful when you swing your leg over, and you'll be fine."

"Playing softball has definitely not gotten me ready for this," Rob said. He climbed up the fence, first handholds, then one foot in, then the other, and then he moved gingerly up. His muscles burned as he pulled himself to the top of the fence line, the little spears of metal pushed low by Moira's pressure. He pulled his legs up as much as possible and looked down at Moira.

"We totally got this. Trust me."

Trust Moira.

Of course.

As he perched near the top, all sorts of questions began to rattle around in his mind, but none of them questioned her. His first leg swung over, and he tried to use as much slow and controlled movement as he could muster. Given that most of his athleticism had departed about a decade ago, it wasn't the smoothest of attempts.

"Halfway there. Go slow."

They were close. So close to being inside, to being able to *really* look for Sunny.

"Now just prop yourself up and bring the other leg over."

His toes turned inward, a perilous grip on the inside of the fence, and his hands helped him straddle the line. Sweat gathered across his brow, and the sheer *stupidity* of what he was physically trying to do really sunk in.

He brought his other leg over.

"Okay, this is really, oh shi—"

Rob's front leg slipped, letting free of what little grip he had. He toppled forward, hands losing holds and back leg smacking the fence line, possibly even one of the barbs.

"I got you!"

A thunderous clap echoed through the loading dock as something smacked against the fence, and something—presumably Moira—wrapped itself around him, slowing his forward momentum but failing to stop it. When he figured out what had happened, he looked straight down into Moira's eyes, his own hands planted on the pavement as he draped over her. "Oh, shit, are you okay?"

"Fine. Everything's fine." She smiled, flashing a grin as her cheeks lifted, and he realized that her arms were still wrapped around his waist. "I told you to trust me."

"I totally do. Thanks for catching me."

"My pleasure."

He stayed perched over her, the veins pounding in his tensed arms.

They remained, silent on the ground, Rob's knees stinging a little from the impact, but it paled in comparison to the surge of hope in his chest, the same one that told him to get closer and press his lips against hers.

Bathed in fluorescent loading dock lamps next to a rusty Dumpster, they kissed, everything else fading away until only the immediacy of the moment remained. Blood rushed to his cheeks, and Rob slowly pulled back. As he did, the world seemed to have changed. They were still on a mission and there was still an outbreak, but maybe it was finally okay for two people like Rob and Moira to stop running from the past and look toward the future together.

She opened her eyes, looking straight into his. "You were right," Rob said. "We totally got this."

CHAPTER FORTY-EIGHT

Krista

Moira's hunch was half-right—things weren't exactly normal in the hospital. The military presence made Krista feel like she got the side-eye from just about every passing uniform. On the other hand, everyone else looked exhausted and apathetic. Even the guy with the giant machine gun yawned. The hospital's stark lighting didn't help tired complexions, and Krista considered whether she too looked worn down. Might as well fit in.

This probably was a good thing, since a lobby TV showed coverage of the front entrance riot—complete with freeze frame of Rob front and center trying to talk to the guard. Krista recognized herself, though an adjacent shoulder obscured her enough to hopefully prevent any passersby from making a connection.

In her pocket, Krista felt her business card holder. She debated taking it out and flashing its contents—not business cards for networking, but the photo booth print of her and Sunny. Would it be easiest just to ask?

But she decided against it. Too much at stake. Instead, she marched forward, face hidden by a mask.

The main directory listed Uncle Dean's office on the third floor, but a quick check showed that he'd recently moved. From the grousing she'd overheard about military and government operations, chances were Uncle Dean was on the higher floors with them, though nothing gave away his location. A little voice tugged at her to turn around, disappear, keep all blood ties severed clean. But that feeling came and went, the weight of finding Sunny eclipsing any raw nerves triggered by being in the same building, the same *city* as Uncle Dean.

Booming male voices broke through the relative quiet by a break room, and Krista walked in, pretending to ponder the vending machine's selection while eavesdropping. "It's overkill," one security guard said to the other. "Military? They're protesters, not zombies."

"Guess we have some extra-smart doctors here to protect." The other one, a stocky Latino man with bushy eyebrows and a patch of unkempt hair on his chin, leaned back in his chair while he raised his paper cup like a toast. Neither of them wore their masks.

"I'll tell you what," said the standing one, a lanky blond kid whose security uniform hung off him, "if military means I get longer breaks, then I'm all for it."

"Oh, I think you two could handle a little action," Krista said, pulling down her mask and grinning. The two men chuckled in return, and Krista put on the same facade she showed clients, particularly the male members of families: polite, humble, and a little flirty. How many floors were in this hospital? Krista grabbed a number and threw it out there. "Are the smart doctors still holed up on the seventh floor?"

"Is it seven now? I thought it was the ninth floor," the kid said.

Ninth floor. "Oh, that's it. Sorry, I'm just tired. Long shift."

On command, she gently laughed with an insincerity only she could detect.

"You and me both," said the sitting man. "If the outbreak crosses the state line, I'm quitting and going home."

"Nah, I'm not scared." The younger man looked at Krista and shot a cocky grin, one that probably was meant to impress everyone listening. "This whole thing is overblown."

"You only say that because you're young. You can't even legally drink yet." The sitting man looked over at Krista. "You see what I have to put up with?"

Like pushing a button, another laugh came out, this one complete with a shoulder squeeze for the sitting man. "I gotta get back. Oh, by the way," Krista said, keeping the smile, "I heard some story about a young girl wandering about. Is that true, or is everyone delirious now?"

"I didn't see her, but I heard they brought her back to the pediatric ward. You know, it's funny, I heard she said she knew Dr. Francis."

"How about that, huh?" she said, offering a flirtatious wink. "You strapping hunks keep us safe, okay?"

Krista turned and had just about reached the open door when one voice called her back. "Nurse?"

"Yes?"

"Can I see your badge?" The Latino security guard scratched the scruff on his chin as Krista spun back around. "It's not hanging around your neck like it's supposed to be."

"Right, that." She leaned against the door and patted her pocket, hoping it appeared as inconspicuous as she'd planned. Her fingers settled on the rigid form in her pocket, and Krista considered the other option of just running.

Instead, she reached in, flicked open her business card holder, and nudged out the photo from the diner. *Here goes something*, she thought to herself before flashing the photo, fingers and thumb hiding as much of the image as possible, with dim lighting hopefully doing the rest. "I keep it in my pocket. One time, it fell into a bedpan while hanging from my neck. Not cool," she said, shoving it back in. From their seats, the two guards probably couldn't see her hold her breath.

"Ugh, keep it over there. I hope you washed it. Say no more," the guard said. "Okay, thanks. I just wanted to show Mr. I-Can't-Buy-A-Beer that we maintain protocol around here."

"Yeah," Krista said. "You keep on that whippersnapper."

The younger guard mocked being offended, then Krista turned around, consciously trying to move her butt with a little wiggle while she walked away. As soon as she escaped from the view of any possible security guard her stride returned to normal, but her pace quickened and the mask went back on. Her hip buzzed from her phone's vibration; she grabbed it and read as she hit the elevator bay.

We're in, where are you at?

Krista's fingers flew over the phone's virtual keyboard. Sunny might be in pediatrics. Avoid security. They will look for a badge ID and Rob is on the news from the riot. I'm going to find my uncle.

She sent the message, and the display flashed in response. In front of her the elevator dinged, and the doors slid open. She stepped inside, pushed the button for the ninth floor, and leaned back against the wall's handrail.

The elevator began to rise.

CHAPTER FORTY-NINE

Moira

Moira did her best *not* to gawk at the image on the TV. "Don't look up," she said under her breath after reading Krista's text. But it was too late—Rob already caught sight of himself.

She should have asked Narc if his group scavenged any wigs from the campus theater department. But there were no disguises now, only masks so thin that Rob's sharp inhale was audible. She couldn't teach him about Code Polka Dot right then and there, could she?

Probably not. Instead, she laughed, a casual one—not quiet enough to seem odd, and not loud enough to draw attention from the military security walking the floors. Rob looked at her quizzically, then seemed to catch on and broke from the screen showing his face. She motioned him forward and began walking with a calm confidence, a stride that projected that she belonged there: not too pushy but not too passive either, the appropriate level of professional weariness.

It was something she'd worked on since arriving in San Francisco.

Rob followed, though whatever anxiety he felt about Sunny, about being in the hospital, about being associated with the mob outside was hindering his ability to blend in. "Casual," she said under her breath, and he nodded, though by now the combination of fatigue and worry carved deep lines in his face. "Fourth floor." Her fingernail tapped against the directory on the wall, the word *PEDIATRICS* in bright yellow.

"You think we should ask? I mean, we made it all the way here." He adjusted the mask covering his face.

"We're illegally in a guarded hospital. Your face is on every TV screen. Probably best to stay incognito." Moira pointed down the hall. "Stairs. Best way to avoid people."

"Stairs," he muttered while the door closed behind him.

"What's that?"

"Oh. Nothing. I'm just not in the shape I used to be. Not like you," he said, starting the march up four flights. "I kinda expect you to just float up these things."

"Well, we'll have plenty of time to get you back into shape once we find Sunny."

"You gonna teach me to jump off walls?" Rob said, his breaths giving way to huffing after the first flight.

"If you'd like. If I can do it, anyone can."

"I don't know about that. I've never met anyone quite like you."

"You mean a celebrity?" She turned and offered a reassuring grin for the trudge up the next flight.

"Yeah. That's it." They moved side by side, the only noise coming from the pounding echoes of metal stairs. Near the fourth flight, though, Moira noticed that the second set of footsteps wasn't there anymore. She turned and saw Rob at the landing, hand against the wall, breath heavy.

But the look of concern on his face didn't seem like physical exertion. His eyes said something different.

The stairs echoed as she jogged down to him. "Need a breather?"

"Yeah." He huffed air in and out. "But it's more than that. Just questions about…everything. Where do we go if we can't go home? That sort of thing." His face scrunched, from lips to cheeks to brow. "Even if we find her, there's still the Family Stability Board. They could take her right back. I'm sure running away to Seattle doesn't help. I mean, can I file an appeal from here? Ask that border guard we bribed to make a statement?"

The Family Stability Board, Frank, all of their troubles in San Francisco. Even though they left it all behind about twenty-four hours ago, it felt like lifetimes. Maybe it was the physical distance. Or maybe it was because everything that happened in that span seemed to change each of their trajectories.

But it didn't mean that those issues disappeared. For now, though, first things first.

"I understand. But we can't worry about that unless we find her. So let's do that, and then handle it."

"There's one more, though." His tone dropped, the sense of urgency changing into something much more vital, personal. "I still don't know what I'm going to say to her. What Elena would want me to say to her."

Rob had hardly talked about Elena. He referenced her in the context of what Sunny did or didn't know, but who she was as a person, a lot of that remained buried in his head. Moira couldn't claim to speak for her, nor was that her place to. Yet this circumstance felt more universal than that. Not just with their little group, but for anyone who suffered from PASD—dealt with or not.

"The truth." Moira turned to him, the statement landing without condemnation or judgment. It was a simple fact at this point. "Even if there's another outbreak. Even if there's another quarantine. That's what we owe each other."

No words passed between them, though standing next to Rob, she felt his body tense. He kept staring at the stairs, eyes down and focused somewhere else.

"When I told Sunny Elena was still alive," he finally said, "I don't think I did it for my daughter." The only sound came from the ventilation ducts above the metal door.

During one of the early MoJo tours, she'd asked Chris about the pace of it all, how it whirled by so fast that her memories seemed to come in flashes, fragments. "Memories are meant to fade," he'd said. "They're built with an expiration date."

She repeated the nugget of wisdom, and Rob finally broke his stance. He looked her square in the eye. "It's okay to move on," she said. "That doesn't mean you let go."

Somehow, despite where they were and what was happening, Rob smiled at her. And she understood why. In the harsh fluorescent light of the stairwell, his fingers locked in with hers.

Moira tugged his hand. "Come on. We'll find her. We'll tell her together."

"No," he said, turning to her. "I have to tell her by myself. No offense."

Moira felt the warmth of his cheek, the scruff of his morning shadow brush by before she pressed her lips against his. "None taken."

Excerpt from *Walking in the Dark: An Oral History of the Fourth Path*:

"I watched them from a cliff, one woman leading a wake of humanity. It was unlike anything you'd ever seen. Wastelanders, people in business suits, children, a whole range of people. It gave me faith in humanity for a moment. I saw all these people looking to one person, and that one person looking ahead, and they were moving together. Something symbolic about it, you know?

"But then they kept walking, quietly. It took about thirty minutes for the last person to leave my view. Didn't stop to eat. Didn't stop to drink. Just kept going. And that was fucking disturbing.

"I don't know if they just kept walking to, like, Arizona, or if they walked into the ocean. Maybe they got beamed up by aliens. Or maybe they're just living happy, off the grid, in like caves or something.

"But they probably all died of dehydration somewhere in the desert. Because they followed one person rather than talking to everyone else there."

CHAPTER FIFTY

Moira

The pediatric wing of St. Vincent General Hospital had the opposite vibe of the ground floor. Whereas protesters created a din that mixed with the lobby chatter, pediatrics resembled a mausoleum. Nobody loitered. No keyboards clicked. No phones chimed. The only footsteps came directly from Rob and Moira. Even the lights were at half power.

"Looks like everyone left in a hurry." Moira angled around to peer inside the nearest room; bed sheets crumpled on the floor while a corner night-light gave a hint to the bright colors painted on the wall. A few steps down the hall showed a similar picture. Four straight rooms all looked and felt pretty much the same.

"Power's off on the systems." Rob tapped on the front desk keyboard. "Phone's not getting anything either."

"I'm going to look around."

"I'll check around here for notes or anything about Sunny."

Sections looked dormant, but not in a ransacked kind of way. Books and toys sat neatly on shelves, though office papers looked hurried and scattered. Moira turned the corner and began her search along the left wing of the floor. This felt familiar; they'd broken into sterile environments like this years ago, places that were abandoned and too much trouble for the casual looter, but ideal for resourceful groups seeking supplies and a spot to rest for a night or two.

Those times didn't have the din of protesters and fear bleeding in from outside.

The first room, a playroom with a large window, stopped her in her tracks. It wasn't the Lego castle on the desk, despite the impressive intricacy of it, or the life-size Pooh Bear in the corner.

It was a backpack perched on the edge of an end table, one oddly out of step with the room's sterility thanks to a bus schedule sticking out the top pocket.

"Rob!" The call echoed across the cubicles and equipment at the center of the floor.

"What is it?" he asked, jogging in. She pointed at her find. "She's been here." Rob grabbed the left strap of the backpack, then sat on the child-sized stool next to it. "This is hers." The main pouch sat half-open, and he pulled the zipper down the side. "Bus schedule. Sweatshirt. Her bunny. Look at this," he said, unfolding a printed sheet. "A map. A map of downtown Seattle. She even marked the line from the bus station to here. I blame her teacher. She just had a big lesson on maps."

"Well." Moira clicked the room's light switch to no effect. "You think she'll come back for it?"

"Why would they abandon Pediatrics?" Rob said, leaning against the front counter.

"The protesters." Moira grabbed a memo off the reception counter and held it up. "It says they wanted to move young patients upstairs so they wouldn't hear too much of it. Sounds like it happened when the anarchists joined the mob. Just says 'secured location upstairs.'" Moira's mind went into overdrive, immediately conjuring what that might mean, how many floors were in the building, which one might be chosen.

Suddenly the door to the stairwell flew open so hard it clanged on the end of its hinges. Moira grabbed Rob's hand and pulled him down below cubicle walls.

"Hospital security," a voice boomed. "Show yourself."

She tried to visualize the ward for possible escape routes. From where they were, they could crawl forward into the playroom across the hall. Then they could wait it out while the guard—no, guards, as she heard two sets of voices, one male and one female—passed, then they could crawl back to the cubicle farm. Depending on the search path of the guards, they could either sprint for the stairs or dash out the main hallway. She stayed in a crouch, trying to remain steady to not create any weight shifts that might cause tiles or flooring to creak, though she angled her head to see the pediatrics funhouse mirror on the wall.

From there, she could see the two guards. Distorted in shapes that would have been amusing to anyone under ten years old, but enough visibility to identify them.

There were three people, actually. One guard dressed in a blue uniform with patches. One woman in hospital scrubs.

And a man in military fatigues, complete with machine gun.

Moira leaned over to Rob and whispered as softly as possible. "When I count to three, follow me. Move as quietly as you—"

She stopped when Rob shook his head no.

In the mirror, the guards began to move, the military man breaking off from the other pair.

"We should turn ourselves in," Rob whispered. "Krista's close to her uncle. We should show ourselves and talk. We're not terrorists."

"That's a bad idea. We can't trust them."

"Then trust *me.* It's time to stop running." Rob's eyes pleaded with her, and though it fought against every survival instinct she'd built up around herself ever since Madison Square

Garden—maybe even since that first press conference—she found herself giving in. Not to Rob's logic, but to his sense of being.

She nodded. And he returned it.

"We're unarmed," he said, gradually standing up with hands up. "We're not protesters. We're looking for my daughter."

She followed suit, listening as the footsteps came around on the floor tile. She tracked them, aware of their locations as they closed in, aware of Rob trying to explain what was happening, aware of everything around them. Except something flipped in her, turning her impulses into something just as alert but lacking the sheer panic that often drove survival mode. The calm in Rob's voice was received with a steady but firm response, and though Moira was tense, vigilant, it didn't surge with the hyper instincts of Code Polka Dot.

This was different.

CHAPTER FIFTY-ONE

Krista

The last time Krista felt nerves like this, her life was about to restart. And not at a hospital but just outside a prison.

Mick had moved back and forth, mewing while tilting the balance of the carrier. Krista tightened her grip on the top handle when a voice called out, "Next."

She walked up to a small desk set up in the front lobby of New York quarantine NY2, where sat a woman with a clipboard and a laptop tied into a solar-powered generator. "Hi," Krista said, setting down her discharge papers. Laptop keys clicked and clacked, and Krista's attention turned to the bus awaiting passengers, ready to take them to the converted hotel set for temporary dorm usage before available property went into public distribution.

The man who'd just finished at the desk stopped halfway to the bus, his rolling luggage catching on a small pebble and hopping before holding static at his side. He looked back, as if the quarantine was a giant as tall as the Statue of Liberty, and the luggage wheels started to rattle. Krista realized that it stemmed from his trembling hand, and despite his broad shoulders and towering height, tears began to stream down his dark brown cheeks, so much so that he collapsed to his knees, knocking over his single bag. His hands covered his face.

Krista glanced at the desk, where the woman kept tapping away, unfazed by the disturbance. "Okay, Krista Deal. Single traveler."

"With a cat," Krista said, nodding down at the carrier in her hand. Mick mewed an affirmative.

The woman acted like she hadn't said a word. "You'll be in the Manhattan temporary dorms, building C-three. They'll assign you a specific room when you get there. Here's your information packet on asset redistribution, claiming old property, and other logistical questions." She rattled off the facts like a flight attendant going over the exit doors rather than providing steps to the world's complete reboot. Halfway across the courtyard, the man still sobbed.

"Should we help him?"

"I see this every fourth or fifth person. Give him a few minutes, he'll calm down. Any questions?"

Krista shook her head, then adjusted Mick again and grabbed her own bag. The man managed to get up and after dusting himself off, his eyes met hers. She offered a nod and a half smile, the same weary kind of assurance that she'd given her bunkmate while talking her through all the feelings that came alongside getting married in the middle of a quarantine following a pandemic. He returned her nod and began marching to the bus.

The bus driver, who'd been sitting on the steps with a book, looked Krista's way. "You're our last one for the day," he called out.

The heel of her shoe ground against the pavement as she turned, doing the same look as the man earlier. She stared at the building, the massive walls and barred windows that seemed to be a time capsule for everyone's pain, as if crossing the threshold of the fence line granted permission to exhale.

But while everyone saw the past, Krista stared at the future—a future free from the bloodlines that tied her to a life and family she'd never asked for.

That afternoon, Krista had spun and marched onto the bus. She'd sat as the engine roared to life, Mick's cat carrier settled across her lap, and didn't look back when they pulled away.

Only forward. Never back.

And definitely never paused.

She wanted to believe in that now. Except to move forward, she had to step back.

It was unavoidable this time around.

In his photo, Uncle Dean looked the same as Krista remembered. Same smug tilt of the head, same beady stare, same awkward smile. Things hadn't changed much since her earliest memories of him or since the last time they spoke, a month or two before the quarantine. "Asshole," she said, the tone as low as the volume. Just like when she was a kid, she'd waited for him to show up and save the day. This time, she was outside the door to his makeshift office, staring at the name tag and photo ID taped on the wall.

Ten minutes passed. It didn't matter, because just like then, he didn't come through—he probably was too busy with other work.

Some things never changed. Consistency was something she prided herself on, probably because every single blood relative had failed at it.

Found my uncle, she typed in a text to Rob, sit tight and stay away from security for now.

She fired off another curse under her breath when something bumped into her shoulder.

"Oh," Uncle Dean said, clearing his throat. "I'm sorry, nurse."

And just like that, Uncle Dean moved past her and walked toward his office door.

Krista glanced behind her, then all around, then checked down the hallway, and while she heard voices somewhere, no one was within view. Maybe they were just all the angry voices in her head. He disappeared into his office, and soon she heard the clicking of a keyboard.

She took a step forward, one foot seemingly caught in the next, and while her mind zipped like lightning, her body reacted the opposite, becoming a clumsy collection of marionette movements. Somehow, she got through the open door, and somehow she closed it behind her.

"Yes?" Uncle Dean said, glancing up from his desk, no mask on his face. "I'm sorry, did you need something? Oh." His eyes widened and he tore his glasses off, rubbing the remaining bits of hair on his head. "The transcripts for the French team. I forgot, didn't I? Give me one—"

"Look at me." Krista tore her mask off and her voice rang out, not loud but with a force strong enough to shatter glass. She took a step closer, then another, until she stood right in front of his desk, her knees touching its metal side. "What's my name?"

His mouth hung open, frozen in confusion while he put his glasses back on and blinked. "Krista?" He stood up, the chair beneath him rolling back and hitting the bookshelf against the wall. "Krista? You're—"

"I'm standing right here."

"You're *dead*. I was at your funeral. I mean, I paid for your funeral myself."

"You wasted your money."

"But we got a note, Kristen and me, we got a note that said you were dead. An official document—"

"From Nassau County," they said at the same time. Krista kept going, though. "Jesus Christ, you're as gullible as Mom. I swear, I must have inherited my survival genes from somewhere else. I paid to have a forged document sent to you. By some guy on Long Island who ran a printing business." His open mouth showed he was reeling, and she wanted to say more, to go for a knockout punch. Yet only silence lingered between them.

"Krista. My God." Uncle Dean's fingers bored into his forehead as his thumb balanced on his cheek. "Why…why would you do that?"

"Oh, don't give me that. Now you care. You know when you didn't care? All those times I waited for you while Mom got hammered. You think it's easy to play, to study, to be a goddamn child when a drunk is screaming at the wall? A mom that fights you off when you try to take a bottle away? A mom that needs you to clean up her puke for her, to wake her up for work? You think that's *normal* for a kid? I still remember the last time we talked. The intervention that *you* didn't come to. 'I don't think it's our place to get involved.' That's what you said." The words began to roll out of her mouth, each laced with poison and fire, propelled at an uncontainable momentum. "I learned one hell of a lesson that day. I guess I should thank you. You taught me to rely on myself."

Uncle Dean sank farther into his chair with each word. She hesitated, just for a second, long enough for him to start to say something before she launched into it again. "So I'm sorry if you thought I was dead, but I didn't think one more death notice would make a hell of a lot of difference to you. Or Mom, for that matter. Neither of you ever cared."

"Krista," he said, his voice barely audible, "your mom—"

"Save it. There's a little girl named Sunny in this hospital, and I want you to bring her to me *right now*."

"The girl." He blinked behind his glasses several times before inching forward, hands placed on his desk. "You know the girl?"

"I'm taking her back with me to San Francisco before anyone fails to protect her." She stood, shoulders up and chest tall, and for the first time in her life, she felt like she truly towered over someone. "*I* care about her too much for that to happen."

Without speaking, Uncle Dean picked up his phone and punched a series of numbers on the pad. "Security? This is Dean Francis. The girl we found, the one who said she knew me. She does know me after all. Or a relative of mine. Can you bring her to my office? Okay. And please let the Seattle FSB know they won't be necessary. Okay. Thank you." He set the receiver back in its cradle but continued to stare at it. "She's sleeping. They'll wake her and bring her up."

"Look at big Uncle Dean," her words were gravelly from her dry mouth, "protecting the little girl he found. Nice to see you add something to your repertoire. What's next, you actually going to cure this new virus?"

Uncle Dean's sigh filled the room. His face changed, the color dropping from a pale blotch under fluorescent hospital lighting to a more ashen tone. "Yes and no," he finally said.

"See, even with this you can't stick with an answer. What the hell does 'yes and no' mean?"

"I'm..." His voice trailed off, leaving only the murmur of the outside hallway to eat up the empty seconds. "There's nothing official yet. But we've been preparing for this situation for close to a year. Medically speaking. I believe governments have had outbreak contingencies in place ever since society restarted. Things happened far before any rumors did. France, Kenya, and Australia have been invaluable. Russia's shutting us out, even though we keep offering to share information. The isolated flu symptoms. It was scary to see, but it gave us a head start. The government's blood donation protocol, we've been able to isolate immunity elements." Uncle Dean's demeanor changed. This was a different type of defeat. "This new mutation, I think we've got a handle on it. But it's going to keep—"

"Oh, should we throw a parade? I'll call Mom and we'll go buy a piñata and—"

"Krista, your mom is dead."

Uncle Dean's words dammed up all of her momentum, causing her to lurch between her anger and her shock. Dead. Her stupid, horrible mother was dead. The very idea of it wore her down to the core, exposing something buried long ago: the little girl inside that just wanted her mommy to do the right thing. But in her place stood a woman who had to accept forever being an orphan.

"Figures. It totally figures," she finally forced out, her voice matching his soft tone despite her best intentions. "I knew she wouldn't make it. She was too stupid."

"Kristen died shortly after we had our funeral for you. The last thing we argued about was the music I chose for it. The Clash, of course. 'Lost in the Supermarket.' 'Should I Stay or Should I Go' was too obvious."

She could feel his eyes searching, looking for some sort of connection but her gaze remained strictly on the floor. "I would have also accepted 'Somebody Got Murdered.'"

"I thought you would have appreciated it," he said, letting out a heavy sigh. "She thought it was disrespectful."

"Disrespectful. Like Mom knew anything about that. She died. I knew she would," she said, her voice getting weaker. "I knew it. Of course I knew it." She squeezed her eyes shut so he wouldn't see, but the tears just leaked out the side. "I knew it. I knew it." She turned away from him, away from Uncle Dean's world of evil and horrible sentimentality. "I knew it."

"Krista," he said. She heard his footsteps on the tile, but his movements didn't register with her, not until they stood side by side. "Your mom—"

"I *hate* you." This time, the words came at full volume without control. In her peripheral vision, she could see the words attacking him, cutting away at his posture until he seemed only inches tall. "You *never* got involved. You knew, you *knew* what she was like and you chose to stay out of it. You let it happen."

She turned again, her knees shaking despite having already collapsed into a chair. Warm palms pressed against her face, tears sliding under them. "You let it happen. You let it happen."

On a certain level, Krista knew how *undignified* her meltdown was, how unlike the person she prided herself on being. But the facts were the facts: she didn't need to mourn her mother, the Kristen Francis she knew. She needed to mourn the idea that Kristen Francis departed the world without ever becoming the mother that Krista Deal needed, as a child or an adult.

That, in itself, was an acceptable reason to break her down for a minute or two.

"Krista? Krista." Uncle Dean must have turned on his doctor voice; it came across as gentle and soothing, the type of thing he was probably trained to say just before revealing to a patient that she had six minutes to live. "You're right. And I have to live with that." His voice shook, each syllable chained to the next through the most fragile of connections. "I'm so sorry."

Despite her proclamation, drumming up the necessary vitriol to truly hate Uncle Dean seemed impossible. His apology broke her stride, stealing her emotional thunder and making it harder and harder to stay on course.

She tried. This was what she clawed for all those years ago, when she left the quarantine and started life afresh. This was why she had a giant stack of cash in a safe. This was why she ordered a falsified death certificate after a bit too much wine. Life without family, without a past, without anything to tie her back to *them* or other unnecessary things, a principle she'd clutched on to for dear life. And yet, with three small words, Uncle Dean somehow opened a new possibility: What if she just let all that go?

Somehow, it worked. Somehow, she found herself sitting, body shaking from the tears of release, and when he put a hand on her shoulder, she didn't recoil or fight. Part of her demanded that she be tougher *right now*, but in that moment she realized that that part was as sad and scared as the rest of her. And while she wasn't ready to hug it out and have Uncle Dean over for burritos, the longest first step was taken.

"Why didn't you help?" she said, finally able to speak.

"Because I didn't know what to do. She always said she just needed one more chance. One more chance. And I believed my big sister. Every time."

"Well, she was an idiot. She'll always be an idiot. And you're a bigger idiot for listening to an idiot."

"I'm not arguing with you there." His grip loosened, and he stepped back.

"Did she even make it to rehab?" In just about every circumstance, Krista would have been mortified to let anyone see her with tear stains and nose sniffles. Somehow, the need to protect against that didn't surface this time.

"What do you think?"

"Of course not."

"You always had a good intuition. No, she went into quarantine with the rest of them. I was taken away to the UN research facility, so I couldn't track her until after things settled down. From what she said, her quarantine got good at smuggling in booze."

"What did she die from?"

"Liver failure." Her palm swept across her mouth in a vain attempt to erase the emotions that burst out. Krista's stare fell straight down, burrowing into her shoes, then the carpet underneath. "Don't waste your energy wondering if you should have forgiven her. She never earned it. She never changed. I still think about that. Did she ever hit rock bottom? Her daughter stopped talking to her, she went into a quarantine, so many people *died*. But through it all, someone enabled her." Uncle Dean rubbed his brow, his palm brushing against his glasses as he did so. "Most of the time, that was me." Each passing word seemed to break his posture a little more, chipping away until the defenses were gone. "You did the right thing by staying away," he said with a sigh.

The sentiment sat in Krista, stewing over a lifetime of rage and neglect. "She wasn't family. She was a relation. Family would do better," she said finally.

Which was Uncle Dean? The question lingered for a moment and the answer wasn't definitive, but at least it was a *direction*.

He'd have to earn it back.

"You are as stubborn as your mom." He laughed, the first laugh of their entire reunion. "You know that?"

"Smarter, though."

"Yes." Uncle Dean let out a heavy sigh, and for the first time she noticed the weary posture of his slumped shoulders. "Absolutely."

A knock arrived from the door, along with a muffled voice. "Security." Uncle Dean looked her way, and she nodded. The door swung open.

"Krista!" Sunny's blissful cry matched the volume of Krista's earlier tirade. She ran toward her, knitted scarf trailing, and Krista scooped her up, squeezing her with enough force to protect her against killer viruses, lying adults, and protesting hippies.

"That's a nice scarf you got there."

"I know."

"I thought you didn't like the colors I used?"

"I don't like green. But I like it because you made it and this way you can come with me." Sunny looked up, head tilted inquisitively. "Are you still mad at me?"

"No, Sun," she said, trying to keep her voice steady. "Of course not. We're friends, remember? Friends forgive each other."

"You didn't bring Daddy, did you?"

"I did," she said as Sunny's feet landed back on the ground. "And Moira too."

"MoJo!"

"Well, I think she'd prefer to be called Moira."

"But you can't spoil my surprise for Daddy. I'm going to talk to Mommy so she'll come home."

"Right. Well, I suppose it's up to him now. Sunny," she said, turning her to Uncle Dean, "there's someone here I want you to meet."

CHAPTER FIFTY-TWO

Rob

Rob wasn't sure how much time had passed since security took them away from Pediatrics. They sat in a small room behind a locked door, a couple of metal chairs and a side table offering little comfort, everything in their pockets confiscated. Only a box of disposable breathing masks and a bottle of hand sanitizer remained, and that probably was for the hospital staff's own protection.

Good thing security didn't know about the bag of things from Narc stashed under the Dumpster. He wondered when they should bring up the guy Moira and Krista had tied up.

"You think they're gonna question us?" Moira asked.

Despite being on their own, they'd sat in silence most of the time. Which, Rob figured, made sense. He *wanted* to spend more time with Moira, to get to know more of the true person who finally seemed to be emerging. But being held in a makeshift detention didn't exactly make for the best arena for that.

Not when they still didn't have confirmation about Sunny.

The door suddenly flew open, and a man in a blue uniform stepped in. "Is your name Rob Donelly?"

That seemed like a strange question considering they took his wallet. But given that they had used fake IDs to get here, perhaps not that strange. "Yes, that's me."

"Sir, I think we found something of yours."

"What's—" A high shriek pounced over Rob's question. The man stepped aside, two small hands pushing him at waist level to shove into the doorway.

"Daddy!"

Words poured out of Rob in a garbled mess while he held his daughter, and the troubles of everything outside the hospital melted away. Another outbreak may have been on the verge of eating the planet alive, but for that moment the world was complete. "Sunny," he said after regaining his composure. "We were all worried sick about you. Why didn't you pick up when I called?"

"Because I wanted it to be a surprise. And my phone ran out of battery."

"Well, you surprised me all right," he said. Moira knelt down next to them, a hand on Rob's arched back, her free arm halfway around Sunny.

"One happy family." Krista popped into the doorway, then walked over and put her hands on Sunny's shoulders. "You've raised a little troublemaker, haven't you?"

"I'm not a little troublemaker."

"That's right, Sunny. You're a *big* troublemaker." In the few weeks since Krista had invaded their lives, Rob had never seen her smile quite like now. And when he stood up to meet her on an adult level, her demeanor clearly illustrated that something was different. An aura of something—weary? humble?—penetrated Krista's space, something in her expression that lacked the intensity of every other encounter they'd had.

"Mr. Donelly, I've got good news for you." A stocky man

stepped forward, and Rob recognized him as Krista's uncle Dean. He reminded himself *not* to use one of Krista's nicknames for him.

"Dr. Dean Francis? Or Uncle Dean?" He held out his hand to shake and couldn't remember in the moment if Krista had ever explained why she detested him so. She held everything so close to the vest.

Though now that he thought about it, they all did. Everyone in this new world.

"I've heard a lot about you," Rob said.

"Well, I hope I can make a better impression in person," he said, taking his hand. "Your daughter's asked me about your wife, and unfortunately I'm not treating her personally. In fact, I'm not sure why the doctors wouldn't let Sunny talk to her, but we'll get that straightened out. I can help."

Even in his peripheral vision, Rob could see Krista shake her head.

Uncle Dean glanced back at the security guard. "This is my niece—" he gestured at Krista "—and her friends. Can we get a few minutes alone?"

"Of course, Doctor." He stepped outside and the door clicked shut behind him.

"Look, I…this is not public knowledge yet. But it will be. Might be a week. Maybe two weeks. Hopefully a few days. That means it's getting out there faster. But this new illness, we have a new antiviral protocol and a vaccine for it."

For someone announcing such positive news, Uncle Dean's expression remained grim. Lines sunk in across his forehead, his eyes squinted, and his shoulders tensed.

"When that's ready for public distribution, then President Hersh will make an announcement. Something we've known for a while. You're gonna hear it soon. It might as well be from me." Behind him, Rob heard Moira straighten up, and her fingers dug into his shoulders tightly. Krista looked at Uncle Dean, a confused expression on her face.

This must have been new to her too.

Sunny didn't seem particularly interested in what the grown-ups were talking about, and instead climbed on a chair to look out the window, the colors of the morning sun starting to beam in.

"The truth is that this cure we're working on, it's not going to last. MGS is the fastest-mutating virus we've ever seen. The thing that's been unleashed, it's going to be around for a really long time. All we can do is throw all of our resources onto it. People think the federal government is a puppet show, and it's not. We are looking at the big picture: the survival of our species. Taxes, education, infrastructure, none of that matters if MGS goes wide again. That's why population centers are under the watch of states because on a national level, we've got a bigger battle to fight, and we have to coordinate it with teams around the world. We knew this—we *knew* it coming out of quarantine. But internationally, it was agreed to keep it quiet under Project Preservation. Can you imagine people finally settling back into some type of normalcy, only to hear right away that something's gonna happen, maybe soon? It'd be anarchy. It'd be like the wasteland gangs, but everywhere.

"No one wants to do another quarantine. The easiest thing in the world is status quo. Changing everything once was a damn miracle. Trying to do it again? Trying to make it a regular option? That's pretty much impossible. We have to stay ahead of it. The *only* thing we can do is stay ahead of it. That's what Hersh is going to tell people. That's how we save lives."

The rumors from the other Metronet feeds and discussion groups, they turned out to be true. Maybe not *exactly* true, but true enough that Uncle Dean's revelation seemed more admission of guilt than whopping surprise.

Of course. If something affected the lives of that many people, it couldn't simply be stuffed back into the bottle.

"There is no new normal. It's going to keep changing, keep escaping from us. And our world needs everyone to know, to step up right now. Complacency isn't an option. We have to move forward. We can't waste a single second."

Rob turned and looked at Sunny, kneeling on a chair, arms crossed across the windowsill. She looked at the sunrise, not down at the rioters stories and stories below. Sunny would grow up in this, knowing that MGS lurked around the corner. And yet looking around him, he saw Krista watching his daughter too. Moira reached over and locked her fingers into his.

The future, as it was, appeared more uncertain than ever before. Not necessarily death. Not necessarily life. But what they made out of it—and how they adapted to whatever might happen, past what might have been.

At least they could do that together.

"The, um, good news is that we have *this* cure in the hospital." Uncle Dean moved to face Rob as he talked. "Sunny tells me your wife is awaiting treatment. If we hurry and she's in isolation, we should have time, and I'll personally make sure it's delivered to her."

The mention of Elena seemed to snap Sunny back into the conversation. "And once I talk to Mommy, I know she won't be mad anymore. Then she'll come home, and *then* we'll have a wedding." She hopped off the chair and tugged on his arm. "That's my surprise for you," she said, looking up.

Moira leaned over to whisper in his ear. "It's okay. We'll give you space."

Rob watched, feeling as though he was floating above his body while Moira ushered Krista and Uncle Dean out. "We'll be right outside," she said, and the door hydraulics whooshed shut.

Rob lifted his daughter, sitting her on the table on the side of the room. "Sunny, I have to tell you something about Mommy."

"Can I help pick out her dress?" She blinked and looked up at him, her eyes wide yet focused. "I learned about wedding planning from Krista."

He'd come up with about a dozen ways to start this conversation, and none of them started with answering a question about Elena's theoretical dress. "Yeah, about that." He cleared his throat and took a breath; that wasn't the right way to start. What *was*? Elena would know. In difficult discussions, she'd start off with one positive thing to set the tone, no matter how ridiculous it was.

Rob smiled, a flash only to himself. She was still with him. She'd always be—and with Sunny too. "Let's back up a little bit."

Through the small window in the door, Rob saw Krista talking animatedly to Uncle Dean. Her voice came to life as soon as he opened the door, and he realized that she'd been telling him about how they all happened to collide into one another. "That's when the Family Stability Board decided—"

She stopped at the sound of the door and turned. Not to face Rob. But to drop down on her knees and meet Sunny.

Sunny looked up at Rob, her cheeks flushed from crying. He offered a smile, one that tried to signal that she was free to do whatever she needed to do.

She ran to Krista.

If things were normal, a choice like that would hurt him, a mix of bitterness and disappointment, first that he hurt his daughter, and second that he couldn't be the one to comfort her. But instead, he watched Krista envelop the young girl in her arms, whispering in her ear.

Uncle Dean was wrong. There was a new normal.

This was the new normal.

"How'd it go?" Moira mouthed to Rob from across the room.

"As well as it could," he said aloud.

"Sunny, I'm so, so sorry." Krista pulled back, her hands wrapping around Sunny's. "I know you're upset. You have to know that your dad only did what he did because he wanted to protect you. He went about it wrong, but he did it for the right reason, and feels terrible about it. It's the thought that counts, right?"

"It hurts. Everything hurts inside."

"Believe me, I know what that feels like. I'll help you through this. I'll be here, and the hurt will go away, okay?"

Sunny nodded while Krista caressed her crimson cheek. "I wish I could have seen her."

Uncle Dean's phone buzzed. He glanced at it, then leaned over to Krista. "I need to get going," he said softly.

"Give me one more second," she said to him, then turned back to Sunny. "Sunny, I know you're mad at your dad right now. But I hope you can forgive him at some point. When he's earned it. Knowing him, that'll be soon. He's taken that first step." Her eyes met Rob's, then turned back to Sunny. "And then it's up to you to decide. Okay? See, relations are people with the same blood. But family, that's different. Family is about who gives you hope, who gets involved. And earns the right for forgiveness. Or at least starts down that path. Right, Uncle Dean?"

"That's right, Krista," Dean said, his voice low.

"You understand?" Krista said.

"I think so." Sunny turned back to look at Rob. "I'm mad at him."

"I get it. It'll take some time. And that's okay."

"Krista, you promise me one thing."

"What's that, Sunny?"

"Don't you go anywhere." Sunny's words came across as equal parts request and demand, and she stood unblinking while she awaited an answer.

"Don't worry. I promise you, I'm getting involved." She held her arms open again, and Sunny collapsed in, giving one of her trademark bear hugs.

Uncle Dean nodded at them. "Let me know if you need anything." His words carried a solemn weight.

Moira had crossed the room and taken Rob's arm as this unfolded. While they watched Uncle Dean start down the hallway, Rob turned to Moira."I've got an idea," he said to her quietly before calling out. "Hey, Dean?"

Uncle Dean stopped and turned in midstep.

"Would you mind writing something for me?"

Excerpt from President Tanya Hersh's speech on the MGS 96 vaccine:

My fellow Americans. It is with great relief that I announce the end of the transportation lockdown as necessitated by MGS 96. A cure for the infected has been achieved, and the most critical will receive the first batches. After that, inoculation stations will be set up around Metros. Reclaimed Territory citizens and those who live out in wastelands are welcome to receive vaccinations. Individual states will provide local instructions and guidelines.

However, while this is good news, I also must inform the public of recent discoveries made by our scientific team. The MGS virus is an evolving challenge, and it is the unanimous consensus of the international scientific community that our priority as a species is to stay ahead of this moving target.

To that end, we have committed our resources as an international community toward this goal; this is known as Project Preservation and has been ongoing since the end of quarantine. I am personally asking for every American to move forward with this in mind. For survivors of the initial pandemic and for future generations, it is time to understand that some things cannot be undone. In this situation, there is no reset. But we as a people can be smarter, better, and more focused on keeping it at bay.

All of us carry this responsibility. It will be hard but I'm confident in our resolve. God bless you, God bless the American people, and God bless every survivor of the MGS virus. We will persevere.

PART 5:

FAMILY

CHAPTER FIFTY-THREE

Moira

The woman leaned forward in her chair, and looked Moira in the eye. Bright lights beamed down from overhead. It felt uncomfortably familiar, but this situation was much different.

Here, Moira was in control.

"Take your time," the woman said. "We'll edit this later for broadcast."

Moira glanced back at Rob who stood in the dark part of the studio next to some people in headsets running back and forth. He offered a thumbs-up and mouthed, "You got this."

"My name is Moira Gorman," she said. "I was born in a small village in southern England and given the name Johanna Hatfield. Popularly known as MoJo. I grew up in Manchester and trained to become a performer before the End of the World."

"And about two months ago, your father began talking with the press about finding you," the host said. She kept talking smoothly despite shuffling note cards in her lap. "He even offered a large reward and promoted it on live broadcasts. So why are you here now?"

Moira shifted in her seat, taking in the small studio space around her. On the surface, it looked like a setup from when she did press junkets. Cameras, cables on the floor, microphones, people. But when her eyes adjusted to the bright lights, other details came through. The equipment had signs of aging, from scuffs on its body to duct tape on its base. Bits of electrical tape acted as Band-Aids on cracked cable insulation. Even the overhead boom mic showed bits of fraying foam.

It wasn't the same now. It was tired, dirtier. But in a way, more real. "I'd been a celebrity, a drunk, an outlaw—looter, I guess. After the quarantine, I guess my version of PASD was trying to be the most normal I could be. New name, new identity. I moved out here and sought a normal life. Or at least, what I thought was normal. When my dad made his announcement, it was like all those feelings I had as a teen came back. But with the last outbreak, I think it shook everyone."

"'Moira Gorman.' How did that come to be?"

"Moira is my middle name. I've always liked it. And Gorman." Moira pictured Chris, his eyes filled with empathy at a teen thrown to the wolves, all while chomping hard on gum. "It's the name of someone who was special to me. He took care of me. My old manager, Chris."

"And you like your life now? You won't go back to being a performer?"

"No. I'm content. You know, Chris once told me, 'Memories are meant to fade. They're built with an expiration date.' I don't need to hide from my past. It's just…part of me now."

"The public found out about this interview yesterday, and today Evan Hatfield put out a statement saying that on the eve of the transportation lockdown, he and MoJo mutually agreed to put off her return until things settled. He claims that this interview is a hoax designed to capitalize on MoJo's fame, and the real MoJo will be revealed soon. How do you respond to that?"

That was new information to Moira. She glanced over at Rob, who was already checking his phone, probably for any Metronet headlines about that. Their eyes met, but rather than concern or confusion or anything in between, she sent him a smile. Not the MoJo smile, but a simple turn of the mouth that signaled everything was fine.

"It really doesn't bother me. He can do whatever he wants. I'm just going to live my life now."

"Do you still sing?"

Behind Rob, Sunny crept forward, her short silhouette lingering next to her dad's body.

"Yeah. Sometimes I do."

Ten minutes later, a studio technician in a mask and gloves was removing the microphone pinned to Moira's lapel when Rob and Sunny came over. "She's right. Here's the statement from your dad. It's on the Metronet." He held it up to show her but she waved it away.

"I'm okay. Really. MoJo is who he always wanted. Not me. So if he wants someone else to become MoJo, they can go right ahead."

The sound of a buzzing phone interrupted her, and Rob looked down again. His eyebrows rose and he turned his phone to her. "This one, you have to see."

Dear Mr. Donelly: The San Francisco Family Stability Board is pleased to inform you that your appeal has been received and accepted. The testimonial from Dr. Dean Francis has sufficiently demonstrated your commitment to your daughter's well-being. We wish the best of luck to you and yours. A full report with findings and official discharge will be sent to your email.

Rob's shoulders slumped, not from stress, but the final release of tension. Moira stood up, her foot getting caught in the microphone cord. Her arms wrapped around his shoulders, and Sunny joined in of her own volition. "Things might actually be fine," he said, face buried in her neck.

"That may not be a lie," Moira said, holding him tighter than she'd ever held another person. "For once."

CHAPTER FIFTY-FOUR

Krista

Sunny put the cheeseburger down, its supposedly kid-sized patty and buns looking like way more food than was fit for a child. She studied the half-eaten behemoth on her plate, then opted to go to the French fries instead.

"Gigantic, huh, Sunny?" Krista took a sip of her peanut-butter-and-chocolate milkshake while she watched Sunny nibble. Moira stared back at her—not in person, but the image of MoJo plastered on Sunny's backpack next to her in the booth. If her own teenage mug had been ironed on a backpack, Krista probably would have burned the thing by now, then stomped on it and kicked the ashes around. Moira, though, seemed to have a greater tolerance for this stuff than she did. Maybe it was the new (or old) Moira, complete with now-permanent British accent.

"Yeah. But it was good."

"Well, we're making up for lost time. I'm glad your dad has stopped being so uptight about—" Krista stopped midsentence, the peace of their meal interrupted by a voice yelling at the TV above them.

"Bullshit," a woman's voice said. "That's bullshit."

"The success of the MGS ninety-six vaccine has been attributed to a worldwide effort at staying ahead of the virus's evolution." The news cut between footage of doctors administering shots and President Hersh talking and shaking hands with other world leaders. "While scientists acknowledge the continuing risk of MGS, the global community feels confident that they will be able to stem any widespread pandemic and keep casualties to a minimum."

"Minimum. Ha." The voice came from behind Krista, and she peered over her shoulder to see a frowning woman with close-cropped hair and a half-eaten salad on her plate. "More government propaganda," she said, her voice low enough that it probably was meant to be a private comment. "What are you looking at?"

"Me?" Krista said. She blinked her eyes and feigned innocence.

"Yes, you. You think everyone's being honest? There are more lies in this world than you can possibly imagine."

"Don't even get me started." She turned back toward Sunny, giving her a quiet smile before sticking her tongue out. Sunny's laugh overtook the blare of the TV.

Sure, Krista worried about MGS. Everyone did. But she also knew that her time with Sunny was precious.

More importantly, it mattered.

"You think this is funny?" The booth bumped as the woman slid out and moved to their table, hands on hips in full disapproval mode. "They lie to us. They're out there to control us, and the more people act like you, the more they tighten their—"

"Lady," Sunny said, her voice direct and clear with its usual sparkle, "you need to get over it." The comment stunned Krista, probably more so than it did the angry woman, and she found herself speechless with pride.

"Young woman, did your mom teach you to be so rude?"

"That's not my mommy. That's Krista."

"Guilty as charged," Krista said, raising her hand. She sipped the last dregs of the milkshake, letting it gurgle loudly. The band of the woman's silicone mask snapped as she put it on, and she slouched away, her grumbles disappearing into the din of voices and silverware.

"Nice job, Sunny."

"Thanks." Sunny's response came in a simple, straightforward tone, like she hadn't done anything particularly extraordinary.

The waitress returned, sliding the bill in between their plates.

Krista marveled at the funny little creature that had somehow become such a big part of her life. She unzipped her purse and reached in for her wallet but got the vibrating plastic of her phone instead. She pulled it out and checked the incoming text message from a strange number.

A New York City number.

Hi Krista, it's Jas. OK, I admit it. I paid Reunion Services for your number. Thing is, I listened to London Calling again, and you know what? I think you might be right. We should discuss this, maybe over breakfast since I'm flying in for a conference? Say yes and I'm there. Say nothing and I'll leave you alone forever. Don't want to cramp your style.

Her default response kicked in, causing her eyes to roll. She tossed cash on the table. "Come on, Sunny," she said, scooching out of the booth, device still in hand. "Let's take you home."

"Who's that?" Sunny pointed to the phone.

"This? Oh. It's just a guy I know." The screen lit back up, and her finger poised to push the Delete button.

"A friend?"

"Yeah. You could say that."

Sunny rolled out of the scrunched vinyl seat, MoJo backpack in tow, then pushed her hands up toward the ceiling in a massive stretch. "Cool. Can I meet him?"

In that moment, Krista realized that her finger hovering over the big red Delete was more of a reflex than anything else, and that, in fact, a real conscious choice could dictate what happened. A flutter ran through her stomach, but it carried a different rhythm than usual. After a few moments, it finally struck her. This wasn't the usual anxiety that welled up when her path crossed with someone from her past. No, this was something entirely different, something that until recently felt like it couldn't even exist.

Anticipation.

A tremble jolted her fingers as they tapped out a short message. Glad you finally came around. It lit up the screen for a flash before the Sent icon appeared. "You know what?" she said, putting her arm around Sunny and taking the first step to the diner's exit. "Possibly. Someday."

As she took Sunny's hand and headed out the door, she considered the possibilities. If Jas of all people could finally see that *London Calling* was a better album than *Walk Among Us*, then maybe the world deserved a second chance too.

It's easy to say that the Greenwoods, the Fourth Path followers, and the multitude of suicides, murders, and other losses during the first post-quarantine years were due to PASD. Many of those people were stuck in Kay Greenwood's way of thinking: that the only paths were Metros, Reclaimed, looter gangs, or some unknown, possibly mystical journey out in the wilderness.

But Kay Greenwood was wrong.

MGS 96 showed us that the paradigm shift wasn't from the outside world, but from within. MGS 96 marked a breaking point, where those paths were no longer silos with hard delineations. Instead, people began to accept that the true fourth path came from blending together. Metros remained the core population centers, but they worked in conjunction with Reclaimed communities, who paid taxes following the landmark Reclaimed Resource Agreement Act: a symbiotic exchange of resources and manpower. Looter gangs still battled among themselves, but even they reached a bit of a truce with the world through federal outreach and distribution programs, and in turn created neutral safety zones for long-distance travel. There was enough space for everyone to live the way they wanted, but the connective tissue of humanity simply had to reboot, especially as the world adjusted to a new normal: staying vigilant against the perpetual threat of new illness.

This shift started the way all movements do. In the months following MGS 96, the collective unconscious of survivors seemed to gradually recognize the living rather than the dead. As a community, we still emphasized the importance of familial ties but finally understood that the definition of family wasn't about blood or even who or what you'd lost. It was about what gave you hope and who was willing to get involved.

Maybe it was always that way. We just saw it more clearly after the End of the World.

Excerpt from the dissertation *Un-Paused: The Greenwood Incident, Family, and Hope in a Post-MGS World* by Sunny Donelly, University of Northern California, Class of 2040

★ ★ ★ ★ ★

ACKNOWLEDGMENTS

First off, thank you for reading!

In 2011 I told some writer friends that I had an idea for a book: What if the world didn't end it just paused? Soon after came a very rough first draft about Krista, Rob, Moira, and Sunny in a rebuilding society. That manuscript took on many forms, first as a post-apocalyptic satire and then through massive story and tonal changes, this book was formed. Getting there needed a lot of people, and they all deserve recognition.

Sierra Godfrey saw this book through many early horrifying revisions, and yet we are still friends. My agent, Eric Smith, then dusted off this old manuscript and had me mash it up with *Station Eleven*'s structure and tone. The brilliant Kat Howard assisted with that enormous challenge. That led to Michelle Meade, who acquired the book, then gave it the tough love necessary to really bring it to life. And Margot Mallinson brought it home with final revisions and continuity checks as a decade of revision fragments finally smoothed out.

Along the way, the following people provided feedback, sanity reads, and world-building ideas: Kristen Lippert-Martin, Charity Hammond, Emily Bierman, Diana Urban, Laurel Amberdine, Dave Connis, Rebecca Enzor, Erica Cameron, and Wendy Heard. Moral publishing support also came in the form of the #TeamRocks Slack, In-N-Out Burgers with Randy Ribay, and panicked texts with Jessica Sinsheimer.

Thanks to Caity Lotz and Tala Ashe for starring as Krista and Moira, at least in the movie I saw in my head.

Fellow indie rock nerds probably noticed a theme with my character names. Thank you to the musicians who provided the blender of character names, especially for the main cast: Kim Deal, Tanya Donelly, Juliana Hatfield, Kristin Hersh, Black Francis/Frank Black, Chris Gorman (and his love of gum), Tom Gorman, Gail Greenwood, Kay Hanley, Dean Fisher, and Dave Narcizo. Extra special thanks to Tanya Donelly, both for being wonderfully supportive and also because the lyrics to "Stars Align" inspired the final dialogue between Rob and Moira when I couldn't find the right words to end the scene.

Finally, this book would not exist without my wife, Mandy, who is the heart of this story directly and indirectly. She is a survivor and an inspiration, and a miracle worker with our daughter, Amelia, when I have book events, deadlines, and other authorly commitments. This story is everything I feel about our journey together, all wrapped up in ninety-seven thousand words.

Mandy, I'm so lucky you responded to my Match.com email all those years ago.